Autumn Leaves, 1922

AUTUMN LEAVES, 1922

A KIKI BUTTON MYSTERY

TESSA LUNNEY

PEGASUS CRIME

NEW YORK LONDON

AUTUMN LEAVES

Pegasus Crime is an imprint of
Pegasus Books, Ltd.
148 West 37th Street, 13th Floor
New York, NY 10018

First Pegasus Books edition August 2021

Interior design by Maria Fernandez

Library of Congress Cataloging-in-Publication Data is available.

ISBN: 978-1-64313-712-4

10 9 8 7 6 5 4 3 2 1

Printed in the United States of America
Distributed by Simon & Schuster
www.pegasusbooks.com

For my family

PROLOGUE

I leaned into the fog that surrounded the ferry. The sky was gray and close to dawn, which meant close to docking in Calais and close to the Blue Train to Paris. My knuckles were white from gripping the railing. The air was freezing but my cheeks were burning. I felt fuzzy, high from lack of sleep, lack of food, from too much sex and fear and not enough love.

The still, damp air ran its fingers over my face. My head filled with the growl of the engine, the slap of the English Channel against the hull, with the long, low call of gulls. Their caws echoed through the fog so that each bird seemed a multitude, each call seemed to come from another world. I imagined these gulls were my mother wailing from the underworld, that she was trapped and needed me to release her. If I could find her final diary, if I could find the reason she left for Australia, then perhaps I could finally understand her and release her memory.

I was still dressed in the thin clothing of an Australian spring, but here I shivered constantly and almost uncontrollably. It wasn't just that the wool of my red coat failed to do its job, or that my scarf invited in every whisper of wind, or that my red gloves should have been leather lined in cashmere; it wasn't just that I had recently returned from a year away in Sydney and I was no longer used to Europe's many-mannered chills.

I shivered because I was finally free of my old life. With every minute on the water, more terribly and irrevocably free.

The ferry's horn sounded, long and low, scattering all my morbid visions. The horn meant France was imminent, yes, the shore was in sight, the sailors had started their fast work of unwinding ropes and aligning gangplanks. I had only the smallest bag with me and I clung to the handle of my slender suitcase. I was first onto the jetty, a jaunty red parrot among the sleepy pigeons. I was first on the Blue Train to Paris, first in the dining car, and certainly the only person to order champagne in the trembling morning.

The fields rolled by, weeds sprouting and children clambering over the abandoned war machinery as if it were ancient ruins. I couldn't stand to see my reflection in the debris of the recent past; I couldn't look away from the craters and unnatural hills of burial mounds and collapsed trenches. I smoked the last of my cigarettes and drank more than was sensible on an empty stomach.

But I wasn't here to be sensible or any of those other words that imprison a woman—respectable, obedient, compliant, normal, good. I was here to smear blood-red lipstick on glasses and collars and skin. I was here to slip off my shoes and my hat and let my neck be caressed by the morning air. I was here to dance wildly, eat ravenously, and laugh at the dark.

I was here to live.

"WHEN THE LEAVES COME TUMBLING DOWN"

I could only get to Paris via Calais, via Dover, via London, and I was in London this October with a mixture of relief and dread—relief that I was finally in Europe, dread that I would be discovered by my relatives and forced to stay in London. I was so intent on leaving as soon as possible that I hadn't even bothered to book a hotel. But as soon as possible could not be immediately. I had to see my patron saints before I could embark on my pilgrimage, patron saints in the form of young veterans and my best friends, Saint Tom of My Heart and Saint Bertie of the Bedroom.

London was charcoal and electric. I always had this feeling when I arrived in the Empire's epicenter. The air crackled and possibility hid in every tiny lane, and I never knew, when I entered a room, whether glory or ignominy awaited me. The dull exteriors of the buildings, in sooty stone and pale brick, the drab clothes of the Londoners, all gray and brown and black, were a ruse. With so many people coming and going, living and dying, in this city, I was always guaranteed to find exactly what, or who, I needed.

I couldn't help but think of who I needed as I rode the Underground to Blackfriars. The crush of bodies made the air stink of warm human trapped in damp wool, a smell so peculiar to London that I almost liked it. It had been like this during the war when I had traveled here on leave, supposedly to visit my aunt Petunia and my English mother's other relatives, but in reality, I had slept through most of the days to creep out each night, with the help of her indulgent butler, to carouse with friends. Then the stink of wool had been from wet uniforms, combined with Woodbine smoke and mud and the odd whiff of cordite. I couldn't help but remember what I had needed then—a warm embrace, so unexpectedly yet expertly supplied by Bertie—and how that mirrored what I needed now.

I wriggled out of the carriage, my coat almost catching in the doors, and feelings from 1917 caught up with me. Then, my edges had been ragged, my emotions overused and oppressed, I needed release yet feared that release would overwhelm and overpower me and I'd never be able to climb back into my uniform. I breathed in deeply, to remind myself that it was 1922, not 1917, and I no longer had a uniform or needed permission to travel. I looked around. The stairs up to the river were full of clerks, not soldiers. My black nursing boots had been replaced by high-heeled brogues in the same scarlet red as my coat. Like me, London had donned a fancy tie and put a sweet flower in its buttonhole, it drank cocktails and it played croquet . . . but it couldn't forget. Memories of the war lurked in every look, in every wracking cough and quick purchase of the newspaper. I was far from immune.

The only cure for these memories was a hug from a patron saint. I had to stop myself from running all the way to Tom's office and in doing so breaking a heel, or my ankle, on the cobblestones. I could hear pigeons trill over the honk and bray of the traffic, I could feel the city tremble through the footpath. The sky was a slate roof too close to the double-decker buses. But Tom, my Tom-Tom, my boy from home, was hopefully just around the corner, just up the stairs, just behind the front desk—

"I'm sorry, ma'am, but Mr. Arthur isn't in London at present. He's on assignment in . . ."

"Turkey!" boomed an Australian voice from inside the office, "Or Greece—it depends who you ask, ha! Anyway, he's filing copy from Smyrna." The booming voice came out to reception in the form of a pre-war three-piece suit, gray hair, gray moustache, round red face and round eyes; all he was missing was the top hat and the can-can dancer on his knee. This must be Tom's boss, the man he only ever called Old Buffer.

"Miss . . . ?"

"Button." I put out my hand to shake his, to his surprise. "Kiki Button. I grew up with Tom in Australia. When is he due back in London?"

"How long is a war?" His grin was more of a leer. "When the fires have gone out, Miss Kiki Button. His copy is too good to pull him out of danger yet. Not that I expect you to know what's happening there—"

"From what I read, it has been happening, with equal ferocity from both the Greeks and Turks, since the end of the war. 'It' being, of course, the siege of Smyrna."

"You're well-informed, for a woman."

"No, I'm just well-informed." I ignored his snort of laughter. "Where's he staying?"

"If he sleeps at all it'll be a miracle," said Old Buffer. "But Shereen here knows where to contact him. Say, you're not one of the girls who keeps him in Paris, are you?"

"Girls? Not in the plural."

I was saved from further leers by Shereen, letting me know that Tom had a bed at the Empire Hotel in the port of Smyrna and could be contacted there. Old Buffer just looked me up and down before heading back into the office with its endlessly ringing telephone and drone of the wireless.

I should have known that Tom wouldn't be in London. Hadn't I been reading the papers all the way from Sydney about the endless fighting on Europe's fringes? Hadn't I read our hometown paper, the one he worked for, every day since I had arrived in Sydney last December? His byline was everywhere, reporting on a skirmish here and mob violence there, as he traveled through the vanquished and victorious nations from Aachen to Archangel to Odessa to Constantinople. Reading that newspaper and following his frenetic journey was, for months, the only link I had to a world outside my grief.

I clipped down the worn marble stairs and inhaled my cigarette with too much ferocity. It was absurd for me to be so disappointed. Yet who else would I want first, after a year away, but my darling Tombola? London traffic whizzed by, always changing and always the same: rushed, crushed, and vibrant. I would have to settle for sending Tom an invitation to Paris via telegram.

I had already sent a telegram to Bertie. If I had tried to surprise him, I could have ended up in a boys-only cabaret in Soho, or drinking gin with lush luvvies in a back alley in Covent Garden, or simply sitting for hours in the reception of the *Star* waiting for Bertie to return from one of his famously long lunches. I needed my job back as the *Star*'s Paris correspondent, I needed to know that the editor had forgiven my long absence and would let me be a gossip columnist once again. I needed to see Bertie, quickly and completely, before I left London. Once I got to Paris, I doubted I would leave.

I walked down Fleet Street to where it met the Strand and Soho. I was now regretting being too impatient to leave my suitcase at Victoria Station, as my right arm had started to ache and I leaned to the left with the heft of it. I would arrive at the *Star* sweaty and puffed with dark circles at my armpits—hardly the best look to convince the editor that I could party with *haute Paris* with aplomb, pizzazz, insouciance. I removed my scarf, gloves, and coat and relished the sharp breeze that teased my scarlet silk dress, its fluttery fluted skirt and huge sleeves moving in conversation with the traffic sounds and air that threatened rain. I took the wooden stairs to the office, the walls covered with playbills, and announced myself to Mavis at reception.

"Kiki?" Bertie called over the office noise, with its clatter of type-writers, telephones, and high heels on a parquet floor. I was about to call back but the call stuck in my throat; I had the sensation of my chest tightening, a lump in my throat that I wanted to cough out, my mouth open but nothing on my tongue but stale smoke. Bertie poked his head around the door and for a moment all I could see was his smile and all I could feel were his long limbs as he wrapped his arms around me.

"Caramel check," I said as I stroked his lapel.

"Caramel cashmere with a chocolate check, actually."

"And your lozenges?"

"Caramels, of course."

He always had a packet of lollies in his pocket, bought new each day to match his outfit. I was so glad that habit hadn't changed; I was so glad he understood what I was saying when I spoke about his clothes. I stroked back the stray strand of sandy hair that had escaped his pomade. He had a couple more wrinkles than last year and the shadows beneath his eyes were darker, he no longer smelled of Woodbines, but some strong tobacco that I didn't recognise, he had a few gray hairs at his temples; subtle changes that told me that age was coming as quickly to him as it was to all of us war veterans.

"Have one." He shook the packet of caramels at me. "You need one."

"I need a cigarette."

"Like you need a bullet in the brain. You do know that, despite the fact you put them in your mouth, cigarettes are not actually food?"

"Are you here to lecture me or to buy me a drink?"

"Mavis," he called over his shoulder as he took my suitcase and my arm, "I'm off to lunch."

"Again, Mr. Browne?"

Bertie only raised his eyebrow in reply.

"DOWN IN MIDNIGHT TOWN"

"So, Kiki, the Ritz or the river?" Bertie flipped up the collar of his caramel overcoat and raised his voice over the traffic.

"The river."

"Perfect answer." He waved away the cab that had pulled up beside us and took my hand as we scurried across the road.

"What's on the river?"

"My boat. Well, barge, to be precise. My landlady was beyond the pale, always asking me why young men came over and didn't leave until dawn, why I didn't come home each night, reading me Bible passages—"

"Acting like Nanny?"

"Nanny introduced me to her dishy godson last Christmas, all pillowy lips and creamy skin, so no, nothing like Nanny."

He tucked my hand into his arm as he led me down little lanes, cobbled and dark, with shops touting second-hand books, maps, shoe repairs, and pawned watches.

"So anyway, thoroughly sick of my surroundings—Chelsea is full of posers, Fitzrovia full of socialists, Belgravia full of snobs—I used to walk down to the river and sit in the freezing wind, watching the boats bob up and down. One day an old waterman, like someone out of Dickens, tipped his cap and offered me his 'nevvy's vessel,' as his 'nevvy' wasn't in a fit state to use it anymore. It was red with black roses, equipped with a bed and sink and table, and I forgot to go back to the office."

"Office? What office?"

"Exactly. All summer I pootled up to Oxford and beyond, to picnic on the riverbank, to let the sun set over my bobbing body."

The Thames rippled gray-blue at the bottom of the lane.

"Alone?"

"Only sometimes." He smiled. "A jug of Pimm's can be shared just as easily with a good book as a handsome lad. I devoured both over the summer, trying desperately not to miss you."

"I think you succeeded."

"No," he kissed my hand, "I only distracted myself, as always. Too many boys . . ."

"And too many ghosts."

His heavy exhale seemed to say everything: the pain that still lingered from the war in the form of stray aches; memories that ambushed ordinary moments; the preciousness of friends, and their absence filled with wine, sex, and cigarettes; life held too lightly, like one of the brittle red leaves that fluttered to the footpath along the riverbank.

❧

"Bertie, it's perfect." I sat on the roof of his barge, a large whisky beside me, my red scarf wrapped tightly against the weather, watching the trucks and buses rumble over the bridges. "What luck the waterman found you."

"It's the only time I'll let myself believe in fate." He gave me a look that was easy to interpret: As opposed to the war when, if you believed in fate, you'd go mad with the injustice of it. You could only believe in luck. Seeing Bertie with the wind in his hair, pushing our floating party to a more secluded spot where we could kiss and gossip, I felt very lucky indeed.

We had to keep close to the bank in order for him to use his punt. We could see all the urchins and amputees as they combed the shore. The smells of London were different here too—river mud, salt, rotting vegetation, diesel, and old fish. Here was a London that my mother could never have known, that I only encountered when I nursed East End privates for the first time in 1915.

"Bertie, you can't expect me to believe that you have spent months punting all the way to Oxford and back."

"Of course not, Kiki. I hired a tug to drag me out of London and punted from there. I don't mind a sailor . . ."

"Who does?"

"But I don't want to be one. As it is, I've had to let out quite a few jackets to accommodate the increased muscle in my shoulders."

"Oh stop."

"Any more and I'd have to get a whole new wardrobe."

"Would that be so bad?" It was too windy for a hat and my hair kept flicking in my face.

"Not if you were here to help me choose it."

"Here I am."

"Until when?"

"Paris tomorrow and then forever."

"Sydney was that awful, was it?"

I raised my whisky glass to him and took a big gulp. I couldn't say more in a shout across the London afternoon. Talk of my extended absence would have to wait for the privacy provided by the moon, stars, and liquid night.

We let the tide carry us along for a while, Bertie using the punt to guide the barge. We were headed to Raven's Ait, a river island that held only a rowing club, various blue wooden buildings, and some bedraggled gardens. Bertie docked quietly at a jetty that hid beneath some overgrown trees. Dead leaves spilled on the river's surface. The city was just on the bank but it seemed barely there, the traffic noise hushed by the swish of water against wood. Dusk appeared over the river, the slate sky darkening, and a chill rose from the water. I pulled my coat closer and tucked my feet beneath me. Bertie handed me more whisky from a box on deck.

"My brother sent me a whole crate from Scotland, it's his new business venture." He settled in beside me. "I don't have any food."

"Do you usually eat?"

"No, not usually. But you'd know all about that, wouldn't you?" He picked up my hand and ran his thumb over the too-prominent wrist bone.

"I thought I might try it again in Paris. Eclairs, you know . . . and cheese . . ."

"There wasn't any cheese in Australia?"

He kept hold of my hand, a lifeline to the world, an anchor in joy so that I couldn't float away into sorrow. I lit a cigarette with my other hand and added my smoke to the hazy sky.

"The funeral was the easy part. They'd waited so long, my ancient aunt had insisted on waiting for my return, that my mother was already boxed up and ready to go. I got off the boat in the morning, threw dirt in her grave at lunchtime, and was on the train to my father's property that afternoon. I was back on the train to Sydney a fortnight after that. It was the long goodbye in the form of packing up her life that was . . ."

"Awful? Dreadful? Woeful?"

"Sorting out her clothes was fine, they all went to local charities. Her books were sold, her furniture went under the hammer . . ."

"Is that what took you so long?"

"A year to sell some books? That took a few weeks at most. No, it was . . ." The crickets chirruped their encouragement. I took a slug of whisky. "I read her diaries."

"Were there many?"

"She wrote almost every day since she left England more than twenty-seven years ago."

"That's what kept you in Sydney."

"I sat in her terrace by the harbor, the lorikeets screeching during the day and the bats squeaking in the fruit trees at night. I read every page, I couldn't stop myself. They were boring and repetitive in the way all diaries are, even her constant trips to Europe, and yet . . . I sat in her house with no furniture but a bed and an armchair, building a picture of a woman it was too late to know."

The terrace had been cool through the summer, shaded and sandstone, while the rest of the city had boiled. The harbor had glittered and shimmied, dotted with yachts that bobbed through the endless syrupy sunshine.

"My aunt came over one day and almost had a fit. I hadn't been out in weeks except to the corner shop for biscuits and sherry and tea that I drank black so I didn't have to bother with milk. I was in my grimy slip, with stains on the embroidered peonies of my mother's favorite dressing gown, using her extensive teacup collection as ashtrays, sherry goblets, tea cups, soap dishes . . . I think my aunt actually screeched, galah that she is."

"What's a galah?"

"An Australian parrot. It's also a nickname for an idiot. She shoved me into my coat and took me to her house to be cleaned, washed, dried, aired, fed, and watered. I had to stay until my hair was brushed shiny, my laundry dried and pressed, and I'd eaten three solid meals—although she scaled down 'eaten' to 'attempted' when I threw up mashed potato and chicken pie all over her carpet."

"What a galah."

"Precisely. The maids looked askance at the ragged adult niece. All except Martha, who just brushed my hair over my morning coffee, and said, 'You've always been a scamp, Katherine. I don't know why the Mistress thinks you'll change.'"

"My mother's maid is also an ally from childhood."

"She used to darn the holes in my stockings I got from climbing trees. She would smile then too. Anyway, after two days of my aunt's shrill harangue I was dragged into recovery. I threw out the black mourning clothes I'd been wearing and bought this red ensemble. I cut my hair short, I ordered a meal I could actually eat . . ."

"Which was?"

"Raspberry tart and cream." I shrugged. "I didn't have the heart for hearty. I sold the house and the teacups—do you know, the teacups fetched almost as much as the house? Apparently, they were rare antiques! Of course, the one I've kept for myself is chipped and cheap, patterned with nasturtiums and as big as a soup bowl. It was always my favorite. I packed up the few things I could take with me and booked my ticket for London."

"And your father?"

"I haven't seen him since the funeral."

"Kiki!" Bertie sounded shocked.

"After the diaries . . . I just couldn't."

"He was a brute to her?"

"Worse. He adored her." A slight breeze stirred the leaves on the water's surface, flashing golden in the streaks of light from the shore. "I couldn't face my father once I knew why he couldn't face me."

"You look like your mother? Mrs. Button never had bobbed hair."

"She kept her long luscious locks to the end. But there was a studio photograph in one of the diaries, from the year before she married. We don't look obviously alike, but there is an expression on her face, her expectant look into the camera . . . I've caught myself looking like that in the mirror more than once." Her hair in a pompadour, shawl slipping off one shoulder to reveal flawless skin, her face full of hope, she seemed to lean forward into the camera with desire.

"But I never knew her to look anything other than disappointed."

"Will he be disappointed that you left without a wave?"

"He will always be disappointed with me, for not . . . well, for not being a 'nice girl,' as he likes to say. But I would've leapt into the waves, shoes and coat and all, if I'd stayed any longer."

In the enveloping dark, the river lapped at the barge, the cricket calls buzzed in the blood.

". . . so, Kiki?"

"So, Bertie?"

"So, who was your mother, then? How did she move from hope to disappointment?" He stroked back my hair. "That's what kept you mired in misery, isn't it? Reading the slow disintegration of a woman?"

I couldn't speak. How did he know, this darling friend? His face was all shadows in the almost-night.

"I felt the same way about Teddy . . . you know."

His true love, KIA in 1916; in this moment I doubted Bertie would ever recover from Edward Greene's death.

"His mother let me read his letters when I visited her. She was relieved that there was someone to cry with, someone who also wanted to go over and over all of her beloved boy's quirks. I think she chose to ignore the true nature of our love. She just needed someone who adored him like she did." I heard Bertie exhale too loudly in the darkness.

"Teddy's letters . . . over the year and a half he was in the trenches he became more and more disillusioned, until he was in despair. He used the worst kind of black humor—you know, the gory jokes of dismemberment that are so funny when you have your foot in a corpse, but truly horrifying when back on solid ground. He wrote these things to his mother. I never noticed."

"How could you have noticed?"

"How could any of us have noticed until it was all over? But Teddy's trench was a grave that he garlanded with flowers. If it hadn't been that mortar, it would have been a bullet or gas or shellshock. He would never have survived the war."

It was too dark to see Bertie now, but I could clearly hear his gulps as he swallowed his sobs. I felt for his hand and he clutched it.

"That knowledge, Kiki . . . it makes the sadness indelible."

"The absence larger but easier to carry. It's wrapped around every limb."

I tipped the final drop of whisky onto my tongue as he pulled me closer to him. Bertie lit a cigarette with trembling fingers and much swearing. The night wrapped around us, now warm and now chill as gusts blew over the water. The banks glinted and fizzed but their light barely reached us under the sheltering branches. Bertie smelled of printer ink and pomade, the air smelt of tobacco, river mud, coal smoke. I needed human warmth, I needed a breathing body with all its sweet and sour smells. Without even really thinking, I started undoing Bertie's waistcoat buttons with one hand, my stockinged leg slipping over his suit pants.

"Do you need some comfort, Kiki?"

And he kissed me.

The cold air pricked my skin as we lay naked in the darkness, the only light from our cigarettes and the flickering moon. Bertie absentmindedly ran his hand up and down the length of my torso, stopping occasionally to run his thumb over my nipples, a trick he had played only a little while before, but now I was too spent to do anything more than move my cigarette to my mouth to inhale. We lay there for a long time, wrapped in each other but isolated in our separate loss. Bertie kept turning to me to stroke my hair and look into my face, as though by staring he could drag himself into the present and its hope of happiness. I gazed back in the intermittent moonlight—his messy hair, his big brown eyes, the stains on his fingers from ink and tobacco and lack of care—I let myself be his anchor, as he was mine.

"You know it wasn't just your mother you were grieving, don't you, Kiki?"

A flash of moon showed just how sharp his cheekbones had become.

"I do, sweet Bertie. Though I didn't at the time."

"Never at the time."

"I was just floating in the underworld—"

"All the ghosts caressing and claiming you in half-waking dreams—"

"When I resurfaced and I realized whole days had disappeared—"

"Whole seasons—"

"It was suddenly late autumn and my hair had grown past my shoulders—"

"You'd missed a birthday and were a whole year older—"

"Then I realized, Bertie."

He leant over and kissed my shoulder.

"It felt pagan, Bertie, almost elemental. All the ghosts wore khaki uniform, they had the King's shilling in their mouth to cross the Channel instead of the Styx. Mother's grave was a door and the war marched back through it."

"As it will, every time." He lit us each another cigarette. The flare from the lighter scratched shadows into his stubble. "So, who was your mother? Did you find out?"

I could feel his breath, the smoke he exhaled over my body.

"I've only just returned from my year in death, Bertie. Ask me in a few months' time. Right now, I'm here for life."

"LIMEHOUSE BLUES"

"Do you live on this boat permanently now?"

"Yes." He smiled; a slash of morning sun in a sky pale with the night's exertions.

"But your suits, your shoes . . ."

"Mavis at reception sends them to be pressed and polished before I stow them away. Look."

He showed me all the ingenious compartments in his barge. We spent what should have been our breakfast hour exploring cupboards and boxes and hidden drawers. I was particularly impressed by the shaving kit that folded out of the bathroom cupboard.

"This is just about the coziest trench I've ever seen," I said. Bertie clenched his jaw.

"Isn't it though." He said it quietly. All I could do was kiss him.

We had to rush all the chores we had ignored yesterday. Bertie hailed a passing tugboat to pull us back to central London, giving us time for a quick wash at his little sink. As he placed the key around my neck, Bertie gave me detailed instructions of how he had maintained my studio apartment in Montparnasse while I was away. Last year, Bertie had secured me the gossip columnist job at his magazine. This year, he brought out all the sales figures, he got Mavis at reception to organize biscuits, I was armed and ready to ask our editor for my job back—all unnecessary as our editor agreed without hesitation while on the telephone. I didn't even get to see him as he closed the door on Bertie as soon as he'd grumbled, "Yes." But it meant I could leave London today, I could catch the Blue Train to Paris this minute. Bertie fed me biscuit pieces as I exchanged Australian pounds for British pounds and French francs. I was going to miss Bertie but felt not a single pang as I left him for the Underground.

But when I got to Victoria Station the train had been delayed. Sheep on the tracks, gulls in the smoke stack, a passenger from Calais had expired en route; no one could tell me anything except that the train wasn't leaving until later this afternoon. I was advised by a guard who was more moustache than man to "go and 'ave some elevenses, miss, it'll be a good while yet."

I had intended to go into the station restaurant for a proper breakfast. I had intended to go to a tea house, a bun shop, a pie cart so that my entire diet wasn't cigarettes, whisky, and the occasional biscuit. But each shop had something wrong with it—this one was muggy with steam, that one smelt of cabbage and soap, another was full of middle-aged women who frowned at my short hair—and I couldn't bring myself to take a seat. I wandered down to the river and stared at the water, last night so magical and this morning so ordinary. I wandered east along the bank until the sign for Westminster Station jerked me out of my reverie. The palaces of Westminster were just ahead. All around me were the government offices of civil servants and ministers and men like Dr. Fox.

I'd had absolutely no intention of seeing Fox, in fact the opposite, I'd had every intention of ignoring and avoiding him. Yet the merest slip of unmarked time and here I was, standing minutes away from his office. Bertie had told me the address last year and, try as I might, I hadn't forgotten it. I had looked up the street, once, and now I walked there even while I argued with myself that I mustn't, I shouldn't, I didn't want to, not even a look, as not even a spare glancing thought should be given to Fox . . . and yet here I was, in front of his building, staring like a tourist at the rows and rows of windows in the gray stone façade.

The seconds passed with treacle slowness. Every window showed a memory of Fox. Here he was when I first met him, in his bloody gown at a field hospital outside Rouen, looking at me with his cold gray eyes as I shivered in my uniform. There he was over the operating table, quoting Wordsworth, his hand out for scissors to snip off the stitching thread. A flash of a person in the window was a flash of Fox as he left my tent, where he'd been watching me sleep; I was told he did this often but I had only caught him once. The clouds' reflection in another window was his steel gray hair as we drove back from Amiens, just the two of us. Full bellies had made us lax and happy, the sun bright in the apple orchard, I had run in to pick up apples that had fallen on the ground. I sang as I gathered fruit in my skirt, flashing my petticoat, and he had smiled, his first real smile.

I couldn't move as more memories crowded the windows. The first intelligence mission he gave me that had me bicycling back from the front line with a notebook in my pannier, sweating despite the freezing temperature. The nights he spent quizzing me on Shelley, Byron, Wordsworth, Coleridge, but especially Keats, growling at me when I couldn't instantly supply the next line from "Ode to a Nightingale." Window after window of the times he made me gather intelligence inside brothels and estaminets, dressed like I was there to work and, sometimes, living up to my costume. The smell of all those men, the creep of their breath down my neck, the stink of mud in their uniforms. The telegram he sent me last April that called me back to him, my spymaster, to resume spying for him. A black window, as dark as the office at the Café de la Rotonde, where he called me last year to give me my new mission, to discuss clues, to make me remember how he had almost tricked me into marrying him. How it took all my willpower to resist his quicksilver voice. I couldn't move as memories from the past eight years flitted by, the war and my return to Paris, bringing with them the discordant smells of disinfectant and coffee, cordite and champagne, the sounds of bombs and moans of the dying, the clink of glasses in the Rotonde, his voice, toxic and beautiful down the telephone line: *Darkling I listen.*

Was that him? I held my breath as a figure looked down at me from an upper window. Gray-white hair, charcoal suit, chiselled jaw; from underneath I couldn't get a proper look. I moved backward and almost tripped into the traffic. I grabbed a pause in the flow to hurry across the road for a better look. When I turned back, the figure turned and walked away. Had that been him? I hadn't seen him since November 1918, when I had left his country house in Kent by stealing his car and driving myself back to London. How had he aged in the last four years? Was his hair now more white than gray? Was he thicker in the waist and thinner in the shoulders? I couldn't remember how old he was; in fact, I might have never known, he always seemed both old and young simultaneously, his gray hair pointing one direction but his good teeth and relentless energy pointing another. Had that been Dr. Fox? I wanted to run inside and demand to see him, when I knew I should calmly walk away. In the end I stood by the side of the road until the growl in my belly made my legs wobble and I knew I had to find food or else fall over. The figure never reappeared, but even the possibility that I had seen him, finally, made me both frightened and elated. I chewed food I didn't taste and stayed tense and floating, until the train stopped at Dover.

Then grief and love and hope called me from the water and beyond. Fox was forgotten. Only Paris mattered.

"WHIRLED INTO HAPPINESS"

French chatter in the streets, the fickle air now damp, now crisp, diesel and cat piss and fried garlic and wine and the occasional waft of a Parisienne's perfume. Is freedom not in leaving your home, but in choosing it? When you can't choose, either to leave or to stay, you aren't truly free—but when you can choose, then the city is yours, it opens up like a new lover, completely and with abandon—is that it? Because that's how I felt when I stepped out at Gare du Nord, crumpled and fuzzy-tongued after a breakfast of champagne and cigarettes. That's how I felt as I waved away taxis and buses and started my walk through the boulevards and alleys toward Montparnasse.

It wasn't a short walk to my apartment, nor a comfortable one in heels with a suitcase. But every step rejoiced, every click of my heels said I was free, I was here, I was home. Cafés were scented with strong black coffee and stronger cigarettes. Corner boulangeries gave the hungering smell of fresh bread. Flower sellers wove between the pedestrians, professional sellers offering hothouse irises, beggars crooning over their wilting wild-bloom posies. Fashionable women, with hats down to their eyebrows, walked their dogs on short leashes. Shopkeepers in pinstripes and waiters in aprons darted back and forth to the footpath to meet, greet, cajole, and farewell. Across the Seine, men leaving the factories for lunch pulled on their flatcaps as they looked me up and down. Butchers whistled while shouldering carcasses. Soon the artists and assorted bohemians began to show up amongst the laundresses and off-duty cab drivers, the women hatless in impractical shoes, men in golden satin and burgundy velvet, all distracted by the cloud they found themselves living on. I moved onto Boulevard Montparnasse to see my favorite cafés, Café de la Rotonde and Café du Dôme, my street just a few more steps away.

The key was warm where it hung on a ribbon against my skin. My heart was beating so fast as I walked into rue Delambre that I had to stop to let it settle. The sky was pearly, the sun flirting with the footpath through the curtains of clouds. Wrought-iron balconies punctuated endless pale stone, shops displayed their salami and cheese, their corsets and stockings, their books and books and books, in windows that shone with golden script and scrubbing. People called in English to friends in the upper window of the Hôtel des Ecoles, people passed by speaking French and Spanish, in the café to my left I heard people arguing in fierce Eastern languages I didn't recognize. Was this really my home? This place with its aperitifs on check tablecloths set on the street, this place where a woman could wear trousers and revolutionaries fall in love and no one would raise an eyebrow? I bought a packet of Gitanes and a newspaper from the kiosk on the corner and walked to number 21 so fast I was almost running. I took the stairs in a little jig of impatience, my suitcase banging against my legs, the smells of soap and whitewash and poor drains that always lingered, to the roof with my little studio apartment—someone had oiled the lock recently, kept the floor clean, the air sweet, and the water fresh, as if I had only just left, as if the apartment itself had been waiting for me. I flopped on the bed and the sheets smelt of rosemary. I splashed my face and gulped crisp water from the jug. I ran my hands over my rack of dresses, so neatly hung, I kicked off my hat and coat and shoes and opened the window even wider. The geraniums were wildly blooming and the eave sparrows greeted me as the life of the party. I hung my legs over the window sill and lit up. Now I was properly home: here, this view over the four corners, over the streets and the gardens, all the way to the Eiffel Tower, here it was and so was I. The sky slid up its skirt to reveal hot blues and pinks but I was already seduced, I had been in love for years.

I smoked half a packet sitting on that windowsill, watching as the breakfast menus were put away and the lunch ones put out, watching hungry crowds emerge from nowhere to drink and talk, watching as the day swelled, as the wind teased the reddening leaves from the trees before dropping them on the road. I even managed to read some of the newspaper I'd bought, catching up on the gossip and politics, until an elated faintness forced me down into the street for food.

A taxi honked at me from across the street as I walked to the Café de la Rotonde. I ignored it; I was distracted by being here, by the meal I would order now that I was finally relaxed enough to eat. I'd even chosen a loose-fitting dress in anticipation of a feast, emerald green cut into a wide-skirted style with a loose sash at the waist, embroidered with black roses at the neckline, with my favorite black velvet opera cape to complete the feast-feasible ensemble. My star-patterned shoes had been waiting in my cupboard and their heels tapped on the cobbles as I tried to decide if I wanted my first meal here to be *moules frittes* or scallops still in their shells or—the taxi honked again as it parked.

"Kiki!" the driver called before his long legs climbed out of the car. I knew those legs, that voice, that face with its flop of dark hair.

"Theo!" I ran across the street and straight into his arms. "Oh goody, you still taste like licorice drops."

"Kiki, you still take my breath away. What a greeting! I didn't realize how much I missed you until this moment."

"Theo, don't you know that ardent desire is not at all elegant?"

"I'm Russian. If I don't have desire, I have nothing."

"You're a prince and a Romanov. You'll always have that."

"What good is being a prince if I have to work half the night for a handful of francs?"

"Only half the night? Then you're doing better than most. Besides, if you didn't have a taxi we might never have met."

"I'd forgotten how much you liked my taxi." His hold around my waist tightened.

"It's my first night back in Paris. We need dinner and drinks to celebrate. You're taking the night off work."

"Yes, ma'am!" He gave a mock salute, then tucked my hand in his arm and walked me to the café.

Amid the glitter and chatter of the Rotonde, Theo made small talk as only a prince can, polite yet gossipy with a perfect memory for all the details of family and fate. In the soft, smoky light he looked exactly the down-at-heel aristocrat, with his expertly cut suit shiny with wear, his shirt-cuffs almost frayed, and his tall, slender elegance a little hollow with hunger. Theo was Feodor Alexandrovich Romanov, nephew to the murdered tsar of Russia, born in the Winter Palace in what was now Petrograd. He was a prince in a family of princes, princesses, grand dukes and duchesses, and emperors just a whisker less powerful than gods. Their fall in the Bolshevik Revolution had been swift and spectacular. Those who had escaped the revolution with their lives rarely escaped with any money. They had washed up in all corners of Europe, abandoning their careers as nobility to become champagne salesmen or fashion designers or, in Theo's case, a taxi driver. Last year I'd hailed his taxi, not knowing we were headed to the same party. Once I found out, naturally I had to know more about this high-class cabbie. That night had turned into a summer spent exploring anywhere his taxi might take us.

"I searched for you last autumn, Kiki, but I was told you had gone home to Australia for your mother's funeral. Please tell me that's not true."

Several answers crowded my tongue but none took flight, leaving me just blowing smoke at the sparkling reflections in the café mirrors.

"Oh, my golden one." He looked at me with proper sorrow in his face. "I'm so sorry. You don't deserve any more suffering."

"Neither of us does. At least I had a funeral to go to."

There had been no funerals for his family, he'd told me, no ceremonies to mourn his entire way of life that had been killed off by the Revolution. As a consequence, much of his family was in perpetual mourning.

This information had been revealed in little flashes through the summer, smoking at my windowsill, under the stars on the beach, wandering a riverbank near the former front line. The long summer afternoons had seemed timeless, or out of time, as though we had somehow survived past the end of the world and it was just the two of us, wandering the earth. Then a car would splutter or a train rumble past, his stomach would grumble and I would need a cigarette and we would return to the present and its subterranean sadness.

I took the cigarette he lit for me and handed him a refilled champagne glass in return, the wine glowing in the reflected, refracted light. Our starter of pâté had been taken away, our ashtray swapped for a clean one, as we swapped sympathetic looks for the suffering we had each endured.

"But I have all my immediate family here." He sipped his champagne; the warm lights of the café made his eyes seem especially dark. "Though sometimes I wish I didn't."

"Quite. Why do you think I came to Paris in the first place?"

"Because it's Paris?"

"Well, there is that . . . are you still living with your sister?"

"It's not Irène I'm talking about. It's Felix."

"I've never met your brother-in-law."

"That was deliberate."

Our *moules frittes* had arrived, spicy with garlicky tomato, messy and sensual. I broke open one of the shells and slid the mussel into my mouth, licking my lips to clean up the sauce that clung to them. I was so glad to be here, with him, the happy patter of the other diners over the accordion playing in the corner, cigarette smoke mixing with the smells of sweet alcohol, fresh tomato, cooked cream. Theo watched me with an expression that wavered between wanting and wistful.

"Oh, Kiki . . ."

"Have a chip." I dipped one in the sauce and fed it to him. "And tell me about Felix."

"Felix," he said as soon as he'd swallowed, "Felix is up to it again."

"Up to what?"

"His obsessions, his political meddling, just like last time."

"What happened last time?"

Theo gave me an incredulous look.

"Of course, Theo, how could I be so dense? Rasputin."

"Rasputin." Theo nodded. His brother-in-law, Felix Yusupov, was one of the men who had murdered Rasputin six years ago. Rasputin was the shaman, seer, holy man that Theo's aunt, the tsarina, had kept at court to help heal her sick son. All Rasputin had really achieved was to make the German tsarina even more unpopular.

"But how is this the same?"

Theo frowned. "Felix had never been passionate about anything except clothing, parties, and Irène. Then he heard Puriskevich's speech in parliament denouncing Rasputin as the Antichrist. Overnight he became inflamed with desire to rid Russia of 'this devil,' as he put it. Felix was extreme in his views and in his actions. It was harrowing to see him change from an urbane prince to a brick-throwing protestor, albeit one in a Savile Row suit. Since then, his extreme views seem to come and go . . . though what I suspect is that he hides his views from Irène, and indulges them with his increasingly extremist friends. Dima—my cousin, Dmitri Pavlovich—was one of his political coterie, and may still be, for all I know. They were always extremely close. Can one say suspiciously close?"

"It depends what you suspect them of."

"Of being lovers." Theo shrugged. "I'm not fussed about that. In any case, I think they left that particular peccadillo behind in London with their youth. But I don't want to see Irène hurt, and she will be, if Felix continues with this obsession."

"Why don't you talk to Dima, your cousin?" Theo shook his head. "I haven't spoken to him since he was exiled. Not since the Revolution. We . . . don't, though I know he's in Paris." Theo dipped a chip in the sauce but put it down with a sigh.

"So, come on—what does Felix want?"

"He wants to reverse the Revolution."

I laughed and Theo looked startled.

"I'm not joking."

"But that's preposterous! The entire White Army couldn't do that."

Theo played with a fork, his head bent so that the lights shone in his dark hair.

"Theo, Russia has just spent two years in a horrible civil war. There were rumors that all their war allies helped."

"I know, I heard that too . . ."

"So, if Denikin and Wrangal and Kolchak, with the help of London and Paris and Rome, couldn't unseat Lenin, how does your brother-in-law think he can manage it?"

"With the Fascists, he says. Have you heard of them?"

I had heard of the Fascists, but not since last year, not since my last mission for Fox. I nodded.

"Well, you're one of the few, Kiki. Where did you—"

"Journalist friends." I waved my hand dismissively; I didn't want to tell him about Fox or Tom or my other life. "Where did Felix meet a fascist? Was it the German or Italian type?"

"Russian, actually, among others." Theo surveyed me with a colder look than I had seen from him before, calculating and regal. "You know your groups, I'm impressed. Actually, I'm glad. The last few weeks have been so . . ." He shook his head and shook off his princely stare, his eyes wandering over the red and gold décor of the café. Some society women tried to catch his eye, they looked like American tourists, but if he saw them he didn't show it. I called the waiter for two whiskies and another packet of Gauloises.

"Explain everything to me, Theo. Unburden yourself."

"Most beautiful Mademoiselle *Bouton*. I don't know how I survived without you."

His eyes had lost their aristocratic courtesy and became windows into the abyss of his loss, a loss that spanned a continent and a three-hundred-year reign. They held me in place as surely as his hand held mine. I might have stayed like that, if a waiter with the whiskies hadn't interrupted my thoughts.

"Felix the fascist. Who does he meet with?"

Theo sent a plume of smoke to the ceiling and leaned back in his seat as he considered the question. "Well, he used to meet with another émigré, some kind of art dealer, called Arkady Nikolaievich. The English we meet refer to him as Lazarev with somewhat of a sneer, and I'm not surprised. Nadya, our maid who's been with Irène forever, called him an absolute peasant, which is her worst insult. I think Arkady Nikolaievich is the son of a school teacher or provincial clerk or some such. Anyway, Lazarev might be a nobody but the men he introduced to Felix appear to be somebodies. 'People like us,' Felix calls them, by which he means princes and dukes and such.

"But Felix hasn't met Lazarev for a while, as far as I know. Mostly Felix meets another man called Edouard. They discuss secrets, it seems, as their undertones stop as soon as anyone else walks into the room, when they either stare at the intruder or pretend they were talking about shooting or riding or the cigars that neither of them smoke. I don't know how Felix can stand to spend time with that Edouard, with his high-pitched voice and soft, insinuating touch. Yes, touch—he seems to be always sliding his hand over his trousers or the chair or Felix's arm. I can't help but think of him as a snake, pale and vicious and obviously lethal."

Lazarev—Fascists—this had too much to do with my previous mission. For a minute, I forgot the past year. All that existed was this city and this moment, as I was plunged again into the excitement of possible spy work. Last year, my spy mission from Fox had been tied up with my gossip columnist work, a mission tailor-made for a society Parisienne. I had a feeling that my next mission would be along similar lines . . . not that I was admitting to myself that there would be another mission, that I not only expected it but welcomed it, that I wanted, even needed, that kind of sweet danger. I could admit none of that. I could not even countenance the idea that I was mining Theo for information. No, I was simply being a good friend, an excellent listener.

Theo had even less idea of what I might be doing, judging by the way he kissed my hand which he then laid on his thigh. I sipped my whisky to stop myself from jumping in with revealing questions, my tension confined to my jiggling foot.

"Anyway, Edouard," Theo picked bits of tobacco off his tongue with too much distaste for such an ardent smoker, "'Edouard'—he wants me to call him Eddy, in the English style, but I refuse—wants us to join him in ridding the world of Bolshevism and establishing a new hierarchy based on, oh something outrageous, 'European purity' or 'blood and honor,' something like that. I can't listen, it makes me sick."

"Why?"

"Why? Kiki, really . . . well, because it advocates more violence, more . . . because I've seen what this type of fervor does, this . . . fanaticism. In Petersburg—Petrograd—whatever they want to call the city, servants we trusted were suddenly roaring outside the doors, they let filthy robbers into the bedrooms via the kitchen, they even ripped the tiles off the boiler and smashed them as examples of bourgeois privilege. Of course, we're far above the bourgeoisie, and they'll just have to replace the tiles eventually as the boiler needs some sort of insulation . . ." Theo rubbed his brow, his eyes wide and staring at a place far away from a sweet Parisian autumn, a place where the snow was bloody and the air filled with screams.

"But I'd seen it before, this rage, this derangement, with Felix over Rasputin. Felix really should have been one of Peter the Great's generals, he has the right kind of ferocity. He thought of nothing else but Rasputin for weeks. He put the plan into deadly effect and didn't recoil from, from . . ." Theo pursed his lips and raised his eyebrows. "This is hardly the talk of reunited lovers."

"My apartment can be our sanctuary."

"It always was." But his slender suited body stayed hunched over his glass. "Well . . . Rasputin's body was fished out of the river with a bullet hole or two as decoration. If Felix didn't actually pull the trigger, he certainly cheered on the man who did. He was banished to his country estate and now he's in Paris with the same preoccupations: ridding Russia of its undesirables through fire and blood."

"Who will light the fire with him? This Eddy character?"

"Yes. Felix can't help boasting about it. Edouard is some kind of minor English peer, but he knows German princes, English princes, all manner of nobility. They all went to the same school, I think, as Edouard never mentions anywhere else, no parties, no country weekends, no marriages, none of the ways I know the sons of other Russian families . . . it seems an odd system, to all go to the same school, but then I have always thought our English cousins were slightly odd."

"Your English cousins?"

"Yes, the current princes, David—sorry, you know him as Edward—and Albert, Henry, and George. Admittedly they're distant cousins, but we tend to keep an eye on each other."

The heirs to the British throne; I lit another cigarette to stop myself laughing or scoffing or in some way betraying my middle-class outpost-of-Empire origins.

"Edouard comes to our flat once a week and Irène does what she always does when she's furious: she hides in the kitchen to eat biscuits, getting under cook's feet and generally making all the staff nervous. She can't stand this Edouard any more than I can, not for his views, but for the way he makes her redundant. Edouard's world is a man's world and women are a nuisance at best."

"And at worst?"

"A hindrance to be disposed of. He brushes her off with breathtaking rudeness. As Felix supports him, Irène feels she can do nothing; she won't be the nagging wife, she told me. I come home from a day in my taxi and Irène is in the kitchen alcove laying waste cook's best macarons, the maids keep dropping things and sniping at each other, Felix and Edouard are in the front room whispering over vodka, and I can hardly stop myself from getting into a fight. I couldn't stop myself, a few weeks ago. It wasn't that Irène was in tears, or that I was exhausted and stank of cigarettes, or that Edouard sneered at me. It was Felix's manner. He's started to treat me like a servant, as though by working I have demeaned myself. This is a man who got himself excused from serving in the war!"

"So what would he know?"

"Exactly. He ordered me to fetch him and Edouard drinks, and then caviar, then he actually dismissed me! I couldn't help myself, I sat down and pretended to be interested in all their nonsense. Felix was furious, he considers me an embarrassment, but the snake indulged me and tried to pander to what he assumed were my notions of lost prestige, hatred of commoners, and desire to restore the old order. His eyes slithered over my dirty work suit and nicotine-stained fingers as he talked. All I could get from him was that he was finding 'like-minded men' to 'restore the world to its rightful order.'"

"A recruitment drive."

"Yes! I hadn't thought of that, I was thinking more of a seduction. But he was recruiting Felix to his cause. God knows what he'll make Felix do. I can hardly bear to watch."

A waiter came and left without an order for dessert. Theo smoked silently, his legs crossed, once again lost in his thousand-yard stare. The society women were, in fact, American tourists and came up to ask Theo whether he was really a Romanov prince. He pulled himself together to address them and I had a moment to think. This really did sound like my last mission. A certain Edward Houseman, or Hausmann, had tried to recruit disgruntled British soldiers to the cause of his German Brownshirts. The Brownshirts were the nickname for the German variety of fascist, a group I still did not fully understand, but it seemed to be composed of bitter old soldiers who felt betrayed by the end of the war. Had Hausmann moved from soldiers to aristocrats now? If so, was he only targeting Russians, or were other nationalities on his list? Why was he still in Paris and not in London, Berlin, Munich . . . but I was getting ahead of myself. I had no mission, I was just here with the lover I'd abandoned last year. The society women fluttered away. Theo finished his whisky and licked his lips.

"That was delicious."

"Another?"

"Somewhere else, perhaps?" He picked up my hand and kissed it, holding my gaze. I was at such a pitch, being in Paris, seeing Theo, the possibility of danger he carried, what else could I do but say yes?

"DEAREST (YOU'RE THE NEAREST TO MY HEART)"

As soon as we left the café it started to rain in huge bucketing gusts. We ran to my building but by the time we reached it Theo was already soaked. He slipped off the hood of my opera cloak and kissed my neck. Not a small peck, or a cheeky bite, but with one arm circling my waist and pulling me toward him, he caressed the entire length of my neck from my ear to my collar bone. With each kiss he pulled me closer to him, so my feet rose off the ground and I had to cling to him in order not to fall. He said nothing, each breath became deeper as he kissed the other side of my neck. He knew this made me quiver and I would quickly say yes to whatever he asked. I lifted his face from my collarbone to read his expression. Desire had wiped out all other emotions.

"Please," he said. I kissed him and he made a little moan from the back of his throat. "Please."

We almost ran up the four flights of stairs to my garret, tripping over my wet opera cloak, my shoes scuffed as he half-carried me over the landing spaces in order to kiss me. I didn't need to worry whether we'd locked the door, as Theo held me against it with both hands under my bum. I just about managed to kick off my shoes and unpin my cloak before I felt my stockings clips snap undone, before I felt him caressing me. He kissed my ears, neck, mouth, his breathing so deep it was as if he was trying to drink me in, as if he wanted to dissolve into me. That depth of desire, so rarely found, is irresistible. It made me respond in kind, it woke me up, I was alive to every sensation of touch and smell and sound in a way I hadn't been since I had received that black-edged telegram informing me of my mother's death. I was alive and I wanted him as completely as he wanted me. I wanted him instantly, I didn't want to wait the two steps it would've taken to get to the bed. I said his name and a shudder ran through his body. I could feel the way he had to hold himself back to make the moment last, how difficult and how necessary that was for him. He was so tall that he could hold me up easily. I wrapped my legs tightly around him and let myself go. He said my name, over and over as he calmed down, his lips on my neck still hot with hunger.

He hoisted me up and shuffled to the bed. We lay tangled together as the autumn night cooled our sweat. All I could hear was the patter of rain on the metal roof above us, its harmony on the window panes, the undertone of whistling where the wind tried to join in our kisses.

I thought Theo was asleep and moved to light the bedside candle and grab my cigarettes, but he propped himself up and took a cigarette for himself.

"Our last ones."

"Not ever, Kiki." He looked stricken. I shook the empty packet at him.

"That wasn't a metaphor, Theo."

"Good." He flopped back on the pillow. "Is it my imagination or do you smoke more than you used to?"

"Much more."

"As do I. Why, though? Is it this city?"

"And all the love and heartache it holds. I never want to leave. If I have my way, I never will."

The candlelight flickered in the draft from the window.

"You don't want to be an *Australienne*?"

"Do you want to be Russian?"

"It's unavoidable."

"Precisely. I'm the *Australienne de Paris*."

"A true émigré, always two people at once."

"Always myself, Theo, and that is true freedom."

I was still wearing my slip, its black silk and lace now sticky and askew over my breasts. Theo flicked his cigarette out the window and, leaning over me, pulled the slip over my head, dropping it on the floor as he gazed at me. I kept smoking, watching his emotions boiling beneath the surface—longing, lust, laughter, a sort of hopefulness. I slid my feet up his chest, moving his singlet up with them, until he took his cue and took it off. He was only slightly muscled, hours in the driver's seat balanced by the occasional repair job and night on the dancefloor. Another cold draught made all the tiny hairs on his body stand to attention, among other things. He leant forward.

"Welcome home," he said and he kissed me.

⊷

Theo left early the next morning, and the next, with a promise to intro-duce me to his brother-in-law, Felix Yusupov. I had told Theo that, if he wanted my help with Felix, I had to hear about his fascist fascination for myself. I had to meet Felix regardless; I could not pass up the opportunity to write about Russian princes for my column.

I spent a blissful couple of days wandering around Montparnasse. I wanted to touch everything and often returned to my studio with finger-tips filthy from running them along walls and fences and signs. I sat at three different terrasse tables at each café, ordering a new coffee at each one; I touched posters and sandwich boards for shoe repairs, sausages, stationers; I walked along the Seine with one arm out, brushing the weeds and wood and stone wall as I strolled. I wasn't interested in *haute*

Paris, in the museums and galleries, in the Angelica tearooms or Galeries Lafayette. I wanted to sit under the falling golden leaves and sip cheap aperitifs, I wanted to hear the rough voices of fishermen as they waited out their old age, I wanted to see shopgirls and street sweepers and seamstresses hurrying to and from work or stretching on their lunchbreak. I wanted the Paris that wasn't just for the perpetual tourist. I wanted the Paris that really was my home.

The telegram boy found me at Café Petit. Petit's was the opposite of the Rotonde. Here, no one wanted to be recognized, to establish their reputation among the avant-garde, or to spot the celebrities of the art world. Here, furriers and cobblers wanted a good cheap breakfast, old men wanted to see their friends for a spot of chess, and expats wanted to read their letters in caffeinated peace. Madame Petit had been so delighted to see me again that she insisted I call her Madeleine. I adored short, round Madeleine, who always swept her hair into a Gibson-girl bun and had fresh hot coffee ready when I walked in. I felt at home in her café, its dark green walls with their photos of pre-war Paris, its wooden furniture worn smooth with use. I had ordered my usual light breakfast when the telegram boy poked his head in.

"Mademoiselle Button?" He gave a grin and a little bow at the door; I clearly had a reputation at the post office. "Telegrams from London."

I propped the little yellow cards against my empty coffee cup. I wanted to rip them open and devour the contents, I wanted to throw them in the bin with the rest of my obligations. There were only a few people who would bother to send me a telegram—Bertie, Tom, Fox, and my father—and all of them had the ability to turn my Paris life upside-down and inside-out. I waited for the pastry, and the extra coffee Madeleine brought with it, before I lit a cigarette and opened the first.

UNBUTTON THAT BUTTON IN PARIS FRIDAY GARE L'EST 1600

I exhaled with a smile. No one called me Button but Tom. These saucy instructions meant Tom was coming to Paris to monopolize my company and my bedroom floor. My delicious boy from home, with his black hair that wouldn't stay in its pomade, stormy blue eyes, and dingo grin . . . I felt a physical pain in my chest and I had to fold up the telegram to stop my tears. I knew I had missed his company, but with my mother's diaries in front of me, I hadn't thought much about it. I could hear his deep Australian voice in these few words. I could almost smell him, soap and sweaty wool and tobacco and something else, his natural scent, a smell complicated by memories of far away and long ago.

The coffee was just the right sort of bitter to offset the sweetness of this first telegram, just the right sort of milky to give me strength to open the next.

DARKLING I LISTEN

Just three words and no sending address. I didn't need one, I didn't need any other markers to know who sent this and why. This was from Fox, quoting Keats' "Ode to a Nightingale" to let me know that a mission was impending, my spy work would resume soon, and he was listening somewhere, somehow. It must have been Fox I had seen in the window in Westminster; that he knew I was in Paris by any other means was too chilling to contemplate.

I watched the leaves fighting with the wind. So, the game was on. This was the summons. Next, he would let me know how to contact him, and then my days would be shaped by secret meetings with shady men. When I had received my summons last year, I almost cried. Bertie had delivered it along with the first payment: Tom's handkerchief, rescued from the battlefield.

My boy from home was in serious trouble. He had abandoned his real name, as Thomas Thompson was wanted by the Australian Imperial Force for desertion and the British Army for treason. Tom hid in plain sight as the reporter Thomas Arthur, but he remained in danger until he cleared his name. The handkerchief told me that Fox knew of Tom's plight; I only worked for Fox to get the evidence I needed to help Tom.

What would be my payment this time? Would one more mission deliver the proof Tom needed? Fox didn't work like that, he liked to hold on to power and strengthen his hold over his agents until they dressed like him, spoke like him, smoked the same gold-tipped Sobranie cigarettes with the same sneer as him. But I hoped. I had to hope, I had only hope, otherwise I was working for a man who wished to imprison me.

I shredded my *pain au chocolat*, dipping each piece into my coffee before eating it. The pastry was light and buttery, the chocolate both sweet and bitter, the coffee softening the whole. Each mouthful was a sensation and kept me anchored in my body, when my mind threatened to drift off into memories of Fox in the war, of Tom in Paris, spy missions almost failing and what I'd had to sacrifice to make them succeed. I concentrated on each mouthful until my swirling memories had settled, until I felt safe in Paris, and not threatened by a sudden return of the past.

"LOVE HER BY RADIO"

I moved quickly to my building. There was one job I had neglected to do since I arrived, and that was check my post. Everyone had a little box on the ground floor of the building. I had assumed that no one would have written to me as no one knew I was here. Bertie had already given me the invitations I needed for my work and the first wasn't until the end of the week. I hadn't yet contacted my nearest and dearest. I hoped to run into my artist friends at the Rotonde, or the Dôme, or even just in the street; in fact, that was the surest way to find Picasso and crew, as I had no idea where they were living now. I hadn't yet contacted Harry or Maisie, my best friends from the war, who both lived in Paris. I knew why I hadn't but I didn't like to think about it. Bertie was a mirror but a forgiving one; he suffered as I did, it was easy to see myself in him and still pour the champagne. Tom knew me too well. To him, I could be neither better nor worse, he'd seen it all. But Maisie, my fellow nurse, would see all my flaws and ask me why I couldn't see them too. Harry, Ms. Harriet Harker, would simply tell me what to do to get over my sadness and organize me into doing it. I needed a little time, a little Paris, a few packets of Gauloises and glasses of Cassis before I saw them and saw, in them, the ravages of grief in my face.

That is what I felt anyway, that is what the nasty little voice at the back of my mind told me. That voice, always so fearful, didn't remind me of the times in the war when Maisie had picked me up from the floor of our tent after I had been working too hard, had taken off my boots and unpinned my hair and pulled a blanket over me when I had been too exhausted to move. It didn't remind me how, last year, Harry organized for me to have a twice-weekly bath in her sumptuous apartment while she took care of my laundry. It was a vile little voice, suspicious of its own shadow, and it kept me away from my two best women, the very people who could help me most.

But those two telegrams were a reminder, a warning, a cooee from the future. My little postbox held only one piece of mail, more like a package, with thick cream paper and addressed in spidery calligraphy: Fox had sent me a handwritten mission. I was caught between feeling impressed and horrified that he should be so particular and personal in his attentions. There was no stamp or postage mark though. Had the envelope been hand-delivered? In Fox's handwriting—did that mean he was in Paris? Surely, he would have summoned me if he was nearby. No, there must be some intermediary, he must be playing some game. I smiled at myself; of course he was playing games, it was the only way he communicated, it was what he loved best and did without cease. I just had to make sure I played as well as he did.

I stood in the street for a moment, spots of rain cool kisses on my face, each spot a mark on my silk dress. I took a seat at the Café Dôme among the working men having their midmorning coffee and the revolutionaries just filtering in after the previous night's debauches. These men looked once but not twice at a society girl in an inky blue beret and coat, shirt dress with buttons past my belly button, and star-patterned shoes that fit like old friends. I had all my tools with me: notebook and pencils, coffee and cigarettes.

The envelope sprang open in my hand. Inside was a single page of cream paper with the mission on it and four photographs. I was still for so long that I almost burned my fingers on my cigarette. The photos were of Tom, in uniform, sprawled in mud surrounded by shrapnel and body parts. In the first photo he was unconscious, eyes closed, arms flung wide. Next to him, face up to the camera, was a German soldier, hand out to pull Tom out of the mud. In the second picture, the German soldier was now actively pulling him, one hand reaching into Tom's tunic. In the third, the German soldier was peering at Tom's identity discs. In the last, Tom's discs hung from the German soldier's neck as he hauled Tom, his head slack, through the mud.

I thought I might vomit. I thought I might crumple into a tiny ball, here on the café floor, Tom looked so broken. Yet here it was, payment before I even asked for it, exactly what I wanted: the next bit of proof that Tom was innocent of those charges of treason.

Or was it? I peered more carefully, hiding the pictures behind my handbag. My first thought was that this proved that Tom had been kidnapped by the Germans, but on a second look, it wasn't clear if they were rescuing a stranger or a comrade. The German soldier clearly didn't know Tom by sight as he had to check Tom's identity discs, but whether he was taking Tom to be a prisoner of war or back to his German *kamaraden* was not evident from the photo.

The German soldier clearly knew the photographer, and perhaps even knew why they were taking the photograph, as there wasn't a trace of surprise on his face. The photographer must therefore be German or known by the Germans in that trench. There wasn't anything that would give away the photographer's identity—no boot, no hand, no accidental reflection. I flipped the photos over. Fox's handwriting spiralled over each one:

Teach me half the gladness that thy brain must know
Such harmonious madness from my lips would flow
The world should listen then, as I am listening now

Shelley; I stared at the lines. Fox should be quoting Keats, Keats was his favorite, and using Keats meant that you were a favorite, a code within a code. Was I no longer a favorite? If not, then why send a telegram with

"Darkling I listen," his most-used line from his favorite poem? It was clever how it echoed the Keats fragment in the telegram—"Darkling I listen" and "I am listening now"—as was the way the lines seemed to reveal my closeness to Tom, my closeness to Fox, the madness of spy work and the madness of love . . .

I shoved the photos back in the envelope. My first question when I spoke to Fox would be how he got these photos. There could, of course, be a clue in the mission. As I blew my smoke at the smoke-stained ceiling, I had to remind myself to be professional, however much Fox provoked me to be emotional, vulnerable, and dependent. I made an effort to ash my cigarette, get out my pencil, and get ready to decode his handwriting.

> An old, mad, blind, despised king rises from the south. Houseboys, dregs of their dull race, would march princes, jewels of their fine race, through public scorn. Mad from a muddy trench, rulers who neither see nor feel nor know, but leechlike to their gas-blind amputated country cling 'til they swell with blood. People starved and shunned from the shelled fields, princes halved and stunned in the drenched fields, make an army whom liberticide and realpolitik make a primed dud to all who wield. Black-clad men who tempt and slay, religion in a brown shirt, a free corps against an empire sealed, Versailles worst statute unrepealed—all are graves from which a leader may march in our tempestuous day.

This wasn't Keats either. The last mission had looked like this, but that had been lines from "Ode to a Nightingale" cut up and rewritten as prose. This was also some prosy nonsense, but . . . was this more Shelley? That opening line looked familiar, "an old, mad, blind, despised king," but there was something off about it.

I looked out the window at the soft rain, the streets black and silver, pedestrians tearing wet leaves underfoot as they hurried. On the back of the photos was Shelley's "Ode to a Skylark." The memory returned: Fox had collected me in a car after a six-hour pass—in 1917? 1918?—and we stopped at an abandoned orchard to gather apples. He had recited

"Ode to a Skylark" over and over, snippets and lines, the sun warm on my blouse as I held fruit in my skirt, his tie undone and he smiled: that memory of his one true smile. The lines on the back of the photographs sounded through my mind in his quicksilver voice, lingered with the scent of overripe apples and uncut grass, so I couldn't properly remember more Shelley. Fox didn't much like Shelley and Byron but I didn't know exactly why. I had assumed that they were too sexy and radical for him. This poem was a departure.

I ordered more coffee and a Florentine to go with it. This departure had to be the first clue. If it was Shelley on the back of the photographs, then it was probably Shelley in the mission. Shelley was a lord who was also a political radical, an atheist, abolitionist, anarchist, and advocator of free love. He had drowned in Italy a hundred years ago but my aunt still frowned on his poetry as risqué. I scribbled ideas down in my notebook—radical politics, Italy, aristocrats, love triangles, *Frankenstein*, rebellion and exile—could the poet's life have some bearing on the mission he had assigned me?

I took a big bite of the Florentine but let it sit in my mouth as the caramel dissolved and the dark chocolate melted, until the flakes of almond sat alone on my tongue. I wrote down all the glaringly obvious things Fox had written in the mission too. Muddy trench, gas-blind, amputated, shelled fields, realpolitik, primed dud, Versailles—all of these clearly referred to the war. Did they also, in some way, refer to the violence in the original Shelley poem? There were other things that seemed to be mission-related, but I wasn't sure—black-clad, religion in a brown shirt, free corps. There was nothing particular about these things, except they reminded me of my chat with Theo about Fascists in his apartment and around Europe. The Germans were nicknamed Brownshirts but called themselves the Freikorps, or "free corps." I didn't know the uniform of the Italian Fascists, or if the British or French had their own fascist groups.

This mission had to have something to do with the war, possibly with the Brownshirts, and as princes was mentioned twice then possibly something to do with them. But they didn't point to the core of my mission:

what I was supposed to do and when. The letter read like a warning, not a set of instructions. Presumably, when I called Fox, I would get the key that would lead to instructions—because I had to call him, no matter how much I worked out by myself. An important part of Fox's games was that only he knew the rules. All his agents had to check with him, constantly, that we were doing what he intended. I loved the puzzle but I hated the game; I loved the risk but the greatest danger was always Fox himself. If working for him as his agent became a permanent job—and, with Tom's future at stake, that seemed likely—could I protect myself from Fox? I hadn't been able to during the war. I was stronger now, I was no longer a naïve girl, but was I strong enough? The only proper answer was that I had to be. If I wasn't strong enough already, I had to become strong enough to resist him.

I looked over the photographs again. They were as much provocation as payment. They were ambiguous and so invited me to be suspicious of Tom. If that's what Fox hoped, then he hoped in vain. I wasn't suspicious of Tom, but of Fox—who took these photos? Who developed them? How did Fox come by them? It seemed incredible that Fox could stumble upon them by chance. Much more likely was that he knew they were being taken, or even that he had organized for them to be taken. But why? I had no idea about that, nor for the poetic lines on the photos' backs. The backs read almost like a plea for love, that "harmonious madness," which was impossible. I tucked the photos back into the envelope with the letter. I would show them to Tom on Friday and see if they triggered any memories.

I buttoned up my coat and paid. I had to work out more of the mission before I spoke to Fox, so my next stop was to find the Shelley poem that the mission had bastardized. I needed to go to an English-language bookshop for that and I could think of no better place than Sylvia's.

"Polyphème"

Shakespeare and Company was only a short walk across the park and around the corner. Sylvia Beach had made a name for herself as the publisher of *Ulysses*, the epic by James Joyce that was too scandalous to publish anywhere but Paris. It was apparently as thick as a brick and just as impenetrable. Unless you were a sophisticated reader, of course, and then it was the key to all literature and Joyce was a genius. Sylvia also ran a lending library, sold second-hand books as well as new ones, stood as a postbox for American writers recently moved to Paris, and was generally big sister to all the Atlantic flotsam who washed up looking for bohemia. I admired her for publishing *Ulysses* but I loved her for the rest. I hadn't been to her new shop yet, I was excited to see it, to see who was there, and to see Sylvia again.

Rue de l'Odeon was peppered with people, speaking English with French inflections and French in all sorts of American accents, as they gathered outside Shakespeare and Company and Adrienne Monnier's bookshop opposite. The creamy façade of Sylvia's shop invited me on and the yellow light invited me in. Sylvia looked up when I opened the door.

"Kiki! When did you get home?" Sylvia's smile extended across the counter, as warm as an embrace. *Home*: the word made me smile in return.

"Only a few days ago! Hello," I held out my hand to the woman seated next to Sylvia, "I'm Kiki Button."

"Nancy—Cunard." Her vowels were as round as a sea-tumbled stone. "I've come for another copy." She indicated the blue brick of *Ulysses* that sat heavily in her lap.

"Nancy's a poet," said Sylvia, "and runs with 'the Crowd.'"

"Do I?" Nancy looked amused.

"Of course you do. Bob, Djuna, Mina, Bryher, Ken Sato . . ."

"Oh, them! Yes. Better add Michael to that motley crew, he's coming over soon. And Tristan, as he's fallen out with Breton again . . ."

"I heard."

"They'll make it up, they always do. They have to, no one else understands these Dadaists." Nancy turned her enormous blue-green eyes to me. "Are you an artist?"

"A gossip columnist."

"Oh, handmaiden to the devil!"

"Kiki's a reader." Sylvia smiled. "Have you come for a read or a chat, dear Miss Button?"

"You come for one and stay for the other, isn't that how it works, Kiki?" Nancy's voice was fluting. She was slender, dressed in black chiffon, and bangles jangled on her wrists. Physically, she seemed like some kind of nymph or fairy, powerfully magical, but there was nothing ethereal about her direct gaze or her sharp words. I'd been fluttering about in my own head, dreaming of poets and princes, and Nancy yanked me into the present.

The walls held shelves to just above head height, after which they were covered with portraits of writers, many of whom had handed Sylvia their photo once she'd put their books in her window. Sylvia stocked so much poetry, both new and in the library; none of the dross that I was forced to read at school, but Romantics, radical Victorians, and Modernists. I had borrowed T. S. Eliot last year and found Gerard Manly Hopkins here too.

I listened to them gossiping about poets as I scanned the shelves for Shelley; "How is dear Tom? When is *The Criterion* out? I've heard such amazing things about his new poem from Ezra." Sylvia must be talking about T. S. Eliot and . . . Ezra Pound? "I've seen some of the draft—it's called 'The Waste Land.' You will be astounded. But, then, Vivienne's worse than before." Was Nancy talking about Mrs. Eliot? I was out of my depth.

"How is Michael doing, Nancy?"

"Oh, you know, his work is successful and titillating and boring." She waved her hand in a gesture that signalled "and all the rest." "He's still a lion in the sack, though, and after holding my hand all through my recovery, I'm not complaining."

"Is *Ulysses* for him?"

"Good God, no. It's for George. Or perhaps one of the men George is trying to impress. He asked me to get him a copy."

"You won't be able to smuggle that in your trousers, like Hemingway's friend did."

"Ha! No. My hat box has a false bottom. I may as well take advantage of my womanly wiles while I can. Wouldn't you say so, Kiki?" She had a wicked smile. "Come over, don't pretend you're not listening."

I cleared my throat to hide my blush. "I prefer corsets myself," I said, "I used my school girdle to smuggle rum out of Sydney. Even if the customs inspectors deign to handle the underwear, they expect a corset to be heavy and don't bother to look too closely."

"Bravo, I'll have to try that." Nancy looked me up and down.

"Especially as we don't wear the contraptions nowadays."

"I have to admit, I still do," said Sylvia. "They help to support my back with lifting all these books. Adrienne too."

"She lifts her own boxes, does she?" Nancy's eyebrows shot up. "I thought one of her poets would do that for her."

Sylvia laughed. "They're even worse! No, we do everything, of course."

"Of course! I'll drink to that. I better go. I promised to meet Tristan this morning to help his sort out this thing with Breton. There's some friend of Emerald's who is hanging around too. I don't want to see him but he'll turn up at the Rotonde regardless." Once again Nancy turned abruptly to me. "Do you read new work?"

"Her library card says so." Sylvia nodded at me.

"Good. Then you'll fit in with all the misfits who frequent this freak show. If you see me in the Rotonde, Kiki, don't be a stranger. I'll see you soon, Sylvia." She kissed Sylvia on both cheeks and glided out of the shop.

"Nancy's a whirlwind but somehow, when the dust settles, you want the chaos back. Have you come for more poetry, Kiki?"

"Shelley."

"Percy or Mary?"

"Percy this time. I'm not familiar with him."

"He's a bit *outré*, that's why. But I do have one . . . here. . . ." Sylvia walked briskly from behind the desk to the bottom corner of one of the shelves. Nestled among books of history and political philosophy was a compendium of Shelley. She wiped off some nonexistent dust.

"This volume contains examples of his other writings, so some bright spark decided to recategorize him. But it has all his major poems." She cocked her head as she handed the book over. "Why do you like the British Romantics so much? You borrow them as often as you buy detective novels or read our little reviews."

She was a full head shorter than me and looked at me how I hoped a sister would have looked at me, how my mother never looked at me. I wanted to unburden myself, to tell her everything about Fox and Tom, my mother and the missing diary, Bertie and the war. A bicycle tooted outside and someone waved hello to Sylvia. In the few moments it took for Sylvia to look, wave, and then return her attention to me, I had pulled myself together. I had to lie; that was a spy's core work, after all, to distract, deflect, and dissemble. I could satisfy my desire to talk a little bit though; after all, the best lies are partly truth.

"I was a nurse in the war and my supervising surgeon recited them over the operating table, quoted them as he smoked his postoperative cigarette in the rain, used them to talk to the men who all thought he'd lost the plot. Just snatches, snippets, flying bits of verse. They stuck in my mind. I've made it my mission to slowly hunt down the full poems to find where all these snippets belong."

"More post-war reconstruction."

"Speaking of, do you recognize the line 'an old, mad, blind, despised—'"

"'—and dying king'? Yes, it's 'England in 1819.' That was a big favorite a couple of years ago, on its centenary. It should be in there. Hello!" She moved off to greet her next customer, but not without giving my arm a little squeeze as she went by. So much was in that squeeze—that she knew I felt more than I said, that she was here to listen but not to pry.

Sylvia was right too, as the book fell open to the poem's grimy page.

> An old, mad, blind, despised, and dying King;
> Princes, the dregs of their dull race, who flow
> Through public scorn—mud from a muddy spring;
> Rulers who neither see nor feel nor know,
> But leechlike to their fainting country cling
> Till they drop, blind in blood, without a blow.
> A people starved and stabbed in th' untilled field;
> An army, whom liberticide and prey
> Makes as a two-edged sword to all who wield;
> Golden and sanguine laws which tempt and slay;
> Religion Christless, Godless—a book sealed;
> A senate, Time's worst statute, unrepealed—
> Are graves from which a glorious Phantom may
> Burst, to illumine our tempestuous day.

This was the poem Fox referenced. The whole poem was my mission, almost exactly as written, with just a few words substituted. The politics of England in 1819, and England in 1922, had to speak to each other; the use of the whole poem almost demanded it. I flicked through and there were other grimy pages of poems well-loved and over-read, "To a Skylark," "Masque of Anarchy," "Mutability." I would need to take this home to study it. Despite the telegram with "Darkling I listen," it appeared that Shelley, not Keats, would guide this mission.

"I'll take this, Sylvia. And a copy of . . . the new Eliot poem?"

"Alas! It's not yet published."

"Keep a copy aside for me when it is." I watched her enter my name in her library index. "Tell me, was it only the occasion of the centenary that made the poem popular?"

"Poem? Oh, 'England in 1819'? I'd only just opened the shop then. I opened a year after the Armistice, almost to the day. I had quite a few veterans come in, English mainly, who wanted to read it. I think they felt its fury spoke to them. Shelley's rage at the massacre at Peterloo translated across the last century to tell them something about the war."

"As all good literature does. Peterloo, of course . . ." The name was a play on the Battle of Waterloo. I dredged up my schoolgirl history. It was a riot . . . of soldiers? Put down by soldiers? According to the poem, it was exemplary government corruption. No wonder it appealed to bitter survivors of our war.

"I'll come back for the Eliot." I got as far as the door when Sylvia called my name.

"I almost forgot! Someone paid for this copy of *Ulysses* for you, Kiki."

"Who?"

"I was hoping you might tell me! I received a check in the post from a John Smith—does such a man even exist?—with a postmark from Westminster, London. Is Mr. Smith a literary lover?"

It could only be Fox. "He was never my lover."

"Well, he has good taste."

"I think he means this to be a joke. But the joke will be on him when I read it and love it."

"Oh, you will, I promise you." Sylvia beamed.

All I could hope for was that Joyce wasn't as cryptic as Fox.

I couldn't work on the letter without more clues. I couldn't get more clues until I spoke to Fox and I couldn't speak to Fox until he provided his contact details. Were they in *Ulysses*? I almost dropped the book on the cobblestones; it would be too cruel, and just like Fox, to hide his contact details somewhere in 900 pages of dense text. All these games . . . how urgent was the mission, really, if he didn't tell me straightaway? The wind picked up the rain remnants from the road and flung them at my ankles. It would also be too cruel, and just like him, to let me waste time unraveling clues, so I would then have to rush to complete the mission. I needed more cigarettes, and a proper drink, and maybe even some food. I wanted warmth and comfort.

No wonder I spent so much time in cafés. They were the only places where I could give the orders.

'RUNNIN' WILD'

It was a jolt to remember that my life was more than spying. More letters had arrived while I was out, all from Bertie, all reminding me that I had other work to do. Among the cards of invitation to various parties around Paris, the letters of introduction to people to confirm my status as a writer for the *Star*, was Bertie's delightful, pointed, personal note.

Have you settled in, dearest Kiki? Have you stuffed yourself with oysters and champagne at the Rotonde? Have you smoked out your old lovers? Have you left your shoes in one parlor and your stockings in another? Because Our Editor, Sir Huffandpuff Himself, wants a column of yours sooner than yesterday. Here are some more invitations to keep you going—diplomatic or American, mostly, but they'll do. In the meantime, send your anxious readers a Hello to let them know you're back. Send me a Hello.

And he was right, of course, in what he didn't say: that Paris and Fox, Theo and champagne, had made me forget what paid for my independence. The necessity of a weekly gossip column on the bright lights of

Parisian society had barely registered, but without it, I was dependent either on my father or on Fox; never again.

I could do better than dull diplomatic drinks though. I was booked to dine with scandal.

⚬∾⚬

Maxim's was fast becoming the most famous restaurant in Paris. It was full, even on a Thursday afternoon. Groups of beautiful women sat at tables in the window. They reminded me of the working girls that sat in the large front windows of houses by the trainline, goods on display as the trains rolled into Paris, except here their clothes were silk and noticeably free of holes. The interior was dark enough that, once inside, you couldn't tell if it was morning or midnight. What you could see were the lush Art Nouveau decorations in red, gold, green, and black. Nude women lounged in murals above the diners. Flowers curled in the stained-glass windows, around mirrors, and their bell-shaped blossoms became lampshades. Each door was round and framed with stylized leaves. It was heavenly, if you liked that sort of thing. The people here clearly did, as did the couple who had just entered and looked around with delight. Their skin was luminous and their dark hair shone, their clothes were perfectly tailored and they gave their coats to the staff without even looking; they had to be Prince Felix Yusupov and Princess Irène, Theo's sister and brother-in-law.

"Felix Felixovitch, Irina Alexandrovna." I held out my hand. "Kiki Button. Thank you so much for agreeing to meet me."

"Who taught you our formal address? Theo?" Felix raised an eyebrow.

"Please, call me Irène, everyone does." Irène's handshake was just a touch, almost as if she expected me to kiss her hand. She wore the palest shade of lilac, a dress so exquisitely cut that it floated around her body, the sleeve slipping over her pale skin.

"This place delights me every time I come here." Irène sighed. "So beautiful and, what's the word . . ."

"Rich." Felix replied.

"No, don't be vulgar." She slapped him playfully. "Sensuous, that's the word. So very French."

Felix was busy ordering champagne and caviar, and she leant forward to me.

"Speaking of, I'm so glad you're taking care of darling Theo. Montparnasse is not really our scene, but Theo seems much happier after a night there. Will he be joining us?" Her inference was in only the slightest of smiles.

"Of course he will," Felix cut in. "Lunch at Maxim's? No one says no."

"But his taxi . . ." Irène whispered "taxi" like the word was something dirty.

"He had better change out of that grimy suit, that's all I can say."

"No need," I said as I saw Theo come in. "It seems he's found a dinner jacket that fits."

Theo strode over to our table, kissed his sister's cheeks, shook his brother-in-law's hand, and kissed my hand with a wink. He had set up this meeting so I could interview Felix and Irène. This was not only a favor to me, as I had said that I would help out Theo by using the interview to investigate Felix's politics. I was, of course, silent about any ulterior motives for doing so. Theo hadn't laughed when I said I had wanted to call the column "Lunch at Maxim's with Rasputin's Killer," but simply said "Be subtle, *chérie*." If the way Felix drained his first glass of champagne and quickly drank another was anything to go by, "subtle" would go the same way as their Russian palaces.

"So, your readers want to know what it's like to have lunch with Rasputin's killer, correct?" Felix grinned at the protests of Irène and Theo.

"They want princes and princesses, Paris, and gossip."

"They shall have it!" Felix topped up my glass. "Shall we give the interview in English? I spent my university days in London, we were in London just a couple of years ago . . ."

"But my English is not perfect," said Theo. "Let's stick to French."

"I'll leave you to describe all of this, Kiki." Felix waved his hand at the rich surroundings. "But how a prince feels about losing his country, well, that's a . . . a 'scoop' as they say in English, yes?"

"As long as it's a scoop of wit and chiffon, Prince Felix, then—"

"You can provide that for your readers. What does Kiki Button want from me?"

I returned his hard gaze. "Blood on the snow and the long trail of memory."

"Excellent!"

Irène pouted as she took a spoonful of caviar. "Felix, be good. Don't make my aunt and uncle seem hapless and somehow ridiculous."

"Of course not, *ma chérie*! But the lady has asked. Besides, it will really give her readers something to think about, *non*? Now, Kiki, can you imagine what it is like to see your queen consort with the devil? His flashing eyes, his greasy hair, his long fingers that soiled everything he touched? The tsarina was—"

"Oh, Felix . . ."

"Really, Kiki, take this with a pinch of salt."

Felix put up his hands. "Alright! I'll be very kind to my in-laws. But you have to admit the tsarina was desperate for a cure for little Alexei Nikolaievitch, for our *tsarevich*, yes?"

"Poor little Sasha, who wouldn't worry?"

"He had the 'Royal Disease.'" Theo lit my cigarette.

"Once he started to bleed, he couldn't stop. Fatal for anyone, but especially for a little boy." Felix spooned caviar into his mouth. "So, the tsarina worried. Everyone worried, the heir to the throne was sick. Then the devil came along and, seeing the tsarina's need, created a little home for himself. He put his filthy fingers all over the boy, then he apparently healed him from hundreds of miles away! They say he was touched by God." Felix made the sign of the cross over himself. "But so was Lucifer before he fell. No, Rasputin's aim was to weaken my wife's family," he took Irène's hand here and kissed it, "and to let in the agents of evil to destroy Russia. I had to do what I could."

Felix said all this while eating and drinking. He was a skilled performer.

"I started to see Rasputin as a patient. I pretended I had anxiety, bad dreams, premonitions. He ran his long dirty nails over my face, he spoke in a gravelly voice that seemed to come from the pit of hell. I had to pretend he put me in a trance and do all he said. But this . . . violation was worth it as it revealed his innermost desire: power. Power was his drug. He would do anything for it, anything to break our rightful hold over Russia and bring in his Bolshevik dogs. I had to stop him.

"I gathered a group of righteous men around me—Purishkevich, Sukhotin, de Lazovert, and Grand Duke Dmitri Pavlovich, that is, Irène's cousin, Dima. By then Rasputin trusted me, he assumed I was another of those who depended on him. His arrogance made him stupid and his stupidity made him weak. When I invited him to my family home, the Moika Palace, to view some of our renovations, he accepted. He came in his usual black rags, hair lank around his face, his dragging step as though his devil's disguise was too heavy for him. He sat in my parlor and smiled with his brown teeth.

"We fed him poisoned wine. We chatted, our nerves were strung tight." Felix froze, acting out his watching. "Nothing. He drank the wine down and nothing happened! How could any human body drink such poison and survive? Not just one glass but three! He was truly a devil. We cast our frightened, incredulous eyes to one another as Rasputin sat there, serene. There was nothing for it. We would have to take more drastic action.

"We invited him to see something in the cellar and he came without demur. Sukhotin was a soldier. He knew what had to be done. He had the revolver in his hand, he called the devil to look him in the face, and he shot. Rasputin's body received the bullet, but did the devil die? No! He shuddered, he rolled, then he got up! He came toward me, he grabbed my shoulder and would have throttled me if I hadn't shot him again. Then he stumbled out into the December night, trailing blood. A bullet was the deadliest thing we had, so we shot him again, that devil, and this time, finally, he went down. His devil's disguise was a stain against the snow.

"Sukhotin took Rasputin's coat and hat and walked to his home, so the people wouldn't know straightaway that the devil had gone. The rest of us took his body and dumped it in the nearby Malaya Nevka River. It was grubby but necessary, as we knew that the tsarina would naturally take time to understand how we had helped her, helped the *tsarevich*, and helped Russia. It did take time—enough time that Dima was exiled to the Persian front, Purishkevich to the Romanian front, and I was exiled to my country estate." Felix had his hand over Irène's, who looked queasy beneath her expression of indulgent boredom. She had clearly heard this story before and didn't like it. "It's hard to convey what it meant to be isolated from the capital. And for Dima and Volodya to be thrown into the war! But we were all glad to serve Russia, however we could."

"Oh . . . you didn't fight?" I asked. I could see Theo trying to hide his smirk in his champagne glass.

"Alas, I could not. I tried." He shrugged. "We set up a home for wounded soldiers at the Liteyney Palace, didn't we, *chérie*? And—"

"Sorry, is that a different palace? How many palaces did you own?"

"Palace is just the name for a home that isn't an apartment, or a shack." He waved his hand dismissively. "We tried to save Russia, we perjured our souls to do so, but in the end, all that effort was for nothing. We were too late. The damage had been done, the Bolshevik dogs had been let into the Winter Palace and, in 1917, they tore it down with their teeth. We fled with nothing but the clothes we stood in."

"And a few diamonds." Theo raised his glass. "And some paintings and so on."

"We had to, Theo," said Irène. "It's his heritage as well as his inheritance. You know this."

"Those peasants could never appreciate its true value anyway." Felix almost spat out his words. "To them everything is just bread, vodka, or a manger to rut in."

"Felix, that's not fair," Irène's admonishment was too gentle. "Nadya isn't like that."

"Nor your chauffeur," said Theo.

"You mean you?" Felix laughed. "You're both right. It's all the fault of the Bolsheviks, poisoning the people's thoughts for years. That's why we need to give them real food for thought!"

"Oh, Felix, darling, not this. We're in France. The French don't talk politics at the dinner table." Irène indicated the chicken cooked in cream and the delicate spears of green beans the waiter had brought to our table. He was placing goblets next to our champagne glasses in anticipation of the new wine that would grace the meal.

"How can we talk about anything else?" asked Felix.

"I want to know about Kiki's fabulous dress . . ."

"But Kiki wants blood on the snow. Let me tell you, Mademoiselle Button, there'll be more blood on the snow before too long. I know people. There are plans afoot."

"Which people? What plans?" I leant forward, imitating the position of his body. He was seated directly across the table from me, so this little intimacy cut off Theo and Irène. Irène sighed theatrically and let the waiter serve her chicken, while Theo kept a little smile on his face. Felix gave me a small nod to indicate that he'd talk once the waiters had left.

"There's a man, a wonderful man—oh, not your type at all, my dear Feodor Alexandrovich—but truly excellent, very committed, beautiful hands. Edouard Hausmann, you know, like the man who transformed Paris from a slum den to this city of modern boulevards. He's one of his relatives, I'm sure . . . Edouard has been telling me about a group of men like myself, like you too, Theo, whether you own it or not. Proper men, noble men of old houses, who want to restore Europe to its glory. Not this fractured, fragmented . . ."

"Rubble ruled by rabble . . ." I goaded. It was all I could do when my heart pounded: Hausmann was involved.

"Yes! You understand. Not this mutilated soldier we have now, but a beautiful Europe, a strong Europe, from London to St. Petersburg—never Petrograd, always St. Petersburg—and not Moscow either, that over-grown village. Edouard knows men who are committed to making this happen. He knows how passionate I am about this and he sought me out especially to join his cause."

"Which cause is that?" I asked. Theo squeezed my knee under the table as a thank you.

"The Italians call themselves *fascisti*, so fascism is the general term. You've heard of this? Good, so you know how important it is. Edouard's been introducing us, so to speak, so that we can work together more effectively."

"Like a Soviet," Theo said.

"Yes, like a—no! Not at all like a Soviet!"

"Theo, don't tease." But Irène matched his smile.

"Like soldiers, a band of brothers." Felix gestured with his fork. "We will take back our lands, our lives, from the rabble who has stolen them. Do they think, just because they are numerous, that they have more of a right to the land than us, who have held it safe for centuries? Like so many rats, they have overrun Russia, Austria, Germany, Galicia, all the way to the Mediterranean. Europe is being ruined by these rats and their revolutionary plague and we must exterminate them!"

"Felix, darling, please calm down."

"And who would run your estate if you exterminated all of them?" Theo raised an eyebrow.

"Alright, alright. These two keep me on the straight and narrow. Just the Bolsheviks, yes? Lenin and that grasping Trotsky and all those dogs. Am I allowed to revile these rabble-rousers? Good. Edouard has a plan. He's so persuasive, such fire in his eyes, perfect Savile Row suit. I'm always suscep-tible to a man in a good suit . . . but really the plan is very sound. A real show of strength. He's telling me about it soon, once all the details are in place."

"Not now?"

"No, well . . . I haven't formally joined the group. It's a requirement, a bit like the Masons, I suppose. Not that I ever wanted to be a Mason . . . but Edouard, he has such conviction, I might follow him anywhere."

Irène rolled her eyes. "Just don't let him lead you here, Felix. Maxim's is our special place."

Felix picked up Irène's hand and kissed it; this was the signal to end political talk and begin the gossip. It was clear that Edouard's persuasiveness was not merely political, with his "fiery eyes" and "beautiful hands." It must be the same Eddy Houseman, formerly Bertie's lover and Fox's agent, the same Edward Hausmann I confronted in my mission last year.

It was also clear that, if he knew anything, a showman such as Felix would have bragged about it. Felix was a prince, my mission statement wrote of princes, Hausmann had reappeared: I had a dreadful feeling that my mission would once again set me up against the Fascists.

Over the rest of the meal—which I noted down for my readers, chicken followed by a dessert of delicate apple flan, cognac, and coffee—we chatted about the delights of Paris. Irène wanted to open a fashion house and was gathering ideas, interrogating me on every detail of my outfit. Theo kept stroking my leg under the table. The other guests were looking at us, some discreetly curious and others blatantly staring. They were quite gorgeous, these Romanovs and Yusupovs, with their pale skin and dark features, graceful movements in luxurious clothes, Irène's diamonds and Felix's loud laugh. Every movement, every word, spoke of power. And of course, with Rasputin's murder and the tsar's execution, they were famous, even for Paris. Bertie was going to love this. I guessed that this was why Hausmann had also made Felix a target.

Even though the *Star* paid for the lunch, Felix left a tip so generous that the waiters bowed to him. As Felix was being helped into his coat, he turned to me.

"So, is our little luncheon enough titillation for your readers?"

"I'm planning on calling the column 'Lunch at Maxim's with Rasputin's Killer.'"

Theo gasped but Felix laughed. "Excellent! Send me a copy."

I was about to follow them out the door when the old man who brought me my coat looked at me full in the face, put his hand on my arm, and nodded to the head waiter.

"It must be," he said.

"Mademoiselle," the head waiter bowed, "I'm sorry to bother you, but you remind us very much of a beautiful woman who used to visit. An English woman, she promised she would return soon but she has not come. I know this is an impertinence, but you look so alike . . . perhaps you know her?"

"Mademoiselle King," the old man said.

"No, Albert, her married name is Madame Cordelia Bouton."

He said my name in the French way.

"That's my mother."

"YOU REMIND ME OF MY MOTHER"

They exclaimed with delight, telling me how beautiful I was, how beautiful she was, how lucky this meeting was, but I could barely move with shock. Theo looked at me, concerned, but I just shook my head and watched him follow his sister down the street.

"Albert, run and fetch the coat. Tell us, how is your wonderful mother?"

"She . . . she's . . ." Thankfully I didn't need to finish the sentence.

"Oh, my deepest condolences, Mademoiselle . . . Bouton, is it not?"

I nodded.

The head waiter looked around at the restaurant, then ushered me into a little alcove, as opulent as the rest, with nymphs and flowers, curling leaves in gold, and dark wooden furniture. He indicated for me to sit on a deep velvet bench set into the wall. Another nod brought a waiter with tea in a delicate green cup. The head waiter produced an ashtray and a lighter before I even realized I needed a cigarette. Albert hurried back with a soft blush-pink coat in both his hands.

"How is Madame . . ." he faltered at the stern look on the head waiter's face. "Mademoiselle, I'm so sorry."

He handed the coat to the head waiter who extracted a book from the pocket, folded the coat carefully, and tied book and coat together with a ribbon he produced from his pocket, placing the bundle on the table in front of me.

"Madame Bouton walked out without this last time she was here."

"That must have been years ago."

"It was," Albert said.

"Nothing is too much for our valued customers. She's visited us almost since we opened. We would do . . . we would have done anything for her." He dropped his head. "I'm so very sorry."

"How did she leave a coat behind?"

"It was a balmy night. The day had had spots of chill rain, I remember, but when the skies cleared at dusk a warm breeze blew through the streets, the kind that spoke of love's bright possibilities."

"Jean's a poet." Albert spoke sotto voce.

"Albert had taken ill and gone home early. I did my best but your mother was, as always, surrounded by friends, being addressed by two or three people at once but speaking only to one of them, intensely, binding them to her with her luminous eyes."

I had never seen my mother with "luminous eyes." His descriptions were as over-the-top as the décor.

"I didn't notice the coat until the next day. She called, asking about it, and promised to pick it up next time she was here."

"This café opened almost thirty years ago. You must have known her well."

"Oh, Mademoiselle King . . ." Albert sighed theatrically. Jean frowned and Albert went back to the cloak room.

"Albert is a little sentimental."

"My mother made an impression, then."

"Of course!" He looked at me sceptically. "You must know that she inspired poetry." He tapped the little book he had tied to the package. It was a slim volume with a dark blue cover, red letters spelling *The London Muse: an anthology*.

"No one wrote verses to her beauty in Australia."

"Ah! Well. Perhaps she was too delicate for all that sunshine."

"Not even 'perhaps.'"

"She was a true beauty, mademoiselle. She came first when she was herself a mademoiselle, surrounded by admirers. She was like one of the women on our walls here . . . in fact, I think she is one of the women on our walls here. She sat for artists, she spent long hours conversing with poets, and at the end of the night she always helped make sure the bill was paid. She had a smile . . ." He breathed in with the memory. "She had a smile that made you feel as though you were the only person who mattered in the whole world. Which wasn't her smile, of course, but the way she looked at you, those eyes with their changing color . . ."

"Who were these artists?" Could one of them have been her secret lover?

"Always a different group, but they included Matisse, Mucha, Russell, Rodin, Valery . . . sometimes those scruffians from Montmartre and Montparnasse would turn up too, Apollinaire, Modigliani, Picasso . . ."

"Even after she was married?"

"Yes, of course. I never saw Monsieur Bouton, but her marriage didn't seem to make any difference to her appeal. The way she became a little . . . wiser with each visit. All of us become sadder with age, except with her a little melancholy only made her more beautiful."

"Sydney doesn't go in for melancholy. As you say, too much sunshine."

"She was perfect for Paris. I never saw anyone who could glide so easily between the pauper painters in Montmartre and the high-society patrons who came here merely for breakfast. Only the war stopped her being the toast of the salons."

"These artists . . . was there one in particular who was her special companion?"

"Not that I saw, mademoiselle. She knew how to be discreet."

"How very Parisian." I looked into his sympathetic face and couldn't see a trace of insincerity. This made me more confused than ever—the beauty he described was not the mother I knew, nor the woman in the diaries—I needed some space to think. I took the package and got up to leave. "Thank you, you've been so—"

"Wait, come with me." He ushered me through the restaurant to a wall near the kitchens. On the wall were photographs, dozens of them, of famous people who had come to Maxim's. I immediately recognized Sarah Bernhardt and Marechal Petain, Maurice Chevalier and Raymond Poincaré. Jean stood by a photo in the corner.

"Here she is, with her friends, in . . . 1894."

"Two years before I was born." I peered at the photo. "Is that Rodin?"

Jean leaned forward. "It is, with Matisse, Russell, Monet, the Norwegian Munch . . . I don't recognize the others, they weren't regulars. The men who flank Mademoiselle King, as she was then, are Rodin, as you recognized, and Russell, with Matisse at the front."

My mother wasn't merely smiling, she was laughing at the camera. She was literally surrounded by men, everyone smiling and touching each other with linked arms, arms round shoulders, silly poses. I couldn't stop staring. The woman in her diaries was disappointed, regretful, and generally blue. This woman was so full of joy, she was in the place where she truly belonged. I blinked rapidly to stop the tears, I tilted my head back as though to roll the offending drops back into my eyes, but they were too numerous and they spilled down my cheeks. Jean softly touched my back and guided me into the kitchens, where he handed me a napkin.

"I'm so sorry, mademoiselle . . ."

"Don't be." I sniffed. "I . . ." But I had to stop or I would simply bawl. Jean promised to try and procure a copy of the photo for me. When I didn't want to go through the restaurant with tears down my face, he kindly showed me the staff entrance out the back, escorting me through the rubbish-strewn alley with its society of stray cats, to the street, kissing my hand and telling me he'd do anything for the daughter of Madame Cordelia Bouton.

"NEATH THE SOUTH SEA MOON"

I don't really remember how I got home, but I suspected I walked, package banging against my legs, all the way to Montparnasse. All I could think of was how I never knew my mother and I could never get to know her, how cruel that was now that I knew how much we might have had in common. I remember only moments: stopping once or twice to hold back tears, leaning heavily on the stairwell wall to get me upstairs, tripping over my own shoes in the doorway. I collapsed on the bed, but now that I had privacy, I couldn't cry. I lay like a corpse on the pillow as my eyes stung, my throat scratched, and my head throbbed from unspoken sobs.

She had only been fifty-one. She could have had another twenty years of loving life, Paris, art, and parties. I could have saved her from her disappointing days. Is that why she wanted to see me, is that why she finally sent that letter last year, asking to visit? It was hard to fit the joyful young woman with the rule-bound sad-sack, the bohemian Beauty with the Matron who sent off her only daughter to get married. Why had she been like that? Why hadn't she encouraged me, why had she insisted I do the usual thing? Admittedly, she had been lukewarm in her insistence, but she'd been lukewarm about everything, so much so that I hadn't even known she'd loved me until I read her diaries. A page from her diaries was burnt into my memory, written in 1899, a few years after that photo had been taken: "I can't do it. I can't leave my little Katherine forever. Here in Paris, even as the life of the streets makes me tremble, I long to hold her, to kiss her soft golden hair, to see her run in from the garden with her skinned knees and dirty cheeks. So, I shall have to go back. I shall have to return, and return, and return. This is my fate, to be Persephone, allowed to live only once a year, and for the rest to be trapped in my antipodean underworld." I had read that over and over, said it aloud as I paced the rooms in her terrace. It explained so much about her.

But not about X, the mysterious man mentioned over and over in her diaries. She had loved him, she must have to have mentioned him so often, but this love was only expressed obliquely, through descriptions of his clothing, or the sounds of her surroundings, or the mutable sky. I still had no idea what made her choose my father; her diaries were curiously silent on that point. I could now guess, however, that X was probably an artist.

I smoked the rest of my cigarettes as I wrote out my notes from the interview. It was all I could do to stop myself crying. I would write up the column tomorrow and send it to Bertie. I felt spent, I needed food but wanted no company. I picked up my copy of *Ulysses* and headed out, not to one of the cafés where I might see a friend and be obliged to chat, but to a little backstreet with an Indochinese noodle house.

The noodle house had no blonde society women in it, no members of the expatriate "Avant-Guard," only men and women from French Indochina looking for a taste of home. Everyone looked up when I entered, but only for a moment, before they went back to their steaming bowls, and newspapers that looked like they were written in French but held not a single French word.

"What language is that?" I asked the man opposite me. The noodle house held long tables, each table with six seats and a corridor down the middle to the kitchen, like a canteen. The man looked up.

"Sorry, I don't mean to interrupt."

"It's Vietnamese," he said. "You've never seen it before?"

"No. I'm not French."

"You're not from Tonkin? Annam? Then why are you in here?"

"It smelt good."

"Better than any café. They all reek of overcooked cream." He looked me over. The waitress came up to get my order but he spoke to her in his language; I hadn't expected it to sound so musical. The waitress nodded and seemed to come back almost instantly with a huge bowl of noodles, another plate with white shoots and green leaves and red herbs, and a pot of tea with a tiny bowl-like cup.

"I ordered you the best," he said, "*Phở bo*, noodle soup with beef. Classic food from Hai Duong. If you like the way this place smells then you will like this soup. Add the shoots in as you wish, and the basil leaves, and chili. Have you seen this before?" He pointed to the red herb.

"Once. In Chinatown, in Sydney."

"It's extremely spicy. Eat with caution. Is that your reading material for this meal?" He pointed to *Ulysses*. "Read with caution." He laughed at his own joke.

"You've read James Joyce?"

"I have no wish for punishment." He laughed again. "I read Marx first in English, but it's not a language I have much love for."

"I'm Kiki."

"Nguyễn." He took a pencil from his pocket and wrote it at the top of his newspaper. "Nguyễn. I'm here every night, except when I attend the Party meetings. Say hello next time and I'll tell you about my country."

"French Indochina? I've always wanted—"

"It's not French." He folded up his newspaper and stood up to leave. "It's Việt Nam."

The soup was delicious. The chili was much hotter than I expected and I ended up drinking an entire coconut to cool my tongue, much to the amusement of the waitress. *Ulysses* sat beside me as I ate, as the soup required both hands, one for a spoon and one for my inexpert use of chopsticks. I had time to look around the little noodle house as I ate. There were photos of Việt Nam on the faded blue walls and the front windows were opaque with steam. The tables were bare of linen and the chairs bare of upholstery, clearly so they could be easily cleaned as I watched the waitress quickly slick down a table between diners. Everyone who came in gave me a glance but no one else spoke to me. I had all the privacy that I needed.

Eventually I was left just with my tea and Joyce. But I hadn't got much further than "Stately, plump Buck Mulligan . . ." when a slip of paper slipped into my lap. I knew that luxe cream paper—I held the tea in my mouth, I couldn't swallow—and I knew that spidery black handwriting. Fox was overdoing it once again. I closed my eyes and swallowed; I did not want my mission to intrude here tonight. I thought this place could have been a haven but Fox had followed me here too. I looked around the little blue café, its photos on the walls, a Buddha figure surrounded by fruit on the countertop. Was it too much to ask for just for one more night to enjoy Paris and all the delights of noodle soup and avant-garde novels it could offer? The letter was heavy in my hands. Apparently it was.

"SHIMMY WITH ME"

It was dark when I returned to my studio flat and I read by candlelight. I flicked the letter over but there was no second page. The letter was, like the mission, only a poem.

Rarely, rarely, comest thou,
Spirit of Delight!
Wherefore hast thou left me now
Many a day and night?
Many a weary nightingale day
'Tis since thou are fled away.

How shall ever one like me
Win thee back again?
With the joyous and the free
Thou wilt scoff at pain.
Spirit false! thou hast forgot
All but those who need thee not.

As a lizard with the shade
Of a lustrous leaf,
Thou with sorrow art dismay'd;
Even the sighs of grief
Reproach thee, that thou art not near,
And reproach thou wilt not hear.

Let me set my mournful ditty
To a merry measure;
Thou wilt never come for pity,
Thou wilt come for pleasure;
Thy happy lot will cut away
Those cruel wings, and thou wilt stay.

I love all that thou lovest,
Spirit of Delight!
The fresh Earth in new leaves dress'd,
And the starry night;
Autumn evening, and the morn
When the golden mists are born.

I love snow, and forlorn forms
Of the radiant frost;
I love waves, and winds, and storms,
Everything almost
Which is Nature's, and may be
Untainted by man's misery.

I love tranquil solitude,
And such society
As is quiet, wise, and good;
One minute past, and

What difference? but thou dost possess
The things I seek, not love them less.

I love Love—though he has wings,
And like light can flee,
But above all other things,
Spirit, I love thee—
Thou art love and life! Oh come,
Make once more my heart thy home.

"Many a weary nightingale day"—nightingale was surely not in the original poem. This poem was in code. It was Shelley, called only after the first line, "Rarely, rarely, comest thou." "Nightingale" wasn't the only substitution. There was also "thy happy lot," "forlorn," "one minute past," and possibly "lustrous." These were all words or phrases from Keats's "Ode to a Nightingale," which I knew inside out. "Nightingale" was the first clue and this was the key; the other words would refer to something within or about "Ode to a Nightingale."

Stuck in the folds of my passport was the copy of "Ode to a Nightingale" that Fox had given me when I first started nursing for him. My copy was now brown with travel and frayed at the edges, spotted with tea and coffee and what looked like blood. But the title was clear: "Ode to a Nightingale (early May)." "Early May" was not usually published as part of the title; in fact, I had only seen it on this copy. I had an inkling that "nightingale" had something to do with "May." I looked at the other words but there was no obvious link between them. Unless it was their position in "Ode to a Nightingale"—"nightingale" was line 1, "lustrous" was line 39 (it was so helpful that each stanza was ten lines), "thy happy lot" was 5, "forlorn" was 71, and "one minute past" was 4. No, if "one minute past" was 4, then "nightingale" couldn't be 1 as the word didn't appear in the poem except in the title. Was "nightingale" actually zero? 0395714—that collection of numbers was nonsensical, unless only some of the numbers mattered.

5714 could be the end of a telephone number—now I felt I was getting somewhere—which left 0 and 39, nightingale and lustrous. 039: another telephone number? A date, a time? That made no sense. What about the words, what could they have to do with each other? Maybe "nightingale" of the title did relate to "may," as a synonym, a substitution within a substitution? May-lustrous? May-beauty? May-fair?

I couldn't help myself, I yelled "Aha!" into the chill night. Mayfair 5714—this must be the number to call Fox. Was it his club? In Mayfair, it was more likely to be his London home.

A cold wind crept under the window frame and wrapped around my neck. He had given me his home number in the poem—home is where the heart is—his heart was in the poem. Shelley and his abstract Spirit of Delight disappeared and I could hear Fox's silvery voice flow like mercury, poisonous and powerful, through the lines to speak to me directly. It was so intimate that I felt sick.

I opened the window wide, the night air damp and wild, moving under my hair and in my sleeves and making it hard to light my cigarette. The view at night was a carnival of light and noise, it was a photographic negative of the subtle elegance of the day. The Eiffel Tower lit up like a beacon, calling all the street life out of their crannies and into the rain-heavy air. I inhaled deeply and considered what the entirety of the poem meant. It was unlike Fox to be so personal, but if he wasn't calling me with this song, then why was it here? That final stanza was too much, he couldn't possibly mean it, I doubt he would ever think of something so over-the-top. I had never made his heart my home and never would; he must know it. No, this "spirit of delight" had to refer to something other than me—our work together, Englishness, King and Country, something. That it seemed to speak to me was just a game, a play for power, it had to be.

The bells in the church rang; it was nine o'clock. If I had to call Fox at his home in Mayfair, and not at his work in Westminster, then now was as good a time as any.

"DER ZWERG"

Telephones were still a novelty in Montparnasse. As I collected my things I tried to think where there might be one I could use—the Hôtel des Ecoles, just up the street? It seemed too cheap to need a telephone. There was one at the Rotonde, I had used it last year, but it was in the manager's office and not at all public. Private residences might have one, of course, but whose? I really needed to find a telephone where I could call Fox throughout this mission, somewhere straightforward where I'd never have to beg or persuade. There was sure to be one at the station.

Gare Montparnasse was only a few minutes' walk away. It was one of those grandiose train stations built last century, before trains were associated with rows of uniforms, lines of bandaged wounded, and forever-goodbyes. A couple of decades ago there had been a spectacular accident: A train had plunged right off the tracks and through the front window, spilling onto the street like a child's toy. The façade of the building still held the scars of this accident, with the stone chipped and the replacement bricks a different color. The station was busy with trains running to and from the French countryside, farmers and weavers, merchants and winemakers, the rural poor desperate for money and well-fed Parisians desperate for space. This autumn night there were people coming and going for the weekend, people drinking at the station bar, ragged boys begging for errands and ragged girls selling matches. I bought a box of matches from a pale girl.

"Is there a telephone inside this station?"

"Yes, mademoiselle."

"Show me." I slipped her a whole franc. Her eyes widened but when I put my finger to my lips, she nodded and put the money silently in her pocket. She wove her way through the departing passengers to a little booth at the far end of the station. It was wedged between the guardhouse and the bar, a glass cubicle with blue frames.

"What's your name?"

"Delphine." She curtsied, her lank hair flopping forward as she did so. She moved quickly for someone with rough wooden clogs on her feet. Her clothes were grubby, with a skirt so full of holes it could masquerade as lace.

"Do you sell matches here every day, Delphine?"

"Yes, mademoiselle."

"Then I might see you again." She could be useful. I felt a pang that I was already recruiting; she didn't need any more hardship in her life. But then again, if she was to help me, I'd buy her some proper shoes and probably teach her to read. Surely that was better than selling matches. She looked at me, pallid and expectant.

"In fact, make sure that I do." I slipped her another coin. She took it with perfect gravity, curtsied like I was her new mistress, and resumed her match-selling. I noticed she had a new ring to her voice as she sang out her wares, she stood a little straighter and ignored the taunts from the boys around her.

"London, Mayfair 5714, please." I was surprised how confident I sounded saying Fox's number, how straightforward the French operator was, then the English operator, the fuzz and static on the line, the operator checking if Fox would accept reverse charges. I kicked out the cigarette butts that littered the floor and shut the door tightly. There were too many people about, but despite this, the station buzzed with loneliness. Under the harsh electric lamps, every unfilled space rang with absence.

"Fox." His voice was steel, not silver, as he answered the call.

"Darkling I listen."

Then he laughed. I was flooded with a relief so profound it felt like joy.

"Hail to thee, blithe spirit!"

"No spirit, nor any light-winged dryad of the trees—"

"Bird thou never wert!"

"I'm flesh and blood, skin and bone."

"And brain. When will you teach me half your gladness?"

"You couldn't know the half of the half."

"That harmonious madness?"

"Precisely. Your madness has rhythm but no harmony. Like a machine."

"The world listens to machines."

"As I am listening now."

"Very good, Vixen." He made a satisfied-sounding hum. "I thought you might have imagined me as Frankenstein's monster, so I'm glad I avoided that allusion."

"You remind me more of Frankenstein himself."

"And you're the monster?"

"And I'm Mary Shelley."

He left a long pause. "A year is a long time for a funeral."

"I got stuck in Sydney in 1899, just as now I'm stuck in England in 1819." I wanted to get away from the personal and onto the professional. I was only calling him to get the key to the mission. With the door closed, the booth stank of stale smoke.

"It's England in 1922 you need to attend to."

"I'm in France, Fox."

Another pause. "Joyce is very poetic, wouldn't you say, in his use of language? He certainly admires poets, spends his time with poets and librettists, calls himself an artist and not merely a writer."

Where the sweet hell was this going? Surely he had not read *Ulysses* . . .
poets and a clever use of language, aha, that was the key to the clues. I
took out the mission letter and read over it once again.

"'England' is a metonym for the royal family."

"Very good, Vixen."

"The princes are real princes then."

"Their mother would say so."

"Mother? Ah, so they're brothers, two brother princes. Soldiers, if all
those war references have any meaning."

"Tinker, tailor, soldier—"

"Sailor—naval men?"

Fox hummed.

"Or one of them is a sailor and the other is a soldier . . . but what
war is there now for English princes?"

"It is a grave situation."

"Grave—that's in the letter, along with all that talk of trenches and
shelling and Versailles statutes." Someone's barking laugh was cut off as
the door to the station bar slammed shut. "While I'm thinking out loud,
tell me: black-clad, brown shirt, free corps . . . have I met these princes
before? Or the houseboys, perhaps?"

"I see I'm going to have to make these clues a little more complicated
next time."

"Or you could just tell me what I have to do and when, as you did in
the war."

"You miss the good old days?"

"They weren't good, as the photos you gave me show."

"'We look before and after and pine for what is not.'"

"Are they payment or a threat?"

"'Our sincerest laughter with some pain is fraught.'"

"'Our sweetest songs are those that tell of saddest thought.'" Fox was
quoting Shelley's "To a Skylark," the same poem on the back of the
photographs. "That's just post-war life."

"Are you sure?"

"Sure of what? That it's life, or that it's post war?"

"These games really are beneath you. I've underestimated you."

"Just tell me what I have to do and when." But I winced at my own impatience. I must never betray my feelings to Fox, even if that feeling was easily understandable frustration, as any such admission gave him too much power. I just had to play the game as he wanted it played, to the very end, or I would never get my payment: full proof of Tom's innocence. I chewed the end of my pencil in place of a cigarette; it was too stuffy in this booth to smoke.

"Teach me half your madness, Vixen."

"Madness? That is the saddest thought."

"But it makes the sweetest song."

He wanted me to "sing" the clues. I put my notebook and the mission on the little bench that supported the telephone.

"There are two princes, brothers, who represent England. They will be 'dragged' by 'houseboys' into 'public scorn,' that is, into doing something that will shame the monarchy. I assume, therefore, that I need to stop that happening. 'Realpolitik' and Shelley's own radicalism mean that this shameful thing they intend to do is political. This something has to do with the brown shirts, the 'free corps' or Freikorps, and black-clad somebodies as well. The title of the poem you use, 'England in 1819,' suggests that this political something is anti-English . . . combined with the brown-shirts, I'd guess it would be something against England's centuries-old democracy."

"I applaud you." He sounded disappointed.

"'We look before and after and pine for what is not.'" "To a Skylark" intruded; there had to be another meaning, there always was. "Is this something to do with the aristocratic resurrection that Prince Felix Yusupov was talking about? Using the Fascists to fight the Bolsheviks?"

"'The world should listen then.'"

"But who wouldn't listen now?" Why had Fox chosen me for this mission? "Some of your colleagues? Other men in government?"

"If you can make them listen about the princes, then I can make them listen about a certain farm boy."

The screech of trains echoed through the station. I pressed the phone closer to my ear.

"They will listen, then, to the gladness of a patriotic colonial, the madness of days lost unconscious in the mud."

He was talking about Tom, how he had been knocked out by a blast at Passchendaele and recovered in a German trench. How Tom wandered back to the line in a daze, only to find he was accused of being a German spy and had been charged with treason. Fox knew so much, but I hadn't mentioned what had happened since 1917. I pulled my scarf tighter around my neck. I was suddenly cold.

"If you are my blithe spirit, Vixen, then such harmonious madness from my lips would flow."

"No one could be blithe enough to counteract you. If I am a bird, then you are a cage."

"Bird thou never wert."

"According to you, I'm a vixen."

"And vixens find their prey. It's time to work."

"I don't like your kind of work."

"I would worry if I didn't know you, Vixen. If I didn't know how much you loved the hunt."

I couldn't fault him. How could I lie and say otherwise, when it was clear I had spent all day thinking only of his letter, his codes, this mission?

"And what would you do for my farm boy?"

"I could do everything to rescue Lieutenant Thompson."

"If I do everything for you," I said, and he murmured assent.

"And why me, Fox? Why send the mission like this? Who are we hiding from?"

"We. You don't often use 'we.' You often assume that we work against each other, not with each other."

"I don't work with you. I work under you and under sufferance. But if I'm hiding, it's because you're hiding, so the 'we' is unavoidable."

"Not a royal 'we' then."

"I'll leave that for the mission. So? Who is after us?"

"You will meet with my man Bacon—"

"Is that Fry? I met him last time."

"He will fill you in on some of these details."

"Surely no one is listening to your private calls. Isn't that why you asked me to call you at home—for privacy? Isn't that why you let me ramble on about the mission? You aren't making sense. Who are we hiding from?"

"Bacon—Fry, as you call him—has other things to give you."

I wasn't going to get more out of Fox tonight. In the time I had been speaking to him the station had nearly emptied. The guards were turning down the lights and all the beggar children had disappeared.

"One last thing, Fox. 'Rarely, rarely, comest thou' . . . why that poem? It's so . . . sweet."

But the operator was on the line; Fox had hung up.

The station was deserted. The last train had departed, the last returned from the country, every traveler had hurried off to the warmth and comfort of their hotel, their local café, their home. The bar held only a few stragglers. A single station guard, an old man with enormous eyebrows, made his rounds. I felt disappointed and strangely alone, that Fox had once again hung up without a goodbye, and I couldn't bear to think what that might mean. I marched from the station to the Rotonde and spent a bottle making acquaintances and speaking nonsense before I was walked home by my neighbors to a fitful, haunted sleep.

"MY RAMBLER ROSE"

"Kiki, this is perfect!"

"Bertie, this is Paris."

"Princes, Paris landmarks, and Rasputin's killer . . . it's so good to have you back."

I was once again at the station telephone booth, shouting over the steam and squeals, the yells and clangs, to dictate my column to Bertie down the line.

"Although, Kiki, I have heard that the postal system between France and England is really very reliable."

"More reliable than reverse charges, you mean? Ask Sir Huffandpuff if the *Star* can buy me a typewriter and I'll make sure all of my columns are on time."

"I can approve a typewriter for you—done."

"By the way, which day is on time?"

"Today."

"And today is . . ."

"Kiki!"

"I jest. I bought a newspaper, I know what day it is."

"We go out on a Friday—that's today, Kiki, just to remind you. I'd like your work by the last post on Wednesday so I have time to edit it, but last post on Thursday is acceptable. It's set and printed in, oh, about half an hour so it can hit the stands this afternoon."

"The *Star* is a weekend publication now?"

"Daily was too onerous. Weekly makes us a proper magazine. We even have an agony aunt!"

"Is that you?"

"'Dear Worried of Croydon,'" he intoned, "'the reason you are unable to find a man is not that there are no young men after the war, but that you have not left your parlor since Armistice. Throw off your slippers and head for the dance halls.'"

"You have found your perfect role."

"No, my perfect role is as your batman."

"My batman?" A batman was an officer's servant in the war. "Am I an officer? Is this the war?"

"Well, I do help you carry out orders from your general."

"Do you? I'm confused, or perhaps still a bit hungover."

"I was walking through Whitehall a little while ago . . ."

"Ah."

"And a certain man caught my eye. Tall, broad-shouldered, lovely navy coat, slight limp. He was going where I was going, so I found myself following him into the underground at Westminster, traveling the few stops to Temple Station, but instead of heading back to the office I followed him up the road into Soho. He walked into one of my favorite watering holes, so naturally I followed—it was lunchtime, after all . . ."

"It's always lunchtime with you, Bertie."

"And he ordered whisky . . . so to cut a long story short, my new lover works for Fox."

"Hold on . . . I think you've cut the story too short."

"I put a bit of your detective work into practice. He smokes Sobranies, he quotes Romantic poets at odd times, and he never relaxes. He says he's a secretary, but even a parliamentary secretary can't work such late hours."

"What's his excuse?"

"Excuses are for schoolmasters and maiden aunts, darling. When I mention the late hour, he just shrugs like the administration of government is too difficult for him to explain."

"How long have you been seeing this man?"

"A couple of months. But it was only when you arrived last week and reminded me of Fox that I started to realize that two plus two makes four. I thought it might be good, you know, to have a little peephole into the inner workings of a silver-tongued, Savile-Row-suited surgeon."

"I haven't had that since the war. I love you. Take notes."

"Like a real spy?"

"Don't wish for it. It's a dirty, lonely life."

"You're not alone as long as I'm alive."

"Ditto."

"You're always a bit dirty, though."

"Send me some soap, then! I like Pears, preferably scented with something spicy." I opened the door and lit a cigarette. "And stay alive, Bertie. I need you."

⎯⎯⎯⎯

It was Friday, five minutes to four. I was at Gare de l'Est to welcome a certain foreign correspondent, veteran Anzac, farm boy, Tom-Tom heartbeat of mine back to Paris. The station was full of people coming and going for the weekend, all in their coats and hats, gloves and scarves, waves of people in black and gray and brown. I received more than one look as I stood at the end of the platform like a glamourous canary—a mustard yellow coat with matching cloche hat, soft yellow gloves that matched my yellow suede shoes, a golden silk dress embroidered with autumnal leaves. I wanted to be noticeable for more than just my golden hair; I wanted to be a beacon, a light, a flame. I was also nervous, stupidly so. As I often did, I dressed brilliantly to disguise my fears, in the hope that this disguise might, for a time, become my true self. My clothing was a talisman for brighter days, as I needed to be so much brighter than I felt—I needed electric blue velvet, parrot green silk, bright pink leather—I craved gold thread holding down little silver mirrors and diamonds around my hem so that I sparkled. That would be my first task when this mission was over: a carnivalesque wardrobe, a neon street-light wardrobe, a wardrobe to ward off the dark.

Trains steamed into the platforms and the crowds surged. I didn't know where he was coming from, I just had to scan the moving throng and trust that Parisians hadn't all grown to be over six foot tall in the past year. They hadn't, as there he was, his blue fedora tilted back on his head so he could do as I was doing, hunt impatiently for the face from home. I watched him for a moment, his head strained forward, his eyes wide and searching, the skin over his cheek twitching as he clenched his jaw. Then he saw me, and I couldn't stop my smile, I couldn't stop myself from pushing my way to him, from jumping into his arms and saying his name over and over. He wrapped both of his arms around me to keep me close, both feet off the ground, his face buried in my neck.

"Button." His voice was muffled by my scarf.

I pulled his head away so I could look more closely at his face. He was much thinner than last year, his cheeks slightly hollow, and his eyes sunken. His skin was pale beneath his soldier's tan, a dirty tan of relentless exposure and not at all healthy. He wore the same suit as last year, a navy wool pinstripe, but it was now fraying at the collar, it was covered with stains and cigarette ash. His eyes, deep blue, looked at me like I had saved him from drowning.

"Yes," I said. I felt the same way.

"Button."

"I'm not going anywhere."

"Not without a good meal and a pint, you're skin and bone."

"You can talk. Do you even own a mirror?"

"You're my mirror." He took off my hat to stroke my hair. "Button, are you . . ."

"Yes. Now I am." Now I'm alright, now that I'm back here. He understood; he smiled, his little boy smile of unalloyed joy.

A cough sounded next to us and a young man with a black moustache looked at us sheepishly. Tom gave an embarrassed laugh and let me down.

"Button—sorry, Hem—Button this is—"

"Ernest Hemingway." He shook my hand firmly and his smile was warm. "I'm with the *Toronto Star*. I met your man Tom here in Smyrna. As we were both coming back to Paris, we decided to share costs, defray the per diems, so to speak."

"Hem, is it?"

"Hem, Hemingway, Ernest . . ."

"Hem's a good writer," said Tom.

"Tom's not bad himself, but he's a better drinker than writer." Hem grinned.

"Just a better barman. Button here's a writer."

"Hardly!" I said. "It's primarily fiction."

"Oh, you write fiction?" Hem looked keen.

"No, no, I write a society column for a gossip magazine based in London. I just have to disguise the truth so much it could work for MI5."

"Ha, right. Sorry, was your name Button?"

"Only Tom calls me by my last name. Everyone else calls me Kiki."

We had made our way to the doors of the station by this point, Hem and Tom using their broad shoulders to create a passage through the crowds. Hem turned to us.

"I'm surprising the wife at the Ritz, so it's goodbye from me. But say, Tom, you're staying in Montparnasse with the rest of us, right?"

"He's staying at my place, on rue Delambre."

"Meet me outside the Lilas tomorrow, at six? We can have a drink then."

He shook our hands and headed into a taxi. People swirled around us, smoking into the late afternoon, their bodies and bright laughter creating a pool of warmth. Tom held my hand. He said nothing, there was almost too much to say—my mother, Sydney, his family, his reporting, my return to Europe, the whole of the past year in fact—I didn't know where to start. I couldn't start, I could only gaze back at him.

"Good meal and a pint, whatcha say, Button?"

"Let's put your suitcase in my studio and begin."

"WHEN YOU AND I WERE
YOUNG, MAGGIE, BLUES"

"Cozy." Tom admired the wood-paneled walls around our corner table. I had avoided the raucous atmosphere of the Rotonde and instead led Tom to the Falstaff. It was dark enough that it felt entirely private.

"Belgian beer." Tom toasted my glass of Kir. "Pity it doesn't come in pints."

"Pity doesn't come in pints either."

"You don't need a pint of pity, Button. You need a good wail, a good meal, and a good dance."

"And you need?"

"Not the wail."

"You need that most."

"Men don't cry!"

"Don't tell a nurse that men don't cry." I wagged my finger in a mock scold. "Or I'll spank you for lying."

"There are other things you can spank me for."

"Settle, petal . . ."

"Lying's not my besetting sin."

"No . . . maybe pride?" I returned his dingo grin. "Definitely pride."

"And yours, Button?"

"Well, it's not sloth! As for the rest, I'm doing my best to sample them all." I took a sip from his glass. "That's good beer."

"Should I get another for you?"

"I need room in my belly for dinner. No, what I need is not a good wail, but a good talk. That's what I've missed: someone who really knows me."

"So not me, precisely, then?"

"But who else knows me?" I had meant it as a jokey riposte but the words settled heavily between us. No one else knew me as well as Tom did; no one else knew me as a child in Australia and an adult in Paris, no one else knew me pre-war, post-war, and during the war itself. Tom was the only person, man or woman, who had taken that journey with me.

"So me, precisely, then." He held my gaze, then sighed like he had just remembered to breathe. "Good. Because I have missed you."

I held his hand. "What's happened?"

"You're meant to be telling me—your mother, all that . . ."

"We have all night. And all tomorrow too, yes? Or Hemingway wouldn't have extended that invitation."

"I don't have to be back until Monday 0900."

"So, a train on Sunday. Can you stay until then?"

"To be anywhere else would be a punishment."

"You know, I feel the same way!"

"I should think so."

"Yes, pride is definitely your besetting sin." I smiled and he laughed, not at the joke so much as our friendship, our easy company, at being together again at last. I drank my Kir and let its warmth run through me.

"I read all your reports while I was in Sydney, Tom."

"Did you make a little explorer's map of my travels?"

"That was beyond me, but I did buy the paper with my sherry and milk every morning."

"Morning sherry—like that, was it?"

"Worse."

"Nothing's worse than sherry, Button, unless it's cooking sherry."

"Or vodka?"

"Potato peel vodka, ugh."

"Tell me about Russia."

Tom looked around at the watercolor landscapes and lithographs of horses on the walls, at the flickering fireplace, at the slowly disintegrating foam on his beer. I'm sure he saw none of it. His stare said he saw somewhere far away and all too close.

"To tell you about Russia is to relive the horror of the war again, except in a strange language with a strange script and two armies dressed so identically it looked like one army fighting itself . . . a nightmare version of our war, Button. I've been there all through the past year. I know it was bad because the sacking of Smyrna felt like relief.

"Though there is almost no fighting left in Russia, there is also no food left—American Aid feeds everyone from the Baltic to the Black Sea. People drift like ghosts along the train tracks, hands out for any scraps that people might throw from the train. I saw people eat orange peels and potato peels. Apple cores are a positive luxury. Old Buffer didn't want to know about any of that—'too much of that already and Belgium is closer' he blustered when I confronted him about it—so I just have to write up what the well-fed officials say in Moscow, Petrograd, and Vitebsk."

"If the country suffers, why are the Reds still in power?"

"The country—that's it precisely. The peasants in the country suffer, they have no food and feel the harvest is stolen from them when the officials ship it off to Moscow. They are the people who are lying down by the train tracks to die, who are giving away their children to strangers at the station to take elsewhere, anywhere, that they might have a chance to live. I look into their ghoulish faces and wonder if I see despair there, or resignation, suppressed rage, or simply hunger.

"The cities, however, are full of enthusiasm. They're creating a new world, they say, a bright future for men and women alike. The Jewish men I speak to are particularly excited. This new Soviet does away with the pogroms they've been afraid of all their lives, there's no religion anymore, they say, they are finally free. Oh, of course, they say, creating a new world requires a bit of hardship at first, but utopia is worth it. Paradise is worth the sacrifice."

"So, the officials are Red through and through."

"It would be infectious, if I hadn't had a dying child's handprint burning my palm since Kiev."

"There's no chance for a Royal revival then."

"Any support the Whites had disappeared with the last of the food."

"'Bread, Land, Peace.'"

"It's a good catchcry. It's all anyone wants, in the end."

"And drink."

"There's plenty of that, though only the rotten homemade stuff. Suicide juice: it's too potent on an empty stomach, people drink it and die." He drained the last of his beer. "Why do you ask about a Royal revival?"

"I have some Romanov friends—I know, preposterous, but that's Paris for you—and there's . . . talk. I want to know how seriously to take such talk."

"In my opinion, not seriously at all. When were they last in Russia?"

"As they're still alive, I don't think they've been back since they fled."

"They're imagining it's the same country, the empire it was for hundreds of years. It's not, it's . . . a new world, just as the Bolsheviks want. Whether it's a better world, well, they have to stop their citizens dying of hunger first. Until then, their new world is just an extension of the hell we've been through since 1914."

"Only until 1918."

"Not there. Some mothers have only just found out their son died at the front; that's seven years without a word. Not in Smyrna either . . . but I need more beer for that."

"Something stronger? Something sweeter? Even some food at the Trianon?" I indicated the fancy restaurant across the road.

"I like it here. I don't have to behave myself. Don't they have a cheese platter or something?"

"I'll see what I can rustle up."

I came back from the bar with two drinks, more cigarettes, bread and cheese, and a promise from the barman to provide us with something hot. There was a little package sitting on the table.

"All done up with string, Tom-Tom?" He avoided my eye, busying himself with the food and drink. "Light us a cigarette, then, and I'll open it."

Inside was a beautiful silk scarf, long and brilliant blue, with heavy tassels and a subtle pattern of flowers. Wrapped up in the scarf were two small glasses, the same deep blue, painted round the top in gold. I placed the scarf round my shoulders and the glasses on the table.

"They probably need a wash," he said.

"So do I. So do you."

Tom gently turned my face to his. "As I thought. The scarf is the same blue as your eyes."

I couldn't speak until he had turned back to his beer.

"Are these from Turkey?"

"From a market on the border with Greece, though whether this particular market is in Greece or Turkey this evening is another matter."

"Thank you."

Tom just nodded, burying his face in his drink, his cigarette, a bite of bread. I wanted to climb into his lap and open him up; I took a deep drag on my cigarette to stop myself.

"I brought you nothing from Australia."

"Not even a letter from home?"

"Oh yes, I have that! Or news, at least, that your sister made me promise not to tell you."

"Oh, Sissy . . ."

"She's worse. I don't think it's her body that's making her sick, though. I think it's her mind."

"She's not mad."

"She's not mad. She's bored."

"Being bored doesn't make you sick."

"You're not a woman. You wouldn't know."

"Then help me to know."

"That's a challenge. Ah, thank you." The waiter brought over two steaming bowls of thick potato soup, with more bread, butter, and a bowl of croutons.

"This smells delicious, Button."

"Doesn't it though. So, how does a bored woman become sick?" I stubbed out my cigarette and took a spoonful of soup. "Oh, that's good. She becomes sick because she loses hope. You saw it in the war, on the wards. I don't know how it happens, but you could see it in the men's faces, that they'd given up and even when they seemed to be recovering, they died. I think Sissy is suffering from that malady."

"But she has . . ."

"Has . . . what? Exactly. There's nothing there for her. There was nothing there for me either, but marriage to some dullard and a life lived at the kitchen sink. Unbearable. And you know, that country . . ." I thought of the red soil, the far horizon, the shimmering heat, and my mother wilting by the window.

"That country?"

"It's not for everyone. It certainly wasn't right for my mother."

Tom reached past the bowls and glasses to take my hand. "Now it's your turn. Tell me."

"She . . ." I shrugged; there was too much to say. "It's going to take me all night and all day to tell all. But I need . . . I need to find her final diary."

"You said that you'd been reading her diaries, in the only letter you sent to me in more than an entire year."

"Sorry."

"You should be. I've been going mad without word."

"I sent a telegram or two . . ."

"Literally two. I just had to hope you weren't dead, or worse, married."

I laughed. "In Sydney? Never." Tom just squeezed my hand.

"So, you know everything about your mother except the end?"

"Where, hopefully, she reveals the man she loved for years, the one she kept coming back here to see."

Tom looked at me, thinking, his spoon resting on the side of his bowl. "She was so . . . she seemed like she came from another world and was halfway back there. Like she was listening to music that no one else could hear. My mother would tease him about it, but my father couldn't stop watching her, like she was an angel or a goddess that had accidentally appeared on his sheep property. Then she'd look right into your eyes and through, it seemed, into your soul. My father was always a bit stunned after a visit to your place, if your mother was there."

"And you?"

"I was looking at you most of the time. I noticed her when I would come home from school for the holidays. She seemed . . . sad is the best way to describe it. She must have had a secret sorrow, as there was no particular reason for her to be sad, as she just smiled and took tea and spoke kindly to our maid Jenny even when she dropped the tea things. You were always so lively, I mostly wanted to get away to be with you . . . but my mother always spoke of her with a mixture of pity and disapproval . . . Yes, that's exactly how she spoke of 'poor Mrs. Button' and 'dear Cordelia.' I never really knew why. I never asked."

"Your sister did."

"Sissy would. And?"

"It was in the diaries. My mother married my father because she became pregnant."

"With you."

"No, with another child by another man. A man who couldn't marry her, but someone had to pay for the child's upkeep, and my father agreed to take the child as his own. That's how much he loved my mother."

"Christ."

"She lost the child on the ship to Australia. Then she was stuck in Australia, married, and then pregnant with me."

"And this other man . . ."

"I hope his identity is in her final missing diary." I toyed with my cooling soup. I couldn't eat, I was too tense. "She refers to a 'big fuss.' Maybe there was some kind of scandal? I think . . . I don't even know if her family knew she was pregnant, but she was very bohemian . . ."

"Like mother, like daughter."

"I know, I know . . ." I sniffed to stop the tears. "She spent her days with artists and poets. She traveled here, to Paris, as a young woman and I don't think she had a chaperone. She . . . her diaries are odd. She came to Europe often . . ."

"I remember. She was always just back or about to leave."

"And she wrote a fair bit when she was here, but many entries are just a series of notes. Then, when she was on the way home, she would write up everything she'd done, detailed descriptions of dresses, artistic analysis, even entire conversations. Almost as though . . . as though she was saving it all up for when she was in Sydney, alone and lonely, so that she'd have something to read over, to fall back on."

"Why didn't she stay here? It wouldn't have been the first separate marriage."

"Apparently she couldn't leave me." Then I couldn't stop the tears rolling down my nose. Tom pulled my chair to his and dragged me onto his lap, hugging me so tightly it almost hurt.

"I knew it." He spoke into my shoulder. "You always hated her but I knew she loved you. You only ever saw the woman who was married to your father."

"Stop . . ."

"But I saw her look at you, so . . . well, sad always, but proud and amused when you challenged Mr. Reginald Button. She especially liked that time you ran away from school."

"She didn't! I got into so much trouble!"

"From her?"

"Father did most of the yelling . . ."

"She related the whole event with such amusement to my mother, who came home shocked that Mrs. Button thought it was funny that young

Katherine ran away from school on the gardener's horse, and managed to buy a ticket to Shanghai at Woolloomooloo docks, before being reported to the police."

"I was only twelve. I suppose it was pretty funny."

"It was magnificent."

"But why didn't she say anything? Why did she let me think she was just like my father?"

"Her diaries don't say anything?"

"They just say 'One day she'll understand' or 'I hope she understands' and various vague statements of that sort."

"I think that one day has come."

"But I don't understand."

"You need the final diary." He looked up at me. "Button, how do you know it exists?"

"Because the penultimate diary ends halfway through a sentence. Where did the end of the sentence go? No, there has to be more." I reached over for my cigarettes.

"You aren't going to finish your soup?"

"I . . . no . . ."

"Well, I'm finishing mine. I'm bloody hungry."

"Oi! Careful! No soup on the dress, you grub."

"Get off, then. And finish your soup—you're skinny as a beggar's purse."

"The look is called *garçonne* and it's very fashionable, I'll have you know."

"Looking like an urchin?"

"Looking like a boy." I tucked the unlit cigarette behind my ear and reached for my soup spoon. I had relaxed just enough to contemplate swallowing some. Tom reached over and tucked my hair behind my other ear before it trailed in the spoon.

"I like it—short hair, short skirts, smoking in public. Drunk in public. You still need a bit more flesh on you though."

"As do you."

"War's not so conducive to health."

"Grief neither."

"Almost the same thing, really."

"Almost." I returned his gaze.

"Button." His tone was soft and happy. The sounds of the bar floated around us—French and English and Spanish and Flemish, old voices and young, curling with the smoke of pipes and cigarettes and the roaring fire.

"I'm here now, Tom-Tom."

⤙⤚

"July last year. That's when I last saw you, Button. When you were about to leave for the coast."

We were sitting on my windowsill, facing each other with our backs against the frame, wrapped in blankets and smoking into the night. Tom's long legs filled the entire width of the window but he left just the right amount of space for me to sit in between them. The lights of the city shimmied and blinked.

"I begged you to join me, Tom."

"The Hungarian coup couldn't wait. I did ask, but the legitimists said no."

"If only they had waited, they might have been more successful."

"I doubt it. The people of central and eastern Europe are sick of kings. They want revolution."

"Does revolution want them?"

"No. It just installs new kings, even if the new king is of the people's choosing." He pulled my foot into his lap and traced the burgeoning hole in my stocking with his thumb. "It's been hell."

"Without me? I understand . . ."

"That wasn't hell. That was simply . . . purgatory, endless dull gray London, with none of the champagne-soaked nights I'd come to rely on for release. No, it's the . . . it's as though I'm being punished for fleeing the war in 1917. I didn't see the Armistice here in France, so I'm forced to travel all the countries where the Armistice made no difference and the fighting continues. Russia, Hungary, Germany, Russia . . . now Greece—or Turkey—I'll just call it Smyrna, it's easier—fire and blood, wailing women, children slaughtered like the little lambs they are . . ."

"Christ Almighty."

"He wasn't anywhere, nor Mohammed. The air smelt of barbeque—wood ash, rosemary, and flesh—and death, you remember, fresh blood and shit and that sting in the nostrils of burnt rubber, of smoking metal, of other people's fear-soaked sweat."

My gorge rose and I swallowed. "I remember."

"They're fighting over a border town, over their version of Abraham's God . . . I can't care anymore." He had been rubbing the hole in my stocking as he spoke, and he leant down to kiss my toe. I murmured his name and he pulled me, foot first, so I was right in front of him, tangled and tucked up against him. He kissed my hair and breathed in deeply.

"Thank God you've come back, Button."

"I'm here to stay."

"In Paris?"

"Too many nosy relatives in London." I turned my face to his chest to kiss him. "I'm here for you, whenever you're in Paris."

"I wonder if Old Buffer would let me relocate."

"From my brief encounter with him, he still has the idea that Paris is a sink of iniquity, you know, lust and gluttony and not a shred of work done. I could tell by his leer."

"He's very leery. I think he has a bad eye."

"He definitely has bad teeth. Probably bad breath too."

"Oh, definitely bad breath."

A breeze fluttered around us. Tom pulled me closer and I reached up to kiss his neck. I could hear him exhale, feel his heart beat a bit harder, feel his limbs relax.

"Just to sit here with you, Button, just to watch the lights of Paris as they bow to the night . . ."

We sat like that, communicating tenderness with our bodies, and watched the neighborhood lights blink out one by one by one.

"BABY BLUE EYES"

I dreamt of kissing him, of course. Just kisses, it was the war, our uniforms were in the way all the time, I couldn't undo all my buttons, he couldn't undo his puttees, our laces and straps tangled together and we could do nothing but kiss. I woke to find that we were holding hands, my hand dangling over the side of the bed, his reaching up above his head so that our fingers were entwined. The day was misty outside the window, we were in a cloud-bound tower, we were a world unto ourselves.

I watched him as he slept. His black hair had rejected all pomade to flop over his face. He was thin, his jawline so sharp it could chop wood, his cheeks sinking, his eyes sinking as though retreating from the horror they had faced and seen. Even his fingers had lost their muscle; his huge hands showed no hint of the soldier, shearer, or horseman he had been. The war had returned for us both, but whereas I was infected by ghosts and memory, he had watched blood flow. I felt a sudden connection, a bridge—to take care of him would be to take care of myself, that I would only get better if he also got better. I squeezed his fingers; he opened his eyes to look at me, upside-down, from his mattress on the floor.

"Button." It was a sigh. "Is it breakfast?"

"Those bells? I think it's lunch already."

"But they'll serve us coffee, right? Your breakfast people? The old woman who fusses like a favorite auntie, her grumpy husband . . ."

"They'd serve me coffee in their nightcaps if I needed it."

"I thought so." He yawned. "I went there once you know, when I stayed here while you were away. It wasn't the same. Everything tasted stale and tepid."

"I do bring a certain zest to daily life . . ." But that sentence ended in a shriek as he grabbed my foot and tickled me. It was all I could do not to slide off the bed and into his arms.

Madeleine Petit welcomed us warmly and let us order anything we liked. We were on our second coffee and third cigarette before I got up the courage to speak.

"You have to know . . ." I couldn't go on, not with Tom smiling at me with such open-hearted pleasure. I reached over and covered his eyes.

"A surprise, Button?"

"A shock. I can't look at your ocean blue eyes and tell you."

He removed my hand with a frown. "I'm ready."

I took out the envelope of photos Fox had sent me and placed them in front of Tom. I watched him inspect the envelope, reach in and get the photographs, the rippled feelings in his face as he saw himself in uniform—shock, disbelief, hurt, anger, fear—I could only remind myself to breathe by smoking.

"Where did you . . ." But he realized as he spoke. "You're working for him again. Fox."

I nodded.

"Why, Button?"

"You're holding the reason."

"Where did he get these?"

"I almost don't want to know, except that it could save you."

"I don't need—"

"Don't you, Mr. Arthur?"

He looked at me, and from his stunned, angry expression, I knew that he knew. He needed help to clear his name and working for Fox was probably the only way. He gave an exasperated groan and held his head in his hands, looking at the photos, then stood up so fast he knocked his chair over as he strode out the door. I knew he wouldn't go far—he'd left his coat and his cigarettes—but I could feel his fury, his frustration, his despair. I could even hear his yell as he let some of it out. I didn't want to work for Fox again either, but the longer Tom remained Mr. Arthur, the harder it would be for him to remove the charges hanging over his head. Madeleine raised her eyebrows but I could only shrug. Everyone else turned back to their newspapers.

I finished my cigarette and let my coffee, no longer hot, soothe my tongue. Tom was all passion and action, so different from cold, remote Fox. I had to admit that he'd be a perfect help in this mission. Reporters were allowed to go everywhere and talk to everyone, and he was probably privy to all sorts of political gossip. He might even know who the princes were.

But first he had to tell me what he remembered about these photos. He couldn't remember anything when I helped him to escape in 1917, he simply shivered when he was awake and screamed when he was asleep. But bad memories are a bit of shrapnel in the blood, they have a way of pushing to the surface. It was almost exactly five years since I had got him out of his Paris hotel hidey-hole and onto a ship home, complete with forged discharge papers supplied by Fox. Now Fox had these photos; Tom needed to search the catacombs of his memory to find something, anything, to help us.

He loomed in the doorway for a moment, dark as a shadow, and he barely looked at me as he walked back to his seat. His forehead had a sheen of sweat on it but his arms were goose-pimpled. He wouldn't look at me until he had lit a cigarette and blown a plume of smoke past my ear. Then he glared at me with his stormy blue eyes, his face too pale even for a chilly autumn day—I could tell straightaway.

"What have you remembered?" I asked.

"In the mud . . . German voices above me, some speaking English to me with an almost-English accent . . . you know, telling me to be still, stay calm . . . the smell of cordite and fresh blood and old bodies and myself, shit and fear and pain . . ." He raked back his hair with a trembling hand. "And one other thing."

"Yes?"

"Fox."

"My boss."

"And mine." He had to look away then, probably from the shock and fear on my face. "Or was. In the war. As I was walking just now, I remembered what I remembered while you were away."

"Yes?" My voice sounded strangled.

"He was the officer who gave me my mission. The one that sent me over the lines at Passchendaele."

"Fox sent you behind enemy lines in 1917, on the mission that led to your charge of treason? Fox?"

"I didn't know who it was at the time. He was just a British officer, speaking with my CO, the Saint, and a couple of other officers. My assignments came from all sorts of officers . . ."

"Wait, assignments, mission—you did intelligence work?"

"You didn't know?"

"You didn't say!"

"I assumed you knew . . . yes, of course, how else could I have been that far forward of the front line?"

"I heard stranger tales from the men I nursed. I assumed you were knocked out and the line moved around you."

"In that mud pit, no one was moving anywhere."

I felt his expression must mirror my own, a kind of appalled surprise that this fundamental part of our shared story was only just now being told.

"And?"

"I worked it out later from your descriptions of him. Silver hair on a young face, deep smooth voice, stood very straight, the scar on his cheek—and then I remembered the pips on his uniform, he was

RAMC—and then I remembered that he called me Thompson before I had been introduced . . . it must have been your Dr. Fox."

The edges of my vision started to swim and I felt queasy. Fox had been between us for so long; I'd had no idea. I couldn't even smoke my cigarette and it burnt itself into an arc of ash.

"You know, Button, these photos . . ."

"He took them." He must have; oh, the bastard.

"I reckon so. Or had a hand in having them taken."

"Oh, he wouldn't have got mud on his uniform! No, he ordered for them to be taken."

"But how did he know I'd end up behind German lines?"

"Because . . ." Something broke inside me, something sank. "No . . ."

"He must have, Button. He must have ordered it."

"How, though? How? He's so King and Country! He wouldn't know any Germans . . ." Except he would, as he was German. I swallowed hard against my rising nausea.

"But didn't you tell me—"

"Yes. His family came to England from Germany when he was little. His birthname is von Fochs."

"So, then." Tom reached over and took my hand. "Your fingers are freezing, Button!"

"So, then, you'll help me." Tom nodded as he blew on and rubbed my fingers, trying to get some warmth into them. "I have a new mission—these photos are just . . . an 'advance payment' if you will. An enticement."

"An entrapment."

"I think entrapment will be my task, not my fate." I fished the letter out of my bag. "Read the mission."

He kept hold of my fingers as he read, rubbing them absentmindedly with his thumb, frowning at the paper. I stared at the basket of bread on the counter, at the coffeepots, at the rows of colored liqueurs that lined the mirror behind the counter, anything to settle the rising anger, fear, pain, whatever was causing the nausea and the accompanying jiggle in my right leg.

"Which poet is this?"

"Shelley. The whole mission is about radical toffs. I have to find—"

"Princes and houseboys?"

"Quite. Fox wasn't as subtle this time."

"But just as gross. What do you need from me?"

"What do you know about fascism?"

"Like what's-his-face, the bloke from your last mission—"

"Hausmann."

"That's the one. You're still following this?"

"Apparently so. Hausmann is clearly the 'houseboys' the mission refers to. He was recruiting for the Freikorps last year. The Freikorps have close ties with these Fascists."

"I remember."

"I need you to keep an ear out for what might be happening with this group."

"My life has been a round of communism, socialism, monarchy, back to communism, all soaked in national pride . . . I haven't heard about the Fascists since I was in Poland last year, when the Germans were still making a fuss. The rest of eastern Europe is staring down Lenin."

"What about Germany? Italy?"

"Germany faces the east too and there was that little matter of the 1918 uprising in Berlin . . ."

"You must have heard something on the road. Other reporters in the hotel bars, like Hemingway, the mates you make to share the gossip and the risk—what do they say?"

"You make us sound like pigeons on the barbed wire."

"Those messenger pigeons are the unsung heroes of the war."

He tapped the letter. "This 'black shirt' clue. Have you heard of Benito Mussolini?"

"Italian?"

"Yes. Lots of the 'other reporters in hotel bars,' as you call us, knew him. He used to be a reporter."

"But what is he now, if he used to be a reporter?"

"Leader of the Italian nationalists, called the Fascists. Other reporters have been saying that he invented fascism, from some Milanese nationalist group or other."

"And they wear black shirts, like the Freikorps wear brown shirts?"

"That's the word around the hotel bars. Lots of chat about how the clash of empires is being replaced by the clash of ideologies . . . not that most papers want to hear about the reporters' analysis. But these professional observers, well, they have a bit of an investment in what grows in the place of a toppled empire. But, as I said, my life's been dominated by black bread and bathtub vodka. I haven't had much chance to eat spaghetti."

"We can get you some here in Paris."

"Or we could go to Italy. I'd love to see the Colosseum."

"And I'd love to get lost on Venice's canals. But not yet."

He sighed. "Not yet." He gave a kind of start.

"What?"

"Button . . . does Fox have a brother?"

"I don't know. He seems to have sprung up whole and complete in British RAMC uniform and Savile Row suit."

"I met someone on the road . . . it was last year, I was just returning from Russia, again, and all I could think about was getting a hot bath and a hearty meal . . . but there was another reporter, at least he said he was a reporter, on the train out of Munich. He called himself a German but had a perfect British accent, said he learned it at school in Britain. He . . . yes, he wore a brown shirt . . ."

"A military uniform?"

"So many do, still, they're the only clothes they own. It's not at all unusual in most places in eastern Europe. But it was his bearing. He was definitely an officer, but his uniform was like that of a private, and he said he was going to London to see his brother. I asked him, 'You're German, but your brother's English?' and he replied, 'Silvius always preferred mother to father, so he remained English when the war started. I was hoping to see my nephew too.'"

"Silvius, he said?"

"Yes, and this man's name was Cassius. The name was so odd that it stuck in my mind."

"Fox's name is Silvius. Silvius Atticus Frederick Fox—or Friedrich von Fochs, as he was born. Not that he ever told me this. I met someone during the war who knew him at school; the man was killed by a sniper minutes later."

"It might be worth doing a bit of spy work on Silvius."

"And Cassius. And a nephew! Whose son? Fox's son, or is there another brother, a sister?"

"A nephew means a mother somewhere too. Sister . . . or Fox's wife?"

"No."

Tom raised his eyebrows.

"Well, he didn't have one during the war."

"How do you know?"

I couldn't look at Tom, the innocent question with the disappointed, hurt tone soon to follow. I lit a cigarette, though my throat was starting to hurt, though my tongue could taste nothing but ash and fire.

"Oh, Button . . ."

"He never said, but surely . . ."

"And he's still after you?"

"He wants me to . . ."

"He's still after you." He took the cigarette from my hand. "I'm not worth it, Button."

"Of course you're worth it." I pushed the photos toward him. "We're so close."

"Maybe I like being Mr. Arthur."

"Maybe you do, but it's not safe. Someone will recognize you one day and then it's a hop, skip, and a jump to the firing squad."

"The Saint is dead, my other OC is dead, it can't . . ." His face fell. "It can." He took a long drag on my cigarette before handing it back. "Right. Fox."

"He could have you arrested."

"Bastard."

"His bastardry is so pronounced it's positively Shakespearean—Edmund from *Lear*, perhaps, or Iago."

"Iago is good; the cunning whisperer."

"But we have whispers about a possible Cassius, a possible son . . ."

"Julius?"

"Or Caligula. I'll ask Bertie, see if he can find out anything."

"Bertie's part of this?"

"Intimately . . . if you know what I mean."

"Like last time?" Tom grinned. "How is Bertie? Good bloke that. I like your taste in friends."

"So do I. Why do you think I returned?"

"OO~OO ERNEST ARE YOU EARNEST WITH ME?"

After an afternoon spent walking and talking, we headed to the Closerie des Lilas. Hemingway was sitting at a terrasse table, a purple liqueur in front of him. He was bundled up against the wind in a navy peacoat with the collar turned up, a thick woolen scarf of a homemade brown, and a black beret. He saw Tom and waved, indicated two seats at his table, and called the waiter over in preparation for our joining him. At his table was a soft-looking woman with short brown hair and a warm smile.

"My wife, Hadley." Hem introduced her with obvious pride.

"Are you writers too?" she asked.

"Tom's a reporter, we met in Smyrna," said Hem. "Kiki here . . ."

"I'm a gossip columnist," I said. "So writer: yes. Artist: no."

"Hadley plays piano," said Hem, his hand on her knee. "Sit down, sit down, we've got a few minutes."

"Until what?" Tom asked.

"Until we meet Gertrude and Alice."

"Gertrude Stein?" I asked. "I've never been invited."

"I was nervous at first," said Hadley, "but Alice is the loveliest wife I've ever met."

"Gertrude's a gun," said Hem, "and Tom, this'll be the real Paris for you."

"It's a salon," I said to Tom.

"And surely the perfect antidote to your recent travels, wouldn't you say?" said Hadley. "I took Hem, my Tatie, out to a Bal Musette last night for 'sweet song and supper,' as Tatie calls it, for just that reason. Paris will cure all our ills."

"And we certainly saw some, in Greece, or Turkey, or whatever it is now." Hem growled through his cigarette smoke.

"Turkey, I reckon," said Tom. "But I dunno if I can talk about all that, not on such a romantically wind-blown night as this . . ."

"We're travelers in an antique land . . ." Shelley, again; I stopped myself. I reached over and took Tom's cigarette.

"If you want antique," said Hem, "you need to get to Italy. Eating gelato under the Roman aqueducts, strolling past the Colosseum on your way to drinks—*bellissimo!*"

"We were there in June, on our delayed honeymoon," said Hadley, with a smile at her husband. "Tatie worked, of course. I'm finding out that you can't stop a writer from writing, whatever food for the body and soul is on offer. Sometimes that even makes it worse!"

"On a story?" I asked.

"No, an interview," said Hem. "With Benito Mussolini."

"Another newspaperman," Tom nodded, but gave me a look. "Always slippery buggers, other reporters, never answering a question directly. Or else they go over-the-top and spill their guts over several drinks."

"Slippery as a whore's promise, this one." Hem licked the purple liqueur from his lips. "I want to like him—no, really, I do—we both fought on the Italian front, both wounded for Italy, both want to see the world a better place than before the war so the war was all worthwhile. But he used to be a socialist and now he's a fascist. He's gone from being an internationalist to a nationalist, an intellectual to a populist . . ."

"And how can anyone trust a man like that?"

"Exactly, Kiki."

"Was he wearing one of his black shirts?" Tom gave a sardonic grin and Hem laughed.

"You know, he really was! That's another thing I don't trust—his showmanship. Show off with words, show off at a rally, but with another veteran, just the two of you? It's too much. It makes the performance not persuasive but pathological."

"So . . ." I smiled in a way I hoped was persuasive. "What did he say that you didn't publish? What's the gossip?"

"Ah, of course, you're a gossip writer."

His smile was patronizing but I didn't care. I needed to know what this black-shirted man was up to.

"Well . . . he sat there stroking the ears of a wolfhound the entire interview. Even as he told me about his half million followers, about how he was going to reignite the Roman empire, he ran the dog's large ears through his fingers again and again. I could see he was getting happy on it; the soft pliability of the ears was doing something to him. When he mentioned, sotto voce, that a 'big event' that was imminent, I almost laughed. He looked offended, but the double entendre was too much."

"What big event?"

"Oh, he was very secretive about it, but he'll gather his followers—all half a million of them, if you take him at his word—for some enormous show of force, popularity, whatever."

"You're not interested?"

"As a newspaper reporter, sure. As a man, no. He's all bluff and nonsense."

"His secretary does make a delicious cup of coffee though," said Hadley. "From a little stove-top pot, which she serves with a sweet, airy biscuit. She did this all while chattering away in Italian, which I don't speak, and did no other work, not even answering the telephone when it rang. I think making coffee was the main part of her job."

"Typical," Tom and Hem spoke together, then laughed, and the conversation moved away from the black-shirted people's prince. But it was enough to go on. I could now figure out where to look next.

⌘

"Hemingway!" Gertrude signaled with a teacup from her chair. "Matisse is arguing with me about socialism, but I've lost track of who's for it and who's against it. You've just been to Smyrna. Tell us about the clash of civilizations there."

I glimpsed a solid woman with a sharp gaze and hair braided around her head. She was seated next to a middle-aged man with pince-nez, looking like a lawyer from the suburbs in his pale gray three-piece suit. Was that Matisse? The walls were covered with contemporary artworks, starting at eye-height and moving to the ceiling, with sculptures placed on tables against the wall.

"Gertrude." Hem gripped his hat with both hands and his nod looked very much like a bow. "Tom here was in Smyrna with me."

"Pleased to meet you, Miss Stein."

"What accent is that? Australian? I met some of them during the war. You'd know about the clash of civilizations, then. Alice?" She nodded at a small woman with a serious nose, bobbed black hair, and alert eyes. Alice, who must be Alice B. Toklas and Stein's muse, lover, and champion, smiled and ushered me and Hadley away to another part of the room.

"Tea is this way," she said and placed her hand on my arm. It was clear; I was not invited to talk politics and art with Stein and the men. I bristled but Hadley winked at me.

"More gossip in this part of the house," she whispered when Alice moved away to get us cups. "And you may get back to the 'big talk,' as I often think of it, when they find out you're not a wife."

"A wife? Is this the married women's quarantine?"

"Gertrude finds the men censor their opinions when their wives are present," said Alice as she handed me a slice of green cake. "It's pandan and pineapple slice, a recipe I picked up from a sailor from Java. Try it."

"I think quarantine is probably too harsh a word . . ." said Hadley.

"Gertrude, and the rest of them, don't properly value the quotidian," said Alice. "Take this slice, for instance. The recipe is a Polish-Jewish-American version of a Dutch cake cooked in France with traditional Javanese ingredients. I bought the pandan at a dockside market where all the peoples of the world meet and trade. The recipe is from the sailor's mother, who worked as a kitchen maid in a colonial house from the age of five. He joined the navy of the Dutch East Indies, ended up with the British navy during the war, then decided to jump ship in Paris after going to a meeting of the French Communist Party with his 'Tonkinese brothers,' as he calls them. In there," she gestured to Stein and the men, "they are discussing the 'clash of civilizations,' of how important, and somewhat self-important, men decide national politics. But their whole argument can be found in the story of this green cake—empire, religion, communism and capitalism, monetary policy, immigration, and war. They talk about it, but here, we live it."

Hadley applauded, as did a couple of other women whom I didn't recognize. Alice smiled.

"But I don't think you've ever cooked a cake, have you?" Alice raised her eyebrow.

"Not beyond the compulsory lessons at school."

"No, I could tell. You're one of these young ones who have fled the so-called 'domestic trappings' of marriage and home."

I could only smile. "What's the giveaway, my lipstick or my high heels?"

"It's the way you hold your cake, like it's poisonous."

"Ignore the green color, it's delicious," said Hadley.

"But not if you live on cocktails and cigarettes, isn't that right, Miss . . . ?"

"Button. Kiki Button." She shook my hand softly. "Yes . . . but no, I love cake. I just . . . I don't even own a gas ring to cook on."

"Nor a spoon, I bet." Alice sighed. "You're the Australian's wife?"

"Just his friend."

"Anyone's wife?"

"It's not my style."

"No . . ." Alice looked me over, assessing me with something that felt like pity. "Well, you can join the men soon. Stay with us a moment longer." She let Hadley introduce me to Mrs. Matisse, Amelie, who was Matisse's main model and knew as much about mixing pigment for paint and stretching canvas as a tradesman. Hadley was a concert-grade pianist, but had no ambition to exhibit. They were formidable mathematicians of household accounts and swapped information on how best to balance credit to live above a meager income. I could see Alice looking at me with her big eyes from across the room, as though daring me to find value in this knowledge. I didn't know what to do except to finish my slice and take another. It was far too sweet for me.

"You remind me of that English woman," Amelie said, interrupting her own advice on how to haggle for a camel in Morocco. "Alice! That English model, I've forgotten her name for a moment, but Henri knows her well, we all know her, she sat for him that time when I was in bed after I lost the baby. You know . . . friends with Rodin. What is her name?"

"Cordelia," said Alice. "I've been thinking that as well. There's a look they share, a sort of . . . yearning. And Cordelia has no interest in cooking either."

Amelie laughed. "That's right! The one time she had to cook for Henri, she managed to burn boiled eggs! She is so sweet though—and she always has plenty of money for cheese, sausage, sweets for Jean and Marguerite—but like a flower, easily bruised. Too easily for Henri. As for me, I'm in my element when the house burns down."

Hadley laughed. "And me, I come alive when the kitty is empty."

"What was her surname?" I could feel my pulse beat in my throat.

"Oh, family names, I never remember those," said Amelie.

"I don't know it," Alice said. "I've only met her a couple of times and, like you, she doesn't value the quotidian. She speaks mostly to Gertrude and Matisse. She never comes here." She scrutinized my face. "Yes, you have a definite look about you of Cordelia. Let's ask Gertrude."

She ushered me away from the tea table toward the men. Gertrude looked up from her conversation and spread out her hands.

"Ah, the scarlet woman! I wondered who you were in that vivid red dress. Are you Pimpernel or Jezebel?"

"Depends on the day. Depends on the hour."

"Is it silk? I never wear the stuff myself, too delicate, but that embroidery is exquisite. You must have bought it here in Paris. Nowhere else in the world would embroider such luminous blooms."

"She reminds me of that model, Cordelia," said Alice.

"Of course! She wore red the first time we met her too, though I doubt she would have shown her ankles then, unless it was on the modeling dais."

"Miss Button here wanted to know Cordelia's surname."

"It's Button, of course." Gertrude smiled. "Are you related?"

The cubist nudes stared down at me from the walls. "My mother."

"Well! Your mother; no wonder you make such an impression. Alice, are you leaving Miss Button with us?"

"I think she belongs here." Alice nodded and went back to the wives and their politics-in-action. I had nothing to add to their conversation but I was strangely sorry to be left. I felt as though I had failed some test of womanhood, cast out from those who might protect me. Above me, a faceless torso cavorted on a sea of sickly green.

"Miss Button." Gertrude waved me over, appraising me as Alice had. She didn't smile at me either, but seemed less concerned that I had no interest in the domestic arts.

"Yes, you have a definite look of Cordelia about you. Almost an air. Well, well. So, you're Tom's friend—from Australia? Come to think of it, Cordelia did mention she lives somewhere out of the way . . . that would explain why she seems to be everywhere one moment and vanishes the next. Presumably she goes home to you and your father. Don't worry, we like her. She's always so lively, witty in that very soft, feminine way that men like. But she has a way of looking at you that makes it seem as though she understands you completely. You know what I mean."

"I—"

"Of course you do, you're her daughter. But her last trip—when was that, a couple of years ago?—she seemed burdened. Why? Oh—Matisse! Matisse, look here, it's Cordelia Button's daughter."

The man in the gray three-piece suit turned and stared at me for a long time, his whole body still, his eyes burning a hole through his glasses. I could do nothing but stare back.

"How old are you?" he asked abruptly.

"Twenty-six."

He stared and then sighed. "Thank you. And my apologies. You have such a look of your mother."

"Doesn't she, though?" Gertrude said. By this time Tom had noticed me and was eavesdropping.

"How is she?" asked Matisse.

I shook my head. I couldn't force my words past the weight on my chest.

"Not dead!" Matisse looked shocked. "No! No, it couldn't be."

They waited for my reply. I cleared my throat, swallowed, took a deep breath against the weight.

"Last year, very suddenly."

"No . . . no . . ." He continued to stare at me.

"I'm so sorry," said Gertrude.

"You knew her well?" I asked Matisse.

"Yes—no . . ." He continued to stare. "She modeled for me. She . . . excuse me." He turned abruptly, grabbed his hat and his wife, and left.

"Well! How rude. I knew there was a reason we don't invite him here anymore."

"Matisse knew my mother well?"

"Well, we always met her in his company, but she was only an occasional model, you know, on account of her living elsewhere. Australia, I mean. I always think like that, there's Paris, there's America, then there's elsewhere. I didn't think news of her would have had such an effect, but then, Matisse has always been wound tight as a clock spring, and just

as likely to come apart if you prod him. She was part of that group with
Monet and Russell and even Rodin, I think—I don't know them, their
work isn't my style, but Rodin was a nice man. Hemingway, did you
ever . . . no, you're too young to have met Rodin."

"Please—can you tell me more about my mother?"

"You don't . . . of course, you miss her." Gertrude nodded. She moved
some books off an armchair which she then pulled close to her own. A
sculpture of a headless female body loomed behind her.

"Sit down." She patted the chair like giving an order. "Hemingway,
would you be a gun and bring Miss Button a cup of tea? Lots of sugar
and a good splash of brandy. Now, Cordelia Button . . . I'll have to check
the details with Alice, but we met her at a gallery opening, or rather,
at the supper afterwards with Matisse, who else was there, that strange
Norwegian Edvard Munch, was Russell there? . . . She was dressed in
red, like you, all flowing fabric and a tiny waist, a real Gibson Girl type.
She talked deeply and intimately with Matisse at the supper and he barely
spoke to anyone else. Every time she spoke to someone else, he was lost
in thought. She listened very politely but had little to add to Alice's
anecdotes of the problems of laundry while traveling. But when I spoke
to her about laundresses in art, she had a lot to say about color and line
and form. She was an unusual woman, looking decorative but without any
decorative small talk. After that night we met her quite a few times—in
Montmartre, in Montparnasse, at the Opera—and then she vanished."

Stein shrugged as Hemingway handed me a cup of tea that smelt
strongly of brandy.

"You said she seemed burdened . . ."

"Yes, I was hoping Matisse could have said something about that. I
suspect he will once he gets over the shock of your sad news. But Cordelia,
that winter . . . she took too long to answer a question, she was always
distracted. It was just a couple of months after the Armistice, everyone
was dying of the flu, no one had much energy and we were all a bit lost
in thought of those we'd lost. I remember I was often concerned about
the state of my car. Cordelia had been nursing someone, I think—was it

Munch, or was it someone else?—or had she been the sick one? I got the sense that she hadn't understood that France was tired and Paris full of absence. It was her first trip here since 1913, she told me, but she didn't say more than that. She didn't need to; her shock and disappointment were apparent. I don't know how long she stayed. I think she might have spent a bit of time with her family in England. Alice was with me then, she'd remember more—Alice!"

Alice looked up from a discussion over the teacups and came over.

"Alice, dear, the last time Cordelia was here—do you remember? I told Miss Button here that Cordelia seemed burdened, but I only remember thinking about my car and how to fix it."

"Yes, that was an ongoing problem. We'd used the car in the war to transport wounded to the hospital and it was in rather a state. Is your cup empty? Come with me." Gertrude turned back to Hemingway and started discussing a writer I'd never heard of. Gertrude and Alice's dance was perfectly executed. This time, I didn't mind going to the tea table.

"I saw that Matisse left," Alice said softly. "I'm not surprised. He had a tenderness for your mother."

"They were lovers?" I concentrated on holding my cup steady for more tea and brandy.

"It would be hard to compete with Amelie. But there was a group of men who held your mother in very high esteem and Matisse was one of them. They are not part of our group. They are mostly older artists whom Gertrude finds too attached to the old ways. I don't mind their art but they don't listen to women, so their art quickly loses its luster. Only Matisse listens."

"My mother, when she was here last . . ."

"Ah yes. Paris was so . . . well, it was still finding its feet after the Armistice. The hospitals were all full of war-wounded and flu victims. She came to nurse a friend, though she never mentioned to me who that was, and then stayed and continued to nurse people in a hospital before she left for England. She paid the rent for Modigliani and Jeanne for the whole time she was here, so I heard, and a good while afterwards as well. She was . . . lost, and in that respect, she fit into Paris perfectly, as she always had. So many of us felt lost."

She cut a slender slice of fruit cake and slipped it onto my saucer. Her look almost dared me to eat it.

"Who were these other men, these artists who admired her? Gertrude mentioned Monet, Rodin . . ."

"You should ask Matisse. He lives in the south, though, and I don't know how long they'll be in Paris."

I wanted to leave, to ask immediately, I had just put down my cup and saucer when Alice put her hand on my arm.

"Don't ask yet. Matisse is a sensitive soul, it will take him a while before he can answer any questions. Come, tell Hadley what you know about seamstresses in Montparnasse. She admires your style." She handed me back my cup and saucer, the slice of cake still placed precariously on edge, ready at any moment to crumble and break.

"THROW ME A KISS"

"You're very quiet, Button." Tom nudged me as we walked home in the cold evening.

"They knew my mother."

"I heard."

"She flits about these streets in my imagination. I keep thinking I can see a woman in pre-war fashions, in last century's corsets, just turning the corner. How could I not have known she had this other life?"

"Perhaps because she was as good at keeping secrets as you are."

"Yet another similarity that I find out too late. Distract me, Tom-Tom. Help me think of something else, at least for a minute."

He looked at me with such longing, it was visible even in the darkness. Something metal clanged, a group of American tourists tumbled drunkenly out of a café singing snatches of music-hall hits. Tom took my arm and held me close as the cobbles clapped beneath our footfalls.

"You missed all the political chat at Gertrude's. Hem spoke a bit about Smyrna, but then said something odd. He said, 'Those *fascisti* in Italy—I wouldn't be surprised if we found them in Paris before long. They're appealing to all the old soldiers who want to continue the old ways.'"

"Old soldiers . . . like exiled princes."

"Especially those who fought. When I fought, I wanted the . . . civilization, for want of a better word, to be there when I returned. Concerts
and restaurants and books and sport, I wanted it all to have thrived in
my absence. I needed it to. How much more so for men who view the
land not with simple belonging but with ownership?" He stared down
the dark street as he spoke.

"What is it, Tom?"

"Nothing—"

"Go on."

His shoulders slumped. "Smyrna. It wasn't the worst thing I've seen
but it is the latest. It's still happening too . . . it feels so odd. I'm here
drinking and laughing, no one here is at war, but over there, men are still
bayonetting each other, children are still howling into the night, there
are still women who roam from cot to cot selling themselves for nothing
but the chance to live for a few more hours. The fires are smoldering and
the cupboards are bare, while here, all is normal. At least in 1916, 1917,
everywhere was at war. Even on leave, the streets were full of uniforms,
there were air raid sirens all the time, food was rationed, and blackouts
made a little sanctuary of every café and pub. My leave was only from
the front, as no one could take leave from the war itself. With Smyrna,
I can. With Russia, too, I just take the train and there's no more war, no
refugees, no famine, there is real coffee and butter on soft bread, there
are clean sheets and running water and people getting excited about
football and theatre and paintings. It only takes a few hours to travel
from chaos to order. I can hardly fathom it. I keep turning a corner and
expecting a corpse, I keep expecting a tap on the shoulder and behind
me are the guns."

He stopped in the dark between streetlights, he pulled me into him,
wrapping his arms around me. I made my body soft so that it fit perfectly
with his.

"You're the only antidote, Button. You let me be here and now and not
halfway between never-was and couldn't-be."

We were steps from my building, I recognized my neighbors as they whistled and argued. Tom's hug was somehow both too rough and too flimsy, a hug from far away.

"Well, that was certainly a distraction from my bad mood."

He laughed but it was water splashing in the gutter, it was rueful.

"I can think of better distractions," he said. "All you have to do is ask."

Spilled light from the windows above made his eyes seem black, his expression intent. He would do anything for me, he would do nothing until I asked him. Did he sense my hesitation, that I was enjoying a life unbound too much to kiss him? Was he politely respecting my mourning? Did he need me to say yes first, to start the tumble into each other? I couldn't tell, except that he was in earnest. I couldn't help but reach up to stroke his face.

"And I will ask, dearest Tom-Tom." I didn't invite him to ask the same of me; I could see, clearly, that our relationship didn't work that way. We stood there for a long time, mostly in shadow with my hand on his cheek, only moving upstairs when the October wind made me shiver.

⌘

We slept badly. Tom was restless and I half woke with his tosses and turns. I drifted in a dream state through the dawn and into the morning, through the church bells that seemed to remind me that all I had believed in was upended and emptied out. The next day we roamed Paris aimlessly, ate absentmindedly, smoked constantly. I felt there was a cocoon around us, a protective space where others couldn't enter, couldn't hear us or see us properly. This space pushed back the sounds of now, the French along the river, the cars and carts and coffee cups. It was filled instead with the sounds of elsewhere, with whipbirds and fire crackles and the caress of the Pacific against sandstone, with howls and blasts and dead silence. This space protected us so we could speak and finally be heard.

I spoke of my mother.

"My mother . . . I am filled with guilt. Then rage. They mix together until I feel as though I have drunk absinthe from the gutter, I am retching and wretched. I have so many questions but they all simmer down to one: Why didn't she let me know her? I think she was preparing to, there are little notes all through the more recent diaries, things like 'When I see Katherine in Paris . . .' or 'I wonder if Katherine would enjoy Chelsea?' or 'Katherine should really meet X, she'll find him amusing.' X is the mystery man. I think if the war hadn't delayed her, she would have joined me here and left Sydney forever. I would have seen who she really was, in her natural habitat. But it was the war—she couldn't get here until I had left—then she died. Did she return in 1919 only to see me? There's something missing, there are connections I can't make. I keep getting glimpses of her, little slices of a total stranger with my mother's name. I need to find that final diary. I need to find X, whoever he is. I think that's the link between the mother I knew and this amazing Montmartre Cordelia."

"How will you do that?"

"Gertrude suggested I speak to Matisse . . . perhaps he'll know."

"Perhaps he's the mystery man."

"He's too young." I flicked my cigarette butt into the bushes. "But I'll find out somehow."

Tom spoke of war.

"Russia . . . I've never seen anything like it." The sun ruptured the clouds for an unruly moment before returning the sky to gray. "It was a front, the whole country a muddy trench. Endless grasses, horizons bare but for fleeing horses, smoke, the occasional explosion. Train tracks lined with wraiths, streets haunted by skeletons with roving eyes. This is the new world, the commissariat said, we all need to sacrifice to create a better earth. But just like in the trenches, it wasn't the bureaucrats who sacrificed their lives, it wasn't the bigwigs who suffered. They'd just left the 'imperialist war' and were inflicting that suffering all over again, a suffering so immense I could hardly think outside it. I thought, this can't be worth it, however cruel the old regime was, at least it was stable, it can't have been as bad as this. My interpreter agreed with me. The son of a police chief in Moscow, he'd studied in London and it was dangerous for him to be in Russia, but he wanted me to see what it was like, he wanted me to tell the world. Then people in the trains, in the stations, in the bars and cafés would speak to us. He wouldn't translate at first, he told me they were talking nonsense, but he changed his mind. Such stories! The serfs had been practically enslaved, they had belonged to their princely masters who starved them or saved them on a whim. Working every day until they died, they had to beg for medicine, for education, for permission to marry. Anything, they said, was better than that. I met quite a few Jewish people traveling to Russia to help the Revolution. Their stories, of pogroms and murders, made even my interpreter cry. Slums in the Pale where hiding from the police was their first childhood memory. Rats for dinner when the pigeons ran out. Fear that every city murder would inspire a mob to set them on fire in so-called 'revenge.'"

The wind picked up the littered leaves and old newspapers and flung them at the backs of our legs, making us scurry into a café. The café reeked of old fat and cabbage, a smell that not even our coffees could overpower. The window next to us was opaque with condensation.

"So, I couldn't say that the princes are right and communism is dreadful, nor could I say the opposite," Tom said. "All it seems is that, in an attempt to remedy a sickness, they have wounded themselves so badly they'll be bleeding for a long time. I do believe one thing though: Hem is right. Europe is throbbing with revolutionary desire, and it's a race to see whether communism or nationalism will win out."

"Nationalism . . . like the Fascists? Are they nationalist or internationalist?"

"The Communists are internationalist . . . although Russia just happens to be 'first among equals,' if you can wrap your head around that paradox. These new Fascists . . . I can't tell yet. They help each other across national affiliations, but the way they operate seems to be tied to their national armies, which makes it more nationalist. We'll have to see how it plays out."

"My mission is clearly about these old soldiers who hate the new Europe."

"I'd say so. These clues aren't as convoluted as last year."

"No," I took a sip of my coffee, hot and bitter. "I've been thinking about that. Last year Fox knew who I had to find, where and when and all the details. He just wanted me to play his game and work it out. This year, I think he knows one or two things—the houseboy or boys, the prince or perhaps two princes—but not the rest. That's why the mission is easier to decode. I actually have to do some proper spy work and find out the details."

"He trusts you, then."

"Probably he has no choice. He sends me to do the work men can't. Which is another clue: what sort of princes are they, that they would let a woman close and not be suspicious, and not arouse the suspicions of their servants?"

"Libertines. Ladies' men."

"That's my thought. Which means they can't be just any old princes."

"The Prince of Wales."

"The Empire's darling."

"Jesus wept."

The last rays of sun refracted through the window's dirty moisture to speckle Tom's face, the shadows under his eyes, his thin skin.

"It could be fun, you never know."

"With you, Button, it's always fun. The question is, how dangerous will the fun be?"

"We're working for Fox. Pack your pistol."

⌘

We stood at the station platform at Gare du Nord. The whistle would blow any minute, the train was filling, and Tom still wouldn't find his seat.

"You want a good one, you're going a long way, get in, for Pete's sake."

"Button, Pete doesn't give a fig about where I sit and neither do I."

"You'll end up squished between Fat Freddy and Gabby Gladys and you won't get a wink of sleep. Go on!"

"Button." He put down his case and took my hands between both of his. "I'll stay here warming your icy fingers until the train begins to move. Stop nagging me."

"I don't nag!"

"I'll get on in my own good time."

"I don't nag. You just don't know what's good for you."

"I know what I need." His voice was low. It made my heart beat uncomfortably fast. The lamps on the platforms were already lit, golden light pooling on the stained concrete.

"I need you back in Paris soon. You're part of this mission now, Tom. Abandon all hope of an easy life."

"Yes, ma'am!"

"Write to me, or telegram or call, from London. I'll need to discuss my breakthroughs with you. I'll need . . ." But I couldn't put into words my jagged feelings of desire and desperation, the will-o'-the-wisp of loneliness, the wildness that made me drink more than my body could hold, pain that tore through my days, ideas forming and reforming like oil on water. Tom squeezed my hands and kissed them.

"Yes, you will," he addressed all I hadn't said. "I'll be back as soon as I can. I'm bound to be sent to some skirmish somewhere and I always, always come through Paris."

"It's not goodbye."

"It'll never be goodbye."

The whistle blew, the train heaved its wheels into the first rotation.

"Last drinks, Button." He kissed me fiercely on the cheek and vanished inside the crowded carriage as the train pulled out in a cough of steam.

"MY BUDDY"

For the first time in a long time my head ached when I woke. It could have been the bowls of Breton cider that one of the waiters at the Rotonde brought out, as a joke, but that had kept us going through the night, crisp and cold, they tasted like the weather. It could have been the entire packet of cigarettes that disappeared into my lungs. But I knew these were mere symptoms of the real disease: Tom was gone, Bertie was still in London, Theo was somewhere or other but I didn't need any more men. I needed my women. I needed Maisie.

I telegrammed Maisie Brown Chevallier but I couldn't wait for a reply. I should have contacted her earlier, I was a fool to take so long to say hello, as I didn't want to wait to meet her, I didn't want to make a polite arrangement to call on her, I wanted her right now, I wanted to run immediately to her strong embrace. I barely noticed the streets of Paris as I clipped over to the river, my teal heels rapping against the cobblestones. I hardly saw the seamstresses assess my peacock blue coat with its tatty fur collar, its sumptuous volume in need of a wash. I simply clutched the coat like a prayer and moved forward into the wind.

Angelina's Tea Room was luxurious gilt and cream, hushed and discreet, and absolutely the wrong place for me at the moment. I was in a dingy-cellar-bar mood, a riverside-pie-cart mood, a mess-tent and biscuits-at-midnight mood. But as I'd practically summoned Maisie to a pot of hot chocolate, I thought this place would be easy for her to find in a hurry. The high ceilings were decorated with Art Nouveau swirls and the walls were mostly mirror. The air smelt of chocolate and expensive perfume. If I hadn't had a packet of patriotic Gauloises with me, I would have felt dirty smoking.

I remembered the first time I saw Maisie, when I was training to be a nurse in London. Matron had decided to bully me, for my "bright face" Maisie decided, so I was punished on the slightest pretext. As an experienced nurse, Maisie showed me tricks with sheets and bedpans so I could be both precise and quick and thereby avoid the worst of Matron's wrath. I remembered when we found each other again at the field hospital in Rouen. I'd been in surgery with Fox when she had arrived, I was exhausted and could barely stand in line at the mess tent. She lifted me up with a big hug and then cajoled and threatened the other nurses until we shared a tent. She then tucked me into bed, and when I woke, fed me chocolate rum cake that had been sent to her from England and made me tell her all the hospital gossip.

At the end of the war, Fox and family had called me to London while Maisie stayed in Paris. I promised to write, of course, but I'm a hopeless correspondent. Her letters told tales that seemed to mirror my life: nursing flu patients, working harder in the peace than in the war, performing emergency tracheotomies that ended up useless. Being in uniform but now also in quarantine. Missing each other's company. Why hadn't I replied? I received her letters at the Sydney Hospital, where I knew no one except by their eyes and walk as we were all in masks and gloves, all the time. I didn't leave that hospital until it was almost 1920.

When I met Maisie last year by accident in the street, her high hair and purposeful stride unmistakable even out of uniform, the world was suddenly sunnier. The world was safer; whenever it looked like I might get lost in cocktails, lovers, and spy work, she led me back to myself. She saw me, she knew me almost as well as Tom did, and I needed her. I hadn't called her as I had been hiding. Now I felt I would fade away if she didn't turn up soon.

"Katie King!" Her enthusiastic wave, her flash-bulb smile: my Maisie. I pushed past the polite tea-sippers to get to her as quickly as possible, throwing myself into her strong arms and hugging her until she squeaked.

"There's only one person in the world who calls me Katie King."

"I came as soon as I got that telegram, though to be honest, it wasn't that hard to leave the household accounts. When did you get back to Paris?"

"A week ago. I'm sorry it's taken me so long—"

"Pfft, don't be silly," she said, as we walked arm in arm back to our table. "You had to find your Kiki-legs, you know, like sea-legs, only for Paris."

"I was called Katherine for a year. The first few times I didn't even respond, I didn't know who they were talking to. But Kiki doesn't fit Australia. It's too . . ."

"French. Which is why you're always Katie King to me."

She smiled, a real smile of love and joy. When I first met her, she'd had little freckles all over her nose, but they had disappeared after the first winter in the hospital tents and had never returned. She squeezed my hand, but when I returned the squeeze it turned into another hug across the table. Although I embraced her with all my might, I was so slight compared to her that I felt like a child hugging an adult. I could feel the muscles in her shoulders and back flex, whereas my strength was simply desperation. She was taller than me, even accounting for her usual bouncing hair, which today was tucked securely away. She pulled back from the hug and smoothed my messy bob. She was wearing a sheer cream blouse and a tight brown skirt, a palette which looked subtle, sophisticated, and very Parisian.

"You're even stronger than when I left, Maisie."

"I'm back on the wards."

"What, they're paying you?"

"Nope, I'm still married."

"You're not working for free? Oh, Maisie . . ."

"It's just so boring being a housewife! I can't do it. I've told Ray, I'd rather lance a boil than spend more than five minutes choosing curtains. You know, the upholsterer came in with six books of samples and a packed lunch? He expected to be in apartment all morning. He was shocked when I sent him off with an order in under ten minutes. It would have been five but he insisted on a cup of tea."

My face hurt with grinning. "And what else, Maisie? What else?"

She winked. "Chocolate first. Here, I'll order."

"Your French has improved then."

"It's had to, working on the wards. Even in the American Hospital." She ordered us pots of chocolate and the famous hazelnut Mont Blanc pastries.

"Now, Katie, tell me all about your mother. I can see your sorrowful business isn't finished. You wear your sadness like a skin disease."

"Charming."

"It isn't."

I laid out the year as a story, from the moment I stepped off at Wool-loomooloo to the moment I reunited with Bertie, the gilded mirrors and the smell of hot chocolate lending a fairy tale quality to my words. She listened as a friend, as a nurse, as one who knows the action of grief. She didn't interrupt, her strong hands cutting the pastries into tiny slices. As I spoke, I felt the Sydney summer, when the humidity sat on the streets like a drunk and I was sunk in darkness. I felt how the colder southerly winds brought the sounds from the harbor and the street and let me breathe. I saw how I was jolted out of my slump by my aunt, a shock that would have broken me if it had come too soon, but instead came at just the right time to set me in motion.

"You're stronger than when you left, Katie. Stronger, perhaps, than you realize."

"It's my only hope." I rolled the chocolate round my mouth, sip by tiny sip, it was so rich and sweet. The pastries were now only crumbs. "How did you cope, Maisie?"

"With what? My mother's death? I only ever knew various nuns and matrons."

"I thought . . ."

"It's the life of a mission kid." She shrugged. "I never knew my mother. I wasn't that lucky."

She returned the squeeze of my hand.

"It's why . . ." She exhaled with force. "It's why it's so complicated . . . my grief when I lost the baby." She couldn't stop her tears then, dabbing at her eyes as though to push the tears back in.

"I didn't want to get pregnant. Ray expects a nanny, he wants to send his children to boarding school. But I can't, I just can't hand over my children to some officious bitter matron, who enforces prayers at bedtime and whacks your palm if you ask for more dinner."

"Oh, her . . . I know that matron."

"You see? Until I win that fight: no kids. But the pregnancy just happened, in the way they do, and I loved the little thing as soon as I knew it existed, imagining it blue-eyed like Ray or brown-eyed like me . . . This was my family, here, I could set things right. I could be grounded in the world in the way I always should have been, so when I woke up with vice-like pain and blood on the sheets . . ."

"Maisie, Maisie . . ."

"He didn't understand, he just said we'll have another, we'll try again—which I know, of course, as a nurse, pregnancies fail all the time—but he couldn't possibly understand that this blood is history, it releases ghosts . . ." She put her face in her hands.

"This place is too polite for what we need to say now, Maisie."

She sniffed, blinked, wiped her eyes on the napkin and her nose on the back of her hand.

"You know all the bohemian cafés, Katie. Take me somewhere where my tears can turn to laughter."

"ANGEL CHILD"

We leaned over the balustrade of the Pont Neuf, Sainte Chapelle behind us, tourists all around us, the silver surface of the Seine below us as it shivered in the breeze.

"Katie, I know you know what I mean, you have to . . . if we close all the doors to grief, life is bright and happy, a little thin, but nonetheless our days are mostly fine. But one breath of despair blows all the other doors open, and all the windows, it blows cold and dark through every moment . . ."

She stared at the river like it was a magic mirror.

"You thought of the war."

"How could I not? Though I don't think I'd thought about it much since I took off my uniform."

"Maybe because you never took off your uniform, Maisie."

"Neither have you."

"The stitches have dissolved and now it's my skin."

"And I'm still nursing, still in France . . . I couldn't even bury this babe, it was too small. Oh, Katie, there was so much blood . . . I couldn't help but think of all the other unburied, the bits and pieces we'd put in the furnace until the back of the field hospital smelt like the devil's barbeque. I couldn't help but think of all those mothers and how they might have cherished Tommy's right finger, or Freddy's half-rotten left foot, anything, just to have a piece of their baby again. Not that I ever thought of that at the time—the best place for a gangrenous limb is the fire—but after the miscarriage, the dreams of blood returned."

"So much blood."

"And much too often." She accepted a cigarette from me and blew the smoke over the water under the overcast sky, gray on gray on gray. "And I thought of afterwards too, you know, the flu pandemic."

"The tears after the celebration."

"How could we have survived the carnage only to suffocate in our beds? I was busier than during the war, here in Paris, working all hours with beds full of teenage girls before their first sweetheart, widowed women leaving orphaned children, crippled boys who were their mother's joy . . . it was like the gas wards, except this time we couldn't tell them that they were heroes, that it was for the nation. It was for no reason at all, it was just senseless and unstoppable."

She flicked her cigarette butt in a long arc into the water, and pulled up the collar of her dark brown coat.

"It was more than a year for me," I said. Traffic honked and grunted behind us. "I nursed on the ship home and was immediately pushed into Sydney Hospital, as my mother was on the board. I didn't see an unmasked face until I escaped to my father's property for Christmas 1919. Happy times."

"Exactly. Who would remember that year if they didn't have to?"

❧

We walked through the Jardin du Luxembourg arm in arm, as much to keep out the wind as to make our chat intimate.

"Sometimes I don't think Paris knows what a park is supposed to be," said Maisie. "All this grass, some flowers, and a great big palace in the middle. There are never enough trees, or nooks, no groves to get lost in, no corners to hide in. The English don't have much style but they do know a good park."

"That's because everything in England is a park, if it's owned by someone. It's only a forest if it's got too wild."

"If I want a forest here, I could always go to the Bois de Bolougne, I suppose, but even there the trees are so . . . polite." She was surprised by my laughter. "You know what I mean! Ray has no understanding that a tree should look like an octopus, or a hawk, or a thin man or a set of veins. To him all trees are neat like Christmas."

Red and brown leaves blew around us, birds pecked at infinitesimal specks on the paths.

"Anyway, this miscarriage—this is where the story gets interesting. So, I didn't go to my hospital, we just ended up at the local, with a midwife I nicknamed Harem Scarem. Not because she was whiskery and severe; I'm not cruel. No, she earned her nickname when she barked, 'One less mulatto baby is one more reason to thank God.' If I hadn't been so weak, I would have slapped her."

"I'd be next. I may still."

"She knew this too and was enjoying herself. 'Does the father even know? Do you even know the father?' Her teeth were yellow."

"Yellow teeth? Unforgivable."

"Ray came in as she said that and chastised her so loudly it brought in the other nurses, who then fetched a doctor. It turns out the doctor knew Ray, they'd served together and hadn't seen each other since some hellhole or other. Verdun, I think. Anyway, Sister Scarum got put on bedpan duty by the matron, for a month, and shuffled away to pour her vitriol out with the sewage."

I laughed, small and sarcastic, and pulled Maisie closer as the wind sent its long cold fingers into our clothing. Maisie pushed back an escaping hair.

"So, while I'm lying there, pale and desperate to leave, the doctor introduced Ray to a third man, who was also with them in Verdun. The man blanched as soon as he saw Ray and ran away. Ray, who's as soft as uncooked meringue, ran after the man to apologize and reassure him."

"Leaving you alone?"

"The doctor had to examine me, prod my belly, check my stitches."

"Brutal."

"Medieval. Anyway, who do you think this man was? It was Michel!" I took my cue. "Who is Michel?"

"Who is Michel indeed! This is where the story goes from interesting to very interesting. Michel is the reason Ray was being blackmailed."

"Blackmailed by whom?"

"Blackmailed by Edward Hausmann."

I stopped abruptly. Maisie had raised her eyebrow just slightly, her expression a kind of furious amusement. She remembered exactly who Hausmann was and now probably knew more about him than I did. I cursed strongly enough that even a passing sailor looked startled.

"I know, Katie King. The man behind your last mission."

The sky seemed to sink lower. "You have to tell me more."

"Then let's find a café, Katie, I'm freezing."

"I WISH I COULD SHIMMY LIKE MY SISTER KATE"

We moved past all the terrasse tables outside the Closerie des Lilas, full of cackling bohemians and ogling tourists, to a little red booth inside. The café chatter reminded me of my final telephone conversation with Fox last year. He had insinuated that Hausmann had Ray Chevallier in his sights, something about cabaret and "Monsieur Chevallier's weakness for the dark and exotic." Fox was too infuriating; I had put it out of my mind. I wish that I had understood his words not as a tease, but as a warning.

The air in the café was stuffy with exhaled breath and the booth was slightly sticky. All I wanted to do was smoke in the low light, but Maisie insisted we order chips and beer. She would have kicked off her shoes too if we hadn't been in public. She licked the beer foam from her lips.

"Katie King, how can cold beer be so warming?"

"Tell me about Michel, Maisie."

"This is a story." Maisie stretched her legs. "At the hospital, Michel went with Ray, blubbering and wailing, his apology composed of excuses.

He hated Hausmann too, but he was scared of him and couldn't take the fear any longer. Over thin coffee in a disgusting café behind the hospital, he told us everything.

"The story starts in the war. In the hell that was Verdun, Ray went a bit mad. 'Crazy Ray,' they called him. Recklessly brave and couldn't stop talking. After one raid he came back with half a dozen POWs and babbled at them all the way back to their lines. He told them all sorts of confidential details including, Ray says, where they kept their stores of munitions. The next day Ray woke up in a puddle, only to find out that one of the prisoners had escaped and the munitions dump had been bombed, killing two hundred men. This man, Michel, was the escaped prisoner."

"He's German?"

"He's from Alsace; French father, German mother. He joined the German Army in 1914 then defected to the French Army in 1917. Anyway, after Michel escaped, he ran straight to his superiors across the German lines and repeated everything that Ray had babbled. The Germans wrote everything down, as Germans are wont to do, including Ray's name. Signed, stamped, the whole lot.

"I found Ray asleep at the dining table with a little note clutched in his hand. I recognized the name Hausmann and I made Ray tell me everything. The note was delivered by Michel and said that Hausmann had these documents."

"What did Hausmann want?"

"Money. What else? Loads of money, all the money from Ray's family estate in Senegal. If Ray didn't cooperate, Hausmann would use the evidence to say that Ray was a traitor, a double agent for the Germans, that he had murdered his fellow soldiers. All nonsense, of course, but when it comes to one's war service, well, mud sticks."

"Especially trench mud. How much have you paid so far?"

"Nothing. Between us, we've done a magnificent job of stalling. We said the cocoa estate was on the verge of bankruptcy. Then we said it all belonged to Ray's elder brother, that we had to consult lawyers, that French lawyers took forever, et cetera et cetera. Our final promise was that we were getting the money, we just needed to offload a particular shipment of cocoa. That was in March."

"And Michel?"

"Hausmann was blackmailing Michel as well. Michel's French now, he has a French wife, a French war service record, and a job in a French hospital, but the only place he truly lives is in fear. Michel doesn't want anyone to know he fought for the Germans, that he even spied for the Germans! When he saw Ray, he assumed Ray would recognize him. He panicked and, over coffee, unraveled. He doesn't want to be a courier, he just wants to live a quiet life with his seamstress wife, in the country somewhere, with his own little vegetable garden . . . sweet, I suppose."

"Were you at the meeting? Weren't you in hospital?"

"I wasn't going to stay in that building one moment longer. I went to that café, I almost started bleeding again and was laid up in bed for weeks. I got so bored that Ray bought a radio, so I could lie on the couch and listen to the news.

"Anyway, once Michel had confessed, then we had something to work with. We took him out to a little plot in the country, and after that Michel agreed to steal the evidence for us, to be paid exactly the cost of that little plot. It was expensive but cost us much less than Hausmann would have. Hausmann tried to keep blackmailing us, he even contacted Ray himself as, of course, he couldn't find his go-between. He turned up at our house and left in a lather when we told him we'd burnt the documents."

"Had you burnt them?"

"Abso-bloody-lutely. But knowing the German Army, there'll be copies."

This didn't sound at all like the type of blackmail Fox had mentioned.

"So, the blackmail had nothing to do with you? Or Ray's past in Senegal?"

"No. Why would it?"

I shrugged, hoping the smoke in the café would mask my confusion.

"Hausmann doesn't like me, of course," she said. "He called me 'colored' and 'coolie' before Ray threw him out of our apartment. But he didn't threaten me."

She took my packet of cigarettes and pushed the plate of chips toward me.

"Katie King, what do you know?"

I didn't want to tell her, but between her frown and my hunger, I couldn't resist. I took three chips, licking the salt from my lips as I contemplated how to say what I barely knew.

"Fox mentioned something last year. He knew that Hausmann was going to target Ray. I thought . . . well, I thought Fox was just winding me up. Apparently not."

"You're working for Fox again?"

"I work for him whether I like it or not. It feels like blackmail, not employment."

"That's because it is blackmail."

I lit up to avoid looking at her. The floor was covered in the burns of a thousand cigarettes.

"Katie, it always was. It's just that his threats used to be undeniable: do this or we lose the war."

"It's not the war now. I don't want to involve you."

"Hausmann has been blackmailing us. I'm involved regardless."

Maisie watched me as I took a big slug of my beer and ordered another, cigarette dangling from my lip, a spot of beer on my bright blue dress. Her look was full of pity and love and I could hardly bear it, I had to turn away. The café's warmth was rent by the sawtooth wind through the ever-opening door. She was still watching me as I stubbed out my cigarette.

"You can't hide from me, Katie King."

I hugged her then, maybe even cried a little, let her laugh at me and shush me and put more chips in my mouth.

"As I eat, read this." I reached into my bag and handed her the note.

"What is it?"

"My mission."

She scanned the spidery handwriting.

"Fox is still being cryptic, I see."

"He can't help himself."

"Don't make excuses for him. Do you carry this everywhere?"

"I have the last few days. Once I work it out, I'll check with Fox and then get rid of it."

She read the note a few times, frowning, her lips moving slightly as she went over the different ideas. I ate mechanically. I was thinking of Hausmann and when I saw him last, cursing me in the Citroën factory, after Tom and I had stopped him from stealing a Picasso painting. Hausmann was going to sell the painting to raise money for his Brownshirt cause, but in the end all he took with him was the bullet I had put in his shoulder.

She took a deep breath. "Houseboys," she said, "that's Hausmann."

"Your recent history with him is my final bit of proof. The 'religion in a brown shirt' are the Brownshirts from Germany, the Freikorps. The 'black-clad men who tempt and slay' are the Italian Fascists, led by a man called Benito Mussolini."

"And the leader? The princes?"

"English princes. As for the leader . . . I don't think anyone knows. Yet."

"With those people, the rest makes sense. You need to find the princes. Hausmann is still recruiting for his cause, and we know he wants important men or he wouldn't have contacted Ray with his diplomatic links. But this leader . . . he's not only a leader of princes. From these clues, he's also a leader of 'people starved and shunned from the shelled fields.' To me that says ordinary soldiers, ordinary men and women, especially those who have been 'shunned' from their fields . . . Ray talks a lot about the violence in the east, the disintegrating Austro-Hungarian empire, the new nations that France now needs to have individual treaties with, immigration deals and extradition treaties and all sorts."

"The Ottoman Empire has undergone the same thing. And the German."

"And what do the Italians call this, what did Ray say—the 'mutilated victory,' that's it. That despite being one of the victors, they have no spoils, and have even lost territory. That would support your idea that this refers to Muscle-man's Blackshirts."

"Mussolini. Benito."

"Right, Benny the Muscle. He's calling to people who have lost everything—which, strangely, is both princes and paupers."

"Learning French has made you political."

"Oh no, Katie, I was always political. I just didn't used to care so much about the tantrums of powerful men. Now, as a diplomat's wife, I have to."

"Well, we always had to sponge their backs and empty their bedpans."

"Ha! We still do, only they call it taxes."

"I've missed you so much, Maisie."

"Katie, you have no idea." She clinked her beer glass with mine. The morning had turned into afternoon, the darkening sky outside calling forth spirits from the bar.

"But here, Katie, this line, 'make an army whom liberticide and realpolitik make a primed dud to all who wield.' Fox seems to imply that these ordinary people are a 'primed dud,' ready to explode but nothing will happen . . . or does 'dud' mean not failure but some unexpected consequence, like a grenade exploding in your hand? Who is in danger here?"

"I think that's a warning, where the mission turns away from 1922 and back to the time when it was written. Shelley wrote the original poem, 'England in 1819,' four years after the end of the Napoleonic wars. England's army slaughtered its own people when they conducted a peaceful protest, in a massacre nicknamed Peterloo. England was about to become the most powerful empire of last century. The danger is to ordinary people who get in the way of the powerful as they create an empire."

"Not the princes you need to save."

"Not in the original poem. Princes are the 'dregs of their dull race,' according to Shelley."

"Who was a radical lord."

"And that's the main link—politically radical aristocrats. All much too clever. However, what I need to do is to find the princes before the Brownshirts or the Blackshirts get them into trouble."

"I still think there's more . . ."

"There's always more, with Fox." But right now I didn't want to delve into how much more Fox meant. "Have you heard anything from Ray about Benny the Muscle? Or the Freikorps? Any gossip at work about a recruitment drive, event, demonstration, a big something or other?"

"Not that I can remember, but I will ask."

"Be subtle."

"Fuck subtle. I don't need that, Katie. Not with Ray and not about Hausmann. Ray's a patriot, to his marrow, and any political schemer who endangers France's borders, or people or forests or oceans, he opposes."

"But didn't he grow up in Senegal? How can he have such a commitment to a country he only knew as an adult?"

"Why did so many Australians want to die for the British Empire? I don't know, Katie. He went to boarding school here and only returned to Senegal over the summer holidays . . . but I think it was the war. Actually, I'm certain it was the war, and his mother's death just before it, and one of his brothers' death in Verdun, and his father bleeding the cocoa company dry, its workers destitute, before he died in the arms of his German lover. It's something to do with all of that."

She gave a perfectly Gallic shrug, complete with pout, her sleeves slipping up her arms as she lit a cigarette. She knew how she looked too, as she raised her eyebrow, inviting me to appreciate her performance. She checked her watch and jumped up.

"I have a shift starting in half an hour!"

"Catch a cab."

"I'll have to! And borrow a uniform." She shrugged on her coat. "I haven't run from beer to bedpans since Armistice. But Katie, we haven't discussed Fox—and Tom, have you seen him?—and all the important things!"

"I'm staying in Paris, Maisie."

"For good?"

"We have time."

"LOVESICK BLUES"

I stayed in the café a little longer, not keen for the rain-checkered wind to follow me home to my unheated apartment. I wanted bright drinks to compliment my bright clothes, glasses of liquid gold and ruby and bronze. I was still not bright on the inside. Maisie helped, Maisie always helped, but Fox was between us and Hausmann haunted our words. Scraps of Shelley and Keats chased each other as I drank and smoked and stared at the windswept outside. Eventually the golden drinks, either too sweet or too bitter, made me feel sick. I needed deep breaths of cold air and the spatter of rain on my face. I wanted Maisie, still, and was in half a mind to walk to the American Hospital to pester her, when a taxi pulled up next to me.

"Kiki!" A Russian head leaned out of the passenger window.

"Theo!"

"Hop in!" He opened the door. "Please?"

There is something about a pleading prince; although I wanted crisp cold rain, I found myself slipping in beside him with barely a second thought.

"Golden one, it's been an age." He kissed me with luxurious slowness. "I've been busy all weekend with driving and family business."

"Business I should know about?" I'd been busy all weekend too, but I did my best not to think of Tom.

"The main business is that you're invited to a ball."

"A Russian ball?"

"Alas, no, not until St Petersburg's winter snows visit Paris. Then, my golden one, I will give you a proper pre-war-style party. In the meantime, my cousin Dmitri's former paramour is holding one. Here's your invitation from Coco Chanel." He took a card from his jacket pocket. "It's in a few days. We were only just invited. You will come?"

"A black and white ball! I've always wanted to meet Chanel."

"And I can see you tonight?"

"When have you known me to say no?"

And I got a passionate kiss to soothe my tender-sore heart.

⟨≈⟩

I spent what should have been dinnertime watching the light leave the sky over the rooftops, watching the windows of the metropolis stretch, blink, and start the night shift. The lights came on in geometric shapes: dark squares in the gardens, bright lines around the boulevards, the Eiffel Tower a triangular lighthouse, a beacon for the expatriate desperate to turn loneliness into solitude into attitude.

I had to call Fox to confirm what I knew and get the next part of my mission. I pulled out all my winter woollies from my wardrobe, but looking at my flimsy, sheer selection made me realize I hadn't faced a proper winter since the final year of the war. I had nothing to protect me from the fierce winds and ravenous frosts that were on their way. I put on literally all my warmest clothes, black suede boots and gray trousers and my black boucle coat. I hid my hair under a black beret that my father had given to me last year, though whether as a joke or not, I couldn't tell. I was just warm enough for autumn.

I was on the watch for newspaper boys, for men in leather coats and wide-brimmed hats, for men who spoke bad French in worse suits, but

I could see no one following me on the way to Gare Montparnasse. Delphine was not at the station, nor any of the beggar children. The last train had pulled in some half an hour previously. Only the café was open and it housed just a few decrepit patrons. The lamps were being doused as I walked in, but the moustachioed guard recognized me and tipped his hat, pointing the way to the phone booth to indicate it was still open. I looked around again, but unless Mr. Moustache was a watcher, I was alone.

The phone pipped through to London, the phone operators talking each other's language with bad grace and grammar.

"Mayfair 5714. Yes, we accept reverse charges." The operator hung up and the butler spoke again. "How may I help you?"

"Is that Greef?" I asked.

"Yes, ma'am."

"Greef, I don't know if you'd remember me, but this is Miss Button."

"I remember you, of course, Miss Button. Shall I call the master to the telephone?"

"If you wouldn't mind. Oh, and Greef, you have an excellent telephone manner."

"Thank you, ma'am." He sounded as pleased as his dignity would allow. "One moment."

But it was more like one second than one moment.

"Vixen."

"That was quick. Are you waiting for someone else to call?"

"Always. But who else could be more important?"

"The prime minister?"

"Who? No, he can wait. Our work is much more important than whatever is happening in Turkey."

"I know a lot of men who would disagree."

"You know a lot of men."

"But not the right men, it seems. I only know those who are true blue, not blue blood."

"Very good, Vixen."

"I've done a bit more digging. Are you ready?" I opened the door and lit up, not bothering to wait for his reply. "The 'black shirts' are Mussolini's Fascists. Hausmann is definitely involved somewhere, as he's still in Paris, still trying to raise money for his beloved—even, should I say, sacred—Brownshirts. If I followed Hausmann, he'd probably lead me to a prince or two, but not to the English ones. So I just sniff around his trail, as there are probably other princes who are part of this posh-boy gang. These princes have lost their influence and wealth in the major and minor revolutions that have shaken Europe, and are now joining forces with their former peasants to restore the old order. These other princes will be the link between Hausmann and the English princes—who have to include, at least, well-known libertine, the Prince of Wales."

I listened, but the station was hush. I could not even hear Fox hum down the line.

"There is more in the mission clues," I had to fill the silence, "to do with Shelley, and you, and the 'tempestuous leader,' but all of that is not immediately important. Only Wales, and possibly another of George's heirs, is important."

"Bravo, Vixen." His voice had taken on a hard edge. "Welcome back."

The light in the telephone booth fizzed and flickered.

"Bacon will leave for Paris tonight and will meet with you to fill you in on more details."

"What? That's it—no more contact?" I was absurdly bereft. After hating Fox's intrusion in my life, it seemed ridiculous that I would miss his banter. "What about Tom? What about the photos? What about my payment?"

"Bacon will have a check."

"Not money, my proper payment. Those photos—who took them?"

"'The awful shadow of some unseen power floats though unseen among us . . .'"

"How did you get them?"

"'Visiting this various world with as constant wing as summer winds that creep . . .'"

"Wait, it should be 'inconstant' not 'constant.'" He was quoting more Shelley, "Hymn to Intellectual Beauty." "Is this to do with the mission or with my payment?"

"'Like memory of music fled, like aught that for its grace may be dear, and dearer for its mystery.'"

I had to take the phone away from my mouth or I would yell in frustration. Why had I rung Fox with only the mission worked out? Why hadn't I also deduced some of meaning of those lines on the back of the photos and how they related to Tom? Why hadn't I asked Maisie for more details of her dealings with Hausmann? The station was almost dark, only the café held some meager light. If I screamed, no one would make a fuss; it was a definite temptation.

"Fox."

"'Art thou pale for weariness, of climbing heaven and gazing earth, of wandering companionless . . .'"

"'Among stars that have a different birth'—oh yes, very good, Fox." Another Shelley poem, "Art thou pale for weariness," that Fox was using to refer to the princes, my mission, my Paris life. Thank goodness I had borrowed that volume from Sylvia, or I would have thought he was trying to sweet-talk me.

"'And ever-changing, like a joyless eye that finds no object for its constancy?'"

"Not pale for weariness, Fox, pale with frustration."

He laughed then.

"As for constancy, I will never have the constancy of the fanatic. I'll leave that to you, Ozymandias."

"Ozymandias? I like your bite, Vixen."

"Who took those photos? How did you get them?"

"You should check your post more often, Vixen. And next time, I might call you."

"How? I don't have a telephone . . ." But my last words were said into the void as the operator terminated the call. I stood outside the booth in the still gloom. Fox wouldn't say any more to me; instead, Fry would

contact me in some irritatingly clandestine way to give me more information on those princes and the mission. Fry's presence seemed to confirm
my suspicions that Fox didn't know precisely who I was meant to find, or
when or where or how. I strode out of the station. I hadn't even managed
to ask about Ray Chevallier and Hausmann.

But that wasn't what made me want to scream. The payment, the
photos, the lines of Shelley, every time I followed a thread it led somewhere impossible. The Monday night streets were damp and empty; only
the cafés provided proof of life. The lines kept teasing me that Fox was
trying to seduce me; that, in fact, he loved me. Which was impossible,
it had to be, I couldn't bear to contemplate that it might be possible.
I backtracked on what he said, again and again, and ended up at that
same idea. I escaped into the final lines of "Ozymandias":

My name is Ozymandias, King of Kings;
Look on my works, ye mighty and despair!
Nothing beside remains. Round the decay
Of that colossal Wreck, boundless and bare
The lone and level sands stretch far away.

My letter box was boundless and bare; no post waited for me. What did
Fox mean, then, when he said I should check my post more often? I took
the steps two at a time to my flat on the top floor. I stripped off my outside
clothes and huddled under the blankets, lines of Shelley going round and
round my head—"Look on my works, ye Mighty, and despair!"—until
Theo showed up with cold cheeks and an ardent desire to warm his lips
on my breasts and his hands between my legs, with seductive murmurs
in Russian and French on breath that smelled of licorice drops.

At midnight, he unwrapped the bundle he had brought with him to
reveal a little package of wood, paper, and twigs.

"This room is far too cold for such a passionate woman as yourself."

I kissed him as he looked around.

"But Kiki . . . where is your hearth? Your boiler?"

"Here." I knocked on the far wall and a panel fell out. Behind it was a little fireplace, dusty and decorated with a desiccated rat. With much laughter on my part, and a look of intense distaste on his, I flung the carcass out the window while he lit a fire. It burned hot, the walls glowed, my rack of clothes embraced the healthy smell of wood smoke. We had to open a window to help air circulate, so the room was no longer stuffy and stinking of stale cigarettes. I had no more need to huddle under the covers, I could be properly naked. With Theo's unflagging help, I could relieve myself of thought. I could, but didn't, as even in the midst of sighs were the sensational lines of Shelley. I was the spirit of delight, the starry night, the Autumn evening and the morn. The fire's hiss whispered: "Spirit, I love thee—thou dost possess the things I seek—thou wilt come for pleasure." The words swirled with the woodsmoke until the fire had spent itself, until all that remained was the echo: "Wherefore hast thou left me now?"

"MISTER GALLAGHER
AND MISTER SHEAN"

I checked my post on the way to breakfast and there it was: a handwritten note with lines from Shelley. I took them to Petit's to work them out.

> I met a traveller from an antique land
> Who said, "Two vast and trunkless legs of stone
> Stand in the desert . . . Near them, on the sand,
> Half sunk a shattered visage lies, whose frown,
> And wrinkled lip, and sneer of cold command,
> Tell that its sculptor well those passions read
> Which yet survive, stamped on these lifeless things,
> The hand that mocked them, and the heart that fed;
> And on the pedestal, these words appear:
> My name is Ozymandias, King of Kings;
> Look on my Works, ye Mighty, and despair!
> Nothing beside remains. Round the decay
> Of that colossal Wreck, boundless and bare
> The lone and level sands stretch far away."

Of course, Fox would use "Ozymandias" as the code. I had teased him with it last night, so now he would tease me by making me repeat this poem until I hated it. I read the note again and again, but this was the poem in its entirety; there was no code, no game, no little jibe. It was his handwriting and there was no stamp. This note must have been hand-delivered, presumably by an agent, and presumably not by Fry as he would have said hello. What did the note mean? Was it just a nasty little "peek-a-boo" from Fox? Was an agent actually following me, would he turn up here at Petit's and I would never have a moment's privacy for the rest of my life? I looked around. The other patrons were the usual old men, most of whom I recognized and who nodded *"Bonjour"* at me when they caught my glance. There was no one new, no one strange.

This was Fox's handwriting. He could not be in Paris, as I had called him in London last night. He was sending an agent to meet me who, even if he had left immediately after the call, could not yet be in Paris. Unless he flew . . . were there commercial flights across the Channel? Was that now possible? Did they fly late enough, or early enough, to get this note here? The clock on the wall said it was almost noon. The only possible way for this note to have reached me from London, since last night, was by air. If the note flew, then Fox could have flown with it. I wrapped my scarf tighter against the chill.

I looked at the note again. There was no meeting place or time. Therefore, the meeting place and time must be in the poem itself. Ozymandias . . . was he a Persian king? No, Egyptian, that was it. "Look on my works, ye mighty, and despair . . ." I could look on the works of the mighty Egyptians at the Egyptian room at the Louvre. And the time? There were no clues. In Fox terms, that meant as soon as the letter reached me. It meant now.

⤙⤚

"So, Delphine, do you understand what you need to do?"

We stood in a corner of Gare Montparnasse.

"Yes, mademoiselle. I sell my matches, I ask the other street sellers what they have seen, then I report back to you and you will pay me."

"That's right. Where are your proper shoes, your boots?"

"I have no other shoes, mademoiselle."

"Hm, we'll have to change that later today."

Her eyes lit up. "Real boots, mademoiselle?"

"Good sturdy ones. Now, here's the money for the metro, keep me in sight but don't let anyone see us together. This is a secret task, understand?"

She nodded and squirrelled away the metro fare, looking around and pretending she had never seen me before. I smiled; I was right to take a little detour to pick up Delphine. I wanted a second pair of eyes, someone invisible who could take the temperature of a place. Delphine was perfect for the task. She was bright, but pale and plain, and could slip into places where I would be noticed. There were always plenty of tourists at the Louvre, and so plenty of street sellers on the forecourt. From them, Delphine should be able to find out something.

⸎

The palaces stretched out magnificently, regally, as acres of windows and curls and creamy decoration rose into view from the metro. The foyer was marble and, as soon as I stepped inside, I was greeted with centuries of collected artworks. As I made my way through the galleries to the Egyptian room, I couldn't help but think this was the most ridiculous place for a meeting. How like Fox to lead me here.

I smiled when I saw the hulking bulk of Agent Bacon peering intently at a mummy as though trying to see under the wrapping. He was the agent Fox had sent at the end of my last mission to hand over my pay check and pick up my quarry—literally, over his shoulder, after he'd knocked the quarry unconscious.

"I didn't know you had silver teeth, Bacon—or is it Fry?"

"I invited you to call me Fry last year and the invitation still stands. I lost the teeth at Passchendaele."

"What a muddy bloodbath that was."

"A bloody mud bath. You were there?"

"You know I was. Where stood Fox, there stood I. I remember having to crack the mud off the men when they came into the triage tent. Is that mummy interesting?"

"Like any corpse. I prefer the future."

"It is our job, after all. Changing the future."

"I prefer noisy drinking holes to quiet museums too. Bloody strange rendezvous point, but Fox said you'd understand."

"Yes. Well. It is a bit whispery in here, wouldn't you say?"

"And I'm hungry. I've been up since yesterday."

"Now, kiss me on both cheeks like we're old lovers, and we'll leave here arm in arm."

He grinned as he crooked his elbow for me.

"You certainly smell like you've been up since yesterday," I said. "Cigarettes and sweat. Now that you're in Paris, Fry, you'll have to stop smoking Sobranies. Gauloises are the only inconspicuous smokes."

"They're what you smoke?"

"And Gitanes." I frowned at him. "Fox didn't tell you?"

"Fox didn't even tell me your name."

"BUGLE CALL RAG"

We went to a cozy café on the left bank, full of brightly colored tourists and housewives concerned with their shopping bags. I fit right in, with Fry looking like my uncomfortable foreign cousin or some such. I ordered their final croissant and Fry ordered the closest the French would do to a fry-up.

"If Fox didn't tell you my name, how did you know I was the contact?"

"He just said you'd be a true blonde. If you notice, there aren't that many in Paris. In any case, as soon as you walked in, I recognized you." He looked me over. "How do you do your work in that costume?"

I wore yellow today—a lemon silk dress, my mustard wool coat and matching cloche, and yellow suede heels—all very much as usual.

"It's so . . . eye-catching." He frowned.

"I work as a society girl gossip columnist. I'm hiding center-stage."

"To each their own."

"Well, I don't think the salons of Paris would accept a silver-toothed pirate as a society girl. Society entertainment, maybe . . ."

He grinned in a way that seemed nasty. "Shall we get down to business?"

"Before we eat? How very British of you." But this was just banter; I was keen to know what Fox had told him. "Nonetheless, patriotic service and all that. My quarry . . . I don't have exact names."

"Neither do we."

"I thought so! This is a first."

"No, this is usual." He looked me over again, as though wondering whether to tell me something. Instead he just forked a pile of fried egg and bread into his mouth. He continued to look at me while he chewed. Was he expecting me to explain my relationship with Fox? There wasn't much I wanted to tell him. I lit another cigarette and returned his stare until, finally, he swallowed.

"Your verdict?" I said but he raised an eyebrow. "To your extended assessment of me."

"I can see why the boss is obsessed with you."

I snorted. Smoke came out my nose like I was on fire.

"Really, Miss Button. I read the note he sent you. Poetry? He recites the Romantics, of course, but using them as mission code? That'd take far too long. But I can see why he likes to bait you."

"If you don't have the names of my quarry, why are you here?"

"Ah yes." He shoveled in more food, wiping his meaty fingers daintily before reaching into his coat pocket.

"Firstly, your expenses check. Apparently, I am to insist that you take it as no other payment will be forthcoming before the mission is complete."

I put the check away without looking at it and Fry raised an eyebrow.

"Secondly, to give you the information and general background that we have about your mission." He wiped some egg up with his bread and washed it down the mouthful with beer. He made me wait for every sentence, a technique that subtly and not-so-subtly indicated his assumed authority. It was an effort not to snap at him to hurry up. I ordered more coffee to hide my impatience.

"Miss Button, we know the end point but not how to get there. The end point is that you distract, persuade, ensnare the prince or princes. I think the boss means for you to seduce them somehow, a ploy at which I would surely fail . . ."

"This is Paris; you'd be surprised."

He laughed in an embarrassed way. "You will work at an arranged meeting place. Then I will collect the quarry and return him or them to England. I have another contact who I'm working with to provide the transportation. As we do not know who the quarry is, we cannot work out the end point yet."

"You must have some idea." I wanted him to show his hand, but he clearly needed some prompting. "They're heirs to the British throne, yes?"

"Who else is a prince in England?"

"There are some Russian princes hiding with their cousins in England . . . you're right, Fox wouldn't care about them. So, Albert, Edward, George, and Henry it is then."

"Either one or two of them, I think. Not Henry, he's too . . ."

"Ridiculous. That voice! But perhaps that's what the Fascists like."

"He's too much a soldier." Fry failed to contain his smile. "Far too patriotic."

"So, a combination of Edward, Albert, and George. As Fox is using me, my money is on Edward, at least." I waited for a response from Fry, but his attention was on his food. "In fact, I mentioned the Prince of Wales to Fox and he didn't disagree."

"Neither do I."

"Wales it is, then."

Fry mopped up the last of his egg with his bread, chasing down every last morsel, thorough and precise.

"The Prince of Wales was in the army in the war. Are Albert and George in the navy?"

"Yes, both. Albert joined the air force though, at the end of the war. George is still in the navy. Why?"

I was thinking of the "Tinker Tailor" rhyme, but this information didn't properly narrow it down.

"Just thinking. How did Fox find out about this?" Fox was a generation older than the princes, more the same age as their father, the king.

"He really does like to keep you in the dark."

"I like to think that because I'm in Paris, I don't get the office gossip."

"It's mostly about the poor luncheon in the cafeteria."

"But that's not where he heard about the princes."

"I think it is gossip though. From his club, or his country house, or one of his ministerial parties. Some blabbermouth minister who doesn't know what Fox does."

"And what does Fox do? As in, what's his job? I thought he was a doctor."

"He was a doctor. I believe he still is to his neighbors in Kent. He works as senior advisor to the Home Secretary, though I don't think he does any advising. For you and me and anyone who knows, he's a secret strategist in British post-war intelligence."

"Houses built of shadows. Very well. Do I work with you to discover the wayward Wales and crew?"

"You contact me about the end point and I contact the transportation. Otherwise you're on your own." He finished his beer to the last drop.

"And you're content with that?"

"Fox must have faith in you."

"Faith? To him, Faith is just a woman's name and, like Grace, Hope, and Charity, the virtue is a stranger."

"You know all his secrets, then."

"If I knew all of them, he couldn't tease me with poetry."

"But you know how he got that scar on his cheek. What is it, a duelling scar?"

"He wants you to think so. It was an accidental war wound. He wouldn't let me patch him up."

Fry nodded. The café smelt sharply of fried onion and soap.

"So . . . he doesn't write code like this to anyone else?"

"Not to me." Fry shrugged. "Not to anyone I've worked with. It's your special privilege."

"Or punishment."

"It could be worse. He could be a Modernist."

I smiled to cover my disappointment; despite his profession, Fry was still old-fashioned.

"How long are you in Paris, Fry?"

"I have some work to do here, so a week or two."

"What work?" He ignored me, as he searched his packet for a last cigarette and, not finding one, helped himself to mine. "Oh, come on. I might be able to help."

"You're working with the nationalist threats—fascists, royalists, and so on. It took a bit of convincing but Fox has allowed me to work on the communist threat."

"A more general threat to British democracy than a specific embarrassment to the crown."

"It's proper intelligence work." If you can sniff smugly, then Fry did just that. "Our government needs this information. Fox's patriotism has always been more about 'England's green and pleasant land' than the grubby business of parliamentary democracy."

"How did you end up working for him? You're the only agent of his I've seen who . . . well, that I've seen this side of the war."

"Yes, he kept you secret."

"Did he recruit you on the operating table?"

"Pretty much. And I was glad of it. I'd given up my scholarship at Cambridge and was disgusted that I was going to be rat food before I could be a historian."

"What happened to Cambridge?"

"Duty got in the way."

The café patrons flowed around us, speaking several languages and in various states of excitement. I felt like an island of serious state business, cold and quiet. I didn't need to wonder why I smoked so much.

"So, if you're here, does that mean there are British Communists in Paris?"

"Communists are internationalists. They are everywhere."

"There was certainly one in the noodle house I visited the other day. A man from Indochina—no sorry, Việt Nam—introduced himself as Nguyễn. He might like a bit of company at one of his party meetings."

He helped himself to more of my cigarettes. "Maybe Fox was right to have faith in you."

"I can let you come with me, if you promise to behave. I need to look at these Communists anyway. It's to do with my princes."

"Russian princes? Surely not English princes, I'd have heard."

"They all know each other. They're all related."

"Of course. Contact me here." He scribbled a number on a coaster as I paid for our meal.

"I'll attend the meeting."

"Bring your flatcap."

"It's my father's."

Outside, the streets were shiny with rain. Leaves glowed on the trees and on the footpath, workers hurried, tourists dawdled, faces red-cheeked and bright-eyed with the coming winter. I was no longer isolated but part of the flowing life of Paris, and it gave me strength.

"You read the note Fox sent, Fry. Why didn't you say hello when you delivered it?"

"They weren't my instructions."

"But your instructions told you to read the note, did they?"

He grinned. "I read it on the flight over here."

"Flight! Is that usual?"

"I fly here often."

"With Fox?"

"Always."

"He's in Paris?" The noise of the street rose to a clatter. Was I cold or were my hands just shaking?

"Almost always, I should say. He sent me alone this time. But I think he comes over at least once a month and always by aeroplane."

"LOOKING ALL OVER FOR YOU"

"Browne speaking."

"Best of all Berties." I looked around at the station, cavernous and gray, people hurrying or lugging luggage but no one watching, waiting, loitering. "When are you coming to see me?"

"As soon as I can. When will you send me your column?"

"After I attend Chanel's black and white ball." Bertie squealed on cue. "Though I have a filler column in the post already. It's about all the chic places to go in Paris."

"You know these?"

"Viper. It's everywhere I didn't take Tom."

"How is our intrepid reporter?"

"Too intrepid for unbroken broadcast. He's full of static and gunfire."

"The handsome ones always are."

"Are you alone? I have a question about a certain doctor."

"Hold on." I heard him chatting to Mavis at reception. "Now that I'm sitting in Mavis's warm seat, I am. Fire away."

"Has Fox been to Paris recently?"

"My man has, but he didn't mention his boss."

"Ask him. I'm told Fox flies here regularly. It would explain . . . things."

"Such as?"

"Such as how he knows what I'm doing when I can't see any watchers."

"No beggar boys? No young men reading newspapers?"

"As almost nobody flies, it's so bloody expensive, it didn't even occur to me that he could. Or would, just to spy on me."

"Like a jealous lover?"

"Too close to the bone, Bertie." I swallowed against the nausea of this thought. "Anything else to report? How is your man?"

"He says he doesn't want to talk about politics in the bedroom. But he can't stop himself, so he goes into my little kitchenette and speaks about it there instead. He fulminates on the inherent moral righteousness of parliamentary democracy anchored by a monarchy. I tease him, of course, and take the side of the Communists, or nationalists, or anarchists, or absolute monarchists, whoever I can, really. It's a wonderful way to see in the dawn. He's hardest on the Communists. He hates them and all the internationalist anti-hierarchy they stand for. He's most ambivalent about chaps like Mussolini and his nationalists, says they can be worked with, doesn't see them as much of a threat."

"Quite the chatterbox."

"Like an undergraduate who's just lost his virginity."

"Keep asking him about Mussolini. Read up on fascism so you can ask him some pointed questions. What is Mussolini doing? Does Britain support him? What about German Fascists? And so on."

"That might take a bit of time. He's away at the moment."

"Where? A flight to Paris?"

"He never tells me. I just search his pockets for matchboxes and coasters and then I know he's been to Dublin or Rotterdam or what have you."

"How lucky you are that he's so careless."

"It's why I chose him. That, and his bedroom eyes."

"One more thing—see if you can find out anything about a Cassius. Some of Tom's static suggests that Fox has a brother."

"Now there's a thought to freeze the blood. Ah, must dash, Himself has returned to the office and we have several overdue meetings. Call me after the ball. I want all the breathless first impressions."

I lingered by the cigarette vendor, smoking slowly and scanning the crowd for Delphine. She saw me but pretended not to, her head raised a little higher as she called out her wares, until she stood by me.

"Two boxes please."

"I have run out of your favorite brand, mademoiselle. But if you come with me, I can find some for you." She led me to a secluded corner next to her little bag of belongings. She handed me a box of matches from her bag; the girl was a natural.

"So, Delphine, what did you see?" I put the money in her hand immediately and she stood a little straighter.

"No one else like me was following you. I asked one or two of the other sellers outside the museum, but they hadn't seen you, they were looking at the tourists. When you came out, I saw one man watching you and your friend until you got in the taxi, then he walked away."

"What did he look like? How did he act?"

"You can tell if someone's watching. He smoked and pretended to look around but his body was always toward you and your friend. He was just kicking the cobbles until you came out and then he was very careful about looking casual." She let herself smile a bit at my murmured encouragement. "He had white hair, a very nice suit, beautiful shoes, so shiny and a deep red color, he smoked a black cigarette . . . it's the truth, mademoiselle!"

I must have looked angry as she suddenly bristled.

"I believe you. I just wish it wasn't the truth." White hair and black cigarette, beautiful suit and shoes—could that be anyone but Fox? If so, had Fry lied to me or had Fox flown here without his knowledge? Was he going to turn up here, at the station, at my apartment?

"Are you sure he didn't follow us?"

"You got in a taxi and he walked the other way."

"Very good, Delphine, I'll need you again soon." I looked her up and down. Her face was expectant above the rags she wore.

"I'll come to the station tomorrow to get you those boots. I can't have you work for me in these ridiculous clogs. Fair?"

"More than fair, mademoiselle." Her pallor receded as she curtsied and moved away to sell more of her matches. I hoped she kept some of the money for proper food and a warmer coat. I hoped whoever was watching us left her alone, but if it was Fox, then the hope was in vain.

25

ˈLADY OF THE EVENINGˈ

Apparently, I needed diamonds. This was Theo's excuse for not meeting me in Montparnasse, for oh-so-gently insisting that I meet him at his apartment and travel with him, Felix, and Irène to Chanel's ball. He assumed I didn't have any diamonds, but his assumption was only partly correct. My diamonds were my mother's and were kept in a safe in a London bank, along with the money from the sale of her house. So, it was true that, in Paris, I had no diamonds. If I was going to wear diamonds, I would need to borrow them from his sister. I could think of worse fates.

A dress, however, was another matter. Balls in Montparnasse meant wearing whatever you could afford, from sumptuous velvet to your only paint-stained trousers, and sometimes both. That would not do for Chanel. Neither would actually wearing Chanel, that would be too sycophantic by half, and wearing Chanel's rivals would only irritate her. Something from my mother's wardrobe would have been perfect, a high-necked long-sleeved floaty stripey piece of nonsense from before I was born, but none of those had survived the turn of the century. After meeting Fry and Delphine, I had gone straight to my neighbor, a seamstress with deft fingers and an eye for the modern, and paid her extra to whip up something for me *tout suite*.

Odile did not disappoint. After only two fittings she presented me with my gown, gloves included, and even helped me to dress. I had to wriggle into the black silk sheath, it was cut so close to my body, done up with only three buttons over my buttocks at the bottom of a very low back. Over the top of this was white silk gauze, so fine it was almost transparent. On the gauze Odile had embroidered constellations, not merely stars but their precise pattern in the northern French sky, "I got it from a book, mademoiselle, the designs were so pretty." She had been doing this work on her own, waiting for the right commission. All she had to embroider for me were the long black gloves that had phases of the moon from elbow to wrist in silvery white thread.

Theo rushed downstairs to greet me before my star-patterned shoes had even emerged from the taxi.

"Isn't this against protocol, Theo? Shouldn't you wait for me to be announced?"

"But how could I let this slice of heaven stand in the street?" He kissed me three times on the cheek. "You outshine us all, of course."

"You don't look half-bad in a tuxedo."

"I had enough practice before we left Russia. So many balls." His sigh somehow conveyed both impatience and sadness. I squeezed his hand as we walked upstairs.

Felix looked as royally dashing as I would have expected, especially as his tuxedo jacket was white. Irène wore white to match him, a long floaty gown that stopped at the ankles, with drapes to and from the wide waist sash. They each had one black pearl object, a pin for Felix and a necklace for Irène.

"My mother's," said Felix. "She knew her jewels." He kissed his wife. "Please be quick, Irène. There are only so many ways I can try to convince your brother to join me and Edouard in our cause."

Champagne was pressed into my hand as we walked through the apartment to Irène's room. The place was a museum to Art Nouveau, all green and gold with red wood carved in curves. Her dressing room was no less lush, dark pink like the inside of a rose or a wound. Her maid placed the jewels on me, selecting them out of a chinoiserie box, while I sat at her dressing table in front of an enormous gilt-edged mirror. First came a hair slide with tiny diamonds in a pattern of stars. Then, on a black velvet choker, a big clear stone. I had never really been excited by diamonds, but this one was so perfect and pure, it seemed to contain all the light of the sun as it sat against my skin.

"You mustn't mind Felix when he talks politics." Irène spoke to my reflection.

"I don't. I enjoy it."

"Thank you, Nadya." She dismissed the maid. "It's so hard for him, after all he's done for Russia, for the monarchy. And of course, the news of our cousins . . . Would you . . ." Her eyes were wide and concerned. "Theo won't listen to me. He needs to give up that taxi-driving. Felix will support him. You agree with me, I'm sure."

While I was wearing enough jewelery to feed Montparnasse for a decade, I thought it best to pretend I did.

"Felix wants Theo to join him in his politics. It will be good for Theo. Our cousin, Dmitri Pavlovich, is part of the group; Felix assures me. Our brother Nikita is too."

"I'll speak to him."

"If you would. He listens to you." And the second clause, *though I don't know why*, hung in the air. "You're welcome here anytime, naturally."

I wasn't very grateful for this afterthought. I just smiled and followed her back to the champagne.

❦

It turned out that Theo's cousin, Dmitri Pavlovich, had found Chanel a ballroom that belonged to a Russian princess. Black and white marble tiles lined the floor. The walls were white, without a hint of gold or silver, not even on a window latch or door handle. Across this unrelenting pallor hung silky black banners from the ceiling like storm clouds. Vases held white roses and macabre black ones. Black lacquer chinoiserie screens, patterned with pale cranes or peonies, stood strategically around black chairs. All the drinks were white, served by waiters dressed entirely in black; they were even masked. The only warmth in the scene were the candles. The ballroom had no electricity, so the golden light and heat from hundreds of candles made the room glow. In the center was Coco Chanel herself, all in black, in a dress shorter than everyone else's, hair shorter than mine, and a ring with single huge black diamond that positively sang of luxury, rarity, and pain. Dmitri Pavlovich was next to her, a proper host. On closer inspection I could see black cats embroidered on her dress, stretching and moving with feline precision, even down the chiffon train that extended from the back of her gown. She smiled lazily, her eyes calculating; I could see how perfect the dress was for her. I imagined how she would have purred against Dmitri Pavlovich, exciting him with an occasional flash of claw.

"Kiki Button," she said. "The blonde *Australienne*. Yes, I've heard of you and not just from Theo." She looked me up and down. "Heavenly," though she couldn't have sounded more disdainful if she really was a princess. "You're our only exotic, Mademoiselle Button."

"I'll place myself on a plinth, then, and be part of the entertainment," I said, but her responding laugh had a cruel tinge.

The masked band played a mixture of sweet jazz, music hall, and dance classics from the last decade. Food on the supper table was all monochrome too—white grapes in gin jelly, black caviar, oysters, white fish in white sauce, blackberry tart, blackcurrant jelly, slices of white fruit that you couldn't tell if it was apple, pear, or melon, until you put it in your mouth. I watched the other guests come in. The men invariably wore black tie, making Felix stand out in his white jacket. The women in black wore white boas and shawls, while those in white wore dramatic black belts and black chokers, all looking like chess pieces on the dancefloor. At one point the waiters served black cocktails made with a licorice liqueur, and the whole room smelt of lollies. I made mental notes of everything, I said yes to every dance, I smiled until my face ached.

As I was being led off the dance floor, Theo caught my eye and nodded toward his brother-in-law. Felix was laughing too hard with a couple of pasty-faced men, all guffawing in a way that reminded me forcibly of my father. Theo came over and whispered in my ear.

"These are his princes, you know, his 'good men.' The ones who'll change Europe."

"Will they speak to me?"

"Kiki, *ma chérie*, everyone will speak to you." Theo grabbed two martinis from a tray and slid in next to Felix.

"Of course, Eddy will be in charge of the organization," said a tall man with a narrow chin. "I mean, we're not secretaries!"

"Exactly!" said a dapper one through his lisp. "We're soldiers."

"We're soldiers of civilization," said Felix and the other men toasted the sentiment. "Ah, please allow me to introduce my brother-in-law, Prince Feodor Alexandrovich."

"Please, call me Theo." I could see by the way he shook their hands that their handshakes were weak to the point of condescension. "And this is Mademoiselle Kiki Button."

"You're soldiers of civilization," I said, suppressing a shudder as they kissed my hand. "Whose civilization?"

"Whose? There is only one civilization."

"Western civilization."

"European Christian civilization, as we've taught to savages all over the world!"

"The savages appear to be in your own backyards," I said. Felix wagged a finger at me.

"Kiki," he smiled as he raised his eyebrows, "don't be cheeky."

"It's my job." I smiled too and just as falsely. "But are you serious? Who else is in your civilizing army? Who is your commander? Surely not Denikin."

There was a lot of bluster and nonsense after I mentioned the name of the commander of the defeated White Russian Army. They started talking about his charm, the look in his eye when he spoke to his men, the rumble of his laugh; he did not sound like the "tempestuous leader" of the mission clues.

"You sound like you knew him personally."

"Of course we do!" said Dapper Lisper. "Don't you know who we are?"

"Well, I might do if I knew your names."

More bluster and wet kisses on my hands as they exclaimed their apologies. Theo looked embarrassed, though whether for them or by them I couldn't tell. Felix looked amused.

"Roman Petrovich." This was Narrow Chin.

"He's our cousin," said Theo.

"Distant cousin," said Felix, "but close ally. They both are. Roman introduced me to Edouard, actually."

"Edouard was at my wedding last year. He needed special dispensation as someone not of royal birth."

The men shook their heads as though they were far more modern than such rules and strictures.

"I'm Prince Gottfried of Hohenlohe-Langenburg," said Dapper Lisper. "Well, my father is the prince, but I'm the heir . . . though exactly what I'll be the heir to in a few years is under question."

"Which is why we're here," said Felix.

"So . . . who is your commander?" I asked. "Edouard?"

"Goodness, no!" Gottfried snorted. "I haven't even met him yet. I heard he'll be at the next gathering."

"He might be at the next gathering," Roman corrected him. "But I think this . . . movement, if you will, has no leaders. We are the leaders, it's our birthright. This movement is simply to return us to power."

"Like the White Army?"

"The White Army was undone by the peasants. This is a movement of princes."

"The Fascists, yes?" I pretended ignorance. "But . . . the fascist leaders aren't princes, are they? I didn't think Mr. Mussolini was a nobleman."

"Oh no, he's rabble!" said Gottfried.

"Vulgar man," said Roman, "But useful. After the Cossacks betrayed us, we have to use what we can to restore Europe to order."

"And who we can, Italian tradesmen, German clerks," said Gottfried.

"And there are some proper German men," Roman smiled at Gottfried, "for all their being on the losing side in the war, who know how Europe should be run."

"I'd love to come to your next gathering."

They looked at me with suspicion and condescension.

"If Theo comes, he might like to invite you," said Felix.

"I believe Edouard is bringing some princes to the next gathering who still own their lands," said Roman. "Polish and German."

"And French? English?" I asked. They laughed; bugger.

"They don't own land," said Gottfried. "Not real land, not like we do."

"Did," said Theo quietly, but they ignored him.

"They think politics is beneath them, that it's for factory workers and paupers," said Roman.

"Especially the English. They think the channel protects them from ideas." Gottfried scoffed.

"It's probably why Sasha likes it there," said Felix. "That's the big brother Romanov. An heir, perhaps, if there was a throne to be heir to."

"There will be." Roman frowned.

"Yes, there will be." Felix sniffed, then held out his glass to a passing waiter. "Ah, champagne! I was beginning to think this wasn't a real party."

"Of course it's a party! We're here," said a handsome face; he looked like Theo.

"Nikita!" Felix exclaimed, "You came after all!"

"I insisted," said the woman at his side.

"My brother Nikita and his wife, Maria," said Theo with a big smile, "And this is Mademoiselle Kiki Button."

"Ah, the blonde *Australienne!*" said Nikita. "Dimka will be happy to see you."

"He's here?" said Theo.

"Here!" and Nikita waved to a young man bounding in the door. And thus, with bubbles and kisses in French and English, politics was banished. I was properly launched into the world of Russian princes in Parisian exile. As Felix winked at me, all I could think of was how Bertie would squeal with delight.

꿍

"Oh, Theo . . ." I had collapsed in an armchair after a particularly fast dance. "I don't know which is harder, the dancing or the politics."

"If only the politics was also over in three minutes. It might be more bearable then."

"Will you . . ."

"No, my golden one. I won't take you to one of those meetings. You'll have to meet your princes another way."

I couldn't think of a way to press the point without giving myself away. As I smiled at Theo, thinking frantically, a gust of icy wind blew in from the window behind us. The window was actually a door to a tiny balcony that hung over the moonlit street. I could see the silhouette of two women in the doorframe.

"Harry!" I called and waved. "Wendy!"

"Kiki, darling!" said Harry and, almost before I stood up, my great friend Harriet Harker had enveloped me in an enormous hug. Her lover Wendy ran over and hugged the two of us, squeezing the air out of me in gusts of laughter, both of them so much taller than me that my feet left the ground.

"How long have you been home?" asked Harry.

"I love that you call Paris my home."

"Of course it is," said Wendy. "We've never seen anyone more at home in Paris."

"Why didn't you call me? Where have you been? Tobago? Timbuktu?" Harry tapped me with her fan. "Don't tell me you've been hiding in the country on some dairy farm, I'll never believe you. Those farmers know cheese but they wouldn't know a cocktail even if gin and vermouth started copulating on their kitchen table."

"Her protégé ran off with a dairy farmer last month." Wendy's clipped English tones conveyed everything her words didn't.

"So, Kiki?"

"I've been in Sydney. My mother . . . for her funeral . . ."

"Oh God, honey . . ." Harry's American accent became thick with emotion.

"I'm so sorry, Kiki," said Wendy.

Harry stroked my arm, then took my face in both of her hands and kissed my nose. "This is not the time or place. You're coming over tomorrow and you can tell me then. Garçon! Double Manhattans all round! And who is this?"

"This is Theo." He had been waiting politely and now shook hands with Harry and Wendy. "Theo, this is Miss Harriet Harker, aka Harry. She was with the ambulance corps in the war and I patched her up one starry night as we discussed the healing properties of champagne for heartbreak and silk underwear for loneliness."

"And when she arrived last April, I rescued her from looking like a dirty bohemian," said Harry. "She came to my apartment and went home looking like a clean bohemian."

"This is Wendy Moore, painter, sculptor, reluctant heiress. She also rescued me last April by making sure I ate proper meals instead of Harry's usual dinner of cheese and gin."

"I've changed!" said Harry. "I've mended my ways."

"Not when left alone," said Wendy. "Very pleased to meet you, Theo. You're Russian? What do you do in Paris?"

"Apart from hide out from the Russian secret police, of course." Harry smiled but dropped it quickly. "Oh God, I meant that as a joke! You're not really hiding from them, are you?"

"It's a bit hard to hide when my brother-in-law is Prince Felix Yusupov." Theo nodded toward Felix, who dazzled in his white jacket next to the black-clad Chanel.

"You're a prince?"

"Harry, you sound so American when you say that."

"Oh, Kiki, how can I help it?"

"I'm a Romanov, no less." Theo gave a slight bow.

"Well!" Harry hooked her arm in Theo's and strode with him toward the supper table, skillfully and brutally extracting as much gossip as she could. If I didn't love her, I would have rescued Theo, but when he looked back at me, I just winked.

"She wasn't impressed with this party before, too much style, not enough substance. But she'll be happy now," said Wendy. "You must come for dinner. As soon as convenient."

"Harry directed me to come tomorrow. Besides, I'm sure I'll need someone to tend my hangover and my sweat-stained body. I still have to pay for my baths."

"Excellent. And bring your dirty linen, real and metaphorical."

⌘

The night ended in Theo's room, everyone else in bed, smoking near the open door of his balcony. The moon splashed on my skin as he slowly undressed me. The room was lit only by a smoldering fire. He said almost nothing, no sweet murmurs or witty gossip, just his intent gaze as he moved his hands down my body with the dress.

"Please." His voice was a rasp. Another "please"—what else could I do but whisper yes as he licked the salt from my skin? What else could I say when every kiss felt like goodbye? Air from the balcony sent its fingers over my curves so I couldn't tell if I tingled from cold or from Theo. All the curtains were open and the full moon's light cut into the shadows at his collarbone, the sharp line of his haircut, his dark eyes locked with mine.

"'TAINT NOBODY'S BUSINESS IF I DO"

Servants make me tense. They shouldn't, I grew up with a cook, kitchen maid, scullery maid, nurse maid, gardeners, and all manner of men who worked on the farm. But sometime around boarding school, I got out of the habit. I didn't want other people around me all the time. I much preferred my independence, even solitude; I wanted to leave books open and clothes scattered on the floor and have them be undisturbed the next day. For most of my adult life I had, in fact, done the work of servants, scrubbing bedpans and floors, washing sheets, the endless tending and mending of bodies. Modern clothes and short hair meant I didn't need someone to dress me. My little studio flat, with its noises and smells and drafts, barely needed cleaning. It was also much more private than this soft, lush, crowded cage. Waking up in Theo's bed, hearing footsteps and murmured voices, pots and pans and splashing water, I was suddenly aware I couldn't wander around naked, or help myself to coffee and biscuits in the kitchen, or any of my other favorite morning-after activities.

In the daylight I could see that the huge glass doors of his balcony looked over a courtyard. Light streamed in, making the room, with its high ceilings and pale walls, seem vibrant even though the sky was gray. The only hint of the overblown Art-Nouveau-museum look that marked the rest of the apartment were his dark blue-green bedsheets and the decorative tiles over the fireplace. I wrapped myself in my opera cloak and took a cigarette out on the balcony.

In the courtyard were the usual chairs and table and potted plants, as well as two different gates that led out to the street. A tall man dashed into one, then dashed out the other, before he returned, looking over his shoulder. I almost called to him to help him out, I expected him to smell my cigarette smoke and look up, but he was so intent he didn't seem to notice. He hesitated then moved straight into Theo's apartment building. He wasn't a servant or a tradesman, as he wore a perfectly tailored gray coat and neat gray hat that covered his face. I wriggled into my ball gown. There was something about that man that was deeply familiar. I needed to know who he was.

"Mademoiselle!" The scullery maid was startled and the cook looked annoyed.

"Mademoiselle, Feodor Alexandrovich has ordered your coffee and pastries. I will bring them to you presently." An old butler-type servant indicated that I should leave.

"Who was that man?"

"Mademoiselle, there is no need to worry."

"Was he a tradesman? The man who just came in here."

"Mr. Eddy?" the maid asked.

"It wasn't Mr. Eddy," said the cook sharply. "Don't you know an Englishman from a Russian yet? That man was one of the Master's Russian friends."

"If he's a Russian friend of Felix's, why is he using the servants' entrance?" I asked.

"He is not a friend," said the butler. "But not quite a tradesman either. He is . . ." the butler pursed his lips, "another exile."

"You don't like the exiles?"

"Felix Felixovitch has not been able to move in the same circles since we left Russia."

"He means the Master has to speak to ordinary people." The cook sneered.

"There is no reason why he should," said the butler, "except that Paris is . . ."

"Too republican?" I asked.

"Quite so, mademoiselle."

"So, who was that man? Why was he creeping around in the early morning?"

"It's eleven o'clock!" said the maid but was hushed by a stern look from the butler. The butler then looked me up and down, as if deciding what was most important: his discretion or the encroachment of the lower orders on his Master's perfect nobility. I was very glad his snobbery won the day.

"He calls himself Arkady Nikolaievitch, but I would never address him as such. I call him as a man like him should be called, by his family name."

"Which is?"

"Lazarev."

Lazarev! As he walked upstairs with me and the tray of breakfast things, I tried to get him to tell me more, but he simply murmured, "I have said enough."

"Ah, Vanya, *merci*." Theo was deliciously sleepy. "Just put the tray there. Kiki, what are you doing out of bed?"

"Cigarette."

"Ah, yes . . . and yes please, though I feel like a kipper, I'm so smoked."

"And fishy."

But his only retort was a kiss once Vanya the butler had closed the door.

"WHEN HEARTS ARE YOUNG"

I loved being with Theo but had no intention of staying at his house all day in a stinking ball gown. I had no intention of staying in his bed when last night's desperate kisses swirled between us with our smoke. I excused myself when more of his brothers turned up for an enormous semiformal breakfast party, slipping safely back to down-at-heel, bonkers, private Montparnasse.

I needed to think about Lazarev. He had been part of my mission last April. He had teased me by seeming to have information about Hausmann, when he actually knew nothing of use. He was excellent in a waltz, though, and drank vodka like it was a vocation. In the end, he had been extraneous. But clearly not anymore, as here he was, sneaking in and out of the Yusupov apartment in the early morning, as though he was a secret lover or a thief. What had he been doing? More importantly, who had he been seeing? It wasn't Theo; I doubt it was Irène; it could only have been Felix or one of the servants in the kitchen. The butler was a snob, the maid was a bit clueless, the cook was sarcastic—unless they were brilliant liars, none of them were interested in Lazarev. He must have snuck in to speak to Felix. Theo had mentioned that Felix saw him sometimes. I would have to get him to find out why Felix was seeing Lazarev now.

Waiting at home was a letter from Tom. I waited until I was washed and dressed, sitting at my windowsill with a cigarette, before I allowed myself to open it.

Button,

London is damp, cramped, and I feel like a tramp in my worn cuffs and scuffed shoes. I only unpack my suitcase to wash the smell of bloodshed and cordite from my clothes. I haven't learned how to go to sleep. I fall unconscious at some point in the night, wake up dry-mouthed and still in my trousers before I haul myself onto a lumpy mattress for hours of bad dreams.

Do you feel sorry for me yet?

It's no wonder I love Paris. It's perhaps the only place I can get a good meal and a proper rest (even if that rest doesn't include any actual shut-eye).

But I'm not writing to whine about my life of travel and excitement. I have news in the form of Fleet Street gossip.

The lads in the bars have also made their way home from Smyrna via Paris, Rome, Vienna, and Milan. They speak about gangs of old soldiers who follow other old soldiers. They speak to boys too young to have fought, who pipe up about a new world order, even while the old soldiers are using the same words to talk about the old world order. The men in Vienna speak about Munich, about the Freikorps and some political party or movement with a long name that I always struggle to remember. Its initials are NSDAP and they wear brown as they did in the war. The men in Rome and Milan speak about Mussolini. These men wear black and live to fight. They are excited. They speak of a big event coming, something new, some show of power. The Fleet Street lads have their bags packed and are booking passages to Rome, to Milan, to Florence, to make sure they're nearby when the big event happens.

Which means I will be there too. Old Buffer wants to send
me back to Greece but I've convinced him that Italy is where
the news will happen, that an eyewitness account will make
him look good and the paper sell well at home. I'm convincing
him that a week or two eating spaghetti and gelato in a
warmer climate will stop me "looking like a cadaver, some
ghost of Banquo." I just need a few more days—to wash
my clothes, to gather more gossip from the pubs and print
rooms—before I will be back in Paris on my way to Rome.

Keep the camp bed out, set up a table for my typewriter.
I'm bringing whisky and gossip and I'm in need of warmth.
I almost don't want to say it but I will: I miss you, Button.
Champagne doesn't fizz without you.

T.

My heart rattled its cage as I reacted simultaneously to all the parts
of the letter.

Something was going to happen in Italy and soon. Were my princes
involved? With Fry, I had narrowed it down to Edward, Albert, and
George; that is, the Prince of Wales, the Duke of York, and Prince
George. But how they were involved was still a mystery. These Blackshirts
didn't sound like sons of earls and men with property, they sounded like
angry villagers and disillusioned clerks. They "live to fight," Tom wrote,
but that kind of physical violence did not suit men in tuxedos or hunting
tweed, even if they were old soldiers. How did the two connect?

Camp beds and typewriters, whisky and scuffed shoes; why did these
make my breath catch? It wasn't the objects, they were just ordinary,
everyday things. It had to be the longing he wrote into them, as though
his grimy cuffs reached out for me across the channel. Which they did,
in a way, as he couldn't and wouldn't say what he really meant. I was glad
he didn't, as I wasn't at all ready for confessions of undying this or deep
unconditional that. Except friendship, of course; I supposed that could
be the most complicated of all.

⁓

I pulled on my only pair of trousers, warm and practical, just right for a head full of passion and last night's champagne. I found my sailor's pea-coat under the bed with a packet of boiled lollies in the pocket—Bertie must have worn it when he was here. But it was covered with dust and smelt of mold, so I grabbed my peacock coat and the soft blue scarf that Tom had brought back from Smyrna. I couldn't find my mirror, so I would need to trust that I had washed off all of last night's makeup. I also had to trust that my feet would remember the way to Harry's as I had forgotten her address. My literal dirty linen would have to wait until next time too. For the moment, it would be enough to relieve my heart of some of its memories.

The air became heavy with moisture and the surface of the river shivered. I could talk about my mother with Bertie, with Maisie, and especially with Tom, but speaking about how I still suffered felt like wading through mud, like extracting bits of shrapnel. When I spoke about her, my memory offered up sections of her diaries, events in my mother's voice from years previously. When I spoke about my suffering, my memory offered up events that had nothing to do with my mother. I saw the crematorium in Sydney, manned by a sweating one-armed veteran. I saw the portholes of the troop ships, rust stains dripping like blood. I saw an amputated leg in a muddy French field, I saw apples rotting by the roadside with no one to harvest them, I saw gold cigarette butts amid the debris outside the surgeon's tent. What else could I do but concentrate on the smells of frying garlic and fizzing wine, on the sounds of French debate and cooing pigeons, on the feel of an European autumn as the dead leaves littered the footpath?

My walk to Harry's gave me the opportunity to call Bertie. I headed into the cavernous and busy Gare du Nord. A guard directed me to a bank of public telephones, such a strange but welcome sight, their little boxes painted blue and yellow.

"Browne speaking."

"Bertie darling, I call you with a hangover and sore feet."

"Kiki! Did you go to the ball? When will there be copy? You don't possibly have a photo, do you?"

"I can't possibly as I don't have a camera. Will you buy one for me?"

"Will Fox?"

"Why? What have you heard?"

"Only that my lover-boy now requires evidence for his various theories. He was fulminating about it last night, ranting really, like a rabble-rouser at Speakers' Corner. His boss, Fox that is, wants proof of what he has heard, seen, read, and understood. He was going on and on about how could he do that without a camera, without a radio studio, why should he show evidence of thinking like he was schoolboy, et cetera et cetera . . . but it seems that Fox might just buy you a camera. He might just have to."

"Or he might just send me evidence of other work he has commissioned. Has your boy been to France lately?"

"Not that I could see. Dublin again, and Italy. He had a wrapper for Italian homemade licorice. I was tempted to buy him more but that would give me away."

"Italian . . . Fox knows more than he's letting on. Not Germany?"

"Who goes to Germany nowadays?"

"The damned. I'm beginning to think I'm one of them."

"Leave the melodrama for your copy."

"I'll send it tomorrow. Say hello to Tom for me."

"With pleasure! But for any reason?"

"Same old. He's on leave from the front."

"By the way, I have a check for a typewriter made out to you. Himself is humming up the corridor; I'll see if I can add a camera to the total. Any juicy titbits from the ball last night that he couldn't refuse?"

"All the Romanov brothers in black and white tuxedos around Coco Chanel in shimmering black. Masked waiters serving white cocktails. A ballroom as big as Buckingham Palace."

"Next time we will have it on film."

"Be here soon, Bertie. I think I'll need you."

"CRINOLINE DAYS"

My muscle memory, it seemed, was reliable. After a little more wandering from Gare du Nord, I recognized Ms. Harriet Harker's apartment building. I had been coming here since the war, when she held an informal drop-in service for serving women. We could come and have a nap, a bath, a cocktail, and smoke with no one checking our uniforms or passes, with no one looking for chaperones or looking for a tryst. As most of the women she invited were part of the Ambulance Corps (unofficially sapphic, and they all looked good in trousers), freedom from male attention was particularly welcome. I was mostly there for the bath and the laundry service and good conversations with free-thinking women. Some of my fellow Voluntary Aid Detachment nurses behaved like schoolgirls on an especially bloody excursion. They survived shelling but were still afraid of their fragile "reputation." Abandoned ambulance drivers were much more my thing.

I stood at the front door and waited for the concierge to let me in. Last year, Harry had redecorated her whole apartment in purple, from pale lilac walls to aubergine bath towels. Would it still be purple or had Wendy managed to tone down Harry's fin de siècle excesses? All I really wanted was to sink into one of Harry's armchairs and let her lecture me on how thin I was, how my clothes needed mending, how I needed better work than the froth of gossip writing, and other ministrations of a friend who acted like a favorite aunt. I swayed slightly, so intense was my sudden desire to be cared for. I steadied myself as I smiled and chatted to the concierge, as I took my place in the clanking lift up to Harry's apartment.

"Kiki! Darling! Wait, let me tip the elevator boy." She rushed out and placed a coin in the waiting palm of the lift operator. "You bohemians, I don't think you'll ever learn. Come in, come in! Excellent trousers, they really suit you. Wendy, look—Kiki's in trousers!"

"Very nice." Wendy kissed me on both cheeks.

"Very warm," I said.

"And good for walking, I can tell by your flush."

"I took the liberty of making pie." Harry ushered me to the lounge. "Well, of asking Annette to make little pies, so you can eat a full meal but only feel like you're eating snacks. Finger food, it's my new craze. I could tell from last night that you needed a proper meal. Have you remembered to eat today? Pull over that ashtray, darling, but first put at least one bite of pie into that piehole of yours. Oh, grief, I was just the same when my mother died. I didn't even like her, but when I heard of her death, I was all unmoored and in danger of sinking. Do you know what put me on an even keel again? I traveled to England and saw a cheese-wheel rolling competition, of all things. It was so much fun watching that enormous wheel of cheese roll down the hill, cheering for the men who chased after it, I found myself forgetting my grief for a while. It got better from there. I met Wendy on that trip too. Find yourself a Wendy!"

I let Harry talk, leaning back into the armchair, looking out the large windows at the ever-darkening sky.

"What was your mother's name, Kiki?" Wendy asked. "Harry couldn't tell me."

"Cordelia."

"Cordelia Button."

"Cordelia King Button, actually. She always included her maiden name."

"Cordelia King?" Harry looked shocked. "Your mother is—was—Cordelia King?"

"*The* Cordelia King?" asked Wendy.

"Is there more than one Cordelia King?" I asked. "Don't tell me you knew her."

"We knew Cordelia King," said Wendy. "Everyone did."

"Here, wait, let me . . ." Harry moved into another room, her purple dress flowing around her curves. "I have a photo—no, no—yes! Here it is. Here they are, I should say."

She returned, showing the photographs to Wendy who nodded, before she showed them to me, one hand on my shoulder.

"Is that your mother, Kiki?"

And there she was. In the first photograph, Harry sat at the terrasse tables of a Parisian café with a group of women. It was clearly some decades ago, as they all wore the fashions of the 1890s, with huge hair and long skirts, except they were smoking and there was not a chaperone in sight. I didn't recognize anyone but young Harry and my young mother, in the same striped outfit that she wore in the photograph at Maxim's. She was smiling with such joy, the position of her body was relaxed and somehow flirtatious and graceful.

The second photograph was very recent. Harry stood next to Wendy, looking just like they did today. There was my mother, looking as I remembered her, with her perfect posture more like a punishment than good form, as though someone had slapped her wrist for slouching. It was here in Paris again, again outside a café. There were no uniforms at the table; it must have been taken on her last trip.

"You knew her for years."

"Decades," said Harry, moving over to perch on the arm of Wendy's couch opposite me. "On and off. She was one of the first women I met when I moved to Paris. That photo," she indicated the older photograph, "was taken in the first month I arrived."

"When was the other one taken?"

"When we last saw her," said Wendy. "About, let me think, 1920? 1919? Something like that."

"What . . ." How could I ask everything I needed to? "What was she like?"

"I'm sure you'd know better than us, Kiki!"

"I never knew this woman." I pointed to the picture of my young mother. "Tell me about her. Tell me why she left Europe and why she always returned."

"Ah," said Harry. "That was a question we often asked ourselves, me and the girls, Natalie, Winnie, Romaine, all the rest. Why would such a vibrant soul, a muse who was working to become an artist herself, suddenly pack up and leave for the other side of the world? She was an adventurer of the heart and mind, she said, and her body was very happy on the Kings Road or rue Gabrielle. She never even said she wanted to be married—she was committed to free living and free loving. She was very advanced!"

"It was one of the reasons she was so loved," said Wendy.

"Yes, she was . . . tolerant is too mealy-mouthed, but her morality was that you could live as you wished. She just loved being alive, being in Paris, going to galleries and dance halls and cafés and, oh, everything! When she left for Australia, we didn't have a farewell party, we had a wake! She didn't even properly say goodbye, which I liked to think was why she kept coming back . . ."

"But we knew it wasn't," said Wendy.

Harry sighed. "Of course we knew. We . . ." Harry pursed her lips and looked out at the glowering sky.

"I've read her diaries." I ground my cigarette into the ashtray with too much force. "All twenty-seven years of them. You don't have to keep her secrets. I know just how unhappy she was. I know that there was a man, a special man, who she came back for. She got pregnant by him but lost the pregnancy after she'd already married my father. That this man couldn't, or wouldn't, marry her, directed the course of her life. Who is he?"

Both women stared at me in a kind of stunned silence.

"This can't be a secret," I said.

"Well, it is, actually," said Harry.

"She always had plenty of admirers," said Wendy, "but when she visited us . . . well, we always thought she was . . ." Wendy and Harry exchanged a look.

"One of us," said Harry. "A sapphic. Or maybe that she didn't make the distinction, man or woman, she loved a person for who they were."

"I read nothing about any woman in her diaries. She only referred to 'he' or 'him.'" We were looking at each other with the same question in our frowns: who was Cordelia, really? These two women across the coffee table seemed to be separated from me not by a few feet but by the chasm of a generation.

"To be honest, we only assumed she was one of us," said Harry. "We never actually saw any evidence of it."

"All the more remarkable then," said Wendy.

"And all the more secretive," I said. "So, who were her admirers?"

"Everyone!" Harry threw up her hands. "She was so vivacious, so sensual . . ." Harry's voice choked up, and she had to stop and dab at her eyes with the handkerchief Wendy passed to her. The pale purple of the walls seemed gray and drab in the dim light from the windows.

"She was beautiful," said Wendy, still looking at Harry.

"She truly was. I can't believe . . . such a loss. Her admirers, alright, let's see." Harry took a breath and appeared to pull herself together. "When I first knew her, before she left for Australia, she was part of Rodin's set."

"Gertrude Stein said the same thing."

"Yes, Rodin, not my thing really, but there you go. The big man didn't attend the gatherings all that often, but the others did, who were they . . . actually, you know, I don't think I ever really knew them. Men, painting and sculpting and feeling themselves so important, older than Picasso and those Modernists. They were working with color and light. Lovely work, but, oh, very old-fashioned ideas about women. I don't know what she saw in them."

I couldn't stop myself from picking at the purple velvet of the armchair, worrying at a little thread until it gave way, bit by bit.

"And in London?"

"I heard about her in London," said Wendy. "It took me years to link the stories of 'Lovely Deelie,' with Cordelia King in Paris. But she was a favorite there too, a model, she was part of the Café Royal set. From what I understood, she would walk into the Royal for dinner, find an artist, and agree to pose for him the next day. After the sitting they'd join the Café Royal crew and the cycle would continue."

I'd been to the Café Royal; it was a hub of hubbub and bohemian gossip. A vision of my mother at the Royal in her striped dress, greeting models in booths and listening to bearded painters, walked across Harry's floor-to-ceiling windows.

"That means . . ." I searched Wendy's face but she didn't reflect my surprise. "There must be hundreds of paintings or drawings of her!"

"I'd say so!" said Harry. "I always wanted to see her own drawings, but she'd never show anyone her sketchbook."

"I got the impression they weren't really sketches, they were . . . something else, ideas perhaps, something domestic or abstract or in some other way provocative," said Wendy, "which is why she wouldn't show anyone her work."

"The domestic was provocative?" I asked.

"Oh yes," said Wendy. "Men sneered at women painting women unless they were heroines of antiquity or naked little girls. You couldn't paint a woman making dinner or hanging washing without being dismissed. As for breastfeeding! Heaven forbid we have bodies that aren't solely for male pleasure."

"But her lover . . ." My head was beginning to whirl with questions like *Where was her sketchbook?* and *Who was her teacher?* "Rodin's set, you think?"

"If her lover was a man, in Paris, that would be my best guess," said Harry. "We would have heard if her lover had been one of Natalie's girls."

"But her lover could have been in London," said Wendy. "As she lived in London most of the time, that would seem more sensible."

"But less romantic, darling," said Harry. "And she was romantic. And in Paris so often too."

"Who were Rodin's set?" I asked. "Apart from Matisse—and maybe Russell?—people never say the same names."

"I've never heard of Russell. You'll need to ask—oh, who is it—Derain?" Harry conferred with Wendy.

"Wasn't Brancusi one of his students too?"

"Isn't Brancusi too young?"

"I can never really tell under their beards." Wendy grimaced.

"Brancusi is too young," said Harry. "You need men at least as old as us. Try André Derain, that's my best recommendation. I think they were friends."

"Do you know where he lives?" Was Derain a Fauvist? My thoughts flashed with bright colors, seeing Harry's dress glow, the stark contrast of Wendy's white shirt against the aubergine velvet couch. "Or where his studio is? Unless he frequents the quarter . . ."

"Ask around the galleries, honey, they'll tell you." Harry sighed again, poured wine, picked up food and put it down again. "So, Cordelia King is never coming back to Paris. I'm more devastated than I like to admit. You know, when she was here last, it was just after the war, we all felt, well, a bit old, a bit creaky. A bit like everything we'd worked toward had been dug up with the trenches and discarded just as easily—votes for women, for example, or freedom to love. We saw her having an aperitif alone at a café, she waved us over, and suddenly we were on a night out."

"She was tired and sad then," said Wendy.

"So were we all! To be honest, I didn't notice."

"You were very tired, Harry, after your ambulance duties extended into the flu pandemic."

"Ah yes." Harry and Wendy exchanged a tender, private look. I looked away, out the window over the rooftops, steel and slate and rust and stone.

"Which is why your mother was tired, Kiki," said Wendy. "She'd been nursing someone through the flu, but she wouldn't say who. She just said, 'He survived, thank God, and he even remembered thank me.'"

"She was witty?"

"Of course, darling!" said Harry. "Not in a cruel way, like those Cunard women, but softly, pointing out the ridiculous, playing with words."

"She was never like that at home."

They looked at each other again, a whole conversation in Wendy's raised eyebrows, in Harry's pursed lips.

"We have long suspected that perhaps you were the only good thing to come out of her marriage, Kiki darling. Our guess is that she would have left the marriage if it hadn't been for you."

"Not to make you feel guilty!" said Wendy. "She loved you, that's what we mean."

"Of course! That's exactly what we mean. You didn't think . . . Someone asked her once, around a table twenty years ago or so, 'What's in Australia then? Don't go home!' but she just smiled her slow sensual smile and said, 'My little girl.' Someone made a comment about how her girl would be a little angel and the conversation moved on."

Was it Harry's loving look that made me want to cry? Perhaps it was the way Wendy ran her hand through her short white hair and stared out the window, or the way Harry squeezed Wendy's other hand with all the confidence of tested intimacy. Maybe it was my hangover, or my empty stomach, but I struggled to swallow even a sip of wine, and I couldn't see the flame of my lighter through my rapid tearful blinking.

"Actually, I do remember some of the people she sat for," said Wendy, coming back to us from the view, "mainly because I asked her to sit for me and she was too busy! Matisse was the person she said no to me for, here in Paris."

"Apparently he's very demanding," said Harry, "which sounds like Cordelia, she could tame anyone."

"In London, well, the Café Royal set centered around Augustus John, so maybe him?" Wendy frowned. "Although he might be a bit young."

"Are you in London much, Kiki?" asked Harry.

"Not if I can help it."

"I feel the same. Dirty, cramped city."

"But I might not be able to help it in the future." I didn't want to explore why with Harry. I had to have at least one part of my life unstained by Fox. "In any case, I have friends there who can help me."

I closed my eyes for a moment, seeing Bertie flirting his heart out in the Café Royal, seeing Tom striding down Fleet Street, collar up against the wintry rain. I opened them to find Harry sitting on the coffee table in front of me, her large silk-clad bottom surrounded by plates and glasses.

"Kiki." Harry leaned forward and took my hand from where it had been lying slack in my lap. "You can lean on us. Truly."

I nodded. My head felt so heavy, it felt like I could hardly hold it against the armchair. Harry kissed my hand, exhaled heavily, then clapped her hands on her knees.

"Anyway, Kiki, eat! You're like a sparkling skeleton from the tomb of Tutankhamun. I absolutely can't let you leave here with this plate empty."

"My heart is too full to eat."

"Rubbish. Try that one, it's chicken and leek and delightfully creamy. Here, have some more wine. Annette! Some of the white from the trip south, please! There are stewed plums and cream for dessert and I won't accept anything less than a plate licked clean." She took my glass to top it up. "Now, tell me about all these princes you were with at Chanel's little party! And did you meet the Germans? They said they were princes too, but unless they fought for France it seems a bit early to include them in a ballroom, don't you think? I still can't hear that accent without a shudder."

Harry shuddered theatrically, making the wine she was pouring splosh over the table. Wendy protested, Harry laughed, and I was able to relax enough to eat. The room was cozy, with its soft armchairs and roaring fire and some kind of extra modern heating somewhere too. Harry gave me all the gossip and news from the past year—where she and Wendy had been on holiday the last two summers, who came to her Sunday salon and who they left with. It was an effort for her to keep up her banter; Wendy held her hand and massaged her shoulders, Harry paused often when her chat is usually seamless. But I could not help her in her struggle. My own thoughts were too distracted by the clues about my mother's lover.

"YES! WE HAVE NO BANANAS"

"Browne speaking."

"Bertie darling, the check arrived."

"Oh good! Now you can send us your copy on time, instead of dictating some beautiful nonsense over the telephone, that Mavis at reception then has to type up just in time to rush it to the printers."

"Is that her real name, 'Mavis at reception'?"

"It's how she answers the telephone. It stuck."

I had left the door to the telephone booth open so I could smoke without fumigating myself. Yesterday's trousers were covered with wine and cold mud splashes where the icy puddles had leapt out of the way of the traffic and onto my accommodating legs. I did not want today's red brogues and scarlet coat to become equally grubby.

"You'll miss it, writing the column with me over the telephone, smoothing the edges and adding the frills. A typewritten column and a couple of pictures will be dull in comparison."

"Everything is dull compared to your physical presence, but it would make my life so much simpler."

"Does it need to be?"

"It does. My man is starting to suspect I'm not with him for his . . . (Mavis, go and get me some caramels, there's a love) for his knowledge of Kodak's Box Brownies." Bertie spoke in hushed tones. "I go through his coat pockets but there's nothing there. I've had to resort to more devious methods—following him in the morning, reading his letters—I even took one of the Hello Girls at the Ministry exchange to dinner, just to get more information."

"What sacrifice! And?" I looked around at the concourse of Gare Montparnasse. Still no newspaper boys or young men with gold-tipped cigarettes. Why were there no watchers?

"Well, he's off to France, isn't he?" said Bertie. "Accompanying his boss, the Hello Girl said. He has to meet with a colleague in Paris . . . Fry?"

"I know Fry."

"Well. You might meet my Roger too. In fact, they might be there already. (Ah, Mavis, thank you.) I need that copy by tomorrow, Kiki." His voice had changed, becoming a touch theatrical; he could no longer speak freely.

"I'll post it today. Send me a telegram with another telephone number we can use."

The evidence was now overwhelming: Fox was in France. This thought ran around my head as I walked through Gare de Montparnasse, the late morning travelers drifting in from the countryside. He didn't come over with Fry, a couple of days ago, but he was here now. Why? What had changed? I was so close to working out all the clues. If he was in Paris, how was I supposed to contact him?

I stopped by the doors, my feet arrested by the thought: Fox would visit me. That's how he would contact me, he would wait for me in a café, he would loiter in my street. I could just imagine him, standing in a doorway opposite my apartment building, hat down and collar up, the smoke from his Sobranies stealing through the damp air as he watched me, at my window at night, or saying goodbye to Madeleine Petit in the morning. I could almost hear his footfalls in his leather-soled shoes, soft and even like a metronome . . . I would have stayed like that for an hour, staring at the Montparnasse traffic and seeing only Fox's shadow, if it hadn't been for Delphine.

"Mademoiselle, would you like some matches?"

"Delphine." I breathed again, I could focus, I could hear once more.

"I have more brands 'round the corner, if you would prefer."

"Ah! Yes." She must have information for me. "Let's go."

"Mademoiselle, I have seen that man you met, the big one with the dark hair and eyes like a thief."

That described Fry exactly; I laughed, partly with relief. "And?"

"He met another man, tall and thin and sniffy, and they went to the station café. They talked for a while but I couldn't get inside to hear them."

"When was this?"

"Last night."

"Well done. Keep a look out for them. Now, I promised you boots. Your feet look frozen and sore in those clodhoppers. Which bootmaker do you have an eye on?"

Delphine grinned and I followed her down a couple of alleyways to a tiny little shop. Its front window was dirty but inside it was scrubbed clean, it smelt of fresh leather and glue and was noisy with industry. A small dark man with enormous eyebrows greeted us.

"Delphine! Back again? Is this your wondrous benefactor?"

"She will pay for the boots." Delphine held herself like a queen. "Are they ready?"

"But of course, Mademoiselle Delphine." The man gave a little bow. "Wait one moment."

He brought out a pair of calf-high black boots in Delphine's size. They seemed ordinary at first glance, but at second glance I could see all the details—a brogue pattern on the toes and up the sides were black embroidered animals. I picked out a cat, a dog, a bear, and a bird in flight, before Delphine pulled them on.

"What wonderfully soft leather," I said.

"Of course, mademoiselle," said the man. "She wanted red boots but we decided, in the end, that black would be more useful. No one would believe she was a match girl if she had red boots."

"And I can leave them here at night too," said Delphine.

"Why would you do that?"

"So my father doesn't sell them."

The man gave me a loaded look; clearly, he kept an eye out for Delphine as well.

"I think I might like red boots," I said.

The man looked at me curiously. "With that coat, certainly. But with your hair, I think golden boots might suit you better, mademoiselle. Wait one moment." He returned with a length of gold leather. "We have just received some of this."

"Oh yes, mademoiselle!" Delphine's eyes glowed.

"Put some aside, I'll return tomorrow. Delphine, I trust you will show me the way here."

She winked. She wouldn't be a match-seller forever, not if I could help it.

"MAKE IT SNAPPY"

I had to cross the river for the type of shops that sold typewriters and cameras and other things Montparnassians were mostly too poor to own. I needed to be able to put the typewriter in a suitcase and the camera in my handbag or else they would be useless. This meant I needed the latest models, not yesterday's machines that could hardly be moved except by two burly men with lots of grunting. I thought about using the typewriter money to pay a typist, but Bertie would expect copy forever and the money for a typist would eventually run out. No, I needed a typewriter and to learn how to type. Life was full of complications.

Complications such as Fox being in France. Who was this tall, thin, sniffy man that Delphine mentioned? Was it a Parisian contact of Fry's or was it Bertie's lover? It certainly wasn't Fox. First of all, although he was taller than me, he wasn't tall for a man. Secondly, when I knew him three years ago, he had been built like an athlete. I doubt he would have abandoned an ounce of strength or a smidge of personal power by becoming thin. And sniffy? If Delphine had said snarly, snarky, or steely, then I might have believed it was Fox. But sniffs were for snobs; Fox was above that kind of class-consciousness. So, if it wasn't Fox with Fry, then where was Fox? Hopefully Fry would tell me.

The typewriter shop was on a street that sold lots of different writing implements. There was a shop selling fountain pens and another selling paper. There was a printer and a bookshop and a shop that sold only ink and wax. The typewriter shop had a small museum of old typewriters in the window, but the inside was bright and clattering as the salesmen and shopgirls showed off their wares.

"I need a portable typewriter, as small and light as you have."

"Yes, mademoiselle. This gentleman here is looking at our latest model, so if you don't mind . . ."

"Nguyễn," I said. It was the man from the noodle house who recommended the *phở bò*.

"Miss Kiki."

"You're a writer?"

"I'm the new secretary of the French Communist Party." He held himself a little straighter in his worn brown suit. "And we need better records of our committee meetings. The old typewriter is too heavy to move and our meetings no longer fit in the president's office. You want a typewriter too?"

"I write a column for a London magazine on all the things your party would do away with—you know, princes and balls and rich capitalists, that sort of thing."

"You need some education. When are you coming to a meeting?"

"Whenever the next one is. Whenever you invite me."

"You're in luck. It's tonight, eight o'clock at the Pigalle Workers' Club. It's an important meeting too. We're making final preparations for the second congress."

"Second congress . . . of the Communist Party?"

"All the committees of the Communist Party in France will meet in Paris next week. You should come to that too."

"Even if I'm not a party member?"

"You will be." His smile was a mixture of sweetness and arrogance. "I'm a very persuasive speaker."

I laughed then. That was one of most ridiculous flirtations I'd heard
to date, along with "How d'you like my cannon, miss?" and "Sister, I
think I can feel my missing leg. Could you check for me?" He knew
it too and grinned, his thin face lighting up. We bought the shop's
last two portable typewriters, both in a serious black with matching
suitcases, while he gave me advice on where else in Paris I could find
proper *phở bo.*

"Until tonight, comrade." Nguyễn loped toward the metro.

On the recommendation of the typewriter sellers, I moved to the next
street filled with other gadget shops, such as radios and microphones and
cameras. I bought the smallest camera I could find, one that fit neatly in
its own little handbag. I imagined photographing Nguyễn at the meeting,
his worn brown suit holding his shiny new ideas. As I stopped in the
street to practice my photography skills, I wondered idly what Theo would
say if he knew I was going to a Communist Party meeting. I wondered
what would happen if all the parts of my life collided.

At home I had two telegrams and a handwritten note. It was the
handwritten note I tore open:

Darkling I listen

Nothing more, just Fox's handwriting to let me know he was in Paris.
I stared at it. Should I scream or cry or laugh or sigh? I looked up and
down the street but no silver hair was sitting at a café table or lurking in
a doorway. It was with heavy feet that I trooped up to my flat to put on
clothes more suited to serious proletarian revolutionaries, to put more
film in my camera, and to pack my new handbag with the necessaries.
Darkling I listen: There had to be more. Why did he only listen? Why
didn't he see? He should have written lines from Shelley about seeing and
knowing, about hunting and finding; he knows I know his handwriting,
he doesn't need to use this line over and over. Unless he really does hear.
Did he mean that he was listening to my telephone calls to Bertie and
eavesdropping on my conversations with Fry? Did it have to do with that

line from the photos, "the world will listen then, as I am listening now"? Was he referring to something I had already done, or something that I was about to do? These games were too much.

I sat on my bed for a moment, listening to the clangs in the street, the chatter in the stairwell, the old plumbing in the walls, anything to stop the downward spiral of my thoughts. Fox might be in Paris but I was not his pet, collared and caged, not anymore and never again. I applied my reddest lipstick like it was war paint. I removed my sensible knickers and replaced them with emerald green silk ones. I ripped up the note and flung it out the window, watching it catch on the spitting wind and scatter, sodden, over the street.

⌾

"Katie King! (Yes, thank you, Gina.)," said Maisie. "What's the gossip?"

I flicked up my coat collar against the chill in the telephone booth.

"Nancy Cunard, an avant-garde poet heiress, just stopped me in the street to invite me to a 'little gathering' she's holding at the Rotonde. I'm calling to see if you're free tomorrow night."

"Count me in. Will there be people there for our 'other' work?"

"I don't think so, but I have information about that. My friend in London . . . Have you met Bertie?"

"During the war, but not since. Slender Soho type?"

"That's the one. He's been doing a little digging for me and has sent me some names via telegram: Carl and Phillip."

"Who are they?"

"Friends of Hausmann, I'm hoping. I also have another telegram from Tom."

"You're practically a post office, Katie."

"More like a dead letter drop."

"What's that?"

"It's . . . not important. Tom's coming in a couple of days."

"He's part of this too?"

"Unavoidably. He's on his way to Rome, where Mussolini is planning a big demonstration with his Blackshirts. How do you feel about a trip south, Maisie?"

"Pizza in a piazza? I'm there." I heard her sigh. "Life is so exciting with you in Paris, Katie."

"Your life was a bit exciting before, what with the blackmail."

"Oh no, that was just fear and tension. Somehow you make it glamorous."

"Put diamonds on my pistol, then. Six o'clock tomorrow outside the Metro, here in Montparnasse? I want you to myself for a moment before we plunge into the party."

"I'll wear all the parrot colors."

I hung up and smoked a cigarette, looking around at Gare du Montparnasse. Delphine caught my eye but shook her head: no sighting of either Fry or Fox. It was good to see her move about in her new boots. She was quicker and lighter and her ready smile meant she sold more matches.

But I needed to find another telephone. If Fox really was listening, then he knew where and how to listen. He would have threatened the girls in the exchange to record my calls. I took a risk today, after the note and the telegrams and my heart going like a racehorse and Nancy Cunard chatting in her chic bangles and having to remember how to be a society girl while my head was split into several fighting factions. I just had to speak to someone, to Maisie, as soon as I could.

I had a new number for Bertie in his telegram:

SOHO 8623 PRINZ PHILLIP & CARL?

"Prinz" was German, I was sure, for prince. I would need to find out how he got these names. His lack of banter suggested that he sent this in a hurry, that someone was with him or waiting for him and he had no time to think of a little innuendo. This was most unlike him; I hoped he hadn't been found out by his lover.

I had a telegram from Tom too:

BUTTON LAY OUT THE CAMP BED WE'RE MARCHING TO ROME.

A little better than Bertie, but only a little; there were no willow cabins, no whisky, no time or date or place to meet. Just the bare ten words of the cheapest telegram.

I sighed, full of smoke. This spy work was threatening to become as serious as the war.

"IN THE LITTLE RED SCHOOLHOUSE"

"Fry." I nodded. We met opposite the Grand Guignol theater. The streets of Pigalle were bustling with people ignoring the cold weather in favor of cheap thrills. The lights from the theater barely reached our side of the street.

"Nice cap," I said. "It looks like it really was your father's."

"Absolutely. You can't actually buy the proper ones in London. As I was traveling to Yorkshire to buy one anyway, I thought I may as well use the real deal. Besides, new boots are always suspicious."

"New high heels, however, are just the thing."

I had given serious thought to my outfit. If I had changed back into my trousers and sailor peacoat, would that have made me look like I was playing at having proletarian sympathies? The most straightforward thing would have been to wear what I had been wearing all day, but even though red was the color of revolution, a scarlet dress with matching coat and hat was just far too noticeable. In the end I did what no true revolutionary did and bought some new clothes. I bought some navy woolen trousers, which I got Odile to fit around my waist, and a thick green jumper to keep me warm. My sailor peacoat and black beret went well with this costume, as did my new tri-tone green heels.

"I wanted to wear the golden boots I'm having made, but they're not ready yet. I have to impress my own flat-cap wearer tonight."

The theater posters screamed of bloody murder. Red lights flickered in the windows of the apartments above us. I checked the directions in my notes and set off.

"You've impressed me," said Fry. "This is quite an invitation."

"This invitation? This is nothing. Now if I'd been invited to tea with Lenin, that would be something."

"If you'd been invited to tea with Lenin, I wouldn't be working with you, I'd be reporting on you."

"Aren't you anyway?"

The Workers' Club was hidden down an alley between a nightclub, a *moulin*, and a couple of brothels. At least I assumed they were brothels, as women lounged in the doors, the windows, on the street outside, chatting to each other across the alleyway, calling out to us in a way that was casually hopeful, seemingly impervious to both the cold and rejection. Fry ignored them admirably but I could see the muscles in his neck and jaw tense in the effort to do so. I pursed my lips to stop myself laughing.

I had expected a self-important hall like the ones I had seen in Sydney, but this club was just a sign erected outside an old stable. Inside it was scrubbed raw. It had clearly only recently been turned into a meeting place, as it was heated by a single gas ring and the door to the main house was a neatly edged hole in the wall. But the lack of heating was immaterial; it was warm with packed bodies. Many attendees looked battered by life—limbless veterans, women with gray skin in gray clothes, teenagers with scars and a gaze that flickered between vacant and fiery. But there was a sizable contingent of bourgeoisie, with their new clothes and healthy skin, keen for some kind of three-piece-suit revolution. At the far end of the stable was a makeshift stage. Nguyễn smiled at me, causing a couple of people in front of him to turn around. I moved up the aisle.

"Nguyễn, I've brought a friend, over from London. He's a brother to your cause."

"Alberts." Fry held out his hand along with his alias.

"Comrade, welcome."

"Inkpin and Shinwell send their regards."

Nguyễn nodded; Fry had established his credentials. "Will they join us at the Congress?"

"Between the police and the election, no chance this year. Next year, we hope."

"Miss Kiki, take a seat just there, you'll hear everything."

The hall hushed as a bald man with bottle glasses and a bushy brown moustache stood up to take the floor.

"Tovarishi!" His voice rung out. "Comrades! Welcome to this meeting of the French Communist Party. As you may know, I have recently returned from Russia as a delegate to the Second Enlarged Plenum of the Executive Committee of the Communist International. The Comintern report that French workers have a special place among the Communist International and our Congress in Paris this year will draw the eyes of the world!"

As he spoke, I looked over at Fry. He caught my glance and gave me a discreet nod; this is what he came to Paris for. I followed his lead and clapped when he clapped, even though much of the terminology was foreign to me: Comintern, dialectic, decossackization, commissariat. Even if I understood the phrases, like "means of production" or "new economic policy," I couldn't always understand the sense. But apart from the ideology of equality, I was beginning to see why so many intellectuals were attracted to communism. There was a whole theory here, a philosophy of life with its own terms and judgements, that sounded nothing like religion or patriotism or any of the ideas that had kept us mired in the bloody mess of the war. The Communists famously had been against the Great War. If I'd heard about them before I started working for Fox, I might have been attracted to communism too.

"Comrade, respectfully, I disagree!"

My thoughts had taken a little holiday but were brought back by an altercation. Fry stiffened as the speaker stared.

"Your criticisms of the Comintern are just the sort of bourgeois rubbish that the Soviets would expect from out-of-touch Parisians!"

Pandemonium. Workers yelled insults about how hard they worked, about ideological purity, mixing French patriotism with Marxist rhetoric. Nguyễn looked shocked, then amused.

"And who are you, comrade?" Nguyễn looked like he was enjoying himself. "Please share your inside knowledge."

"Lazarev, Arkady Nikolaievitch." Lazarev stood up, looking so unlike the man I met last year I couldn't stop staring. Gone was his cane and perfectly tailored suit, his shiny shoes and smooth manners. He wore loose rough wool in gray and navy, a cap in his hands, and a grubby neckerchief round his throat. He could have played a worker in a Soviet propaganda film. Fry leaned forward and I hid behind his bulk. I did not want Lazarev to see me.

"I can tell you that Moscow is not happy with the way you have been conducting your meetings here and are considering removing France from the Fourth World Congress of the Comintern!"

More yells, but Nguyễn put up his hand. He had a great natural authority, much more than the man with the bottle glass specs.

"Please, Arkady Nikolaievitch, do go on. You were no doubt sent to educate us."

Lazarev coughed uncomfortably, his bluster suddenly gone, his lack of commitment for a moment transparent. He was in disguise, Nguyễn had seen it, and now we saw it too. Lazarev blundered on.

"The VTsIK is under direct orders to make sure that the Comintern follows Comrade Stalin's directives. I have them here." He held up a piece of paper, in Russian with a big red star at the top. "For everyone to read and follow!"

The meeting fell into disarray as the main speaker tried to contain the anger and mayhem Lazarev had caused. Eventually the meeting broke up, to convene again on Sunday evening. I stayed in Fry's shadow until

I saw Lazarev physically escorted from the hall by two burly workers. Nguyễn packed up his typewriter and turned to me.

"Well, Miss Kiki?"

"Well, Nguyễn, if I wanted to see a cockfight I'd have gone to the ring down the road."

Nguyễn smiled and Fry smirked.

"There are always imposters," said Nguyễn. "They try to break us up, like tonight, but it never lasts. The party will prevail."

"Do you know him? Tonight's troublemaker?"

"Lazarev? No. He's obviously Russian, but he seems to be a White in masquerade, wouldn't you say, Alberts?"

"I don't know about these Parisian imposters. In England their jackboots are a dead giveaway."

"Jackboots?" asked Nguyễn.

"Oh! Are the troublemakers in England, ah, *fascisti*, is it?" I smiled; hopefully he knew I was thanking him for introducing the topic.

"They are," said Fry. "And not always factory workers neither."

"I haven't seen that here," said Nguyễn. "Just disgruntled Whites wanting to reverse the revolution." He shook his head, as if at such foolish behavior.

"When's the Congress?" I asked.

"In a week," said Fry.

"It's for party members," said Nguyễn with a big smile. "Join us."

"Not tonight, dear, I have a headache."

He laughed then, thank goodness. Fry, in the guise of Alberts, got a few more details from Nguyễn about the conference before accompanying me out of the hall.

"Alberts: I like it."

"It's how I'm known at the Party meetings. My family thinks I'm a mad red."

"Instead, we know you're just mad."

He gave me the briefest smile as we passed a *moulin*, the red lights outside casting a bloody glow on his skin.

"Lazarev," I said. "I know him."

"But you're chasing Fascists, not Communists."

"I know. Last year he was involved with the Fascists, or one Fascist—Edward Hausmann."

"Hausmann!"

"Of course! You'd know him from the war."

"Fox hates the traitor. We all do."

"I don't think they were close, Lazarev and Hausmann, but Lazarev liked to bandy Hausmann's name about to get closer to the aristocracy and their money. He had some kind of art dealership going."

"So, what's he doing in a Communist Party meeting?"

"Exactly. Especially after he was at Prince Felix Yusupov's apartment yesterday morning."

"How do you know that?"

"I was there. With his brother-in-law, Prince Theo Romanov."

Fry laughed so hard he stopped in the street.

"Oh, come on Fry, it's not that funny." But apparently it was. "You just need to spend a bit more time here, you might find yourself a princess."

"I wouldn't know what to do with her."

"I'm sure she'd let you know." Cue more laughter. "And you can let me know: why didn't you tell me that Fox is here?"

Fry's mirth stopped abruptly. "Fox isn't here."

"He certainly is. Unless someone else delivered a handwritten note this morning?" Fry stared at me but I couldn't detect any signs of lying. "I know Fox caught a plane to France yesterday. Why is he here?"

"How do you know he caught a plane?"

"Why is Fox here?"

Fry lit two cigarettes and gave one to me. "This is why you hate him, isn't it?"

"I didn't say that."

"No, he did. He seems to take pleasure in your hating him."

"I suppose because he knows that's the best he can get."

Fry looked me up and down, as if deciding something. I could hear glass smash somewhere nearby, and the sharp smells of old wine and urine.

"Part of my mission here is to report on you."

"You shouldn't be telling me this, Fry."

"No."

Girls in shiny fabrics watched us from windows and doorways. Music scattered through the spots of rain in the air. I stubbed out my cigarette and took Fry's arm in a way that demanded intimacy.

"So tell me more."

"He spoke about you as an inexperienced agent, 'Make sure she follows protocol,' that sort of thing."

"Bastard, I worked for him all through the war!"

"He never said." He nodded. "Of course."

"I'm not inexperienced, just reluctant and untrained. He couldn't have me turn up at your meetings and training sessions to learn Morse code, signaling, all the other official things. It'd give me away."

"You're only useful if you're a secret."

I could feel him looking at me, but in the neon hoots of the boulevard my mind's eye saw only Fox.

"He taught me a few things—how to shoot, how to ride a motorcycle, a few codes that he thought might be useful. All the poetry he liked. I learned easily enough."

A car backfired, a firework banged into green flame; that time in the woods with his pistol, Fox's hand on my wrist, his voice just behind my ear as I focused on the target.

"And during the war, you know, I had a 'nuns fret not' attitude."

"'Nuns fret not at their convent's narrow room, and hermits are contented with their cells . . .'" Fry quoted the Wordsworth sonnet; Fox had, no doubt, forced him to learn it too. "I think we all did."

"I'm not a nun anymore. The convent room is far too narrow."

"So why do you continue to work for him?"

I laughed and it tasted bitter.

"Yes, yes, stupid question," Fry said. "He must have something to threaten you with."

"If he wanted, he could threaten me with my favorite color, my eye color, my childhood. In fact, I'm waiting for it."

We had moved away from the chaotic noise of Pigalle to a cold boulevard. Some cafés spilled their light on the footpath, but no one sat outside in the fickle sleet. There was no need to stay close to Fry now. I flicked up my collar and shoved my hands in my pockets. The only noise was the moan of the wind as it chased the occasional car.

"So, you think Fox is here to . . . haunt you?" Fry asked. He had flicked his collar up too, his hands also in his pockets, though I couldn't tell if the imitation was intentional. He frowned into the darkness.

"I'd love to think Fox had some legitimate reason to be in Paris. But with the only evidence one tiny note, I can only think he's doing what he's always done."

"I have to report to him soon. I'll call him."

"You'd be a double agent for me?"

"Someone has to keep a check on power." He stood like a street-side sentinel, a bastion of righteous Englishness despite his morally murky profession. He scanned the road for a taxi like he was deciding strategy.

"Lazarev"—I didn't want to be bundled into a taxi for safekeeping, I wanted Fry to look at me and work with me—"will you question him?"

"No, you will. You're right, we need to talk to him."

"Does 'we' include your tall thin friend?"

"How do you . . . You aren't inexperienced at all, are you?"

"Is he working with you from London, or is he a Paris man?"

"Both. A London man who lives and works here in Paris. I'm sure you'll meet him soon. Not at the interrogation though. That's our bit of fun."

"The only interrogations I've done have been in a low-cut dress with a bottle of champagne."

"You'll have to learn how to do them in a grimy cellar with a spot of blood."

"I've done a lot of things for Fox, but I didn't sign up for that."

"None of us do."

The taxi door closed before I could say any more.

⤫

"Bertie."

"Kiki, darling." He sounded exhausted, even over the clattering night noises at Gare du Nord.

"Is your Roger tall and thin?"

"He is. Or was, I haven't heard from him."

"Probably because he's in Paris." I heard Bertie grunt. "What are his other distinguishing features?"

"Missing pinky on his left hand. His jaw clicks. He's pigeon-toed too, it makes for quite a distinctive walk."

"I feel I should be using a code name with you now, Bertie."

"How about Tristan and Isolde?"

"I love you, but I was thinking more Mephistopheles and Faust."

"And Fox is the devil? I didn't realize you were damned, Kiki."

"Neither did I until I found myself in a field hospital on the Somme."

I heard him sigh heavily.

"Are you alright?"

"Sorry, Kiki, I'm . . . not alright. As you guessed."

"Has your lover found you out?"

"He suspects. I wasn't quite subtle enough in getting those names."

"You mean of the 'prinzen'? They came from Roger?"

"He caught me reading his papers. Admittedly, he did leave them scattered on the table, but I was breezy and silly and accepted his very poor excuses without even a snigger."

"But it isn't Roger who's robbed your voice of its color."

"A couple of others suspect too. Luckily Soho boys in Soho bars all have secret lives. The barman thinks nothing of being my receptionist as long as I pay for the best whisky in the house."

"Who suspects?"

"Mavis at reception, for one, but she'll keep mum for me. And a man in a beautifully cut black coat who always seems to be reading the newspaper when I come out of various watering holes. I would have approached him already but his gold-tipped cigarettes put me off."

"Another Fox cub."

"I'll have to give up Roger—well, that's what he told me his name was—but I'd love a little help in shaking my Savile Row shadow."

"Quote Keats at him and he'll think you're one of Fox's agents. Even if it only confuses him for a moment, it'll buy you enough time to hop on a train to Paris."

"Of course! Paris is always a good idea. I need to be with you to take photos!"

"That might actually be the truth."

"Someone needs the telephone. I'll telegram my arrival time."

Bertie had a Savile Row shadow: Fox was closing in.

"QUEEN O' HEARTS"

I settled into Petit's for breakfast the next morning, but my thoughts were far from the creamy coffee and crisp croissant in front of me. The only way to get rid of Fox was to get rid of this mission as soon as possible. I had my notebook with me and opened it to review everything I knew so far.

The mission: The Prince of Wales, and possibly one of his brothers, were being courted by the Fascists. To find out how deeply they were involved with the German Brownshirts, I had to follow the people who were courting them—namely Hausmann, the German princes, and the Russian princes. These courtiers were all going to some big event, and there was a big event coming up in Italy, with Mussolini. I doubted there were two big fascist events in the next few weeks, so I needed to find out if the English princes were planning to go to Rome. If they were, I had to stop them before they embarrassed the British government by proclaiming to be anti-democratic and pro-German.

With these clues laid out, it was clear that I needed to keep following Felix and Theo until their royal connections led me to the English princes. That meant using Theo; I winced. Theo was such a sweet lover, a lovely man, I didn't want to exploit him and his connections. But as he had

asked me to look out for Felix, there wasn't any way around it. I would
see if I could get Theo to Nancy Cunard's party tonight.

I would also ask him about Lazarev. Why was Lazarev at Theo's apartment in the early morning? When did Lazarev stop being an art dealer—or
had he never stopped, and was now leading a double life? The more I knew
about Lazarev, the better placed I would be when I questioned him, a prospect about as enticing as nursing a flu patient through his death rattle. Fry
could say what he liked; I wasn't going to use physical violence.

The threat of pain called forth memories of Fox. His silver voice over
the operating table, the air reeking of the butchers', the floor slippery
with blood.

I pushed away the memory; I was in Paris, I was home. Madeleine gave
me a little nod and a smile, she was getting used to my whims and lack
of routine. I ordered some bread and cheese; I needed a bit more inside
me today than just smoke and pastry. Was it the crisp air whipping up
an appetite, or the distances I walked in Paris? Was it simply time, that
I was getting further away from my own heartbreak? I spread the soft
cheese thickly on the bread. I was sleeping better than I had for months,
neither passing out with exhaustion, nor fretful and fitful. I still had the
usual bad dreams of the war, but here I was in company, I wasn't isolated
in my terrace. One of the old men nodded hello to me as he caught my
eye, before going back to his game of chess. Whatever Fox wanted, here
I could survive it.

Which meant I had to bait him, draw him out somehow. He had left
a note for me in my letter box. Could I do the same? Did he have copy of
the key? Awful if so, but useful to know. I scrawled a little note for him:

Art thou pale for weariness

Just that, the first line of a Shelley poem. That would tell him all he
needed to know and would hopefully conjure up a meeting place, time,
or telephone number. The thought of getting the better of Fox sharpened
my appetite.

❧

"I'm so sorry to have woken you this morning, darling Theo."

He kissed my hand and settled into his chair at the Rotonde. I had chosen a table outside, the heater behind me warming the collar of my coat, the four corners of the boulevards busy with cars, horses, and people.

"As I said, you are allowed. *Un café crème, s'il vous plaît.*" He turned back from the waiter. "Actually, there is a long list of people who are allowed—Irène and Felix, all my brothers, my dearest Mama of course, but she stays in bed longer than I do, Vanya on my instructions—and of all of those, you are the best of all. But you usually don't wake me up, you wait for me to get bored of ferrying rich opera-lovers, bourgeois philanderers, and stinking pimps and come knocking at your door."

"Well, I thought you could skip the stinking pimps for today. Will you come to a party with me tonight? It'll be a rough and ready bohemian party, right here at the Rotonde, thrown by heiress Nancy Cunard. You won't need your dinner suit."

"Or my tuxedo manners."

"But you might need your aristocratic nose for family. You've been worried about Felix, the company he keeps . . . at this party, there will be some Russian artists, exiles, Whites. I need you to see if any of them have been going to political meetings with Felix."

"They wouldn't tell me anything."

"But they might tell me. Just introduce me, I'll do the rest." I swigged the last of the coffee in my cup to avoid his gaze. "By the way, what did Lazarev want the other morning?"

"Lazarev? You mean Arkady Nikolaievitch?"

"Yes, him. I saw him at your apartment, the morning after the ball."

"Do you know everyone?"

"By reputation at least. I thought Lazarev was an art dealer. Early morning is an odd time to negotiate a sale, isn't it?"

"Felix brought some art with him from Russia, to much fanfare—two paintings by Rembrandt. He sold them last year, to an American, I believe. They're the only people still with money! Arkady Nikolaievitch wanted to know what else Felix had to sell . . . but I haven't seen him since, well, not for a long time."

"Can you ask and tell me tonight?"

"As you wish, mademoiselle." He gave a mock bow. The trees on the boulevard stroked the pale stone.

"Drink up, Theo. You've got a shift to get through before we meet again."

Under the table, he flicked up the hem of my skirt to stroke my thigh. "Do I?"

He finally left to get ready for the party, giving me just enough time to post my write-up of the Chanel ball to the *Star*. I felt strangely proud that I had managed, after much swearing and crumpled paper, to type it up without mistakes and strangely sad that it wouldn't be Bertie who'd open it and giggle first. I checked my letter box multiple times but there were no telegrams announcing Bertie's or Tom's arrival, and the note for Fox was still there.

"THAT DA DA STRAIN"

I watched Maisie as she ascended the Metro stairs. Her look had changed so much in the past year. Her clothes were a better cut and she wore them with more confidence. Her dress was black and plum and she wore a black velvet coat over it, without ostentation or excessive ornament. Her outfit drew attention to her graceful neck, her bright eyes, and her height. When those bright eyes saw mine, she grinned; that hadn't changed. I thought she might laugh where she stood.

"Katie King, you're like a syncopated ghost."

"I'm not too waifish today then?"

"Not more than I expected. I like this jazzy red number you have on. You look like a neon nightclub sign."

"Or a brothel lantern."

She laughed. "You're too discerning. But you can be a sailor's delight if you like."

"I wouldn't mind a sailor, if you have one handy."

"You should leave that to your Soho friend." She kissed me on both cheeks like a proper Parisienne. "But really, Katie, I think you must have been eating."

"People are feeding me."

"It's good to know some things don't change."

"This way." I linked my arm in hers and pulled her toward a quiet café. "We have a couple of things to discuss before the party."

"Political things? Or gossipy things?"

"No difference in my world. Or yours either, I guess." We took a seat at a terrasse table and I ordered us some food.

"Chips with champagne? Katie, are you mad?"

"It's my favorite! Bubbles and salt: what could be better?"

"Ray would have a fit."

"Ray's French." I shrugged. "Sydney would think I'm sophisticated."

"You've spent too long away." She gulped her drink. "Now, tell me everything."

I went over all the clues I had so far. Maisie nodded, taking everything in. She behaved differently to last year, just subtly, she was more focused, more used to using her intelligence to take in ideas, remembering names, filing away important details. When we were discussing fascism last year, she kept forgetting the names of the Brownshirts and other factions. Now she remembered everything and brought information of her own.

"This might help you, Katie. I asked Ray to gather any gossip about the Fascists for me—here, in Italy, in Germany, anything that came his way."

"Ray . . . supports you working with me?"

"Of course! He wants Hausmann out of Paris and preferably out of France. But he hasn't heard much about fascism. It's too small, compared with how much everyone is looking east to the Bolsheviks with a shudder. They suspect Paris is full of Cheka spies, Russian exiles who are being blackmailed, that sort of thing."

I immediately thought of Lazarev at the Communist Party meeting.

"But he has heard that Weimar has a headache about Munich. Munich is increasingly, what was his word, 'agitated'—they declare themselves to be a Free State, their streets are crawling with Brownshirts, and fanatical newspapers and pamphlets crowd out the more temperate publications.

It's a slender link, but if there's any way we can show Hausmann is German, Ray can have him quietly deported."

"I think it might be easier to find Hausmann at this Rome event."

"And you think that this is where the princes are headed? It sounds like a good place for Felix and company to show their allegiance to the forces that oppose Bolshevism."

"I'll bring my camera. We'll gather evidence." I played with the chips on the plate. "What else have you heard from Ray?"

"I haven't heard anything about your mother, Katie." She squeezed my hand across the table, a sleek movement that started with a loving look and ended with her finishing her champagne. "I move in the wrong circles."

"I expect I'll find out more tonight. It's time, Maisie. Let's go."

"Wait! I haven't finished the chips!"

⟡

Henri smiled broadly when he saw me and led me through the café to a private room upstairs. I heard the party from the bottom of the stairs, jazzy guitar and screeches of laughter, thumps and scrapes, and the jangle of bangles.

"Mademoiselle Kiki, I believe your party is just this way."

"Henri . . . will I need whisky for this, or will champagne suffice?"

"I think champagne will suffice, mademoiselle," he said as we climbed, "For now."

Henri gathered some empty glasses and plates before heading back downstairs. The hostess caught sight of us and moved our way, her eyes obscured by a little veil from her hat.

"Kiki!" Her voice held harmonies. "So glad you could make it and at such short notice. Not that short notice matters very much around here, artists will go anywhere at the end of the day. Poets are even worse, I should know! But I don't know whether I should ban you writing about this party in your column or encourage it." Her silky black sleeves rippled with the rhythm of her bangles.

"You won't have a choice. But my readers are mostly interested in film stars and princesses. Being a king in the art world won't mean much to them."

"And to you?" Nancy said in French, turning to Maisie, her blue-green eyes demanding and critical.

"This is Maisie Chevallier, my oldest friend from the war." I returned us to English. "Maisie, this is Nancy Cunard, our poetess hostess."

"It means the world to me," said Maisie. "It's one of the reasons I stayed in Paris after the war! That, and my husband." She smiled and I had to hold in my laughter. I had never heard her talk about art or even seen her read more than the latest thriller as we relaxed after our shift.

"You'll be overjoyed to hear, then, that later we're having some readings from Eliot's new poem, 'The Waste Land.' I'm trying to persuade Fujita not to join in. I don't think it'd have the right gravity."

"Why not?" asked Maisie. "I've never met him."

"Fujita's voice is like a Japanese lullaby, soft and high. If he intoned 'April is the cruellest month,' everyone would think of their mistresses and leave the party."

"Will you read?" I asked.

"That goes without saying." She floated off in a swirl of silk and veil.

Maisie raised her eyebrows with her champagne.

"Since when do you like avant-garde art, Mrs. Chevallier?"

"Since I needed some cultural cache at our cocktail nights with Ray's colleagues. Yes, cocktails; we have to show we're modern and forward-thinking. Our walls were bare and it was remarked upon. When I wasn't on shift, Ray and I spent a few Saturday nights at galleries. Here in Montparnasse, and a few on our side of the river too. We look for new French artists, of course, so even if we could afford a Picasso, we wouldn't buy one because he's Spanish. We would love a Matisse but he's too expensive. We have—"

"Maisie, I had no idea!"

"I like it! Seeing the work, meeting the artist, seeing that odd mix-ture of arrogance and gratitude when we bring out the checkbook. My favorite is the Robert Delaunay we have. I like his wife's work better, but of course, she's not French. And all the Fauvists, they're so colorful."

"Well, yes, that's the point. Maise, I have to admit, I'm impressed."

She raised an eyebrow archly, then grinned. "They'd be a bit taken aback on the mission, whaddaya reckon? I have to admit, I impress myself. More importantly, we impress Ray's colleagues, who now think Ray is a man of the now, and with a future, because our artworks are avant-garde. Luckily I don't give a fig for all that French subtle-is-elegant crap."

"But that's how you dress."

"Clothing's different. I leave the sartorial fireworks to you, Katie King."

The night came in kaleidoscopic color. Maisie's limbs loosened with the jazz and wine, she blew smoke rings from her cigarette and so attracted the red-headed artist next to us. Henri came up and down the stairs with plates of chips and sausage, oysters and smoked salmon, pâté on toast and tiny little pickles and even an entire wheel of cheese that the partygoers attacked with spoons. I met Fujita, dressed in a golden gown, chatting to a suited Man Ray. It turned out they're my neighbors and they insisted I join their discussion about negative capability. Maisie found her Fauvist playing the banjo in a corner. More cheese and salami found their way into my mouth than would have been possible even a few weeks ago.

I saw Theo's regal height in the doorway.

"Kiki, darling." He kissed me on both cheeks and the lips.

"Welcome to our motley crew!" Nancy Cunard had come up behind us. "These are the aristocrats of art."

"It's a pleasure to be among such majesty." Theo's voice rumbled as he kissed Nancy's hand. She smiled like a pixie.

"I'm sorry I don't have a real Red here," she said, "to have a proper political discussion. We only have champagne socialists."

"Equal distribution of champagne is the only socialism I can toast," said Theo, accepting a glass from Henri as he passed.

"We do have some of your fellow countrymen . . . over there, that's Zadkine and that's Vasilieff. Surely you know Marie, everyone does."

"Even poor princes? It's true," said Theo. "Kiki, shall we?"

We followed Nancy over to a man and a woman deep in conversation in a mixture of Russian and French. The woman, short with curly hair, was explaining something about a studio and lessons and helping, but the amount of Russian in her sentences meant I couldn't understand much. The man, skinny with a mop of dark hair, listened intently to the woman, until he saw Nancy and looked up, a bit dazed.

"Theo!" exclaimed the woman before Nancy could speak, grabbing Theo by the arms and pulling him down so she could kiss him on both cheeks. "How wonderful! I didn't know you knew Nancy!"

"Oh, he doesn't," said Nancy, "but exiles are always welcome."

Theo bowed and extended his hand to the dazed man. "We haven't met. Theo Romanov."

"Oh!" said the man, shaking hands, "Really? Sorry . . . Osip Zadkine. How funny!" He gave a nervous high-pitched laugh. "After never meeting anyone more noble than the local mayor, you're the second prince I've met in a week. Though the other prince was German . . . Do they still count?"

"As princes or as people?" asked Nancy. "As princes, yes. As people, debatable."

"Oh well, he was certainly a prince. Courteous but huffy with a very funny accent to his French. Worse than mine!"

"Yours isn't nearly as bad as you think," said Marie. "Really, we can understand you when you don't pepper it with Russian."

"I only use Russian when I speak to you, Masha!"

"Who was this prince?" I asked.

"Ah . . . Phillip? Someone else introduced him with a 'von' somewhere in the name and then everyone called him 'sir.' He was here from Italy, he's an interior designer, of all things. Do princes need a job nowadays?"

"They do indeed," said Theo with a theatrical sigh. "When revolutionary governments take your lands, houses, artwork, and career in the military, then we have to start using our university educations."

"Sounds dreadful." Nancy's voice dripped with sarcasm and Theo laughed. "I'm sure I'll never use all my lessons in embroidery."

"Darlings, you should have run away to art school, like I did!" Marie gestured so that her sleeves threatened to empty glasses. "My father was a tyrant too, I simply defied him."

"It wasn't father who was the problem, it was mother," said Nancy.

"Same," I said. "I wonder if these princes have problematic mothers."

"They do," said Theo. "But this Phillip . . ."

"Don't tell us you're related," said Nancy.

"It's not merely possible, it's likely. The tsarina was German, after all, and the tsar was my uncle."

A hush descended over us. Even the most revolutionary soul would have been hard-pressed to resist the simple sadness in Theo's statement.

"Long faces are for horses." A head popped up at Nancy's elbow, with dark hair and pale skin punctuated by a monocle. "Neigh!"

"Tristan!" Nancy kissed him. "This is Tristan Tzara, Dadaist extraordinaire. We're talking princes. Have you met a German one lately?"

"Oh, that Phillip fellow at the salon last week?"

"Yes, him!" Zadkine looked like he'd been saved from jail.

"Prince Flip-Flop von Lessen Messen Nessen. Thought he knew all about art because he'd spent a few months in Italy. Spoke about beauty like it existed. *Idiota!*"

"Prince Phillip von Hessen?" asked Theo. "I do know him. He's in Paris, is he?"

"People appear in this city and then disappear and then reappear and then dance through your dreams," said Tzara. "Flip-Flops are lower than the stars, they can never grace the gutter."

Nancy laughed. "You're wonderful."

"For you, dearest dragon, I would sacrifice all garbage and lie with the fishes." He kissed her wrist, to her obvious delight, and she grabbed a bottle and pulled him away to a quiet corner.

"We must ask Irène about Phillip," Theo said. "She might know where to find him."

"How is your dear sister?" asked Marie. "I haven't seen her in an age! Or Felix."

"Felix Yusupov?" asked Osip. "Oh, of course!"

Theo nodded, casually negotiating Zadkine's starstruck awe. Marie and Theo quickly fell into a semi-private chat about who turned up at Marie Vassilieff's studio, here in Montparnasse, for tea and blinis. I turned to Zadkine.

"It appears that Marie runs a community exchange for Russian exiles alongside her artist's studio," I said.

"I've certainly used it, when I needed a taste of home. Vodka with pickles and a sad song, that sort of thing. I'm not very Russian, to be honest. I'm a French citizen, I was a stretcher-bearer for France in the war, and I spent my youth in England. But occasionally, I hear a note, feel a tendril of cold, and the need comes upon me. And Masha is wonderful company."

"And others too, I imagine. Is that where you met Prince Phillip?"

"God no!" He laughed. "Though I wouldn't know a prince unless he told me. I met my wife Valentine there and often my neighbors, Fujita and Leger . . . No, it was very strange meeting a prince, talking to me solicitously as though he thought I was a real person. They didn't used to in Russia, you see, they sort of talked down or around or just pretended you weren't there. Here, of course, they've all been pulled down to street level and have to acknowledge us ordinary folk." Zadkine shrugged. "Princes: who needs them? Tell me, how did you get invited to this bacchanal? Do you know Nancy from England?"

That was clearly all I was going to find out about Prince Phillip von Flip-Flop and our conversation turned to chit-chat until Theo rejoined us. Theo leaned down to kiss my cheek and whispered, "I have more on that prince for you," before he left to find us more champagne.

"Katie!" Maisie hooked my elbow and pulled me toward her banjo player in the corner. "You have to meet André. He reckons he knows a Cordelia King."

A natty man with a pencil moustache sat tunelessly strumming a banjo. He smiled when he saw Maisie.

"Hello! It is delightful to be flattered by such a beautiful, knowledgeable woman," he said, "though I think her knowledge is more flattering than her beauty."

"I should hope so," I said. "Beauty fades but knowledge can only increase."

"True beauty never fades," he said with a flirtatious smile at Maisie.

"This is my friend, Katie King Button. This is André Derain."

This was the artist Harry said I should find; my handshake was too eager.

"Call me Kiki."

"She's the daughter of Cordelia King Button."

"Aha!" André said. "Your friend is a tireless advocate. You want to know about her? First tell me: is she really dead?"

I nodded. He sighed and played a discordant chord.

"That is truly terrible. Have you told Matisse?"

"Why?"

"You must! She sat so patiently for Matisse, hour after hour, as he threw away his work, as he had his usual struggle to get everything exactly so. Henri is like a wind-up toy, all tension and a clattering pace until he needs his pipe, his dinner, and winding up again. His wife is an absolute slave to his work, but he had a soft spot for Cordelia. Her patience was divine, she seemed to grow more beautiful and more spiritual as the hours wore on. It was uncanny. Most people are the opposite, they become objects, no better than the chair they sit on. Not Cordelia; she commanded that you look, that you like, that you worship. She was so kind about our worship too!" He looked into a pitiful distance.

"Was Matisse . . ." The party laughter crowded in on me, I couldn't properly frame my thoughts. "Were my mother and Matisse . . ."

"Lovers? They could have been. They certainly spent enough time together—and she never accepted my advances, so it must be so! No, really, Matisse could be very jealous. Every model knew it was either

Matisse or the rest of the world. He'll be in town again next week, he's coming to dinner with me. Join us! At least for apperitifs. You too, Madame Chevallier." He kissed Maisie's hand, then turned to a man half a room away. "Constantin! I have dreadful news!"

A man with deep set eyes and a salt-and-pepper beard came over, drinking from a bottle of red wine. André lit him a cigarette as he topped up André's glass.

"Andrusha, don't leave me in suspense," said Constantin.

"You remember Cordelia King Button?" said André.

"An angel."

"She's joined them, according to her daughter here."

He kissed my hand. "Mademoiselle, I am infinitely sorry. What a blessing to have had her for a mother."

"I'm trying to find out who . . ."

"Who were her *cher amants*," said André. "She was close to Matisse, wasn't she?"

"I saw her with Rodin . . . but she wasn't a muse for Rodin. But yes, Matisse. Matisse would know. They were friends, all that group. Always going off to paint in the countryside. I prefer it here, in Montparnasse . . . She hasn't really gone, has she?" He tutted at my nod. "This is a tragedy. I have a bust of her in my studio still. You must see it."

André smiled. "You haven't introduced yourself, Constantin."

"Apologies! Constantin Brancusi. I have a studio just a short walk away. Pop in any morning, I'm always working."

"Always clockworking, always lurking, always berzerking," Tristan Tzara popped up between André and Constantin.

"Tristan!" Constantin laughed. "Where have you been?" He switched to Romanian and the party flowed on.

I stood still for a moment. These men knew my mother. It seemed that everyone knew my mother, either well or by reputation. She had been painted by Fauvists and sculpted by Cubists. Anyone else would have boasted about how cosmopolitan they were, how bohemian, how modern. Even her diaries never said exactly what she had done. As I watched Maisie flirt expertly with André and Constantin, and Theo smooth back his hair as he talked to Nancy, I wondered if my mother never properly wrote about it as a way of not acknowledging what she was missing. Paris and London were the center of culture, then and now, and my mother had been a star in both. Surely, in this milieu, a pregnancy would not have been enough to scare her across the world? But then, she didn't have a war to loosen bonds and break ties. She wasn't free in the way I was now free.

"Katie." Maisie pulled me close and kissed my cheek. "Enough brooding, we can do that tomorrow. Tonight, we dance."

"DANCING FOOL"

And we did. First me and Maisie, then Theo and Maisie, then Tzara and Brancusi on the tables, then Theo and Vasilieff and Zadkine in a Cossack dance, and on and on until the champagne ran dry and our feet were blistered and the cheese wheel was stamped into the floor. We bundled Maisie into a taxi before Theo and I strolled up the street to my apartment.

"Let us always be something to each other, Miss Kiki Button," said Theo as we reached my building. "I need your vitality in my life forever."

"Do you smell that?" I was sure I could smell Fox's cigarettes.

"I smell your sweat mixed with your perfume, some garbage . . . ah, some cat piss . . ."

"No, no, that tobacco smell—Sobranies, a Russian cigarette."

"I can only smell my own," he said as he lit up. He held one out to me but I waved it away. All the doors were locked on my side of the road. I ran over the other side, my heels clicking down a little street searching for . . . I realized I was looking for a glowing ruby of cigarette end set against silver hair. I was being utterly ridiculous, but I couldn't stop myself, I scanned the street for any sign of life. All I saw was tabby cat stalk across the cobbles, its white fur flashing at me.

"Well?" The shadows from the streetlamp gave Theo a bruised look.

I shrugged and took the half-consumed cigarette from Theo, tapping off the long plume of ash, to mask the Sobranie-smell that lingered in my memory. Fox couldn't possibly be here, in Montparnasse, watching me . . . except he could, he absolutely could. I scanned the street one more time; I heard nothing, I saw nothing, everything was as it should be, except me. Theo watched, his head to one side, but I couldn't figure out his expression in the darkness. I blew a plume of smoke into the sky and kissed him full on the mouth, teasing him, enticing him to bend forward and hold me close so he could kiss me properly, a piece of seduction designed to distract us both.

"Well." He grinned.

"Well then." It worked; I thought only of his buttons now. I flicked away the cigarette, took his hand and we hurried upstairs to rid ourselves of the last raiments of night.

⤬

"So, Theo, are you really related to Prince Phillip von Whathisface?"

"Ah yes, I said I had more on that prince for you, didn't I?" He put his croissant down and wiped his fingers on the napkin. We were breakfasting together at a suitably midday time, Theo's suit still smelling of last night's champagne, remnants of party makeup still haunting my eyes. I hadn't been able to find my brush and my hair was as bouffant as my dress was sleek. Madeleine Petit suppressed her smile when she saw us.

"Well, yes, I am related to Phillip von Hessen, though distantly. The simple summary is that we're all related through Queen Victoria, but the longer explanation . . . well, the longer explanation is very long, but the kaiser is Phillip's uncle, the tsar is my uncle, and the kaiser and the tsar were both grandsons of Queen Victoria, the same as your king."

"Have you ever met Prince Phillip?"

"No, but it would be easy enough to do. Felix may have met him, my mother may have, someone would know something about his being in

Paris. The aristocracy is like a rural village—everyone knows everyone's business and feels obliged to have an opinion."

"Even when you've escaped halfway across a continent?"

"Phillip hasn't, he's only come from Frankfurt. That's a few hours away."

"How does it feel to have fought against your own family in the war?"

"How does it feel to have my family killed by Bolsheviks? How does it feel to be an exile, a taxi driver, living through rolling revolutions?" He stared at his croissaint. "I take each day as it comes, golden one. If nothing had changed, I'd be married by now and living in a beautiful apartment. A safe life, comfortable and dull. Now my life is exciting because it is insecure, unpredictable, unexpected. I know freedom and ecstasy and despair." He sighed. "Most of all, I realize I can't change it. Felix is wrong. The monarchy will not return. We royals . . . we need to find a new way to contribute to the world, now that the people no longer revere us as gods."

The old men argued over their chess and today's newspaper fluttered on the counter. I pushed Theo's croissant toward him.

"This is quite intense for a breakfast conversation."

"*Ma chérie*," he took my wrist and planted a lingering kiss. "We were brought up to believe family is everything and our duty to our country is the price of privilege. The Bolsheviks, the Weimar revolutionaries, the trenches, blew all of that up. Every day Felix rises and looks out the window with a sigh. Our lives are limbless and gas-blind. This is what the wars have done to us."

Yes, I thought, whatever happened, we would always be something to each other. His dark eyes demanded it.

"And Lazarev?" I asked, "Why was he at your house?"

"Felix denied he was there." Theo shrugged. "I'm sorry to disappoint."

"You never disappoint, Theo, especially when you can introduce me to Prince Phillip von Hessen."

"You want to meet him?"

"I have a suspicion that Felix's friend, Edouard, has him on his list. If I find Phillip, I can help Felix."

"I see." His tone of voice said that he didn't believe me. "You want to write about him, don't you? For your magazine."

I grinned sheepishly; please, I thought, let him think that this was my ulterior motive.

"Would that be so bad?"

"Nothing you do is so bad, Kiki."

"Not unless you request it."

And he laughed, then, loud and deep, stretching as he remembered last night. We chatted through the rest of breakfast, the clouds low outside, a tin hat on the day. I don't know if it was his long pauses and longer gazes, or the knowledge of approaching winter with its short, dark days, but there was a farewell feeling between us. I think he felt it too, as when he got in his taxi, he demanded to know when I could meet him and soon, his hand on my hip through the window. "I have a column to write!" I teased. I also had a mission to complete and for that he could only be a hindrance.

"I GAVE YOU UP JUST BEFORE
YOU THREW ME DOWN"

I had the princes in sight. I was sure that these German princes would lead me to the English princes. Theo had said that all these royal houses were related, but the German and the British were more intertwined than most. Some British princes had been stripped of their titles in the war because they fought as Germans. The British royal family was more than half German—if Theo could get me introduced to even one of these German *prinzen* then I was a good way to completing the mission.

And a good way to getting the real payment from Fox. I checked my letter box again, standing in the doorway of my building, the cold eddies blowing dust around my ankles. No letter from Fox, and my letter to him was still there. What had he meant by contacting me with that hand-written note? Had I really smelt Sobranies last night or was I becoming paranoid? And what about those photos: "teach me half the gladness that thy brain must know." Maybe that was simply an invitation to do more spy work . . . except that he had evidence that Tom was innocent.

He knew, for a fact, that Tom was not a traitor, even if he was a deserter. Fox could change Tom's life—but at what price? This is what scared me.

There was another letter, delivered that morning. I didn't recognize the handwriting.

CALL ASAP FRY

I clipped quickly to Montparnasse station, my black suede boots rapping on the cobblestones, my black boucle coat and black silk dress making me feel like a true Parisienne. I had no problem with Fox listening to this call. I caught Delphine's eye as I entered the station but she gave her head a little shake: no news. I made a note to buy some matches on the way out.

"Bacon."

"Fry, it's Kiki."

"You need a code name."

"'She' will do."

"She who must be obeyed?" I could hear the laughter in his voice.

"And why not?"

"And who is Kalikrates, then? Who is Holly?"

"Take your pick. But I didn't call you up for literary banter."

"No. We have Lazarev. Come now." He started rattling off an address as I scrambled to scribble it down in my notebook.

"But . . . that's a canal on the city limits."

"Bring wellingtons. It's going to get a little . . . slippery."

I lit a cigarette outside the telephone booths. I didn't like the sound of "slippery." Fry seemed intent on making me Lady Macbeth. Was this on Fox's orders? Was I supposed to be tarnished, stained, compromised in some way? If I participated in some violent act, it would certainly put me more in his power. I had managed to get through the war without firing a gun, priming a bomb, hitting, kicking, or in any way hurting my quarry. Fox wanted to change the dynamic, or Fry did, or they both did as some sort of initiation. I smoked my cigarette too quickly. I jumped in a taxi but barely paid attention to the driver's chat. I didn't give a fig about initiation. I could get better results without it. The halting, jolting traffic flickered in the window frame. I would not spill blood. I would actively resist.

⟨⟩

I turned up at a dockside warehouse in the same clothes, cigarettes restocked, and a dash of whisky for courage from the café nearest the canal. No true Parisienne would walk through the streets in gumboots; that was for horsey women in the British Home Counties, not sophisticated society girls on the ancient cobbles. If there was going to be dirt, then the black would hide it, but I was determined that the only dirt I would get would be the gossipy kind. The warehouse windows wept tears of rust down the gray wooden walls. Inside, wet concrete floors were streaked green and black, a dripping tap somewhere mixed with the thuds and grunts coming from deep inside the cavernous space. The warehouse was empty but for some broken furniture, open crates, and a light that crept out from behind a far wall. That must be where Fry was holding Lazarev. I moved forward carefully so my boots wouldn't make a sound. I wanted to hear what they were saying, maybe even see what they were doing, before Fry presented Lazarev to me. I could hear nothing but heavy breathing then the occasional thud followed by a groan.

Lazarev sat in a chair, his head hanging on his chest, his arms bound behind his back. There was blood on his face and on his light gray suit, along with rust, dirt, and mold, as if he'd been dragged along the floor to this spot. Fry sat behind a wooden table a good few meters away from him, smoking and watching. Fry slammed his hand on the table and Lazarev said, "No," as he flinched; this accounted for the thuds and moans. I couldn't see a second agent; did Fry work without backup? Or was I the backup? The only weapon I had with me was my camera and that was more metaphor than blunt instrument. Lazarev panted and Fry drummed his fingers on the table.

"Nice suit." I lounged against the doorframe and lit a cigarette. Both men turned, Fry quickly with a frown, Lazarev slowly lifting his head. "My apologies, Arkady Nikolaievitch. We interrupted you on your way somewhere."

Lazarev nodded with obvious discomfort. Fry curled his lip.

"Off to see your handlers, were you?" Fry said in heavily accented French. He slammed his hand on the table again. Lazarev flinched and whimpered. I would need to take control of this interrogation before Fry's ham-fisted, hyper-masculine routine reduced Lazarev to a useless, speechless wreck.

"We saw you in Pigalle," I said and Lazarev looked at me, scared. "At the Communist Party meeting, as they tried to organize the congress. You caused quite the commotion."

Lazarev stared, his eyes wide. I could see that his lip was split and there was blood in his mouth too. The cold damp room smelt of fish.

"Before that I saw you enter the Yusupov apartment, in a beautiful suit, not unlike the one you're wearing. Which is looking a little worse for wear, I have to say. I can recommend a good laundress if you don't have one already. I'm never quite sure how Bolsheviks feel about laundresses—tell me, are they workers to be lauded or still just one rung above prostitutes?"

I looked at him as though he wasn't bleeding and tied to a chair, as though this was ordinary drawing room small talk. He cleared his throat.

"Lauded . . . workers." His voice was rough and choked. Fry smiled at me, his teeth glinting from his black beard, then crossed his arms and leaned back in his chair. He wanted to watch me put on a show; very well. I would show him just how much damage I could inflict with a charm offensive.

"You need a glass of water, Arkady Nikolaievitch. That's such a long name for my English-speaking tongue. May I call you Arkasha?" He nodded forlornly. "And you need a cigarette too, no doubt."

I saw a tap in the corner with a bucket underneath. I was relieved when it turned easily and clean water came out. There was even a little cup in the bucket; this must have been left here by the men who cleared the warehouse. I took the bucket back to Lazarev, standing by him expectantly. I knelt down with a cup full.

"Now, Arkasha, I have something I need from you. I think you know this."

He grunted.

"I would love to give you this water and a cigarette. Maybe even undo your handcuffs. You'd like that too, wouldn't you?"

He nodded.

"So, will you help me? We do have . . . other methods of persuasion, but I would hate to use them. You'd hate for me to use them, wouldn't you?"

He whimpered like he might cry.

"You'll help me." He nodded. "Very good."

I stood up and turned to Fry. "My chair." Fry nodded to another warehouse corner, but when I didn't move, he just grinned and fetched my chair for me, his walk a little jaunty, a little light for his bulk. He was clearly enjoying this show, or perhaps he was enjoying what he assumed would be my failure.

"Unlock him, please."

Fry followed my orders with only a smug grin on his face. I was close enough to Lazarev that he could have grabbed me if he'd wanted to. But as soon as Fry uncuffed him he hunched over his hands, rubbing his wrists, eyes down, head bent. I'd seen a lot of men in different moods during the war, from tinderbox rage to catatonic and all the tears and fears in between. Lazarev didn't strike me as someone about to lash out. He could hardly drag a cup of water to his mouth from the bucket, his wrists were so sore. I lit a cigarette for each of us to his mumbled thanks.

"Your friends, the Yusupovs, might be surprised to see you here."

"They aren't my friends."

"I gathered that, from the way the servants speak about you."

He gave a bitter half-laugh. "They're such snobs. Just because they stayed in service."

"And you didn't?"

"I was never a servant!"

"You were an art dealer last time we met, trying to bamboozle me at the Café Gogol. What happened?" He hung his head. "Was it Hausmann?"

He sniffed; he was almost crying. He covered his eyes.

"Did Hausmann blackmail you?"

He looked up. I tried my best to look sympathetic; it worked.

"He . . ." He rubbed his face, as though to rub out the anguish. "I thought we were partners, I thought . . ."

"He's a weasel, that one."

"A scoundrel! He only wanted to use me to get to men like Felix Felixovitch, Feodor Alexandrovitch, all of their family . . . he knew, I don't know how, but he knew Felix would be receptive to his 'ideas.' Ideas! Politics! I thought I would be safe in Paris. It's been an awful year, I just want it to end . . ."

I passed him another cigarette and lit it for him, looking at him with my best listening face. I used all my nursing training to ignore the rank smell of his sweat and where he had pissed himself. His eyes were bloodshot, both suspicious and needy. I couldn't see Fry but I heard him shift in his seat.

"You . . . you work with him?" He nodded at Fry. "You can help me? You can help get me out of Paris, out of this life?"

"Tell me what I need to know."

He looked from me to Fry, spending longer on me, searching my face. Last April he had been a flirtatious raconteur, kissing my hand and licking jam off his fingers in the café, twirling me around a dance floor and toasting me with vodka. Now his suit was stained and crumpled with some poorly darned patches at the cuffs. His hands were bruised and scraped, his nails bitten to the quick, his wrists red raw and he sat at an odd angle, as though protecting a pain in his side or back. He took another drag of the cigarette and blew the smoke over his knees with a huge sigh. Brutalizing a man had never been my method, but to protest at his treatment now would give Lazarev room to wriggle away. In this game of fear and shadows, I had to pretend and pretend. To show our true size would mean we wouldn't get the information, I wouldn't find the princes, Tom would remain in danger. It was also clear that Lazarev was ripe for talking. I pushed down all my fury at Fox and the ways he continued to manipulate me, to become a soft shoulder for Lazarev to cry on.

"I'm sick of it." Lazarev's voice held tears.

"Tell me." I could hear Fry cough at my soft, gentle tones.

"I'm sick of being scared." Lazarev exhaled more smoke. "I'm sick of looking over my shoulder, pretending, lying, sick of the whole business."

"You're a spy."

"I am an art dealer."

I cocked my head in subtle skepticism; Lazarev picked up the inference at once and began to exonerate himself in injured tones.

"I was an art dealer before the revolution! I tried to pick up the trade when I moved here. It was hard. The Russians I knew had sold most of their works already and the French had their own dealers. But I was beginning, slowly, as more Russians joined us, as young artists started to need someone who wasn't German or American, who could properly understand them. I met Hausmann at one of the parties at the Café Gogol. Eva . . ."

"I met her last year. She brought me to the Gogol."

"Yes . . . yes, that's right. She introduced me to Hausmann, said he was also interested in art, et cetera et cetera. Snake, snake that she is! She's working with him, with those Fascists . . ."

"Those Fascists . . ." I shook my head. Lazarev nodded as excitedly as his bruises allowed.

"It was all a trick! Liars! Hausmann knew a lot of rich people but knew nothing about art except its cold-blooded monetary value. He said he wanted to buy art from me. I had been cultivating relationships with the Yusupovs, Romanovs, any other Russian family who had fled to Paris and might be looking to sell their treasures. I knew no one in England but I knew there was plenty of money about. Hausmann implied that he could make those connections for me."

"But he never did."

"Nothing of the sort! Just after the summer, last year, Hausmann came to me with a very different proposition. I would steal the artwork for him, and, in return, he would not expose that I had lied about my war service." His voice had become smaller than the tap dripping in the corner. Fry scowled and made a tsk noise.

"Have a few fake medals, do you?" Fry called from behind the desk. Lazarev gave him a quick, dirty look. I hoped Fry would interrupt again; much as I hated it, a little bit of menace from Fry would help us keep the upper hand.

"No." Lazarev's eyes searched the room's corners, as if his gaze probed for an escape.

"But perhaps you didn't correct other people's . . . assumptions." I did my best to look like this was normal behavior which, in fact, I suspected it was.

"Russians don't care, the revolution has obliterated everything else. But the French, the British, people here in Paris are very particular about who fought and how. I . . . let people think I had been on the front line in Galicia. In fact, I was in Petrograd until 1917, when I fled. Exposure would have ruined my contacts . . ."

"And hence your fledgling business, and left you . . ."

"Penniless! Exiled even from my exile. I agreed to Hausmann's plan, I had to, at least to his face. I had no intention of carrying it out. That would have been beyond stupid, when it would be much more worth my while to sell the picture for him and take commission."

"You're all heart." Fry's sarcasm made Lazarev scowl.

"What would you know?" Lazarev spat blood on the floor. Fry slammed his hand on the table and Lazarev flinched. Lazarev flung an angry, scared glance at me. I decided to sigh theatrically.

"I have no control over my colleague here," I said with a resignation that I didn't need to fake, "so perhaps it might be best if you keep to your story."

He looked sulky, glancing between me and Fry as he started to suspect that I was not the angel of mercy that I seemed. I smiled in a tired way and handed him an unlit cigarette. He played with it but I didn't offer him a light. Eventually he understood that I wouldn't light it for him until I heard a bit more of his story. He coughed wetly.

"But I was contacted again, another horrendous proposition."

"The Communist Party?"

"The Cheka. They found me. It's every exile's secret fear, a threat that underlines all our days. Their agents here in Paris saw me at balls, saw me with nobles, and saw an opportunity."

"Who? Which agent?"

"I only met my handler, Smirnov." He snorted. "Smirnov! He had a Georgian accent, he was no 'Smirnov.' He'd be Smirnashvili or Smirnadze or whatever passes for Smirnov in that backwater."

"Tell me about Smirnov."

He shrugged and played with his cigarette until it drooped from the dirt and blood on his fingers.

"Not much to tell. Average height, average build, so a bit smaller than me on both counts. Georgian, but trying really hard to be Russian, to be Bolshevik. He always wore either brown or gray and looked like a factory worker—thick wool pants, wool waistcoat, neckerchief, flat cap, blazer. Black eyes and black hair. Oh yeah, he had a missing front tooth and the tops of these fingers," he indicated the ring and pinky on his left hand, "were also missing. Clean-shaven, which he lamented." Lazarev reached shakily down for some more water, spilling it on himself when Fry slammed his hand against the table once more.

"Come on! More details! Where did you meet him, when, how often—we haven't got all day!"

Lazarev cringed and a shiver went through him. "Every fortnight. After the Communist Party meetings—which he also attended—we'd choose a bar in Pigalle, a different one every time, always dingy and full of drunks. Otherwise we'd meet in Belleville, where he had a room, in a different café or bistro each time. I would have to get changed into my 'worker's costume' before I met him. Can you imagine this suit in Belleville?"

"I can now." Fry sneered. Lazarev was still trembling. I lit his cigarette for him.

"He made you join the Party. What else?"

"I had to report on the activities of certain noblemen and women to Smirnov. This included reporting on Hausmann. In return, no payment, not even of expenses. They simply would not kill me or my family still in Russia—my brother and his wife, my nieces, my ancient mother. I haven't seen any of them for years, obviously, but he showed me photos of my nieces going to school in their little uniforms, my sister-in-law waiting in a bread line, my mother haggling for tobacco."

"And your brother?"

"No photo. They said he was working for the government in Novosibirsk. He's a teacher; I have no idea what he should be doing there." He dragged hard on his cigarette. All was still but for the dripping tap, the sound of the canal outside.

"So . . . you had to ingratiate yourself with noble families for both the Cheka and for Hausmann. You had to report on them for the Cheka and pretend to steal their belongings for Hausmann. Correct?"

Lazarev nodded. "Hausmann's threat was nothing compared to the Cheka's, but if he exposed me, I would no longer be useful to the Cheka and they would kill my family. So, I had to pretend to be useful to Hausmann, and to pretend to deal in art, to go to balls one night and meetings in Pigalle the next. I'm a good salesman, but these lies were a tough sell, even for me."

"But someone found you out."

"No one found me out! Except you." He glanced angrily at Fry. "Hausmann changed his mind about stealing artwork when he realized that he could just charm the princes into giving him money. Felix Felixovitch has handed over more than one check. I know; Hausmann showed me when he boasted. He's trying to bring all those Romanovs into the movement too. Hausmann made me go to a meeting of his Brownshirts, his

Fascists—all bloody Germans, all noblemen, all old soldiers." He spat
on the floor again, cleaning his mouth of bloody mucus.

"You loved it," said Fry.

"No." Lazarev scowled. "I hated it. Almost as much as the Communists, both of them so . . . blind to who people really are. The Fascists
talked about restoring monarchy, restoring order, bringing Europe back
to civilization, reducing the rabble . . ."

"The opposite of the Communist Party meetings." I smiled. Lazarev
looked pathetically grateful.

"There were some Germans there, princes or dukes or some such,
speaking to Hausmann in English and wearing their brown shirts.
They—well, him, really—he gave the best speech. Hausmann introduced
him as Carl Eduard, or Charlie Coburg."

This made Fry sit up with a scrape of his chair. Lazarev looked at
him, scared, and Fry stood up and walked slowly toward him. Lazarev
shrank into his seat.

"What did Charlie Coburg say?" Fry's voice was like a rusty knife.

"He said . . ." Lazarev gulped and tried to pull his voice down from its
fearful pitch. "He said they were on the cusp of achieving true power. He
said that they were to prepare for a big event, a meeting, soon."

"Where?" Fry took a step closer.

"In Rome." Lazarev didn't try to control his voice now. "A big march
with the Italian Fascists in their black shirts. It's supposed to show the
world that Bolshevism has a new and powerful enemy."

"When is the march?"

"I don't know—"

"Find out."

"I can't!" Lazarev wailed. "Someone will have seen me talk to you!
They're going to kill me! You have to get me out of Paris! I've done
everything you asked!" His squeaky voice was surely irritating, but Fry
didn't need to stop it with a slap, certainly not one that brought blood to
Lazarev's lip. Lazarev cowered against the chair.

"When did you find out about the meeting?" I asked.

"You said you'd help me." Lazarev's face had become slack with fear. I pushed away my growing repugnance for this game so I could finish the interrogation.

"Tell me more about Charlie Coburg. Tell me why you saw Felix yesterday."

"I tried to find out more about Charlie Coburg but I couldn't because Felix wouldn't see me and Hausmann wouldn't see me." Lazarev's voice wheedled. "I found out about the meeting last week. I told Smirnov all this yesterday . . . You have to help me. I'm not useful to Hausmann anymore, and my family in Russia . . ."

"We will, of course," I hoped. "But you might need some more regular meetings with my colleague here to inform him of your dealings with Smirnov and Hausmann."

"But . . ." He glanced at Fry and leaned forward to me. "We should work together, you and me. I've seen you with Feodor Alexandrovich, I've seen you with all those artists, you could be an art buyer, a would-be princess with taste and discernment, you're a much better cover. Please. Please!" His voice rose in pitch as Fry dragged him away. I stood and tried to look sympathetic, but I was furious at Fry for being so heavy-handed. A man, who had silently and disconcertingly appeared in the doorway, stepped forward and put handcuffs back on Lazarev. He had some other kind of fabric in his hand, but then Lazarev was around the other side of the wall, his voice was muffled, and I couldn't see what was happening. Fry watched from the doorway, then came over to the bucket by Lazarev's chair to rinse his hands.

"Well, that got us some useful information. Very well played too, Miss Button. I enjoyed our nice-guy, tough-guy routine."

"I know you bloody well did," I said and he had the gall the grin. "I thought it was vile. What the hell did you treat him like that for?"

"These kind of men . . ." He waved his hand dismissively.

"These kind of men respond very well to charm, as I have shown. He was dying to talk. I could have done it all without a drop spilt, without all this ridiculous subterfuge."

"You do realize that you're a spy, don't you? Subterfuge should be second nature."

"After the war, the only second nature I want is an increased tolerance for whisky. And who was that other bloke, the shadow at the doorway?"

"A friend."

"Oh, you can't tell me? You rough up Lazarev in front of me, you expect me to do the same, and you won't tell me who I'm working with? Is this directive from Fox or is this your own little bit of manipulation?"

"Settle, petal . . ."

"Give me Fox's contact number here."

"I don't have it."

"That is enough!" I was yelling now, the sound vibrating through the empty warehouse. Fry stood up, surprised, but I was in full flight. "I don't even take this kind of treatment from Fox, and next to him, you are nothing. Give me his number."

Fry blinked a couple of times. "Look, we have to . . ."

"Now!"

Fry exhaled, puffing out his cheeks, raising his eyebrows, trying to make comic his real discomfort. "He stays with the ambassador. I send word to him via the embassy. I ask him to meet me at Angelina's for tea and then he returns my call from a private line."

"Thank you." He could hear that I meant *I hate you* and winced slightly. "I'll be in touch."

He called after me, some excuse or other, but I answered only with the ring of my footfalls as I marched out of the warehouse.

"WHO CARES?"

"Fox." His voice was steel once again. This was clearly his work voice; it seemed he kept his quicksilver just for me.

"I think we should meet at Angelina's for tea, don't you? It's been such a long time."

I heard a sharp intake of breath; could it really be that I had made him gasp?

"Vixen."

"As you hear. Art thou pale for weariness, wandering companionless, like a joyless eye that finds no object for its constancy?"

There was a long pause.

"Was Fry supposed to keep the code secret? You must know I'm a little more resourceful than that, my Ozymandias."

"Yours, am I?" His voice held a slight croak.

"My stone in the desert, my trunkless legs? Sure, why not."

"Why not . . ." I could hear him light up. "Where are you?"

"Saint Germain 7562."

He hung up without a word. I had never before seen a street-side call box, a thing so novel I made the taxi driver drop me off beside it. It was

the perfect place to call from, as Fox could only call me back at my command. Which, seeing as I could only just command my voice not to be
furious, was probably just as well.

"Button." I answered as coldly as my hot fury would allow.

"Vixen."

"You know, a male fox is called a dog? Somehow I don't think I should
start calling you Dog. It doesn't seem right." There was a long pause where
I heard him exhale; for some reason, I expected him to bark.

"Most agents call me 'Sir'. Enjoy your privilege."

"Privilege or bondage?"

"You don't like my missives?"

"Some privacy would be better."

"Think of them as in lieu of reports."

"I'm happy to report, Fox. It's your subversive missions behind enemy
lines that make me wonder if I'll lose consciousness, status, and my
name."

Silence. Now he knew that I knew that he had sent Tom off on the
mission that had cost him his reputation.

"Do you take pictures of me too, Fox? Will I find some compromising
photographs in my letter box that seem to say that I too am a threat to
England? Will you send them to me with some Romantic poetry on the
back? 'Bliss was it in that dawn to be alive . . . '"

"'But to be young was very heaven.'" He spoke softly. "I would con-
gratulate you on your powers of deduction, but I expected nothing less."

"Fry expected less. Why did you send over an agent with such a low
regard for women?"

"How is our esteemed colleague Bacon?"

"His palm's a little itchy and he likes to scratch that itch against
another man's face. Very vulgar. But he's no Lady Macbeth, the blood
will wash right off."

"You really have been wandering companionless."

"Oh no, he's a fine companion, especially when he uses your money
to pay for my drinks. Speaking of, I'll be clinking glasses with a couple

of German princes soon—hopefully a Prince Phillip von Hessen and a Charlie Coburg."

I'd thrown in Charlie Coburg as a guess, as these names fit the telegram from Bertie. I had no idea when I might meet Charlie, but Fox's silence made me bold.

"I assume they'll know their relatives, English princes Tweedledum and Tweedledee, and we can follow the jolly gang down to Rome for a bit of a mad hatter's tea party. Or a blackshirt tea party, if you will."

"Phillip and Carl Eduard," he murmured. "You have been busy."

"And in need of funds for this jaunt. Will Fry dispense them or will they turn up like a little hand grenade in my letter box?"

"So, you don't like my missives." There was a plaintive note in his voice. Was this a reaction to my barely concealed anger?

"I never know which one's a dud and which one will explode in my face."

"I would never send you a dud."

"So, the payments you send me are valid?"

"Bacon will organize what you need."

"I mean my other payments." A pause: good, I had stopped him from hanging up. "The handkerchief, the letter, the photos—are they duds or will they obliterate the charges against Tom?"

"Don't hunt quarry that's too large, Vixen. Stick to the hens in the henhouse." His voice had turned to steel again.

"But then how can I teach you half the gladness that my brain must know?" If I was going to keep his attention I realized, suddenly and awfully, that I would need to show him my soft underbelly. "I work out this mission . . . is that all you're asking of me? I guess not."

"You guess correctly."

"So . . . tell me."

"Such harmonious madness . . ." His voice had turned silver again, it was almost wistful, there was light and laughter in it as it trailed off.

"I am listening now, Fox."

But he had gone.

"It was all I could do not to slam the phone down in frustration!"

"What does he want from you?" Maisie poured me more wine.

"I dread to know."

"But you can guess."

The combined effects of a hangover, an interrogation, and Fox were making me drink fast and smoke even faster. I'd only just bought a packet of Gitanes and I was already halfway through. I had turned up at the American Hospital just as Maisie was finishing her shift. We were sitting at a café near the metro station, where few visitors and even fewer staff ever drank, probably because it smelt strangely of crème de menthe and stale sweat. I sent up a funnel of smoke up to the stained ceiling.

"It's his voice. His voice and his handwriting are all I've had of him since the war. Everything is communicated in his quicksilver tones and spidery calligraphy."

"You make it sound almost sensual."

"It is . . . his voice runs down my back like a drop of water. His hand-writing plunges me into the cold dark Atlantic."

"Jesus. You need more wine."

"It's through his voice that I get most of my information. In the war he was always in control of himself, every aspect of his person, even his anger was used deliberately to manipulate others. But his voice on the phone is not always . . . under control. I heard him gasp on the phone today, such a little thing, but I was shocked that he was shocked. He keeps hinting that maybe he isn't such a vampire, that maybe he has a heart after all, his handwriting on little quotes from Shelley or Keats that speak of love, his voice with little glitches and hitches that suggest he means something else."

Maisie frowned as she dipped a chip in tomato sauce and mayonnaise. "And you're thinking of his marriage proposal from the end of the war."

"Yes. No."

She took my cigarette and replaced it with potato. "By the way, if you want to avoid getting scurvy, you have to eat more than just chips and pastries."

"A lot has happened in the past four years, but I doubt Fox has become more sanguine about rejection. He refuses to lose. More than that"—I leaned forward to get my cigarette back and to lower my voice—"Tom remembered that it was Fox who sent him on the mission that ended in his charges of treason. I confronted Fox about it just now, but he didn't scoff or deny it. He didn't even really speak."

"That means that Fox has been trying to get rid of Tom since . . ."

"1917."

"But . . . that means he'll never give you the information you need to rescue Tom's reputation!"

"It's why I dread to know what he really wants. In case the answer is: Everything."

I gulped more wine. It was having almost no effect. I thought voicing my fears would make them smaller but instead it just made them more real. Maisie finished the chips and ordered asparagus, artichokes, all the vegetables they had in the kitchen.

"I'm not hungry."

"You have to eat, Katie. Seriously, you're still much too thin."

"Too thin for what? I'm not entering any beauty competitions."

"Too thin for continued health, Sister Used-to-be-a-nurse, and you well know it."

I shrugged and let her swap my cigarette for an asparagus spear.

"Anyway, Bertie's coming tonight . . ."

"He'll feed you?"

"I'm hoping he'll have some information I can use against Fox. Maybe something about a possible traitorous German brother? But yes, he'll likely feed me whatever the chef at the Ritz will send up to his room."

"Good. A possible German brother, eh? Are you indulging in a little light blackmail?"

"I like to think of it as arsenal."

"And the mission? Anything against Hausmann?"

I relayed what Lazarev had told us about the fascist meetings.

"If we can send Hausmann back to London with his tail between his legs, I'll be satisfied." Maisie sighed. "Communism versus fascism, the workers versus the nobles. I can't see this ending peacefully."

"Speaking of nobles, I saw Theo on the way here. He's letting me interview his cousin tomorrow, Prince Phillip von Hessen, and another cousin, Duke Carl Eduard." Theo had pulled up beside me, ignoring the complaints from his passengers, to ask my permission for Carl Eduard to join us. I'd been hard-pressed not to whoop at my good fortune.

"Is this for the gossip column or for Fox?"

"Both, I imagine." I coughed and my hands smelt of grime.

"You should smoke less too, Katie King, you'll breathe more easily."

"And fidget more easily and bite my nails until they bleed."

"Oh yes! I forgot you used to do that. You've been a smoker for so long." She smiled at me a little thoughtfully, as though she once again saw the scared teenager in the London hospital where we began our training, that cold first winter of the war. I wanted to hug her until it hurt, I wanted her to take me home and tuck me up in front of her new radio to fall asleep listening to the crackle and static of news from London.

"Give me some good news, Maisie. Tell me that you're going on holiday, that you've got a new puppy, that your maids did something hilarious, anything."

"Ray thinks I need a puppy, you know, to help with somber moods." She rolled her eyes. "It's Ray who needs the puppy. But Gina did do something hilarious, though how she got the teapot in the car engine to begin with is anyone's guess . . ."

She soothed me, just as I needed her to. I laughed on cue, but I hoped she could see in my face, that she could feel in the squeeze of my fingers, that I adored her, that I couldn't do without her. More people came into the café, they sat under the advertisements for Belgian beer and Dubonnet, the room filled with the heat of wool-clad bodies and garlic and cigarette smoke. The wine must have started to work, as my tongue thickened and my limbs felt heavy, although I was still as awake and jazzed up as ever. I think she understood, from the return squeeze of her strong hands, from the way she kept my glass topped up without me saying a word.

Just as we were paying, Maisie said quietly, "When will you go and see André and Matisse? To ask about your mother."

"I don't know. When I can. The mission can't wait, and my mother won't be any less dead tomorrow."

Maisie caught me in a huge hug and I closed my eyes against the noise, the chill draught from under the door, the exhaled smoke of others.

"Isn't it always the way, Katie King? Absence is eternal."

"MY WORD YOU DO
LOOK QUEER"

I waited in the lobby of the Ritz. Bertie hadn't given me a time and I
didn't know where I was supposed to collect him. He usually arrived on
the afternoon Blue Train from London, but he could have come via Liv-
erpool or Amsterdam or even Jersey in order to shake off Fox's watcher.
He could have even flown, like some message from the future. I didn't
know how to contact him either, so I bought a bundle of magazines
from a news kiosk and settled in to wait. I was still wearing the clothes
I wore to the warehouse and they smelt, I smelt, of cigarettes and mold
and wet concrete. I wanted a proper wash in Bertie's room, I wanted a
proper cuddle and a soft warm bed. When all this was over, I thought, I
might actually need to spend some of Fox's money on making my studio
a little cozier or I wouldn't survive the winter.

French gossip magazines were much too polite; I missed the breathless rumor of Fleet Street. I had to settle for looking at the pictures and
wishing I had a detective novel to pass the time. The concierge looked
over at me frequently and I had to check that my stockings weren't

laddered or my makeup smudged, or anything else that might make it look like I was in the lobby fishing for business. Eventually he came over.

"Mademoiselle."

"It could be madame."

"Not without a ring, not in this lobby."

I smiled at his perfect poker face.

"Please, can I fetch you some refreshment?"

"My friend hasn't called, has he? They told me Mr. Browne hasn't yet arrived."

He shook his head. "You are English. I will fetch you my grand-mother's favorite, English tea with brandy."

"Sounds like a waste of brandy."

He bowed slightly. "Please trust me, mademoiselle."

Maybe Bertie wasn't coming today, maybe I had misunderstood him. The lobby was hushed and plush, unsmiling staff in pristine red uniforms, all standing to attention for people who expected their staff to appear and disappear as though they could read minds. It made me fidgety. The concierge reappeared almost silently, holding a tray with one enormous cup on it.

"I took the liberty of pouring, mademoiselle. My grandmother insisted on a very particular recipe."

"For tea? Intriguing." I took a sip. He was right; the warm tea, the soothing milk, the reviving sugar, and the pep of brandy were just what I needed.

"You're a marvel. What's your name?"

"Jean-Marie." He nodded a bow and allowed a smile to brighten his face before he went back to the desk. He could watch me openly now and I smiled back at him in his dark suit and neat hair, calmed by the tea, calmed by being taken care of without a single comment on my weight, my smoking habit, or my broken fingernails.

I had just taken the final sip when Bertie almost fell into the lobby. I ran to him and he almost collapsed. He was shaking and grubby, with scratches on his cheeks and hands.

"Bertie darling, what on earth happened?"

"Oh, Kiki . . ."

"Monsieur." Jean-Marie appeared at our side. "Please come this way." He ushered us immediately to the lift, then down a carpeted hall to a room in the corner, next to the staff stairs. I suspected that he had quickly changed Bertie's room when he saw him, as the room was not only very private but huge.

"*Merci, merci* . . ." Bertie muttered.

"Your first aid kit please, Jean-Marie."

"Shall I fetch a doctor?"

"No need, I was a nurse in the war. A bottle of Scottish whisky is the only doctor we require. And his assistant, Gauloises Bleu."

"Of course, mademoiselle."

"Call me Kiki." I smiled. "I have a feeling we might be talking to each other quite a bit in the next twenty-four hours."

Jean-Marie gave me the number of his private telephone before he disappeared back downstairs for the necessaries. Bertie stripped to his underwear and I tended to his scratches and bruises, poured him whisky, and lit his cigarette. I tucked him up in bed and sat by his feet, the ashtray between us, as I waited for the whisky to take effect. The room was warm and the reflected light from the creamy walls had already given Bertie a better color, even if it hadn't improved his wild, bewildered stare.

"You look like you've been chased through a hedge by a pack of dogs. What did you do, run here from London?"

"If by running you mean sailing and railing, and from London you mean via Rotterdam and Loos with a final sprint from Gare du Nord, then yes, I did run here."

"You actually ran!"

"I haven't moved so fast since the war. I'd forgotten what it was like to run with a pack, or in this case, an ostrich-skin suitcase. It's rather thrilling."

"I didn't realize ostrich skin had such a revitalizing effect."

He gave a shaky laugh.

"Were you chased by your watcher?"

"He smoked Sobranies, but other than that I couldn't tell. Which was disconcerting, as I'm usually excellent at remembering elegant young men."

"But he chased you?"

Bertie nodded and exhaled.

"Come on, Bertie, give it up. The whole kit and kaboodle."

"Yes, ma'am!" he said in a bad American accent with a mock salute. "So, as you know, I stopped sleeping on my boat—I didn't fancy meeting any strangers on the dark water—and took up temporary residence above Monty's bar. I forget its real name . . . but Monty has had a soft spot for me since I gave the bar a good review in print and . . . in person, shall we say."

"I'm familiar with your reviewing technique."

"You've had so many reviews, I'm arguably your biggest fan."

"Arguable." That raised a smile from him; the whisky was working.

"Anyway, my watcher—is that what you called him?—he must have been following me, as he found me at Monty's straight away."

"It wasn't your lover, was it?"

"Roger? No, too short. But 'not Roger' is my only conclusion as to his identity, and I've had a lot of time to conclude that over the past two days in transit." He gazed out the window at the black night sky. I caressed his cheek and brought him back from his reflections.

"After I chatted to you from the bar, I convinced Himself to send me to Paris for a few days, to be your photographer and, frankly, to have a bit of a holiday. I did my best to shake my Savile Row shadow—jumping aboard the train at the last minute, changing my destination at Dover for Rotterdam, hopping off the train suddenly at Loos—which I thought was all rather ingenious until I saw him behind me again and again. I couldn't figure it out until I realized there were two of them. They were so similar I think they must have been twins."

"But why are they chasing you? Watching, I understand. Chasing across borders, I do not."

"Fetch my bag." He pointed to his neat little suitcase at the door. It was so light that it seemed to have nothing in it.

"Look at this." He passed me an envelope, a bit tattered at the edges. I gasped.

"Yes indeed." He looked smug as he smoked his cigarette. He deserved to. I held in my hands a photo of Fox and his doppelgänger, both young men, both in German military uniform. They stood on some kind of parade ground, judging by the number of braids, belts, buckles, and shiny buttons they had on their persons. Bertie leant forward and pointed to the man who wasn't Fox.

"Do you think that might be Cassius, Fox's brother?"

"Where did you get this, Bertie?"

"I followed Roger to his office—ah yes, I told you that. The Hello Girl I took out was unbelievably friendly. She told me an awful sob story about her fiancé who'd survived the war only to take his own life . . . of course I sympathized, how could I not? I led her around to talking about her work, her boss, I said it was for a story, and she showed me some of his personal effects."

"How?"

"We went back to the office. It didn't seem to occur to her that it was unusual to research 'unsung heroes of the war' at nine o'clock on a Wednesday night. I had to take notes about her service too, and her fiancé . . . but it was worth it, as she said I could take the photo with me."

"How did she come by it?"

"She said a man who looked just like Dr. Fox had been in only the week before and had left some things behind, including this photo. The man didn't say who he was."

"To have gone to military academy, even if only for a while, as well as medical school . . . that'd make Fox older than I thought. It'd make him almost the same age as my mother."

"He can't have known your mother, Kiki."

"No . . ." But I was never sure of anything with Fox. "So, Fox knows this photo is missing?"

"Why else am I being chased across borders, as you say, unless my Hello Girl said more than hello to her boss and he knows I have this photo?"

"What about Roger? . . . No, even if he raised the alarm about you, Fox wouldn't bother to chase you, he'd just wait for you to appear by my side and then . . ."

"And then?"

"One of Fox's agents showed me his interrogation techniques. He looks to the Middle Ages for inspiration."

Bertie gulped his whisky. "Don't tell me."

"No, it's best if I don't. Any news about a possible wife and son?"

"The Hello Girl—I should use her name, Jane—Jane didn't mention anything. But if you didn't see them during the war, then I say they don't exist. Perhaps they're his brother's wife and son. Or perhaps they're dead." Bertie tapped the photo. "But you can use this, can't you? I haven't sprinted through Paris chased by twin thugs for nothing, have I?"

I stared at the photograph. Fox looked so young, younger than me now, his face smooth, his hair already showing his trademark silver. There was something about him that looked so vulnerable—he was standing too straight, perhaps, or the way his eyebrows tended slightly up in the middle like he was confused or upset. Or perhaps it was the man next to him, clearly a bit older, a bit bigger, and a lot more confident. That anyone could be more confident than the Fox I knew was incredible.

"I didn't want to say or write anything about it as it seemed too likely to be stolen or intercepted or some such."

"It's amazing. You're amazing, Bertie."

Bertie's smile was almost boyish. "Also, look . . . that looks like Eddy in the back corner, doesn't it? I mean it can't actually be Edward Hausmann, he's too young, but a brother maybe? A cousin?"

I peered at the face, a little blurry, but with an uncanny resemblance to a certain Edward Hausmann.

"If it is, Bertie, then that would explain why Fox has put up with him for so long, and why he hasn't arrested Eddy already."

"Oh, you think maybe Eddy has dirt on him too?"

"German traitor dirt."

"He needs to show that Eddy is an even bigger traitor before he makes his move . . ." Bertie flopped back on the pillows. "Oh, Kiki, why do I sleep with such unsuitable men?"

"Because you love danger."

"No, that's why I sleep with you."

"No, you sleep with me because you love me."

His skin was still cold and covered with goose bumps, despite the warm blanket, the warm room, and all the whisky. I slipped off my coat, dress, and stockings, and slipped down next to him, smoothing the goose bumps from every inch of skin, giving him multiple reasons to make his flight from London just a memory. His appreciation was vocal and lasted for hours, until we were once again in our most comfortable spot, smoking naked in each other's arms. I blew a plume of smoke above us, the blue cloud not coming anywhere near the peach and gold light fittings on the high ceiling.

"I'm sorry, Bertie, that this little taste of the spying life has scared you so much. There's going to be much more."

"I'm sure I'll get used to it. We got used to the war, didn't we?"

"It seems we can get used to anything."

"Not quite anything. I'm absolutely famished."

"That's a call to action. What do you think they'll serve us—lobster? I really just want a cheese sandwich."

"Yes! Let's be awful Brits and insist on sandwiches for dinner." He kept his hand on me as I made the call to room service.

"I tell you another thing I could get used to: your friend Tom."

"Oh, Tom-Tom . . ." I sighed involuntarily.

"Yes, he's like that, isn't he? I think I can call him my friend too, now, especially after the welcome hug he gave me when we met for a drink, oh, last week I think it was. The way he acted, you'd never know we'd met only last year. He misses you."

"He misses life."

"He said he was hoping for a permanent European posting, that all this traveling to and from London was too much. He garbled some nonsense about wanting to support you in your grief—really, I've never met anyone as comfortable with discomfort as you—but when I prodded him on this, he gave that deliciously sheepish smile he has and admitted, 'I don't have many friends here and no family. Button's the best I've got. I want to see her more than once a year.'"

"So, he really is missing me, then."

"Are you surprised?"

I couldn't reply. Sweet missives and whispers were one thing, confirmation of Tom's need was another. I sank into the soft white bedding.

"Speaking of your grief, Kiki, do you know who your mother's mysterious man is yet?"

"Would it surprise you to hear that there are several contenders? It surprised me. I just wish I had her final diary. Then at least I would know everything she had committed to paper. I would know more precisely what I don't know."

I knew there must be the traffic noises from the square but they didn't reach our hushed room. Bertie stroked the skin on my belly, but he didn't see my belly button, or the sharp jut of my hip bones, or the fingerprint bruises he had left.

"I saw Teddy's mother again, our annual afternoon tea, when Mrs. Greene comes to London to refresh her wardrobe and see to her charities." The only person who suffered more than Bertie from Edward Greene's death was his mother. "She had been going through his boyhood room, finally, and handed me some of his schoolboy diaries. She'd read them, they made her happy . . . but they're awful. The schoolboy poetry he wrote . . ."

"Is schoolboy poetry?"

"In the classical mode, all heroic gestures and jingoistic martyrs. He also wrote about his crushes on this daughter and that daughter of the local grandees. Apart from the vaguely eroticized descriptions of soldiers, there is nothing to suggest that our love was anything but an anomaly. Was it only due to the war? If he had survived, would he have left me in Soho to become a red-faced squire with a horsey wife and six kids? I suspect that he would. I suspect I have been tending a flame for a man who didn't really exist."

"He existed, Bertie."

"But only for that moment."

"But what a moment."

"Yes . . . I suppose I should be happy that I knew some happiness. But what now? What next?"

"Existentially: God only knows, and perhaps, not even Him. Literally: some proper sleep, as tomorrow you're coming with me to photograph Princes Phillip von Hessen and Carl Eduard, cousins of the English princes and my lovely lover, Prince Theo Romanov."

"My God, Kiki! This is gold. Remind me to force Himself to double your salary."

"A dress budget would be nice. I'm practically in rags!"

"Rags fit for royalty."

"Well, needs must."

～

When I woke the next morning, Bertie was still curled up in the sheets. He didn't move when I got out of bed, or when I used his bathroom, or even when I called his name to tell him I was leaving. The last few days had clearly come down on top of him with a crump.

I was freshly showered—the Ritz bathrooms were almost as good as Harry's—but my clothes still stank of yesterday's adventures. I thought about this in the taxi on the way home. Paris's pale walls were like a layer cake, a maze, a puzzle. I hoped Bertie's pursuers were lost in them, were wandering like tourists dazed on sweetness, were not immediately at the embassy speaking to our boss and about to descend on the Ritz.

The Seine sighed in her bed as the traffic ran over bridges. I had the photo of Fox tucked into my coat. This photo was a hand grenade. I wasn't sure how I could use it, but I would use it, and soon. The more I thought about it, the more I was sure Fox could release Tom from the charges of treason. The more I thought about it, the more I was sure Fox had created those charges himself.

"DO IT AGAIN"

"Matches, mademoiselle?" Delphine was perky, perhaps because her feet were now warm in her lovely boots.

"Of course." I handed over some money. "Any news?"

"Mademoiselle." She stepped closer. "I have seen the tall thin man again, with the big man and two other men, they looked like twins . . . in fact, all the men looked like brothers, or part of some group, they all dressed the same and they don't speak French to each other."

"When did you see them?"

"Last night, after I had left my shoes with Monsieur Levi, you know, the shoemaker, and on my way home . . . it was late, about nine o'clock."

"Do you usually work that late?"

"Madame Levi gave me some dinner." She smiled a shy smile.

"Where did the men go?"

"I think to a café . . . I didn't follow them. I didn't know when you would return."

"That's alright. Here." I handed over some more money. "All work requires payment. Treat yourself to a proper lunch as well."

"Oh no, mademoiselle. I'm saving for a new coat. A red one."

But I wasn't at Gare Montparnasse to gossip with Delphine, though her gossip proved that I was right to come. I wanted to call Fox while the photo was still hot in my pocket.

"Fox." His voice cut down the line.

"Would you care for tea at Angelina's today? How about one o'clock?"

"I've been expecting you. Give me your number."

"You might know it already. It's the public telephone at Gare Montparnasse."

"Very good, Vixen."

He rang back in less than a minute.

"Teach me half the gladness that thy brain must know, Vixen."

"Such harmonious madness? I rather think so. Today I meet with a couple of your friends, Princes Phillip and Carl."

"I have no German friends."

"I thought you might have been at military academy together. In Prussia, isn't it, German military training?" There was a heavy silence at the end of the line.

"Anyway, I'm hoping Pip and Charlie will lead me to their English cousins. Thank goodness you're sending me and not Fry, though. These men love flattery and Fry's about as flattering as a dose of the pox."

The silence continued. I heard nothing from his end, just the tooting of trains here, footfalls and yelled French, the squeal of wheels and rush of steam.

"Did you stay at the academy long or did you cut out early to go to medical school? How is your brother, by the way? I'm surprised you didn't introduce him during the war. Of course, you couldn't have if he'd fought for the Germans . . . a German brother, well, well, the world should listen then, Fox."

"As I am listening now." He sounded almost human.

"Have you been wandering brotherless among the stars that have a different birth? Or are you like a dying lady, lean and pale, who totters forth . . ."

"Vixen." His voice was raw, his pauses pregnant. "Vixen . . ."

"Oh, I won't tell anyone, don't worry. But you might want to call your dogs off Captain Browne. He was just acting on orders and I'd hate to have to avenge him."

"You're threatening me."

"Just chatting. It really would be much better over chocolate at Angelina's, you know . . . I think we could both do with a bit of sweetness."

He laughed then, an actual hoot, that made my heart jump, that made me grin despite myself.

"Oh, very good Vixen. Hail to thee, blithe spirit!"

"I think you can send me some proper payment now."

"I don't have it here. You'll have to wait until I return to London."

"I don't think I can."

"And yet you will." There was a new tone in his voice, a softness, a warmth. I had threatened him with exposure and he had laughed; he liked it. I liked that he liked it.

This is not what I had expected at all.

"I'll confer with Fry for all the details of the princes," I said. "I have a feeling that a notepad, not handcuffs, will secure the information we need. Will Roger be with him?"

"Roger?"

"Ah, so it was an alias. A tall thin man . . ."

"You'll meet him soon, no doubt. Bacon will deal with the details."

"Fry will? If you don't want the details, what are you doing in Paris?"

"What indeed." And he hung up.

"PHI-PHI"

"Kiki, darling." Theo kissed me on both cheeks but pulled back after he kissed my lips. "What's wrong? You're as jangled as a set of keys."

"As a jazz chord, as a bombed bell-tower." The traffic outside the café gave me good cover. The trees' branches were bare, their spindly fingers grasping at the wind. I shrugged in a way I hoped looked suitably insouciant and Gallic.

"I'm just nervous to meet your royal cousins, I suppose."

"You weren't nervous about meeting Felix."

"Wasn't I? Ah, but he wasn't German."

"I see." He raised an eyebrow. "Kiki, for a gossip writer, you aren't a very good liar."

I took his arm, turning away from him to look in the endless windows of the café. My reflection showed that Theo was right, I did look worried.

"Some things can't be hidden." I had to change the topic. "Does my costume pass muster?"

"Like you were on parade."

"I am on parade, Theo, only when I present arms, I whip out my pen."

He laughed. "Very well, don't tell me now. I'll find out soon enough." He leant in with a whisper. "We have ways of making you talk."

If only he knew.

On Theo's suggestion, we were meeting the princes at the Café de la Paix near the Opera House. He had left a note for me at home, with the time and place and details of how to address Phillip and Charlie, that I collected as soon as I got home from talking to Fox. With Theo's note was also a telegram from Tom:

1600 GARE DU NORD READY OR NOT BUTTON

Tom would be here this afternoon. I would have to somehow extricate myself from Theo and his relatives in order to meet Tom on time. Theo could give me a lift, of course, but I wasn't quite ready for Theo and Tom to meet. I might never be ready, but in the next few days, I didn't think I could avoid it. I needed both men to pull off this mission.

But between Fox and Tom, Bertie's chase and Theo's expectations, the lack of dinner and the excess of whisky and cigarettes, my hands were shaking. As I'd got myself dressed, I'd had to abandon my sheer navy number as I couldn't do up any of the buttons. I opted instead for a gray silk dress with silver, red, and gold embroidered fish that swam from the shoulder down the front and back to the waist. I wasn't really a fan of gray but this one slipped over my head and was still neatly pressed from when Odile had taken it in and mended it. I had picked up the dress at the flea market, and the fish covered the moth holes. Red shoes, red coat, red hat, red lipstick that I just about managed to keep on my lips and eyeliner that I'd had to hold my breath to apply. Before I met Theo, I'd had just enough time to telegraph Tom back:

PACK YOUR RIFLE DIGGER. ORDER A DOUBLE FOR ME

Tom would know what it meant . . . I hoped. I also hoped that the train conductors at Calais would give the telegram to him, as telegraphing a moving train was always chancy. Walking along with Theo now, I realized I should have stopped to get myself a croissant or glass of milk or anything at all to line my stomach. It probably wasn't the fact that Fox seemed to say he was in Paris to spy on me, or that we laughed together, that made me jittery. It probably wasn't that Tom was arriving in just a few hours that made me feel keyed up. It was probably that I was simply hungry, as I tried to make my body survive on reviving poisons. Maisie was right, I had forgotten my training and wasn't taking my own advice. Thank goodness we were going to a café and the *Star* was paying.

"Where are they?"

"Not here, it seems." Theo scanned the café. "They've taken the princely prerogative to be late."

"How very un-German. It works for me though. I wasn't keen on scoffing breakfast in front of them."

"And you've taken the royal prerogative to eat disordered meals."

"Just call me Queen Moon." Now, why was I quoting Keats's "Ode to a Nightingale"?

The waiter ushered us to our table. Theo had rung ahead to organize something discreet and we were walked past the terrasse tables, the tables in the window that looked out at the terrasse tables, the large tables in the middle of the room, to a quiet place in a corner, with no other diners around us, lit only by the warm glow of a single lamp. The place outside was busy with traffic, other diners laughed and chatted, but in this golden corner, we were alone in the world. I ordered coffee and a dense little orange cake as Theo pushed in my chair.

He sat beside me. "Do you really think Phillip and Carl could help with Felix?"

"Your Edouard is targeting noble families."

"How do you know?"

"I asked around. A gossip columnist always knows people. Anyway, bitter German princes are exactly the sort of men Edouard loves. But I need to get them talking about politics to be sure."

"My mother wouldn't let you, but these days, amongst young men, anything is possible."

"Amongst young women too."

"Oh, that was always the case." Theo smiled. "Cake for breakfast?"

"And scandal for lunch."

"I think that's Prince Phillip von Hessen at the door." Theo did up his jacket button as he stood up, straightened his posture, set his jaw; subtle little movements that transformed him from a Montparnasse taxi driver to someone close to the Russian throne. The café was grand and traditional, with solid columns, gilt-edged murals on the walls and ceiling, and a highly patterned carpet. Theo not only looked at home in it, but made it look homely; I had a strong urge to take his hand and run all the way back to Montparnasse. The man at the door nodded briskly and followed the waiter over to us.

"Theo," the man said, and shook Theo's hand with a little click of his heels. "It is a pleasure to finally meet you. I have not met any of my Romanov relatives and, for this, I am ashamed."

"Revolutions can do that to a family," said Theo. "Phillip, let me introduce Mademoiselle Kiki Button, society reporter for the *Star* in London and a great friend."

"London! It's a pleasure. Shall we speak English?" He looked to Theo for guidance. "I'm just as comfortable in English as in French."

"Your comfort is our only desire," said Theo in stilted English. "Please." He indicated the chair. Phillip sat too straight, his pointed chin held up as he looked about him.

"I just love Paris," Phillip continued in French. "I can never get here often enough. I was last here with my friend Siegfried—the poet, Siegfried Sassoon, do you know him?"

"I know him as the war hero who threw his medal in the Mersey," I said. "Tell me about Siegfried."

"Ah yes, your interview!" He smiled. "He's an art connoisseur, just like me. He's a lovely man, very cultivated . . ." Phillip waxed on about Sassoon and Italian classical art, playing with his wineglass stem, smiling at the cherubs on the walls. I saw Theo's jaw twitch with mirth at this little display of Anglo-German friendship.

"Your life has been so fascinating, your highness, I wonder if—"

"Phi!" A rough voice boomed across the restaurant and a small man with an energetic moustache strode ahead of the waiter.

"Charlie! So good to see you again!" Phillip shook his hand in both of his. "Please, this is Prince Theo Alexandrovitch Romanov and Miss Kiki Button. This is Carl Eduard, Duke of Saxe-Coburg and Gotha, or Charlie Coburg to you Brits."

"Oh, are you British? Are we speaking English then? Excellent! Garçon!" Charlie Coburg ordered appetizers, more drinks, and generally took over the proceedings. He was the opposite to the art-loving, soft-spoken Phillip. He looked and sounded like he'd never left the parade ground, except perhaps for the soapbox. He was loud for such a French place as the Café de la Paix; the gilt edges seemed to shudder at his vulgarity.

"Oh yes, went to school at Eton. I was also the Duke of Albany, Earl of Clarence, and Baron Arklow until 1917 when parliament took away my titles. I was born in Germany, and that is where I am the residing Duke. Picking a side just seemed the proper thing to do. But we've always been internationalists, haven't we, Phi? Royals generally are, always marrying royalty from a different country and then spending our time shuttling back and forth." He somehow managed to eat, drink, and talk simultaneously, with the only mess being the crumbs bouncing on his moustache.

"Is that what brings you to Paris?" I asked. "Family?"

"Family in France? Ha! The French would never admit to that. Besides, we're not Catholic, those families would never marry ours. No, no, doing a bit of political work here actually. Ah, don't write that in your little magazine, eh? Our movement is very powerful but still young, not yet ready for the tender minds of English working girls."

"You might be surprised at what the minds of English working girls are ready for."

"Not just pretty dresses and beaus, eh? Phi and Felix, staunch men, they'll back me up—we're waiting for you too, Theo—but our movement, well." He blew out his cheeks. "I have to say, it's going to change the world. It's bigger than Bolshevism."

"Cheers to that!" Phillip lifted his glass.

"Which movement is this?" I asked, pen poised. Charlie waved my pen down.

"I'll give you some proper gossip in a minute, but this is a special tidbit just for you. Perhaps tell some of your men friends, hmmm? It was started in Italy but, as we all know, the Italians are far better at food than at fighting. It's properly a German movement—English too, if they know what's good for them. It is the last word in anti-Bolshevism . . . or will be. It's called fascism."

I let him run on, nodding enthusiastically as I sipped my wine. I glanced briefly at the other princes—Phillip was listening hard and nodding, while Theo's face, except for his frequent looks to the door, was so impassive it might have been carved from stone.

"Mmm, this pâté is good. The French, they're another people who are better at food than at fighting, though they did put up a good show when they were defending those sodden marshes in the north. Our leader—oh yes, we have a leader, I see your skeptical look, Miss Button, but we're very organized—our leader is the most phenomenal speaker. He could talk Christ down from the cross. Not that he would, he's a good Christian . . . a very precise Christian, if you know what I mean."

He stuffed more appetizers in his mouth as he gave me a loaded look. I did not like the idea of a "very precise" Christian.

"You should remember the name: Adolf Hitler. I met him recently, when he was in Coburg, at the *Deutscher Tag* we held there recently. So many of his people—our people, I should say—came and showed their support! I haven't seen anything like it since the start of the war and, to be honest, I didn't expect to see anything like it for years to come. Not in Germany, at any rate. It was . . . well, I probably shouldn't say, not here in Paris with you and Theo, ha! But I know you hate Bolshevism, Theo, there's no point in denying it. Trotsky and his cabal, that rascal Lenin, they have destroyed your magnificent empire! They murdered my cousin Nicholas. They are devils. If you have any sense at all, you will see that fascism is not a threat to you—in fact, you're just the kind of man we need! Fascism is only a threat to the Bolsheviks, and the middle-class doctors and lawyers who support them."

I had a sinking feeling that Charlie Coburg's rhetoric was supposed to inspire another pogrom. He gesticulated like a ham actor, his fists and pointed fingers at odds with the delicate blush on the murals' reclining nudes.

"Our leader has really hit the nail on the head, how the world has been undermined by the Bolshevik revolution. Civilization has fallen apart under these demonic ideas. We must band together and fix the problem. You've heard of 'The Protocols of the Elders of Zion'? No? Illuminating reading—now there is something proper for the minds of young English girls."

Charlie smoothed down his moustache, gulped his wine. I was right; a "very precise" Christian was code for a new kind of pogrom. I stole a look at Theo, but he was still made of stone.

"Not that the weak Weimar government approve." Charlie glowered. "They think we're rabble-rousers. As if we'd have anything to do with the rabble! But they are too ineffectual to do anything about the Bolsheviks. Unlike us." He smacked his lips and wiped his fingers, looking at me the whole time. I took my cue.

"How so? What effect are you having?"

"I'm glad you asked." His smile was smug. "We're going to Rome to join in the march with Blackshirts. On Saturday, actually, but it's very hush-hush. We'll be wearing our brown shirts, it will show everyone that fascism is the answer, not only to Bolshevism but to the endless fragmentation of our current world. The treacherous end of the war meant that empires collapsed! The peasants demanding to run the country when they've never even run their own farm! So many good men, ready to lead their country to greatness, men who were born to rule, were stabbed in the back by a conspiracy of . . . well." He raised his eyebrows significantly, as if to indicate that we all knew who ran this conspiracy. Although I didn't agree, unfortunately I knew exactly who he meant.

"We need as many men as possible to join. Phillip here is coming. Theo, we're relying on you, and bring your brothers too."

"Will Felix join you?" Theo was far too polite.

"I hope so! He's an important member of our group!"

"A truly international group of soldiers," I said. "What other nationalities do you have?"

"Well, I shouldn't say this, but . . ." He leant forward so much that Theo was obliged to lean back out of the way. "My young cousins, the princes David and George, will be joining us. David—that's Edward, the Prince of Wales, to you—he's got a sound head on his shoulders, he knows how the world should be run. He's just the man to do it, and seeing as he'll be King of England and Emperor of India, he probably will too! His brother's still a boy, but a very charming boy, who'll do excellent work for us under David's guidance. So, there you have it!" He tapped the table with a triumphant look on his face. Glasses and cutlery clinked, laughter erupted at the table behind us, but Charlie paid no attention.

"We are in the lap of power! All my doing too. Even if their stuffed-shirt father won't see me—I mean, we played together on Granny's lawn at the palace, for heaven's sake—those boys know that we're living in a new world. The Bolsheviks changed who was friend and who was enemy, shook up the whole hierarchy that had persisted for centuries! This is the beginning; you men are right here with us at the very beginning. Together we will change the world." He held his arms wide to encompass both Phillip and Theo.

"My deepest apologies!" Felix stopped up short and bowed theatrically. "I can't tell you what a time I've had to get here. Where were you when I needed you, eh, Theo?" Felix smiled and winked as he shook hands with everyone.

"Dear Felix." Charlie bowed and acted the host. "I was just finishing telling Miss Button about our little organization."

"Pooh, ladies don't want to hear about that!" Felix kissed me on both cheeks. "Nor do the readers of the *Star*, I'll wager. They want to hear about the Marchesa Casati's party. We're going, and I have it on good authority that the English princes will be going as well."

"By 'we,' do you mean . . ."

"But of course, you're coming, Kiki! The readers of the *Star* absolutely must know how fabulous we can be! All these cafés"—he waved his hand in dismissal—"these are nothing. The Marchesa knows how to put on a show. You will see the best of us!"

Just as Felix intended, the conversation veered away from politics and onto parties, all the royals in Paris, intricate familial connections, what was on at the opera, the best places to eat. Felix, in his beige suit and two-tone shoes, was the unannounced leader of the group. Despite having the lowest rank among them, he had the most charm, the most conversation, and the most money—and that last point, I could see, was what swayed Charlie. It seemed he wanted Felix in his fascist club in any way possible.

At the end of the meal, I was glad to see Bertie come through the door, his camera in hand.

"Please, can I introduce my editor and traveling photographer, Bertie Browne. If you wouldn't mind, we would love to take a picture for the piece."

The princes posed—Theo serious, Charlie leering, Phillip almost shy, Felix flamboyant. I could see he was flirting with Bertie, subtly enough that Charlie didn't notice, but not so subtly that Phillip did and smiled along with me.

"Bring your camera along to the Marchesa's party—Bertie, was it?— and anyone else that takes your fancy. It's a costume party: the theme is the Circus." Felix leaned in and touched Bertie's wrist just for a moment. "I'm going as the Bearded Lady."

We said our goodbyes at the door and Theo kissed my hand.

"Theo, this was just perfect. I can't thank you enough."

"But I know how you can try." Theo took up my other hand. "I have to leave with my cousins, golden one."

"Just quickly, tell me—Phillip, Felix, are they . . ."

"Not with each other," he said with a wink. "Will I see you tonight?"

"I have a friend, and another friend, and work for the *Star*. Perhaps . . . I'll see you at the party?"

Theo looked quickly at Bertie and back at me. I may have imagined it but it seemed that his face fell just a little bit, that his smile became a little heavier to hold in place.

"As you wish, golden one."

Bertie took my arm and steered me to one of the many cafés that surrounded the opera house. He took a seat at the bar under a huge sign for Cointreau.

"Bertie—cognac, *merci*—I've only got a minute. Have your watchers found you?"

"Not a golden cigarette butt in sight."

"Good." But also, what was Fox up to?

"So, Charlie," said Bertie. "I didn't fancy him."

"Charlie is a dyed-in-the-wool committed fascist. It was all he could talk about. We only talked about culture and society because Felix insisted. But Charlie gave me the gold. I know for certain who the princes are." I smiled. "Wales and young George."

"No!" I delighted in Bertie's delighted shock.

"I have all the clues now. All we need to do is stop them before they get to Rome."

"Before? But I was so looking forward to a spot of the sunny South."

"If my plan works, we still will."

We finished our drinks and our gossip. Bertie took hold of my shoulders and kissed me softly on the lips.

"Take care of yourself, Kiki darling. Don't trip over that devil-may-care attitude of yours."

'THRU THE NIGHT'

I toyed with the idea of not calling Fox. I was full of food and booze, I was keyed up and exhausted, I was already running late. But if I didn't call as soon as I arrived, then I would need to call Fox with Tom next to me, with Tom listening to my banter, seeing my smile . . . it was not something I liked to admit to myself, the fun I had with my manipulative boss, the pride in proper work and solving puzzles and winning wars, the pleasure in making my spymaster my spy-servant, even if only for a moment, those seductive games. Because seduction was the game; only who was seducing whom? I looked out the window of the taxi and saw nothing but memories. Fox in dress uniform, looking every inch the soldier, looking me over as he passed by with the visiting commander. Fox resting after surgery, laid out on the grass in the dawn, blood even on his cigarette, eyes unfocused in the hazy morning light. Fox in his house in Kent, the moonlight in his silver hair, watching me watching the stars before he kissed me. Fox in the apple orchard, again and again, his collar open, his sunshine smile. My heart beat uncomfortably, but whether it was from excitement or fear, I couldn't have said. Perhaps I could no longer tell the difference between the two.

⟨≥⟩

"My apologies, miss, Dr. Fox left for London about an hour ago."

"Left! But . . . do you know, is he traveling by train, by plane . . ."

"I couldn't say, miss."

"Couldn't or wouldn't? Do you know?"

I heard a muffle on the line. "It seems he left for the train station, miss."

I thanked him absentmindedly and hung up. Fox could be here, Fox could be in this train station, waiting to get the Blue Train back to London. Surely, surely he would have taken a flight if he was used to flying, because why would he take the long way home? Only if he knew Tom was coming, only if he wanted to surprise me, scare me, shock me after not seeing him for so many years . . . no, it couldn't be, he wouldn't. I struggled to control my breathing but found I could not. Two minutes until Tom's train arrived. Which platform did the Blue Train back to London leave from? No, Fox wouldn't wait on the platform, he'd wait inside. I scanned the station bar and the café. No, he wouldn't wait, he'd get to the train in the nick of time . . . out of the corner of my eye I caught sight of some silver hair. I moved forward, drawn to it, the head turned—it wasn't Fox. My legs felt weak from relief and disappointment. The whistle blew, steam blasted the platform: Tom's train was here. Was Fox at Gare du Nord or not? My thoughts rattled, I kept seeing and unseeing silver hair and a straight posture, until I saw black hair with a tilted hat, a worn navy suit on a too-large frame, a grin, now boyish, now like a dingo, that ploughed toward me. I jumped into Tom's arms.

"Button."

"My Tom-Tom."

We stayed that way for a long time.

⟨≥⟩

"You're here to stay."

"I like how that isn't a question, Button."

"Of course it isn't a question, but I'd like confirmation all the same."

We'd walked straight into the nearest welcoming café. Tom's bag was at our feet as the warm light flowed over and around us. The café was full of train workers, guards half in uniform, boiler stokers, ticket sellers, cleaning ladies with their buckets of brushes next to them. His worn-out suit and wild-eyed stare fit right in. It was only my silk and embroidery, suede and high color that looked out of place, but then again, it'd look out of place anywhere but Montparnasse. I was beginning to realize that I looked like a bohemian artist—colorful but scruffy, eccentric and too modern—too declassé for the Café de la Paix, too luxurious for a workers' bar, too fragile for the streets, too robust for the drawing rooms. In Sydney, I wouldn't be served, and in London, I would be stared at. In Paris, however, I got a single glance and people went back to their drinks. Was this real freedom? I ordered another round of beers from a passing waiter and waited for Tom to lift his eyes from the table.

He fiddled with his beer glass. "I can't give it to you, not yet. I want to stay, I've argued with Old Buffer that I should stay—and I should, it'd save me time and save the paper money—but it depends on this next story."

"Smyrna?"

"Rome."

"You're coming with us."

"Us?"

"Me, Maisie, Bertie, Fox's other agents."

Tom frowned and looked confused.

"They're my mission unit. I think it's a given that I'll be going to Italy for this Blackshirt gathering, even if my mission is completed beforehand. I'm sure Fry will go too, and his helper, aka Roger the Dodger. Maisie and Bertie want to go as well . . . in fact, I might need them to."

"Button, you're speaking in riddles. How do you know all this?"

"You told me! In your letter. Fascists and princes, it's what my mission is all about . . . you know this!"

He shook his head and stared at the table again. "Yes. No. Perhaps I do. It's been . . ." He looked around as if the unspoken part of his sentence was obvious, his eyes unfocused, as though he couldn't really see the sweat-stained uniforms around us.

"It's been what?" I linked my fingers with his. He picked up my hand and kissed it but his look was still far away.

"Are you having nightmares, Tom?"

He closed his eyes and his hold became a grip.

"Every night. Sometimes during the day too."

"The war—our war?"

"I don't know. Some war. It changes. I'm caught in the crossfire of Germans, Turks, Russians—I'm surrounded by starving children and dead children and bodies that are more mud than blood—it's freezing, it's boiling . . ." The hand linked with mine had started to tremble and his other hand shook violently. I held both and looked into his face.

"I can't . . ." His voice shook too and he exhaled loudly. "I can't . . ."

"Have you told Old Buffer?"

"Ha!" His face twisted. "He's one of those moustachioed warmongers we used to rail against. He almost called me a coward once, when I asked not to go back to Russia, when I said I couldn't stomach seeing any more dead kids."

"He would surely understand that . . ."

"How could he, when other people are just objects to him, just numbers, copy, pounds in the bank? It's not even worth mentioning."

"You'll get a good night's sleep tonight at least."

"Promise?" He couldn't look at me. I kissed his knuckles.

"I promise. But how does relocating to Paris help?"

He looked at me with his stormy face, his eyes like the ocean, like a drowning boy.

"I need you, Button." His voice was very small.

"You have me, Tom. Always." But he wasn't the drowning one, I was, I was falling into him and unable, unwilling, to resist. I could smell his soap and his tobacco, I could feel his breath on my cheek—

If a plate hadn't smashed next to us and made us both jump, we would have kissed. But as it did, all the food on the floor, the waiter angrily apologizing, the customer trying to clean her splashed shoes, we pulled apart, blinking as if we had both come up for air. I saw Tom anew, like he was unscarred and shiny clean. I felt a part of him, not merely connected but somehow joined together. I almost didn't need anything more; a kiss would simply be a rubber-stamp on what had already happened. The waiter cleared up, people yelled and tutted, and we gazed at each other. Eventually we let go of our hands, we picked up our drinks and lit new cigarettes.

"So, Button, explain to me about Italy—why you're going, what you know, all the details please and thank you."

I reviewed everything I knew so far—the princes, Charlie Coburg, the big event in Italy, Lazarev and Hausmann, where the Russians fit in, how Bertie and Maisie were involved. I even managed to impress him with my descriptions of Lazarev's interrogation and the photo of Fox. I could see him slowly calm, his shoulders pull back, his posture straighten, his legs stop their jiggling and stretch out underneath my chair. I chatted about all my parties and gossip, I filled him in on what I knew about my mother, and he came back to this world, this day, this moment. He found his smile again.

We headed out in the night, clear and cold, stars hiding behind the city's lights. All the way home to Montparnasse he kept close to me, touching me with a linked arm, playing with my hand, foot to foot in the Metro. It wasn't supposed to be seductive. He just needed to be near me, he needed my body to anchor him to the world, and frankly I felt the same way. Tom pulled me close as we dawdled up my street.

"Have you put up my camp bed, Button?"

"I haven't had time."

Tom was silent, his feet dragged, he stopped by my building door.

"Do you need time?" His voice was strained, but I couldn't tell if he was excited or scared, I couldn't tell what he wanted the answer to be. I could only be honest.

"Tom, there's only one cure I know for nightmares, and that's another warm body. I plan to hold you tight, through the thrashing and the screaming too, until the ghosts depart."

He put a hand over his eyes and gulped down a sob. I hugged him as he tried to control his tears and failed. I held his hand and took him upstairs where I undressed him, putting aside his filthy socks and suit for the laundry tomorrow. I washed him, his skin too pale, his frame too thin with his knees bigger than his thighs. I could see his ribs swim up his back with each breath. I brushed his hair, combing out the brilliantine, I massaged his head and neck and shoulders. We said almost nothing, just listened to the night noises, clinking glass and laughter, French burbles and cat hisses, footsteps and the thud of pipes. When the last of the lights outside had blinked out, we climbed into my little bed together, with me curled around him even though I was so much smaller, my face between his shoulders as he held my hands and fell into sleep.

It didn't last long. He hadn't been exaggerating about his nightmares. They were the worst I'd seen since working the wards in the war. He sat bolt upright screaming, he was covered in sweat, his eyes staring unseeing. He yelled in Russian, French, and some other languages I didn't recognize. For hours he bobbed up and down, yelling and thrashing, whimpering and shaking, pursued by his memories. Each time he bobbed up I hugged him, contained him, spoke through his nightmares, I stroked and patted and soothed. As the church bell chimed in the cold, black hours before dawn, his shaking calmed and he collapsed across the bed. I couldn't wake him. I moved him roughly, rolling him into position so that we both had room to sleep, even to the point of lifting his head so that I could rearrange the pillow, and he didn't stir, not even the flicker of an eyelid. He could have been unconscious, except when I finally lay down next to him, again snuggled against his back, he sighed and held my hands.

"PACK UP YOUR SINS AND GO TO THE DEVIL"

Tom looked up eagerly as I walked through the door of Petit's. He'd left me a note; he'd apparently woken at a normal hour and couldn't wait any longer for food. His table was covered in newspapers.

"Button, you've been an age. I almost had time to take in a tour of the city while I was waiting for you."

I settled myself gingerly in a chair. "It's only midday."

"Don't you know, all the news happens before dawn?"

"Yes, in the small hours, when I was busy."

"Ah, yes . . ."

"I think my favorite moment was when I had to pretend to be a German private, begging for my life, so that you could release me back to my trench. I wonder what the neighbors felt about me yelling 'Bitte! Kamarade!' in the middle of the night."

"I don't remember that."

"Or perhaps when I had to be a Greek nun and absolve you of some sin or other, I couldn't catch what, but I had to hold your hands and pray for you, in Greek, before you'd calm down. I don't know any Greek at all, so I just intoned 'Athena, Odysseus, Kalamata, Spanakopita,' and anything else I could think of."

He started to laugh, but as he looked over my tired body in the chair, he looked away.

"Thank you, Button."

"No need to thank me, or to look so ashamed. It would've been funny if you put it on stage, but alas, the sparrows weren't much of an audience." I took his coffee and sipped it, but it was tepid already. "I'd have done it for any man, as I did when I was a nurse. But for you, I'll do it again and again, every night for the rest of our lives, if I have to."

"Button . . ."

The ache in his voice. I swallowed hard, nodding to Madeleine for coffee, trying to light my cigarette and failing as I couldn't seem to catch my breath. I didn't know why but, in that moment, I almost couldn't hold myself together—Fox in Paris, Tom in my arms, my mother's lover somewhere, my mother's ghost, all the ghosts invoked in this new clandestine war—Tom's tender heart was too much to carry. He must have also seen my hands tremble as he handed me a lit cigarette and took the half-burnt one from my fingers. He thanked Madeleine for me and again when she brought aspirin. It was my turn to stare at the table.

"I don't think you could do it every night, Button."

"Oh, I could. I just couldn't if every day involved meeting fascist princes and wondering if I'll bump into my boss."

"Bertie is here?"

"Bertie is here—I'm glad that makes you smile—but I meant Fox."

"Fox! In Paris!"

"Apparently he comes often. By plane. I was told yesterday that he'd left again for London, but I don't trust the information."

"Bastard! Can't he leave you alone?"

"I won't let him as long as you're working as Mr. Arthur."

"Then maybe I should work as Mr. Button." But his eyes widened, as though he'd realized what he'd said, and he looked away with an embarrassed laugh. I wanted to jump into his lap and cover him with kisses. I wanted to pick up my bag and run away, as far away as possible.

"It'd ruin your byline." I took a huge gulp of coffee to avoid his eye. I needed to steer us out of these stormy waters and back to the mission.

"Speaking of, what's in the news? What do the papers report today?"

He exhaled shakily and picked up a paper. "Your sort of thing—the Kaiser's new bride."

"Ha! A royal wedding and German resurrection, exactly my sort of thing! It only needs feathers and champagne."

He laughed; thank goodness.

"What else, Tom-Tom? Germany, Italy, Benny the Muscle, brown shirts, black shirts, top hats, big moustaches . . ."

"There's still some news on the Brownshirts in Coburg, but relegated to back pages . . . French troops are occupying the Ruhr . . ."

"The Brownshirts will hate that."

"Talks about Turkish sovereignty—I'm interested in that but it doesn't help the mission—civil war continues in Ireland . . ."

"What a peaceful post-war world we live in. I'm so glad we fought."

Tom laughed then, both delighted and bitter. "Oh yes, one or two of the papers were reporting on Mussolini's movements, *Le Figaro* but also *Action Française*. Broadly supportive of noises in the south, though *Figaro* is not as keen on Blackshirt violence. I don't think they go in for the cleansed-through-bloodshed thing anymore."

"They could hardly be seen to, at any rate. Has there been much violence?"

"Enough to earn me a ticket out of London, but not enough to land me in hospital."

"So, just the perfect amount of fisticuffs, then."

Tom shook his head with a smile. "What have we become, Button?"

"HOT LIPS"

We spent the day getting ready for the party. Downstairs Odile was busy, so Tom and I had to organize our own costumes from the flea markets and fabric shops of Montparnasse. We had enormous fun gluing beads and sewing satin, waxing and curling and painting and primping. Sometimes we chatted, about his work, about Bertie, about Paris life and London life and life as a roving writer. Sometimes we were quiet, just breathing easily for once, in each other's company.

"The thing I remember most about your mother is her air, you know, her sense, her . . . presence."

"Oh, like an air of wistfulness?"

"Definitely that. Wistful, somehow sad and happy together. If something bad happened, she sympathized but with a little smile in her eyes that suggested life was still worth living. If something good happened, it was as though she could feel in her bones how fleeting happiness is."

"Bloody hell. I never got that."

"I don't think you could have seen it, even if she gave it to you. It was something she did for strangers, and I think you were the only person who wasn't a stranger in her life."

"You could have fooled me."

"I could tell you how fiercely she loved you. Her face lit up when she looked at you. But I couldn't tell you why she deliberately estranged you."

Nor could I. In fact, all I could do was light another cigarette and blow the smoke over the view, not seeing the glory of Paris but seeing instead warm sunlight on Sydney Harbor and my mother's cold embrace.

"Do you reckon one of your relatives might have her final diary?"

I couldn't decide between *Oh God no* and *Yes, absolutely*; all I could do was shrug like a sulky child.

"Will you ask them?"

"I suppose I'll have to. I like them about as much as my mother did, for about the same reasons. But once this mission is over . . . the end of the story calls to me."

He squeezed my foot and passed me the spangles.

⤲

I also tried to find Fox. I rang him at Westminster, at his club, and at his house in Mayfair, but he wasn't in any of his usual London places. I called Fry, twice, but I couldn't get him in to the Casati party for love (via Theo) nor money (via Felix).

"They're off to Italy with cousin Charlie," I said. "If I set it up tonight, I think we can get them on the train south."

"Always messy, train abductions. Besides, they might drive. They might even fly. The Prince of Wales is apparently a keen pilot."

"I'm sure no one else is keen for him to be in the air."

"I'm sure no one else is keen for him to get as far as Italy. It should be tonight."

"Tonight? At the party? Without you?"

"Call me. I can be your cab service."

"What if they don't turn up? And what about Rome?"

"Steady on—"

"What have you planned?"

"Events are moving too fast for plans. We'll have to wing it."

"WONDERFUL ONE"

"Bertie—a snake charmer!"

"I knew you'd be an acrobat, Kiki darling. All that gold! And Tom as the strong man. How apt."

We were a brightly colored crew that gathered outside Theo's apartment building. Bertie was in what could only be described as an electric green suit, with a green turban, and a huge fake green python sewn around his body, its head sticking out lewdly at his hip, connected to his wrist by a string. Tom wore a tight, striped bathing costume with a leather belt and leather wrist cuffs. We'd spent ages making a fake barbell out of paper, with little compartments in the bells so that it functioned as pockets for his cigarettes and cash. He'd even stuck on a false moustache. I was entirely in gold—gold cap, gold satin cape, gold leotard embellished with gold beads, tiny gold skirt and gold leather boots, courtesy of Mr. Levi the shoemaker.

The journey to the party was a whirl of champagne and laughter. The Romanovs were everything that is ignoble. Theo was a tattooed man and we spent ages finding all the designs painted on his body. Irène was a half-man-half-woman, her left side wearing a tuxedo and her right side in a ball gown. Her brother Dmitry was her mirror opposite: they almost looked like twins. Cousin Roman had sewn an extra head onto the shoulder of his jacket, and he used a little lever to make the mouth speak. But the most extravagant costume was Prince Felix, the bearded lady, wearing an enormous beaded pink dress, diamonds on his fingers and wrists and neck and turban. Made up like Widow Twankey, he made his entrance to cheers from his family. Bertie was thrilled; Tom was stunned into laughter; Felix was clearly in his element, taking the champagne bottle from Vanya the butler and pouring it directly into our mouths.

Just as we were leaving, two young ladies also dressed as a carnival folk, the older with a fortune-teller's ball and the younger with a pack of cards, arrived in time to get into one of the cars with Theo.

"Who are they?" I asked. Their arrival had shunted me into the second car.

"The Princesses Paley, Irina Pavlovna and Natalia Pavlovna," said Irène. "Mama sent them. She's hoping Irina and Theo get along well enough to want to marry each other."

"And you?"

She sighed and patted my hand. "We're still royalty, dear Kiki. Sometimes duty comes first." Then she took the bottle from Felix, absorbed as he was in talking nose to nose with Bertie, and poured some champagne into my mouth, wiping the drops from my lips with her soft fingers. I felt dizzy—this was clearly the end of my affair with Theo—how strange to have it end this way. Perhaps that was the meaning of Theo's expression when he said goodbye yesterday. Had he been here before and could see what was about to happen? Or had he already been ordered to do his duty by his mama? In that case, it wasn't strange at all, it was just right, just timely. Nonetheless, I felt unmoored. I looked around the taxi. Tom was trying not to laugh as Irène poured bubbly into his mouth and Bertie kept playing with the snake puppet at his hip. I lit three cigarettes, passing them on to Irène and Tom, before embracing the floating feeling by grabbing the camera and taking snaps for the *Star*.

I couldn't have said whether it was the parrots or the elephant that was more spectacular, but by the time we arrived the party was alive with jazz, rainbow feathers, elephant trumpets, and radiant costumes. We had driven for over an hour to the outskirts of Paris, through Felix's impatient complaints, to a country manor that was festooned with lights and flags. In the garden behind the manor, an open big-top tent held the band on a stage, and tables had been set up as a bar. From the house, lines of waiters, dressed as clowns, passed around trays of food, keeping their poker faces even in clown makeup. At the other end of the garden were the animals, of which the elephant was the star. "Just a small elephant," as Felix said, it had a pink saddle and pink feathered headdress, and knelt down continually to let partygoers up on its back for a ride. High-stepping horses, in ribbons and bells, pranced around inside a paddock. An enormous cage was filled with parrots, green and red and yellow and turquoise, screeching and squawking. In between the animals and the tent were the circus performers. A tightrope had been set up between two trees, with a trampoline underneath it, and acrobats took turns displaying their skill.

"No trapeze?" asked Tom to a passing waiter-clown.

"I believe the tree's branches are in the way, monsieur, and cannot be cut down," said the clown with his poker face.

But we were here to work. In this caravanserai I had to find the two English princes with their fascist cousin and somehow charm them into leaving the party with me. In a café that would be easy; riding an elephant above an acrobat with a cocktail in my hand might take a bit more skill. I also needed abundant photos and pithy quotes for a double-page write-up in the *Star*; if I didn't do that, then even Prince Felix the Bearded Lady might work out that I wasn't just a gossip writer. I grabbed two fruity pink concoctions from the bar and presented one to Felix.

"They just called this fruit punch, Felix, but I think we can come up with a better name."

"Pink!" He sipped. "And tart. How about Young Love?"

Bertie sipped my drink. "Soho Sweetheart?"

"Whore's Secret?" I ventured. Felix clapped his hands in delight.

"No, Kiki, it needs to be something that tastes of tonight," said Bertie.

"Then it has to be the Bearded Lady," I said.

"I taste like tonight," said Felix. "Yes, please." He kept one hand on Bertie's arm, only moving it to stroke the snake puppet at his hip.

"Speaking of tonight, are your German cousins here?"

"Charlie and Phi? Oh . . . they're coming. They're a bit straight for this sort of thing, you know, a bit . . . Prussian." He wrinkled his nose in distaste. "Nikita is bringing them—Prince Nikita Alexandrovich, the youngest of Irène's brothers. Irène, darling!"

The lady side of his wife turned toward us.

"Is Nikita here yet?"

"Not yet! What are you drinking?"

Irène promised to introduce me to her brother and his guests when they arrived. Both the English princes loved a party but were notoriously unpunctual. Irène assured me I probably had hours until they showed up.

I moved through the party sometimes with Bertie and sometimes with Tom as my cameraman. I kept losing and finding and losing people in the ever-growing throng. People lounged on giant silky cushions and smoked enormous hookahs. A dance competition started up, couples locked in an embrace. The Marchesa Casati was both an aristocrat and an artist, so the place was not only full of princes and duchesses, but also of painters, sculptors, writers, Dadaists, anarchists, and assorted avant-garde.

"They tell me you're Cordelia King's daughter," said a dark woman in a tattered red satin gown from the Belle Epoque era. She looked me up and down. "I can see the resemblance."

"So can I," said her spangled companion. "Juan Gris, painter."

I shook his hand. "You painted my mother?"

"No, I never did."

"But we saw her often," said the woman. "At the cafés, the clubs . . . everyone pointed her out. Just as they point you out."

"She is here. In your . . . your expression."

"Yes, in the eyes."

"No, Charlotte, nothing so bourgeois. It's the air of this woman, it's just Cordelia. Vivid and brilliant."

"Remember that time she danced at the Lapin Agile?"

"Those high kicks!" Juan smiled.

"My mother danced . . . on stage?" I couldn't believe it.

"Only the once, that I saw," said Charlotte.

"It was for . . . Kisling?" Juan turned to Charlotte.

"No, it was for Amadeo."

"Yes, that's right, she was always helping Modigliani."

"He always needed help, that's why."

"A franc for every kick. After her performance, he ate like a king."

"If only he'd used it for medicine." Charlotte scoffed.

Tom took a couple of pictures of the scruffy pair before a high tumble from the acrobat stole their attention.

I moved over to where Bertie was chatting to a tall, thin, grizzled man dressed as a peacock. His suit was black and blue with painted feathers. From his back stood a big fan of peacock tail feathers attached to his elbows on strings so that the fan moved with him. Standing next to Bertie, it looked like the two animals were trying to hypnotize each other.

"Kiki darling, Rupert Peacock here—"

"Bunny."

"No, it's Bertie."

"Bertie, I know—no, I'm Bunny. Rupert Bunny." He shook my hand. "I'm Rupert Bunny. I'm a painter, that's how I fit into this circus."

"I think I prefer Rupert Peacock." Bertie jiggled his snake puppet.

"So do I."

They were definitely trying to hypnotize each other.

"Rupert says he knew your mother."

"I'm so sorry we're saying 'knew' and not 'know.' Until a few minutes ago I would have said I know your mother. Such a beautiful woman."

"Everyone says she was beautiful . . . is that because you're all artists and that's all you care about?" I tried to sound sweet but the words soured on my tongue.

"Kiki . . ." Bertie put his hand on my arm.

"Everyone comments on her beauty, sometimes her charm, but never her wit, her politics, and I can't find out that she did any kind of work at all."

"I didn't think her kind of woman did any work," said Rupert.

"What kind of woman is that?"

"Wealthy bohemian muses."

"Is that all she was?"

"Clearly not, if you're here. But that's the role she played whenever I saw her. She played it superbly. I never saw one tantrum, one sulk, one moment when she demanded more."

"I'm clearly not my mother's daughter, then."

"None of your generation are. Not that I'm especially sorry about it. I'm always more in favor of good work than good posing. But there was a particular moment, at the end of last century, when women were free enough to come to our studios and sing and dance and debate and love freely, but they hadn't yet picked up their pencils en masse. And there was Cordelia King, the uncrowned queen."

The elephant trumpeted and a cheer rose into the bunting. Rupert's face was tinged green and blue with the lights from the lanterns. My mother felt both very close and very far away.

"I heard she did pick up her pencil, just a little bit."

"If she did, she did so very quietly. But I got the sense that she treated her profession as muse seriously, you know . . . professionally."

"Did you know her long?"

"Oh God yes. She was only about eighteen or so when I first met her. I was living here, in Paris, when she walked into the Café Royal in London and picked up her first sitting. I don't remember who discovered her . . . but she was one of John's first models."

"John?"

"Augustus John. By the time I met her, it was as though she'd been born to that milieu. She was sweet but not cloying, she was patient but not passive, she could listen for hours and ask intelligent questions, she loved to drink champagne and dance until dawn, but knew when to leave one alone."

"She doesn't sound real."

"When an artist dreams of the perfect model, they dream of Cordelia King. In that sense, she wasn't real, she was the embodiment of a dream.

Even when she became Cordelia Button and disappeared for months at
a time, always returning a little heavier, she was still perfectly in tune
with what you needed. That was her genius, really—to intuit what you
wanted and provide it without fuss or fanfare. Have you had everyone
tell you how much they loved her, how much they miss her, all the rest?"

"Not even one snarky sneer." Bertie took the camera from my slack
hands and turned away to the spangled women and jugglers that swirled
around us.

"I can believe it. The only people who didn't like her were jealous
models, and once she married, their jealousy evaporated. She should have
stayed in Europe, though. I have no idea why she went off to Australia."

"No one does."

"It wasn't the right place for her—and I would know, I grew up in
Melbourne. What on earth was she thinking?"

"You don't have any idea?"

"I had some idea that it was due to a failed love affair and some family
business, complicated Victorian-morality nonsense that seems so foreign
now, after that bloody war. But still . . . if London was too claustrophobic,
she should have just come to Paris. It's amazing how much space the
Channel provides. She knew that." He shrugged. "Still, she was here
almost every year. For us Parisians, it was as though she lived in London.
For the Londoners, it was as though she lived in Paris. She was the only
person who could make Australia seem not that far away."

"Who was the failed love affair with?"

He shook his head. "She was never one to boast—about anything, let
alone a lover. But I always suspected that it had some link to Australia.
Otherwise, why flee down under? There were plenty of Americans about,
even some Canadians, there was no need for her to go to the other side
of the world."

"Unless she was proving a point."

"Quite, though it wasn't like her to be spiteful like that. She was . . .
determined, though, in a very feminine, subtle kind of way. She stuck
by her beliefs."

"Which were?"

"People first. Art above all." I must have looked bewildered, as he put his hand on my shoulder with much tenderness, his feathers stroking my arm. "We never really know those closest to us. Especially not our parents. When they go . . . it can only ever be tragic."

Finally, I met the Marchesa, the hostess, Luisa Casati. She was tall and thin, with a sudden savage laugh that scared the parrots off their perches. Her huge round green eyes overwhelmed her pale face. Her hair was a mass of writhing green snakes, made from some kind of rubber, and she wore a shimmering skin of green.

"Marchesa." I bobbed a curtsy.

"Ah yes, Cordelia's daughter." She took my hand and looked me up and down. "I've been hearing of you all night, and the news of your lovely mother too."

I had wanted to interview her for the *Star*, but all I could do was stare.

"That's why you're here, isn't it? To ask about her?" A chorus of gold bangles tinkled down her arms as she spoke.

"No, actually, I'm a society reporter, I'm here to . . ."

"I knew her, of course." The Marchesa took two green drinks from a passing waiter and passed one to me. "Not well, you understand, but our circles overlapped. They were all in love with her."

"Who were?"

"That group who went down to Belle Île all the time. Monet, Matisse, Rodin, all of them. They couldn't stop moaning when she married. Are you your father's daughter?"

"Yes . . ."

"Hmph." She looked at me skeptically and sipped her drink. "I heard otherwise but I could be wrong. I also heard that she married for love, only it wasn't the love of Signor Button. She was such an open, genuine person. That marriage was perhaps her only false action."

She reached over and took my drink from me; I hadn't touched a drop. I had to remind myself to close my mouth as we stared at each other. Her look was appraising, even amused, and mine could only have been dumbfounded. I could not imagine my mother next to this fierce woman, so vibrant and costumed, with snakes in her hair, on her bangles, painted on her dress . . . one of the snakes in her hair caught my eye as it seemed to be moving. It was moving—it was a live python. She saw me watch it and flung forth her harsh laugh, picking up the bright green snake and crooning to it. Tom was next to me, taking photos and asking all the right questions, leaving me to smoke and pick up the pieces of my wits.

"SAY IT WHILE DANCING"

This party was proving to be much more work than I'd anticipated, and as I was completing a mission for Fox, I had anticipated violence. The festivities lent a Dadaist, almost nightmarish edge to these revelations about my mother. I caught sight of a tattooed Theo and my first impulse was to run up to him, but he kissed Princess Irina's hand and I drew back. I could see Bertie introducing Rupert to Felix, but Tom, despite his height, had disappeared into the crowd. It didn't matter anyway, as Theo had seen me.

"Golden one." He bent low and kissed my hand.

"So . . . is your mother a good matchmaker or is that fortune-teller just another royal bore?"

"A royal chore . . . but not a bore and not unpleasant." He shrugged. "It's duty."

"I thought I would be the only one on duty tonight."

"And your photographers." He kissed my hand again and didn't let it go. "Darling Kiki, we both knew that duty would call us soon."

"Yes, but . . ."

"Your British photographer and Australian strongman only confirm that 'soon' is now." He smiled sadly. "I'll miss you too."

"Will you still be around Montparnasse? Because I couldn't do without you completely."

"Nor I you. I'm not sure you'd like Irina, she's too . . . sweet."

"So I'm your bit of tart?" I grinned. "As long as I don't have to be sour or bitter, I'm happy to oblige. Salty is just to my taste."

"Button." Tom appeared beside me, a little flushed, a little rushed, a little square around the shoulders as he squared up to Theo. "Are they here yet? The princes."

"Only this prince." I switched to French. "Did I introduce Tom earlier tonight?"

"Only to say hello." Theo spoke in English. "I had an English nanny."

"I had a French mistress," said Tom.

"So did we all," I said and they both laughed. Please, I thought, let them keep laughing. "But Theo, are your English relations here yet?"

"Irène always knows what everyone is doing."

He looked around and spotted her over by the band. He grabbed my hand and I grabbed Tom's and together we snaked through the crowd. Irène was dancing with her other half, her brother Dmitry, but very happily let Theo cut in, so that all three were dancing together in a kind of hoppy jig.

"Does he really drive a taxi?" Tom asked.

"How else could we have met?"

"My imagination runs rampant." A fleet of acrobats ran across our path. A bear danced with a lion and a swan sipped two cocktails at once.

"Felix knows Hausmann, Tom. That's why we're here."

"Hell. Button, last time with Hausmann I ended up bloody and bruised. Is this going to be the same?"

He was watching the Romanov siblings laugh as they danced, but exchanged a quick look with me, clear-eyed and open. It was unmistakable: yes, I'll go anywhere with you too, Tom, at any time. The party-goers cheered but I wasn't paying attention.

When I turned back to the Romanovs, I could see Felix and Bertie had joined them, Felix handing out kisses with abandon. Theo waved us over.

"He's over by the elephant!"

"Who is?"

"Our brother Rostislav," said Irène. "He's the escort for the European cousins."

"I won't join you," said Felix. "Charlie's like a splash of cold water and Phillip like cold porridge, when tonight is for warm brandy and petit fours. Besides, Bertie promised me a dance."

Bertie winked at me and took Felix in a tango hold. I saw Tom go hunting for the camera, to be my photographer, as Irène took my arm.

"Have you met Slava?"

"Not yet."

"He's a sweet boy. Mama is hoping he might get along well with Natalia Paley. Slava!" She waved her suited arm and a slender body in a tuxedo bounded over. His entire face was covered in hair so that all I could see were his eyes and lips.

"Oh, Slava, it's even worse than I imagined! I can't see your face at all!"

"Here." He lifted his beard to reveal a sweet smile of white teeth, and kissed his sister's cheek. "But it's good, isn't it? I look like a real wolf!"

"It's marvelous," I said.

"This is Mademoiselle Kiki Button, society reporter," said Irène as Rostislav held out his hand. "She is one of Theo's Montparnasse friends."

"I keep asking him to take me to the Café Rotonde and introduce me to everyone but he won't. He says he's too busy."

"I'd be happy to oblige," I said to his hungry look. "I know most of the bohemian layabouts there. But in return, I need you to do something for me."

Irène raised her eyebrows but Rostislav bowed.

"Did you accompany some of your German and English relatives here tonight?"

"Oh God yes. The English are great guns, but the Germans!" He rolled his eyes. "They laugh in shock at the most ordinary things—a lady's knee, a rude parrot. It took them ten minutes to calm down after seeing me, and then they couldn't shut up about it the whole trip! They clearly haven't been to Berlin recently."

"And when have you?" asked Irène in a big-sisterly tone. Rostislav grinned.

"With Felix, silly Rina!" He pretended to growl when she put her suited arm into a boxing stance. "You had better say hello too, Rina, or Charlie will be offended."

"Oh, is he like that?" I asked.

"Yes, only more so."

Rostislav moved us through the party to the throng under the tightrope. Even I recognized the Germans from behind, both standing far too straight in the midst of such louche gaiety. They wore the most paltry costumes—Charlie wore only a carnation in his buttonhole, like it was 1890s London, and Phillip had an old-fashioned Venetian mask tied to his head with a black ribbon. They greeted us with much laughing and leering.

"A moustache, Princess Irène! How extraordinary!"

"How did you get half a suit onto half a dress?"

"And where is the other half?"

"Oh yes, the other half!"

"Mademoiselle Button, your outfit leaves almost nothing to the imagination!"

"I expect you up there on the tightrope any minute!"

And more of this sort of anemic wit. Irène, I could see, was bored by it, her voice even more languid than usual. Tom came up with the camera and the Germans allowed him to take their photo. Rostislav was almost hopping up and down with impatience at this polite chit-chat. I smiled at Rostislav, to invite him to speak.

"Look, the princes—they're on the elephant!" He pointed to the elephant as it rose from its knees. On its back, riding together in the saddle, were two handsome and familiar young faces. A short sandy-haired man with a cigarette clamped between his teeth was grinning crazily. He wore black dress trousers, shiny black shoes, a red tail coat and top hat. The man behind him, clearly still in his teens, wore a loose blue satin tunic and trousers, a bright blue turban, golden slippers, and a long fake beard that kept falling off his face with the rhythm of the elephant.

"He's getting in some practice," said Charlie with a smug smile, "for when he becomes Emperor of India."

"But presumably, in Rajasthan, he won't ride an elephant with a martini glass."

"Oh no. In India, he'd need a gin and tonic."

"I see the Prince of Wales is the ringmaster." I had to change the topic. "But what is Prince George dressed as?"

"I suggested he was a fakir, but he said he wouldn't be an ascetic even if God came down from Heaven and instructed him. He said he was a magician . . . but I think he just liked wearing the satin trousers. He kept stroking his thighs like a nancy-boy on the drive here."

I liked Charlie Coburg less and less.

"I would absolutely love to chat to them, even just a few words, for my magazine." I looked at Charlie with what I hoped was a sweet, pleading face. It must have worked as he grinned unpleasantly and looked me up and down. I could feel Tom bristle behind me, just as I could feel the heat in my face. I hoped Charlie Coburg took it as a virginal blush, and not the flush of fury it really was.

"In those knickerbockers, Miss Kiki, I'm sure they'd be enchanted." He laughed in a dirty-uncle kind of way. I only bit back my rejoinder when Tom put his hand on my shoulder.

The princes bounced around on top of the elephant. I didn't need to feign excitement at seeing them, as with every elephant step it looked like they might fall off. Even the elephant minders looked worried as the cocktails splashed down the side of the animal and Prince George's golden slippers flipped off his feet and were stamped into the ground. The princes were clearly having enormous fun, but this sense of fun was only shared by random bystanders. The rest of us, who knew who they were, held our breath and willed them to hang on.

But the elephant knew its job, the princes stayed in place, until eventually the animal knelt down to let off its passengers. I felt sorry for it, doing such demeaning work in such a tiny space. I imagined its eyes held the boredom of the endlessly oppressed—or maybe that was just me, imagining myself in its place. I smiled sweetly at Charlie and moved closer to him as he waited for the princes to dismount.

A waiter-clown came up to Charlie, bowed low, then whispered something in his ear. Charlie's whole body tensed—he seemed to have snapped to attention. He called Phillip over and whispered to him, and Phillip had a similar reaction. They moved toward the princes quickly. I hurried after them, with Tom holding the camera behind me.

"Is everything alright?" I asked Phillip. Charlie had charged on ahead. Phillip started to lag behind to answer me.

"We've had word that a couple of spies want to abduct the princes."

"Goodness! Who?" I cursed inwardly.

"British spies, no less."

"That's an extreme form of chaperonage."

"David was just saying on the way here that they never get to have any fun . . . though Charlie thinks it's more serious. With his political movement . . . you know."

"Oh yes?" I tried to sound as innocent as I could, and to keep silent the long string of expletives that clanged through my mind. Abducting the princes was supposed to be my plan, but they clearly didn't suspect me . . . so this must have something to do with Fry, he must have changed our meager plans without informing me. I cursed all know-it-all men and their secretive ways.

"Phillip!" Charlie rapped out. Phillip hurried over and took instructions, nodding and yes-ing, backing up whatever Charlie was saying. I could see that the Prince of Wales had noticed me. I smiled as I walked toward him. Charlie kept looking around. I followed his gaze to some shadows behind the elephant enclosure. Two of the shadows emerged into the dappled lantern light and I recognized them immediately—there was Fry, dressed in his worker's outfit, and a tall thin man dressed as a clown. He was never a waiter; he must be Bertie's lover and Fox's agent, the man Bertie called Roger. They really were trying to abduct the princes from the party. As much as I hated their poorly planned action, I was bound to help them. I walked more quickly toward the princes.

"My apologies, Miss Button, but we have to go." Charlie was firm.

"Cousin Charlie, please, let me at least say hello to this lovely girl . . ." The Prince of Wales kissed my hand and kept hold of it. I did my best to look flirtatious and coy.

"Only if she can keep up. Phillip!" Charlie nodded to Phillip and they took the arms of the two princes, almost marching them toward the entrance. When the Prince of Wales let go of my hand, I hurried around to his brother, holding my hand out to him.

"Hello, Golden Girl." Prince George smiled. "What's your name then?"

"Kiki Button, your Royal . . . oops! I can't curtsy when we're hurrying like this."

"Never mind about that—help us stay!"

"But how, sir?" I hurried along, trying to keep a hold of his hand. His arm was outstretched and he laughed at the silliness of the situation. Where was Fry? I tried to pull the prince over to the house, but even as the prince moved toward me, Phillip held on tighter, begging me to let go. Charlie barked at them to hurry, Prince George kissed my hand and they ran off to a waiting car. I hurried after them, mentally cursing my costume for not letting me sprint, for not letting me carry something more persuasive than my person—like a gun, perhaps.

"Button, have they gone?" Tom caught up to me.

"Not quite."

Tom ran with me to the front of the property, but the car doors were shutting, and as it pulled out of the driveway, the princes wound down their windows to call out to me, "Goodbye! Next time! *Au revoir!*" Phillip was left on the lawn; I could only vent my frustration with a particularly heavy exhale.

"Well! They were fairly hustled away," I said as lightly as I could manage. "When I told my editor I'd chase after the princes, I never thought I'd do it literally."

Phillip turned to me. "Yes, a sad business, really. I so wanted David and George to meet Felix. I think they'd enjoy his company immensely."

"You couldn't persuade Charlie?" I didn't mention that Felix was currently in a dress and dancing tango with Bertie. "Not that he really gave you time for any nuanced argument . . ."

"Oh no. Charlie is somewhat impervious to persuasion. Besides, it was all arranged."

"What was?"

"This escape. The flight to Italy."

"You're flying to Italy?"

"Not literally—ha! Charlie would have a fit. He was always so jealous of von Richthofen—the Red Baron, you know. No, taking the princes to meet the other Brownshirts at the Italian rally. Charlie mentioned it at the café."

He looked vaguely around the party, the bunting and the strings of lights, the parrots in their cage, as though taking the princes to a fascist rally was nothing out of the ordinary.

"I'm so interested in his politics," I said; anything to keep him talking, to get more information about the trip to Rome.

"He's so enthusiastic about it." Phillip spoke to the bunting. "After the gathering in Coburg—his dukedom, you know—he was so inspired, he just had to go down to Italy to support Mussolini's fascism. Or is it to enquire secretly about the *squadristi*? You know, I'm not entirely sure. I'm not a Brownshirt. Yet, as Charlie reminds me; he can be very persuasive, just ask David! But the Brownshirts, they're too . . . well, Mama would say I have a strong sense of what is expected of my class. Charlie would call me a snob who would rather be royal than German."

"They're . . . not noblemen?" I opened my eyes so innocently wide I thought it almost impossible that I could be taken seriously. Phillip did not seem to notice.

"Papa has called them beer-swilling peasants. I can't imagine how their politics and mine would dovetail. I'm sure Charlie will tell me how they do, though."

"Are you going to Italy too?"

"Oh yes, but I live there. It's only David and George who have to bamboozle their minders. The rest of us are a little more independent."

"And not heirs to an empire."

"Yes, quite. Regardless, I'm in charge of accommodation. I think the *fascisti* are marching from Naples to Rome at the moment . . . I've booked our rooms at the Hassler. Have you been there? It's once more in German hands, so Charlie will feel at home. They leave tonight."

"And not you?"

"I leave tomorrow." He smiled. "Unlike Charlie, I love to fly. I'll be there well before their train gets in."

Phillip saw Felix wave to him and was lost to anything other than exclamations on Felix's daring as a man and beauty as a woman. Tom caught up with me discreetly as I walked in the opposite direction.

"Did you get all of that, Tom?"

"Does that mean we leave tonight as well?"

"I think we must. But first I have to find Fry and grill him on that bungled kidnapping attempt. Really, what was he thinking? He's meant to be a seasoned operator."

"Seasoned ham, more like it."

I went back to the elephant enclosure to see if Fry had accidentally been stomped on by the elephant, which was the only excuse I could think of for his nonappearance. There was no gathering of people around a mangled body, but there was a man sitting at the base of one of the trees, head in his hands.

"Fry . . ."

"Kiki . . ." He groaned, then noticed Tom. "Who the hell's this?"

"This is Tom. He's part of my team."

"Since when did you have a team?"

"Since I decided I wasn't going to find myself bleeding under a tree, at a party, after a botched mission attempt."

He snorted. "A hit, a very palpable hit."

"Tom, do you have a . . . Thank you." I took Tom's handkerchief and started cleaning Fry's head. "What happened?"

"I was betrayed."

"By Roger?"

"Who?"

"The tall thin man dressed as a clown, the one who stood next to you."

"Yes, but his name is Claude—or Klaus, as it turns out. He was meant to be a double-agent for us, reporting on Hausmann, but it turns out he went to school with Hausmann and has instead been reporting to him on us."

"So he's the one who told Charlie Coburg what you were up to."

"Right before he hit me with something large and heavy and left me here under the tree. Little did he know that my head is my least vulnerable spot."

"There is still a lot of blood though. You will need stitches."

"Then do it."

"I don't have a kit here . . . or anywhere. I know who would though."

"Part of your team?"

"Oh yes. She hates Hausmann too. You can rely on her."

"Does our esteemed boss know about these people?"

"Will he know that you bungled this kidnap? Will he know that you came to do the job that I was already here to do?" Fry said nothing as I cleaned the last of the blood off his forehead. "I didn't think so. We have each other's secrets. There, all done. Let's go. We need to get to Italy."

Fry groaned as he stood up, leaning heavily on the tree trunk, on Tom, and on me.

"Fox was right," he said, "you are perfectly capable of running this mission on your own." With the way he was limping, this was all too true.

"Ah, but a little muscle goes a long way."

"I thought I was a lot of muscle."

"But little used." I laughed at his feeble attempt at a smile. "Come on. Tom, can you get a taxi? I'll fetch Bertie."

"THREE O'CLOCK IN
THE MORNING"

"Katie King! It's after midnight . . . ah." She held the door a little wider when she saw Fry limping through the foyer, leaning heavily on Tom. She was wearing a pink dressing gown, her hair untamed, but she was completely awake.

"Maisie, my love." I looked around for a servant but we were alone. "We need a few discreet stitches and I don't own the right kit anymore."

"And you thought I would?—No, not there, you'll get blood all over the new upholstery, go into the kitchen—well, you happen to be right, Katie."

She ushered us all into her apartment, past the loungeroom, and into the kitchen. It was bare and scrubbed, the white tiles on the floor and walls reminding me strangely of a morgue. Or perhaps it was the one, large, bright white light that glared at the pinewood table, stained and shiny with overuse.

"I stole new thread from the hospital only last week."

"You've been using it up?"

"Our maid found the knives too sharp when she did the washing up, poor thing. Yes, just there, by the table. It's been covered with all the kitchen fluids—fat, bleach, blood—so I'm sure it can handle a few more stains. Boil the kettle, Katie. Tom—it is Tom, isn't it?"

"Maisie." He pulled her into a hug. "It's been years."

"I almost didn't recognize you in your swimsuit. In my head, you're forever in uniform."

"In my head too."

"Here's the brandy." She took a bottle from a cupboard. "Dose yourself first."

"I'm Bertie." Bertie held out his hand. "Don't mind the snake."

"I never do. So good to finally see you again!"

"And Maisie." I put my hand on Fry's shoulder, where he sat heavily at the kitchen table. "This is Agent Bacon, but everyone calls him Fry. He had a little disagreement with a now-former colleague."

"I've seen a few of those before. We'll fix you up."

"You're only a nurse." Fry's voice growled.

"Only!" Maisie feigned offense. "Well, I can get a seamstress if you prefer. My maid does a lot of darning—shall I wake her up?"

"I thought you were taking me to a doctor, Kiki."

"If I was going to take you to a doctor, I'd send you back to Fox." I raised my eyebrows but he merely looked at the table, rubbing his finger along the grain. Maisie had taken off her dressing gown to prep, unselfconscious about her pink striped pajamas.

"Trust me, Fry, this is much better. Free, quiet, and quick, and all you'll have to show for it is a neat little scar under your hairline."

"I can see why you might be worried, Fry," said Maisie as she washed her hands and put on her apron. "Why would a bourgeois housewife know how to stitch skin? But after the Somme, when I worked forty-eight hours straight assisting all the over-burdened surgeons, you shouldn't be worried. I could stitch cuts like yours in my sleep."

"And did, in fact."

"Hmph." Fry looked sullen. "I don't suppose I have much choice."

"That's the spirit."

Fry submitted with poor grace to Maisie's ministrations. I held my cape tighter around my shoulders. This kitchen smelt of soap and old fat and was too spartan for circus clothes. Bertie had taken a seat opposite Fry and peered with undisguised interest. Tom stood close to me, watching Maisie with her box of surgical bits and pieces, working quickly and neatly.

"There!" said Maisie. "All done."

"What?" said Fry. "But . . . I didn't feel anything!"

"I know! Good, isn't it?" She packed up her box in a few deft movements and took her needle to be disinfected at the sink. "It's a new local anaesthetic. I apply it directly to the affected area of little jobs like this. My maid, Gina, is so clumsy and such a wimp, if I didn't dose her up, she'd cry for the rest of the day over one little cut. You looked like you could do with the same care."

Fry did nothing but scowl.

"Maisie, we're heading to Rome tonight."

She looked at me, scanning my face, then smiled broadly.

"Do I have time to pack a thing or two?"

"If I can use your telephone."

"In the living room, with the rest of the drinks."

I nodded to Tom and left Bertie to light Fry a cigarette.

"Is Bertie safe with Fry?" He looked back through the kitchen door.

"I think you mean, is Fry safe with Bertie?" I took off my cap, finally, itchy after the long party. "They're big boys, they can take care of themselves. Especially if you take in whisky."

"They only have rum . . . Carribbean spiced rum." He frowned at the label next to the drinks cabinet. "And you?"

"Just a cigarette."

He lit one for me and waited, his eyes flicking over the green décor, the small modernist pieces on the walls, the big radio in the corner next to the dark green easy chair, the streetlights through the curtains, anywhere but at the mirror over the fireplace that showed our ragged reflections, anywhere but at me. I took his hand and kissed his knuckles. He moved closer, so we were only a handspan apart.

"Tom . . ."

"Do you have to call him?"

"You don't want to hear me play his games."

"I don't want you to play his games." He looked at me with such intensity.

"He won't hear me otherwise."

As he left, I had to turn away to force myself to focus. I stood at the window, looking at the Parisian streets lit up like a photograph under the fat moon. My skin felt prickly with cold; I was light-headed with hunger. I inhaled deeply on my cigarette through the French and English operators, through Greef's polite concern.

"Vixen." His voice was silver, soft and soporific.

"Don't you ever sleep, Fox?" I suddenly felt very tired.

"'I follow the waning moon, like a dying lady, who totters forth, wrapped in a gauzy veil out of her chamber . . .'"

"Yes, yes, alright—though aren't you pale for weariness of these Romantics?"

"'Nuns fret not at their convent's narrow room . . .'"

"I'll take that as a no." Not just tired, but cold and alone. I touched the radio like it was a good luck charm. "So, *bella Roma*: Put your man there on standby. You do have a man there, don't you? Because I'm traveling there tonight. I'm takin' the bacon."

I watched a single taxi trundle up the road.

"Take him to the aerodrome. I need you to fly."

"I have other passengers. I need them to complete the mission."

Fox's pause stretched to breaking point. "Why?" His voice was steel again.

"To be lads and ladies for the ladies' lads."

"Find some Italians."

"Sure, and I would . . . if I spoke Italian, or the princes spoke Italian."

"How many other passengers?"

"Three."

"At the aerodrome in Paris, Bacon knows what to do. At Rome, insist on only Vittorio. Anyone else will either sell you to the Communists or the *squadristi*, whichever side they're working for."

"And your man in Italy? Will I know him by his Sobranies cigarettes?"

"I heard that another of my men has joined Hausmann."

"You clearly inspire them."

"They teach me half the gladness that their brains would know."

"How is the fascist cause 'harmonious madness'?"

"Because the world is listening now."

"So, it's all part of your plan . . . that sounds incredible. I am incredulous."

"You will know my man by his Sobranies cigarettes." I could hear the smile in his voice. My cape provided no protection against the night's chill.

"When's the flight?"

"How's the sky in Paris?"

I moved aside the curtains to stare above the streetlamps. "Clear as a heavenly highway."

"Then as soon as you arrive. Be there in an hour."

I waited but there was no click, no beep, no operator barking at me in either English or French.

"Fox?"

"I expect a full report on this mission, Vixen."

"And you'll have it, when the mission is complete." Is that all he wanted to say?

"Such harmonious madness . . ."

"Do you think this mission is half my gladness?"

"More than half, blithe spirit." Then he hung up. I stared at the receiver. Not more than half, not even half . . . yet I couldn't help but feel that it was true, partly true, some shade of true. Why else would I feel happy that Fox was happy, even if it did make me feel sick the moment after? I hunted through the loungeroom until I found some cigarettes and lit one with shaky fingers. "Blithe spirit" and "harmonious madness" were from "To a Skylark," and I couldn't help but think of other lines from the poem: "We look before and after and pine for what is not, our sincerest laughter with some pain is fraught." Pleasure in pain, pain in pleasure; this was a perfect description of Fox and everything he touched. I felt ashamed that I enjoyed it. I leant against the window and let the cool glass soothe my cheek. But it didn't really matter, all this nonsense with Fox. All that mattered, in the end, was that I did all I could to get Tom's charges cleared. Even if I had to walk through fire, I would do it.

"Katie King." Maisie popped her head in. "What's next?"

It was Ray who ran out to find us taxis, a blonde angel in a blue dressing gown, hailing the cabs and kissing his wife in the street. I think all of us looked on with a pang at his obvious passion for Maisie. I needed to go home and put on some sensible warm clothes, as did Bertie and Tom, then we all needed to go to the aerodrome on the city's outskirts. Fry said he had "business to attend to" and would meet us there, though I had a suspicion that his business included a bottle of gin and a quick private sob. He looked hangdog as he gingerly lowered himself into his taxi.

"Headache," said Bertie once we'd settled in the cab. "I offered to give him some morphine I had in my hotel bedroom and he looked at me like I'd suggested something lewd."

"Had you?" I asked.

"He may be built like a sailor but he certainly doesn't act like any of the sailors I've met." The streets were empty in a way that felt like metaphor, like prophecy, as they whizzed by the cab windows.

"No, I think he's less sailor and more fly-boy," I said.

"You know, I've never been in an aeroplane."

"Nor me," said Tom.

"Nor me," said Maisie.

"I understand Fox wanted to get us there quickly, but all of us, with no experience of air travel . . ."

"We'll be fine." Tom shrugged. "What more have we got to lose?"

"I'LL BUILD A STAIRWAY
TO PARADISE"

Fry was waiting for us at the aerodrome. He looked like he was off to explore the Arctic—huge boots, thick wool trousers, leather jacket with fur collar, woolen cap, and huge goggles. He made the rest of us, in our city suits and little suitcases, look like refugees or gullible tourists. He handed each of us an oddly shaped metal bucket.

"Unless you've weathered a storm in a dinghy, you will find the sea-sickness on your first flight unbearable. Be sick into this."

"Why is there a tube? Wouldn't an open bucket be more useful?" Maisie was always so practical.

"If you're feeling sick, it's because the aeroplane is bouncing around too much. No point vomiting into a bucket for the sick to bounce out and slop all over you. Be sick down the tube. Don't miss or you'll wear it." The rickety metal stairs, the hard bench seats, and the exposed metal frame of the aeroplane did nothing to expel the tension created by Fry's statement. Nothing could expel that except the view.

Is there anything more spectacular than your first time in an aeroplane?

When the possibility entered my head that I would need to go to Italy, I knew immediately that I would take Tom and Bertie and Maisie. But I had imagined a leisurely train trip south, changing at the border, ordering hot drinks and biscuits from the tea-lady, my head on Tom's shoulder as we gazed out the window, or whispering to Maisie about life and love while Tom and Bertie were asleep. Not for one second did I imagine gripping a vomit bucket, my suitcase clenched between my feet, as we put our lives in the hands of a man who had recently got stitches to his head.

We submitted to the terrifying takeoff, where the whole machine rattled like a bomb had exploded and Fry cursed so loudly and continuously that what he thought of the aeroplane and its makers could be clearly heard over the roar of the engines. But after this, I forgot to be scared, or practical, or even to care that Fry could be woozy with concussion. I was absorbed by the transcendent beauty outside the window. The lights of Paris as we left the city behind us. The moon on top of the clouds. I had never thought I would see the other side of clouds or the endless star-bright sky above them. All the constellations were visible in the velvety night. Maisie took a quick look, smiled wanly, before curling up and willing herself unconscious as I'd seen her do many times before. Bertie cradled his little bucket like a long-lost lover, his face pale and sweaty. But Tom, iron-tum Tom, had his face as close to the freezing glass as he could go. We couldn't speak, the engines were too noisy. We didn't need to. Tom held my hand tightly as we stared out our separate windows, occasionally pointing out this star group, or that cloud, as we flew by.

We were flying into sunrise and saw the sun start to lighten the sky. The ground came back in sight, a quilt of green and brown with threads of black road and blue river. The Alps appeared in all their splendor to our left. We flew through the gray, pink, gold, orange, and finally blue of the new day. Silver cities rose from the ground, beetled with cars. Tom actually laughed with joy. It was magical.

We saw the aerodrome below us. I was aware of a tiny thank-you that rose up, to Fox, for these hours of wonder. But any gratitude I might have had for Fox vanished with the descent into landing. We were dice shaken by a furious hand, we were dumped by a wave, we were an eagle shot from the sky. I even checked to see if Fry had lost control of the aeroplane, but he turned and gave me the thumbs-up. Tom made the "he's crazy" sign at his head and I had to agree with him. The landing strip rushed up to us and I wanted to scream, but we bumped and thumped across it and the aeroplane came to a stop without crashing or catching fire. I could see signs in Italian by the side of the landing strip.

We were in Rome.

"ON THE GIN GIN GINNY SHORE"

"I've only been here once before," said Fry. He stood, arms akimbo, enjoying the flashes of sun on his face. He stood exactly like an explorer, his discovered territory the Rome aerodrome with its huge tin hangers and oil-stained concrete. I looked around for a pie-cart, a tea-stand, even a tap to ease the aftereffects of queasiness, but all I could see were the signs in Italian first, then French, then English, pointing to the west hangar, east hangar, passenger passport control, information. The air stank of fuel.

"Prince Phillip von Hessen told me that the princes are staying at Hotel Hassler," I said, "so perhaps we might camp next to the quarry."

"The Hassler? It's lucky Fox has deep pockets." Fry spoke gruffly as he took my cigarette and carefully put it out.

"Fox is paying for this? I'd have thought the palace would be happy to bear the expense." I took out another cigarette. "And why can't I smoke?"

"I think the palace probably will, in the end. Fox doesn't stay rich by being kind." Fry took that cigarette too and tucked it behind his ear. "Too much fuel around. Second rule of the aerodrome."

"And the first?"

"Learn how to land."

I looked back at my team, shaken and woozy and still trying to find their land legs.

"We haven't slept, we haven't bathed, we still smell of elephant and martinis, with top notes of vomit and aviation fuel." No one had come out to greet us, but Fry didn't act as though he expected anyone. "We need to get to the Hassler."

"1500 hours, I'll be in the foyer to organize things."

"I think you should come with us now. You need a check-up. I can't believe you piloted that plane."

"Our man here knows a doctor and where to get pharmaceuticals. Maisie is excellent but . . ."

"Not a drug dispensary. Speaking of, I have some ideas for tonight."

"Heaven help us." He caught sight of someone and waved. "Vittorio!"

A small dapper man walked swiftly toward us. He wasn't smoking Sobranies, or smoking at all actually. I looked around for a man who, if not smoking, looked like he would smoke gold-tipped cigarettes. The empty tarmac, the huge aircraft hangar, and the distant woods didn't provide many places for a man to hide.

"Our man isn't here yet," said Fry. "Fox told me it'd be Tinker."

"That's his name?"

"Like mine is Fry. His parents called him Brabazon Tailor, so he only ever gives the nickname he acquired at school."

"And Soldier and Sailor?" I asked, that rhyme again, but Fry ignored me as the small dapper man had reached us, his hair in perfect, unmoving waves above his charcoal pinstripe suit and wide, quick smile.

"This is Kiki Button," said Fry.

"You're Vittorio?" I asked.

"Sí, signorina." He bent low and kissed my hand instead of shaking it. His touch was gentle for such rough hands.

"Well, if all of Rome is like this, I don't think the mission will be too hard."

"Just don't flirt with the *squadristi*," said Fry. "Their idea of flirting is to club you over the head and drag you to a meeting."

"Shoot first and ask questions later? Unfortunately, I'm used to that."

⌘

I had six hours until I met with Fry and Tinker and I needed to prepare. By prepare, I meant sleep. We hired two adjacent rooms that opened in the middle to create one large apartment, with beds at either end, an arrangement that excited Bertie ("It's like some kind of Baroque orgy"). The rooms had ornate ceilings, striped upholstery, and a cream and gold color scheme. There was even a cream and gold telephone. Bertie's excitement was somewhat subdued with the aftereffects of severe nausea; in fact, we all headed straight for the bathrooms to rid our skin of the stench. We kept the doors closed, me and Maisie on one side and Tom with Bertie on the other. I wanted to sleep, but all I could manage were spots of dozing.

It would have been easy to spirit the princes back to London from Paris. Now, despite the increased distance and our complete lack of Italian language, we had to somehow manage it from Rome. Could we physically bundle them into a car? No one would appreciate the princes returned with bruises and split lips, even if that was Fry's preferred modus operandi. It would be much better if they were enticed, or tricked, into leaving their German cousins behind. The frescoes on the ceiling cavorted and jiggled as I moved in and out of sleep. I knew what had to be done, I just didn't want to admit it, I didn't want to have Fox use me once again . . . but it was too late now: I would have to seduce the princes. Some heavy flirting would probably suffice, especially if I provided enough alcohol and other intoxicants. I probably would not need to reenact the mission from Madame Rouge's brothel. I tossed and turned, the blankets heavy enough to smother me. I could do it, especially with Maisie and Bertie and Tom. It all depended on getting Charlie and Phillip out of the way.

"A BROWN BIRD SINGING"

I was sitting in the square outside the hotel at five to three. I had left the others in bed, each sound asleep. I felt shaky and electric and was very glad of the coffee and pastry and cigarettes that the waiter brought out to me. The day had been spitting rain and I wrapped my red coat closer to my neck. Odile had done a beautiful job, lining the coat with silk so it was now warm enough for a European autumn. Bicycles trilled their bells across the cobbles until the children scattered. Women called from upper windows to the fruit sellers as they crossed. The square was lined with shops, from the useful newspaper kiosk to the decadent purveyor of Florentine leather to the stall with touristy postcards. My pastry was heavier and sweeter than I was served in Paris, but the coffee was black gold and I quickly ordered a second.

I almost laughed when Fry walked over with Vittorio and a man who could only be Tinker. He was medium height and strongly built, his hair slicked back so you could see the streaks of gray, scars on his cheeks and rigid posture, smoking a black gold-tipped cigarette. For all Fry's irritating amazement that I, a woman, could actually be competent, at

least he wasn't one of these Fox lookalikes. I lit a cigarette and prepared
myself for a fight.

"You must be Tinker." I didn't get up, merely extended my hand, which
he shook with more force than necessary. "Take a seat. Fry, Vittorio." I
nodded my greetings.

"Fry filled me in." Tinker's voice was clipped and stern. "It was foolish
to bring a team of amateurs to Rome. It compromises mission security."

"Yet to be without them would compromise my security." I exhaled
into the gray sky. "During the war, Fox often left me to scramble home
at mission's end. Once I cycled a hundred kilometers across two stretches
of front, flirting my way through the checkpoints. I can see you're just
the same as him . . . so now I bring my own guard, to make sure I'm not
stranded on the Spanish Steps like some half-baked Keats."

"And why are you in charge of the mission?"

"Because it needs a woman. The princes aren't interested in your
sort."

"My sort?" Tinker's scowl made his face ugly.

"Prison guards. Prefects."

Fry couldn't keep the smile from his face; clearly, he didn't like Tinker
much either. Vittorio looked between us, barely comprehending.

"But seeing as you are in charge," said Fry, "what's your plan?"

⤮

"Well, well, Miss Button, what a delightful surprise!" Charlie Coburg
leered at me. I put my hand on his arm and smiled my coyest smile.
Bertie coughed away his laugh from where he stood at the other side of
the hotel bar. The bar itself was stuffed with armchairs and couches, the
walls marble and mirror, so that Charlie's leer repeated itself ad nauseum.

"I had to come, I just had to see it for myself." I turned up the
breathless-girl patter. "The march! The new political force! You painted
such an entrancing portrait of the new world order, and their handsome
uniforms. I knew our readers wouldn't want to miss it!"

Charlie laughed in an arrogant way. I got the sense that it would never occur to him that he could be less attractive to others than he was to himself.

"But . . . how did you know we would be here?" He leant in and said, sotto voce, "Have you been spying on us?"

"Me?" I opened my eyes wide and he laughed at the improbability of it.

"Phillip mentioned it." I leant in and whispered. "I have an excellent memory for luxury."

"All ladies do, don't they?" he said and I smiled through clenched teeth. The bar was too claustrophobic, so I steered him to the café outside, chattering about Paris and fashion and parties. I was wary of overdoing it; I hated this breathless-girl disguise and felt the urge to pull into parody by hyperventilating or falling over. I managed to keep my head until I got him onto the small matter of the *fascisti* march, then I reduced my act to nodding and yes-ing. Charlie was the type of man who not only couldn't conceive of a woman spy, but could barely conceive of a woman being able to understand the nuances of politics. He boasted, secure in the delusion that I would do nothing with the information. The lights disappeared down the Spanish Steps.

"Tomorrow is the big day." He drew in his breath, as though to inhale the history of power in this city. "We've had word that the *squadristi* were marching from Naples a couple of days ago. Literally marching, up the roads to the capital, like this was Ancient Rome and they are coming to petition the Caesar! They bring Caesar with them, of course."

"Their own Caesar? Who might that be?"

"Look at this square." He gestured to the waiters and newsstands, the children lugging grocery bags and men on bicycles.

"You wouldn't know that the country is under siege, would you? Yet that's what they're saying, that's what the Italian prime minister understands, it's what the king fears! Even now the Blackshirts are at the gates of the city, even now they are preparing Benito Mussolini to take over as prime minister! How do you like that, eh? Our movement, global in nature but national in character, has begun its ascent to power. We're going to take over the world. By we, I mean, of course, German fascism. This Italian stuff . . . I like to think of it as a test run. However far Mussolini can get, our Leader will get twice as far. That's just the German character, to be more organized, to follow an idea through to completion. These Italian ideas will find their fullest expression in Germany, I assure you. Our movement and our Leader will guarantee it.

"But you're here to photograph strong young men in their smart black uniforms, aren't you? You should be able to get plenty of that tomorrow. If the *fascisti* demands aren't met today, the Blackshirts will enter Rome and head straight to parliament. That's where we come in, us Brownshirts and National Socialists. We will parade with them."

"In solidarity."

"Solidarity? I'm not having any of that Bolshie nonsense! No, no, as allies, so they can parade with us if ever needed. Not that we will ever need them, our movement is growing at a fantastic rate. But we're also here to observe them, you know, check their strength, check their discipline, meet their leaders. Are they as passionate as they were in Fiume, and as decadent? Are they as iron-willed as the Freikorps have been in Silesia? That sort of thing. And Rome, well . . . a little warmth and sunshine at this end of the year doesn't go astray."

"Are there many people here with you?"

"Just the boys . . . oh, you mean from Paris and Germany, non-Italians . . . I don't have exact numbers but a few, yes, quite a few. Felix is not one of them, unfortunately, not this time . . . Hausmann is taking care of all of that. A fellow traveler, a Brit who's seen the light. He's organizing transport, uniforms, that sort of thing. I have my own uniform already, of course."

"A Brownshirt uniform?"

"A National Socialist uniform. But yes, it includes a brown shirt. Proud to wear it . . . yes, very proud." It was strange to hear this English public-school voice quaver with emotion, to see this prematurely aged man mist up at the thought of a uniform. His so-called authority was simply age and bluster, but his commitment to his new ideals was genuine. Even though his suit was beautifully tailored, he looked out of place, a dark stain on the warm stone.

"So, will you join the Blackshirts tonight?"

"That rabble? No. Tonight I'll introduce Phillip and the boys to some of the Ras, the leaders, and perhaps Mussolini as well. Much better for us to stick with our class of men. Tomorrow, if and when the Blackshirts enter the city, then we can put on our uniforms and make a show of force. The world will listen then."

"As I am listening now." I couldn't help but quote Shelley.

"Of course you are," he patted my hand. "Now, how about a hot chocolate? Or are you sweet enough already, eh?"

"A KISS IN THE DARK"

"Did you do it?"

"Of course I did it, Maisie."

Bertie opened the doors between our rooms. "Did you do it?"

"Bertie, please, do you even need to ask?"

"Did she do it, Bertie?" Tom called out from the other room.

"Oh, ye of little faith!" I pulled out a bottle from my voluminous coat sleeve. "Now, come and get some of this, ah, Campari, before the night begins."

"So, Katie King, when do the princes get here?" asked Maisie.

"Pre-dinner, so . . . within an hour, but they're notorious for being late. That will work to our advantage as I want the party to be roasting nicely when they arrive."

"And the dancers?" asked Tom.

"Fry's dropping them off at the staff entrance at six." I poured everyone glasses of Campari to which Bertie added soda water. "We're going to party for our lives."

We transformed the two rooms into one large room by folding back the interlocking doors, pushing the beds against the walls, and moving the chairs and couches into little groupings around the tables. Maisie dressed in a flowing emerald green silk dress that caressed every curve and showed off her strong back and arms. She immediately became the hostess, ordering prosecco and red wine from the bar, ordering cheese and charcuterie from the kitchen, making sure there were enough cigarettes and glasses and fresh air. She even managed to bully the concierge into sending up the jazz trio that were busking outside the café downstairs, arranging them in the corner and telling them to play whatever they liked. Bertie, after putting on a light gray wool suit with a huge pink rose in the lapel, turned up with half the cast of an opera, who had been performing a little show, for free, in a nearby piazza. Tom turned up with the dancers, all in tiny pink tutus with huge feather fans and satin shoes.

"You really need a new suit, Tom-Tom. Look at that cuff."

"The girls didn't seem to mind."

"That's because you're acting like an excited puppy."

"Maybe that's how I feel."

"Do you need to be put on a leash?"

"I'm not about to lick anyone's face, don't worry."

I burst out laughing.

"And as for soiling the carpet, Button, I think your cigarettes will be the worst offender."

"Maisie's ordered extra ashtrays."

"You'll ignore them."

"Yap yap yap."

And he growled at me, but it wasn't an angry growl, not with that look.

"Kiki! You need a matching rose," Bertie called. "Though it will hardly go with that little red number."

"I like a bit of pink and red," said Tom.

"Ha! You would," said Bertie. "Have a rose. It might enliven your very tired suit."

"Why is everyone worried about my suit?"

"Because of what it says about the man inside it," I said quietly. Tom looked at me, stricken.

"Come, come, enough of that," said Bertie. "I believe there are some feather fans calling you, Tom. You work on them, I'll see about my operatic blow-ins."

Both of them looked over their shoulder at me as they walked off, Bertie with a wink that hid his sadness, Tom without even the wink. It would take more than this red silk dress, backless and short though it was, to enliven the mood. I took a swig of Campari, a puff of my cigarette, reapplied my lipstick, and gave Maisie a huge hug.

"What's this for, Katie?"

"For being fabulous. For the work we're about to do."

"Oh that, no worries. It'll be easy compared to hosting the German ambassador and his hollow-eyed wife, their atrocious French sour with defeat. I thought they'd never smile, especially not when they saw my Vlaminck. Luckily they had a sweet tooth and the foot-high lemon meringue pie did much to soothe the jangling aftershocks of the peace treaty and modernist art." She said all this while adding prosecco to my Campari, relighting my cigarette, and using a well-hidden hanky to wipe off a bit of smudged lipstick on my cheek.

"You do your job, Katie. I want to enjoy Rome tomorrow without worrying if I'm going to be co-opted into some political cult."

The band took their cue from the dancers and played music that had floated over the Atlantic, become tangled in the Mediterranean, and offered itself up as Italian-accented jazz. The dancers loved it, the opera singers loved it, everyone's shoulders relaxed as they had another drink and then another. I checked the clock on the table; it was time for the princes to arrive. This meant that Charlie and Phillip would probably be waiting for them in the foyer. I peered out the window. Fry sat at a café table with an English newspaper; that was a nice touch. Tinker should be inside, persuading the Germans to join him . . . yes, there they were, Charlie straight as a pillar, Phillip slender as a willow, Tinker marching beside them. I could see from the set of their shoulders they were already talking business. Fry stood up and shook their hands, folded his news-paper, slipped it over to Charlie—clever, Charlie would eat up all this clandestine stuff—and Charlie picked up the paper and read the note Fry had tucked inside, stashing the note into his jacket pocket. Tinker called for wine, Fry offered cigarettes, all four sets of elbows were on the table as they leant forward to talk. I exhaled in relief. Charlie and Phillip had taken the bait, they were conferring with Tinker and Fry about how best to meet Mussolini and the other Ras leaders. Tinker and Fry clearly knew what to say, though I kept my place by the window. I wouldn't feel safe until the princes were with Fry, and Fox confirmed that they were on their way back to London.

"Katie!" Maisie called from the door.

There they were, the Prince of Wales and his youngest brother, known to their family as David and George. David looked arrogant, his blue eyes glinting, but as his gaze swept the room a lost look swept his face. His brother, young and dapper, dark-haired with a coy smile, accepted two drinks and a cigarette with a laugh of pure glee. The trio played a little faster, the singers fluted their greetings, and the dancers flapped their fans so the lights dappled. I put on my sweet-socialite face, grabbed a bottle of prosecco and rushed up to them.

"Your Royal Highnesses." I curtsied, bottle in one hand and glass in the other.

"Very nicely done!" The Prince of Wales grinned as he looked me up and down.

"I say, no need for all of that, curtsying and whatnot."

"No, indeed, it rather puts a dampener on things."

"Just a hello is enough. And some of that champagne."

"It's prosecco, sir."

"Please, it's George, call me George. Oh! You're the golden acrobat!"

"Porgy, you are slow! She invited us here."

"Oh, I see! Well, some of that prosecco would be nice anyway. I rather liked your golden knickers . . . but this little red thing is rather nice too."

"Thank you . . . George." He returned my smile very readily.

"You can still call me sir," said the Prince of Wales.

"Though only until ten o'clock," said George. "After that, it's David, Davy, Wavy, Smiley . . ."

"That's enough, Porgy."

"Well," I said, "let's drink to ten o'clock then."

"Oh no, we have to have dinner with—"

"They'll wait for us, George." The Prince of Wales turned to me and clinked my glass. "To ten o'clock."

They walked with me into the party and were immediately surrounded by fans, spangles, and song. The opera singers and dancers tested their English and exercised their French by chatting to the star guests. The princes looked pleased, David expectant and George thrilled, at the attention they received. Maisie worked with the singers, conversing in French and topping up their glasses, making sure they had enough to eat. Tom organized the dancers, introducing them to the princes, making sure the musicians had enough booze to keep them playing, encouraging the dancers to sit by David two at a time. Bertie sat down next to George and immediately began a long and intense conversation that I could see, even from across the room, was becoming quite flirtatious. I chatted and drank but I had to stay near the window.

Fry and Tinker were still talking earnestly to Charlie and Phillip. Phillip listened politely but Charlie's body movements were much more expressive, changing every time I looked. He leant forward across the table, jabbing his finger into the tabletop. Then he leant back, arms folded across his chest, head down. He read the note again with affected nonchalance. He checked his watch and indicated that he had to go. He tried to get out of his chair—I was stuck by the window, the jazz and laughter faded, the wine stopped working—but Tinker caught his wrist. Fry stood abruptly as Phillip jumped up, taking the prince by the arm. Phillip and Charlie were outraged, Fry turned and signaled to . . . Vittorio, who came running over, nodded, and ran back to where he'd come from. All four men spoke earnestly, clearly trying to keep their voices down. Vittorio returned with a man in a black uniform and a ringmaster's moustache. This Blackshirt gave a salute, heels together and arm straight in the air at a 45-degree angle, palm down. It was a strange, arresting, powerful salute; Phillip and Charlie stopped trying to get away, they shook the Blackshirt's hand, they began to talk at him, particularly Charlie. Fry looked up at my window then, just long enough for me to understand that he saw me, and he gave a tiny nod. Now was the time.

"FATE"

I caught Maisie's eye and nodded. She gave the signal to Tom as I slipped around to the door and rushed down the end of the corridor. There was a shiny new fire alarm in the hall in a glass box, with a little hammer next to it. I checked the hall—empty—took the hammer and swung, smashing the glass and setting off the alarm. An unholy wail filled the hallway. I rushed back to the room, entering by the door at Bertie and Tom's end and slipping in behind the band.

"What's that?" asked George.

"Of all the damned . . ." The Prince of Wales looked furious.

"It's the fire alarm." I said, "We need to evacuate."

"Sir," said Tom, "we could follow the dancers, but perhaps you might prefer a more . . . private exit?"

"Very well, come on." The Prince of Wales was cross.

"This way," said Bertie as he touched George's wrist.

We moved into the corridor, away from the concerned, cranky, slow-moving guests, to the other end of the hallway, to the heavy door and poor lighting of the staff stairwell.

"Hello," said George. "This is a bit exciting. I can't see a thing."

"What is this damned place?" David's voice rang down the stone stairs. "The staff entrance?"

"Precisely, sir," I said. "None of the other guests will see you, this way, nor see how friendly you are with the dancers."

"I don't give a damn if they see me being friendly to dancers! I won't be pushed down the staff stairwell!"

"Come on, David, they can hardly pull out the red carpet in an evacuation."

"It's unseemly! It isn't proper!"

"It's happening regardless," said Tom under his breath. We could hear voices in the corridor, strident, vaguely German.

"Do you smell smoke?" I asked.

"Yes . . . I think I do," said Bertie.

"Let's go," said George and started to bolt down the stairs with Bertie. We set off after them, but I turned to see David still at the door.

"Please, sir." I hoped my voice sounded soft to him and not the whine it sounded to me. "I'm sure . . ."

"You aren't sure of a thing. I can't smell smoke." He turned back to the door. I rushed up; he couldn't leave by the main entrance and risk seeing Charlie and Phillip.

"Sir." I was breathless. "Please . . ."

I was breathless from nerves and alcohol, and I let this settle into a melodramatic chest-heaving. My desire to get him down the stairs to Fry, my need to complete this mission, I let these things widen my eyes, part my lips, restrict my breath. He paused, just enough to take a step closer, wary but curious. A door banged somewhere above us. As he looked up, I took his wrist gently and started to run down the stairs. He tripped slightly and the momentum of almost falling meant he had no choice but to run down the stairs behind me. We wound down and down, only a few flights but it felt like descending from the roof of St. Pauls. Our footsteps were loud, our breathing was loud, there were clangs and bangs that seemed to come from inside the stone. David looked fierce, angry and frightened, but I couldn't help that. Eventually I felt some fresh air from outside, I heard Bertie and George, I saw Tom standing at the door, holding it open. I felt David pull back, pull his wrist out of my hold, but the forward momentum of going down the stairs meant he barrelled past me, out the door, and ran into his brother.

"Davy! I thought you weren't going to make it."

I saw a car pull up from a side street.

"George, these people—it isn't right!"

Fry jumped out of the passenger seat and ran toward us.

"Don't be silly, they're only . . ."

Fry put his hand in his jacket pocket—was he really pulling out a gun?—no, it was some kind of paper or certificate. He stopped in front of the princes.

"Who the hell are you?" David's ears were red.

"Your Royal Highnesses, from the Home Office."

"Oh no . . ." George pouted at Bertie. "I feared this might happen. We never get to have any fun."

David snatched the paper from Fry and read it quickly.

"Who the hell is this 'Fox'? I've never heard of him."

"Sir, the car is waiting. This way."

"No! I bloody well won't come!" Did the Prince of Wales just stamp his foot?

"Oh, come on, Davy. There's no use arguing."

"Who is this Fox to order us about, I'd like to know!"

"What does it matter? Fox, Weasel, Salamander—they're taking us back to the Lion and Unicorn."

"Mother is not a bloody unicorn."

"And Father is not a lion, though he will maul us if he finds we've been . . . having fun, with Uncle Charlie."

"Sir, if I may . . ." Fry indicated the car. Yes, the Prince of Wales did just stamp his foot. Tom and Bertie had faces so expressionless I knew they were calling on all of their army training to restrain themselves. The car started inching across the square.

"So, it's Uncle Charlie who is the problem, is it? Our own flesh and blood?" David read through the letter again. The car flashed its lights.

"Davy, we must admit defeat."

"Yes, Charlie bloody well is the problem."

"Come on, Davy, Rome's been here a couple of thousand years, it'll wait a bit longer for us." The car was only a few meters away. I could see Tinker behind the wheel.

"Impertinence! Parliament telling us which members of our family we may and may not speak to!"

"He did fight for Cousin Willy, Davy . . . not really that much of an ask, that the English princes remain patriotic and all that."

Tinker got out of the car and walked nonchalantly toward us. George saw us watching and turned.

"Hello," he said. "Are you nanny?"

Tinker nodded. "Your Royal Highness."

"Very well. I say, you don't happen to have a drink in the car, do you? Only having begun . . ." George chatted to Tinker as he climbed in the car. Bertie followed, making sure George got in and stayed in. The Prince of Wales glared, fumed, then turned on his heels and headed to the front of the hotel. Tom raised his eyebrows, then he set off with Fry at a run. The prince had no chance. They caught up to him in moments, both of them so tall, they took the prince by the elbows and marched him to the car, the prince protesting as much as his dignity would allow. Fry bundled him in the backseat like he was a criminal in a police car, locking the door as he did so. Fry nodded to me and they set off, the car squealing and growling.

"I can't believe he actually made a run for it," said Tom.

"I think Fry was hoping he wouldn't have to touch him, you know, royal protocol and all that. But it seems that abductions are abductions, whoever you are."

"What was that bit of paper Fry had?"

"I didn't see, but it had an official header. Something official?"

"Some spy you are." Tom grinned.

I could hear Italian in snatches of song. I could smell garlic and tomato alongside the petrol and cigarette smoke. I heard German spoken with force and saw Charlie rush around the corner with Phillip behind him.

"Where are they?" Charlie was red in the face.

"Who, Your Grace?"

"Don't play dumb with me!" His eyes roamed the square. "The boys! David and George—where are they?"

"There was a fire alarm . . . I assume they went with the others."

"The others said they went off with you."

"Yes, those opera singers . . ." Phillip was breathless.

"Oh no," I said. "They must be . . ."

"Listen," Charlie grabbed my arm. "You will take me to my young cousins or—"

"I don't think so, mate." Tom moved in front of Charlie, half a foot taller and half a foot broader, giving me time to disentangle myself. "If Miss Button says she doesn't know, then she doesn't know."

"Don't you know who I am!"

"No, and I don't care."

"Well, you should." Charlie reached around his waistband and pulled out a revolver, pointing it at Tom. All the sounds in the square disappeared. I was more shocked than scared that he had actually pulled out a gun in the street like a common thug. Tom stood straight, Bertie froze, Phillip stood panting. I kicked myself that I had left my own little pistol in our hotel room.

"Now." Charlie turned to me, the gun still on Tom. "You will take me to my young cousins."

"Do you have a car?" I asked.

"Why would we need a car?"

"To chase them down, of course."

"Phillip." Charlie didn't take his eyes off me. "Hail a taxi."

Phillip ran to the other side of the square. We all waited, watching Phillip out of the corner of our eyes as he ran to the café and asked the waiter to order a cab. I had no intention of getting in any such vehicle with Charlie and his gun. I didn't dare look at either Tom or Bertie, but I doubted they would let Charlie get that far either.

"Where do we direct the taxi?" Charlie's plummy tones were chilling. "The station is only two streets away."

"And the train doesn't leave until tomorrow, and trains are notoriously insecure—too many doors to escape from." I did my best to sound nonchalant. "No, the princes are being driven home."

"And we're expected to take a taxi back to London?"

"I expect nothing of the sort. I expected you to have a car."

"Carl!" Phillip called; the taxi had arrived. Charlie pulled me into a kind of embrace so he could stick the gun into my ribs as we walked toward the cab. I didn't need to pretend to find it hard to walk, the gun in my side did that for me. I could see Maisie creep around the corner of the hotel as we moved toward the car. Our progress was slow as I limped with the pain of the gun.

"Hurry up." Charlie spoke through clenched teeth.

"Impossible with that extra rib you've given me."

He would shoot me; I could feel his resolve in his grip around my body, strong enough to drag me into the car if necessary. Phillip looked frightened, awaiting orders by the passenger door. As we got to the cab, Charlie motioned for him to go around the other side. I cursed inwardly; I had been hoping to get away by jumping across the backseat and out the road-side door, but that would now be impossible. I didn't dare turn my head to see what Tom, Bertie, and Maisie were doing, to alert Charlie to their plans, if they had any, or to stop looking where I was going. The irony of being abducted in revenge for abducting the princes was perhaps the only thing that stopped me from being overwhelmed by panic. The only thing I knew was that I absolutely could not get in that taxi. If I did, I doubted I would ever get out alive.

Three more steps; here was the curb.

"Get in." Charlie growled in my ear in a parody of a lover's whisper. I could feel the gun bruising me. I turned to his face, ready to do anything, to bite him if necessary, my body tense as I resisted his push to get me into the cab—

I heard thudded footfalls. I saw Maisie appear beside us and I brought my knee up to Charlie's groin as hard as I could. Charlie groaned and Maisie whacked him with an empty grappa bottle. Another set of hands—Tom's—reached in and grabbed the gun as it fired into the cobbles, burning his hands and grazing my calf. I stumbled, it stung like first heartbreak, and Tom dropped the gun. I lunged for it, as did Charlie, but Maisie hit him with the bottle again, bringing the duke to the ground. Bertie had run to the taxi to get Phillip, but at the sound of the gunshot the taxi driver had sped away, with Phillip inside the cab, the door open and swinging as the cab rounded the corner. Bertie ran after them, correctly guessing that Phillip would get out of the cab as soon as possible and run back to help Charlie. But Charlie was on the ground, being sat on by Maisie and Tom, his arms twisted around his back. Phillip held his hands up as Bertie approached him, unarmed and unresisting.

"Let me see how Carl is." Phillip's voice was wheedling, especially compared to the coarse curses and grunts coming from Charlie.

"Not if you begged me," said Bertie, "though you're welcome to try."

"Please," said Phillip. "He's a duke. This is most undignified . . ."

"A duke who shot at us!" yelled Tom.

"How dare you! How dare you!" Charlie's curses had deteriorated to outraged claims about his dignity. I unloaded the gun and tipped the bullets into the gutter.

"Get a cab, Bertie. These men are leaving us."

"Never! Never! You will pay for this! The Leader will get you for this!" Charlie's curses went on and on. Phillip stood trembling and bewildered, as Bertie took him firmly by the arm and watched for a cab.

"Get him up or the cab will never stop for us," I said. Tom nodded to Maisie. They both took Charlie's arms and hauled him to his feet. Charlie was woozy, still cursing even though his knees frequently gave way. Tom had somehow lost a shoe and acting the strong man in his socks made the scene almost a joke. His bright red palms were not a joke though, nor was the throbbing pain in my calf. I didn't dare move in case I found I couldn't walk.

The cab came; I heard Bertie give directions to the station that ran the intercity trains. Phillip got in meekly but Maisie had to give Charlie's arm a little twist before he got in. His face was red with hate, glaring at us through the window, his head leaning against the seat, rubbing his shoulders as the taxi pulled away. They rounded the corner and we waited, a beat, then another.

The mission was complete.

"Have we done it?" Bertie asked.

"We've done it." The gun was suddenly almost too heavy to hold. In fact, I felt tired in every limb and had to close my eyes to stop my head from swimming.

"Button." I felt Tom beside me and I leant into him.

"Katie, you're bleeding."

I opened my eyes to see a small puddle of blood at my heel. Tom's hands were glowing.

"How much do they hurt, Tom?"

"A bucket of ice water and a double vodka should let me sleep."

"I can arrange that." Maisie went off to get the ice while Bertie took my arm. He stopped and turned. "We're not going out, are we?"

"I can't, Tom can't—"

"I won't," called Maisie.

"You can, Bertie, if you can find a sweet corner of this city. How's your Italian?"

Bertie grinned. "I left him in London."

"AGGRAVATIN' PAPA"

The mission was over. I was too exhausted even to call Fox. Maisie tended my graze and gave detailed instructions to Bertie for Tom's hands. My graze looked worse than it was; the bullet had broken the skin but not deeply. The red of my dress made the blood glisten like paint and my limp made my wound seem dramatic. Tom's hands were rather worse than they looked, with stripes of burns from the gun barrel across his palms. It was all we could do to stop them blistering, sending up for new ice every hour until midnight, when the choice became either burnt hands or frostbite. Maisie wrapped Tom's hands carefully. Then we crawled into bed and the others slept so soundly they barely stirred.

I wish I could have said the same. My leg throbbed in waves. My heart couldn't stop jumping, floundering around inside my ribcage even while my limbs were too heavy to move. Tom's bed was on his side of the connected room, too far away to talk. I watched his shape in the darkness and I knew he was facing me. Was he awake, like me, still and watching? If Bertie and Maisie hadn't been asleep, I think we would have . . . I don't know, I couldn't even think of chatting when I was so worn out. But I couldn't turn away, I stared at his form every moment my eyes were open through the night. I didn't remember going to sleep.

But then it was morning, silvery light filled the room, it was damp-cold and overcast. The room smelt of spilled prosecco and cheap perfume. We had decided to watch the march before we headed back to Paris, to see what all the fuss was about. My graze was healing nicely already and no one would notice it under the trousers I had brought with me. I went downstairs to order us coffee and some more ice for Tom. I went downstairs to call Fox.

"Vixen." He didn't say hello, of course, he'd been expecting my call.

"I am pale for weariness."

"You find no object worth your constancy? I know you don't wander companionless."

"That would mean I was a dying lady, led by the insane and feeble wanderings of my fading brain. I am the opposite of these things. No, I'm just pale for weariness." I opened a new packet of cigarettes in Fox's long pause. I caught the concierge looking at my trousers. No, it had been my limp, as he came out from behind the front desk with a little stool for me and an ashtray. It was so considerate that I had to look away, blinking at the green marble and brass fittings of the foyer.

"This is half my gladness, Fox, this companionate weariness."

"Rarely rarely comest thou . . ."

"Speaking of rare occurrences, have the two young princes left with a beaker of the warm south?"

"Fry landed a few hours ago. Bad winds crossing the channel but no bodily harm done."

"I can't say the same here. Tom had his hands singed."

"Are the Spanish Steps proving harmful once again?"

"Harmful? Ah, you mean Keats?" Keats had died of tuberculosis here about a hundred years ago. "No, we're suffering from bad dukes, not bad drains."

"We?" A little tension in his voice.

"Just a scratch, though I don't intend to come any closer to a bullet."

I thought I heard him murmur "bullet" but some hotel guests crossed the foyer just at that moment and I couldn't be sure.

"Cousin Charlie is quite the Berlin Bear. Did you know him?" Another long pause, as I expected. He would say nothing until I showed my hand. I had to hold my nerve. My smoky exhale looked endless in the mirrored mirrors.

"You know, Fox, at military college? You're the same vintage, aren't you?"

"I believe he was still in England when I was in Prussia."

"But your brother must know him. Or is your brother older?" I was being impertinent and, in that respect, this banter was dangerous. But his answer would tell me what I needed to know. If he wanted me in his life as more than an employee, he would talk about his family. If he saw me as just a sweet combination of toy and tool, he would not.

"My brother is older. By six minutes."

A twin; my throat hurt, I felt choked. Not only were there two Foxes in the world, but this one, on the telephone, wanted me to know it. Only when he answered did I understand that this was the answer I dreaded. I couldn't even smoke, my hands were shaking too much.

"I haven't seen my brother since . . . since before the war." I didn't want to know, I didn't want any part of his family history. "He chose the losing side."

I couldn't speak. Fox had just told me that he was German, that he still had family in Germany, that he had chosen to be British and all that went with it. He had admitted to going to military academy in Prussia, he admitted to being human and not a specter at the end of a telephone line. Information was power and he was giving me information. There had to be an ulterior motive; he would only give away power now to gain more power at some later date. My brain raced, trying to find a reason for him telling me about his brother, some reason that related to my work for him, but I kept stumbling over the idea that he wanted me in his life. I felt sick, my hangover amplified. Words withered in my mouth before I could give them breath.

"I think you'll like your payment." His voice was quicksilver again; what had he heard in my silence? "Tailor will deliver it today, before you leave Rome."

"We're watching the parade." My voice shook, I couldn't control it.

"Oh, I don't think today is going to be anything as neat as a parade, Vixen." He hung up, leaving the operator to bark at me in Italian.

"MARCH WITH ME!"

We didn't need to find the march; the march found us. The tension in the air was palpable. We all felt it, like the night before a big push, like the vibrations of reconnaissance planes that would give away our position. People hurried, head down to their destination, they spoke in close groups of two or three, they looked over their shoulders at phantoms. No one smiled and certainly no one laughed. People at the café downstairs ate quickly and drank their coffee standing up. One or two tourists loitered, but they quickly hurried back inside, thinking that they didn't like the overcast sky, or their throat hurt, or they felt unaccountably tired. Unlike yesterday, I did not see a single child. The hotel staff said nothing but *Si* and *Non* and hurried about their business. We sat at the café, ordering too many coffees and pastries, waiting for a break in the spotted rain to venture forth.

Then, midmorning, the first Blackshirts filtered into the square. Their boots were black, their trousers were black, their shirts were black and covered with medals. But it was their strut that pronounced them to be *fascisti*, *squadristi*, followers of Mussolini. They came in twos and threes until there was a steady stream, singing songs with a distinct military tone. To my eyes they all seemed short and pugnacious, like the photographs I had seen of Mussolini himself, but perhaps that was just the effect of standing next to slender Bertie and tall Tom. By the time there was a stream of black uniforms, women came out of the shops and leant over balconies, throwing flowers to the Blackshirts and yelling "Bravo!" and other Italian phrases I couldn't understand. The streets around the square were soon stinking with trampled blooms.

"Well," said Maisie, "are we going to follow them, see what it's all about?"

"I think I must," I said.

"Then we all must," said Tom.

We followed the lines of men as they headed to the center of the city. None of us could speak Italian and the Blackshirts didn't seem inclined to chat to our little touring party. We soon realized that they were headed to the Italian parliament building. The main boulevards filled up with thousands of men in their black shirts and medals, their black boots striking the cobbles. A thousand arms raised, giving that strange, powerful salute I saw last night—arm straight out and up, palm down. Bertie told us it was the old salute of the Roman army, which seemed an odd choice. Odd unless the Fascists were planning to build a new Roman Empire, a thought which did not in the least comfort me. In fact, I was filled with foreboding. Only at Armistice had I seen such crowds, only during the war had I felt such tension. All these men in their home-sewn uniforms seemed to augur a new type of war, a very different understanding of peace.

Progress was slow, as I could not walk fast or far without rest. Tom was also tired from his injuries, though his hands now only needed light bandages, leaving his fingers free. The four of us kept in a tight little knot, unwilling to move away from the slight protection we provided each other. Bertie had the camera with him and took photos of the crowds. As we approached the parliament building, we could hear cheering, a loud roar that rolled around and around the stone walls, rolled on top of us and shook the shopfronts. We turned the corner and there they all were, a sea of Blackshirts, arms straight up in that salute, roaring their approval, their anger, their power at the man on the balcony of the parliament building.

"Is that Mussolini?" Tom asked.

"I can't see properly." Black shirts filled my vision.

"I can't see anything but bedraggled *fascisti*," said Bertie.

"This doesn't feel right," said Maisie. "Have you seen what you need to see, Katie? If so, I think we should go."

"Back to the hotel?"

"Back to Paris."

The figure on the balcony gave a final few words and the Blackshirts erupted, saluting and waving and cheering as the figure retreated. The enormous energy of the crowd was battering, deafening, it overflowed and we heard smashed glass. Blackshirts were looting the shops around the piazza. We heard more smashed glass, the cheer had turned to a bellow, Blackshirts were running toward buildings, hurling café chairs at each other, digging up the cobbles and throwing them at the shop windows.

"Back to Paris it is then," said Bertie.

We linked arms and almost ran back to the hotel. We saw news vendors bolting and newspapers burning on the ground. Women were running upstairs and down. We were injured and unarmed and each distressed Roman was pursued by a gang of men. I didn't think about being hurt by the marchers, or the pain in my leg, or that Charlie and Phillip may well be caught up in this riot. All I thought of was obscuring doorways to hide fleeing women as the Blackshirts ran past, of ushering children into foyers and courtyards, of linking arms with old men as we helped them down the block. As we forged our way back, all I thought was, this is what I was fighting against, this violence, this chaos, this hate.

"FAREWELL BLUES"

Blackshirts roamed through the train station, looting cafés for wine and abandoned ticket stalls for cash. We ran to get on the train, without tickets, as it pulled out of the station before its departure time. We threw our bags on and Maisie pulled me, Tom, and finally Bertie onto a rapidly moving train. We had no food with us and no water, no blankets or Italian cash except a few lire. But we were traveling north, back to Paris.

The country was on fire. Only in spots, only here and there, but there were plumes of smoke in the gray autumn sky that had nothing to do with farming. At every village station we could see groups of people, sometimes small and sometimes a crowd, as they surrounded the stationmaster's office, some in the black shirts of the *fascisti*, some wearing medals on old uniforms. We could see down the main street of some villages, the local post office surrounded by people, by Blackshirts, with the postmaster in the street bloodied and bruised. The train was slower than it should have been, the tracks were busy and no one was manning the signals. We had our own carriage in first class, we shared with no one else, but we were silent nonetheless, watching the countryside react to the coup. I was under no illusion now; these *fascisti* meant to change the world and they didn't care who they hurt in the process. The sun set and all we could see was the occasional farmhouse light, the occasional riotous bonfire.

We'd had no food for hours. The train hadn't stopped and clearly no snack-seller or tea-lady had boarded with us. I don't know why but this made me think of the package I had been handed at reception as we left the hotel.

"What's that?" Tom asked over my shoulder.

"My payment." I felt Tom tense.

"Payment? Pay day's not until Wednesday," said Bertie.

"It's from Fox."

The lights in the cabin flickered but still provided enough light to see. The air was stuffy with smoke and the wooden floor was slightly sticky and covered with cigarette burns. No one pretended to give me privacy. Tom, Maisie, and Bertie all knew why the package was important.

I heard Tom gasp at my shoulder. I had only taken out one photograph, but I could see why he was shocked. The photograph was of Tom, in uniform, in a trench with three officers, one of whom was Fox.

"Is that when . . ."

"Yes," said Tom. That was when he was given the mission that sent him into no-man's-land and landed him his charge of treason. I passed him the photo and kept looking through the contents of the package. There were more photos of Tom, in uniform, on leave in Paris.

"When are these?" I asked Tom.

"They look . . . 1916, maybe? I can't tell."

"I'm not in them." I breathed deeply to push away the wave of nausea.

"Why would you be?" asked Maisie, as Tom passed her the photos.

"Fox sent me a photo, last year," I said, "of me and Tom in Paris at a café. Just the two of us in a café, but the implication was, of course, that he had had me followed. Awful, but in keeping with what we know about Fox. These photos seem to show that he had Tom followed separately, without me; this suggests that he had a plan for Tom."

"A plan?" Bertie frowned at the innocuous photos. "I don't understand."

Tom explained what had happened to him, how Fox had been there at the start of the mission, how his mission had gone wrong, and why I kept working for Fox. His retelling was biased and I had to interject frequently, but Maisie and Bertie looked at the photos with a new understanding. Nothing was written on the back of any of them. They were simply wartime photos of Tom.

"Who could have taken them?" asked Bertie. "These were clearly taken by a friend."

"Not necessarily," said Tom. "There were always lots of men around, anyone could have taken them."

"Not anyone," I said. "A Fox agent."

"Right." A gloom settled on Tom's features.

Next was a series of telegrams.

"These are almost exactly five years ago," I said.

"Passchendaele," said Maisie. "The battle at Passchendaele was almost exactly five years ago."

Tom exhaled heavily, like he exhaled ghosts. The telegrams read ominously next to the photos. They were each sent a day or two apart.

MISSION STAGE ONE COMPLETE EVIDENCE GATHERED

MISSION STAGE TWO COMPLETE

MISSION STAGE THREE COMPLETE PAPERWORK TO FOLLOW

Then was a letter, written on official British Army paper, about a complaint against a certain Corporal Thomas Thompson, seconded from the 45th Battalion AIF for intelligence work and reconnaissance. The letter asked the recipient to put Tom on charges of desertion and treason. It cited photos, which sounded like the photos Fox had sent me a few weeks ago, of Tom in the mud with some Germans. I passed the notes to Tom.

"What are these?" Bertie asked. "What mission?"

"Is this the charge that still hangs over you, Tom?" Maisie asked.

"Yes." Tom's voice was a croak. "Desertion I can't argue against, unfortunately, but treason . . . that's a lie."

"But you only deserted because you were going to be shot for treason, right?" Maisie asked. Tom nodded.

"I think the 'mission' in the telegrams is . . ." I looked at Tom, his drowning eyes in the swaying, blinking carriage. "I think Fox created the charge of treason. I think these photos, the telegrams, the letter, are all pointing to the fact that Fox deliberately set out to get rid of Tom."

"But . . . why?" Bertie looked at me. "Not the proposal . . ."

"What proposal?" Tom's voice was sharp.

"It's nothing." I shrugged.

"It's bloody not!" said Maisie. "Fox proposed to her, at the end of the war."

"Propose is perhaps the wrong word," said Bertie. "Wasn't it more of an order?"

"And Katie answered him by stealing his car and driving back to Sydney."

Tom was very quiet. "You never said."

"No," said Bertie in the tense stillness. "Well . . . she wouldn't, would she."

"Wouldn't she?" Tom's voice was strained. In my peripheral vision, I saw Maisie and Bertie exchange a glance, but I wasn't as interested in Tom's game of jealousy as perhaps I should have been. The letter in the package had almost all my attention.

"Tom." I passed the letter to him. He took it without looking at me, but I wasn't interested in that either. It was the contents of the letter that interested me, that shook me.

"Is that Fox's handwriting?" asked Maisie.

"No," I said. "The letter's from a man called Bobbs."

"Bobsy." Tom's voice was now a whisper.

"Yes, I think it must be," I said. I had to concentrate to light my cigarette.

"Who's Bobsy, or Bobbs, or whoever?" asked Bertie. "Come on, don't leave us in suspense."

"Last year, Fox gave us, gave me, a letter from Tom's commanding officer to a man called Bobsy, boasting that they had got Tom on a charge of treason. It was partial evidence that showed Tom was innocent of treason, all we needed was a bit more proof and we could contact a lawyer and see if we could clear his name. But this letter . . ." How could I even explain? "This letter . . ."

"Mission report." Tom's voice was rough. "Internal enemy neutralized. Unconscious agent St. John Sinclair instrumental with mission completion, as per instructions. Double agent Thomas Thompson indicted on charges of treason and desertion, for immediate imprisonment and trial upon discovery, as per cable from HQ. All evidence of mission progress enclosed, cf ten photographs, three letters, two cables, handkerchief, uniform patch. Signed by an R Bobbs and his ID number." Tom let Bertie take the letter from him and lit himself a cigarette. The guttering cabin light made the seats look stained and seedy.

"I don't understand," said Maisie, "but I think I need a cigarette too."

"This letter is proof that Fox created the charge of treason against Tom." I said, trying to keep the tremor from my voice as I held out the lighter for Maisie. "I had my suspicions, but to have proof . . ."

"St. John Sinclair was Tom's commanding officer?" asked Bertie.

"He was," said Tom, as he opened the window to clear out some of the smoke. "He died, after I deserted."

"So . . . Fox deliberately separated you two."

"It seems so." I gave up, my voice shook.

"Which means . . ." said Bertie.

"Which means"—I swallowed hard—"that I was wrong. I thought I could work for Fox and be paid in evidence, evidence that would free Tom."

"Isn't this the evidence?" asked Maisie.

"This is the evidence and also the destruction of hope. Because how can I use this? Who would believe that Tom was not a double agent, as the letter claims? Who would believe that Dr. Silvius Fox, senior officer in military intelligence, now senior something-or-other in the civil service, smeared an Australian soldier for . . . what? Personal gain? To scare off a rival? There's no motive in the letter. Only I, only we, have any clue as to his motive." The cabin walls seemed to close in, the door and the windows rattled, the wheels screamed on the tracks. I felt a huge pressure on my chest.

"But more than that," I said, "by showing me that he created this charge of treason, he shows . . ." I had to blink hard to stop myself from crying. "It shows that he . . . that I can't . . ."

"That you can't win against him," said Bertie.

"Jesus," said Maisie. "But it's been five years! More, even. That's a bloody long game he's playing."

"And I'm his only opponent." My head felt so heavy. "And I can never win."

Fox's power over Tom's life, over my life, the potential he had to threaten the well-being of Maisie and Bertie, hung in the carriage with the cigarette smoke, unmoving, stinking, and choking. I could feel Tom beside me, a tremble ran through his body as though it was too much even to sob. Fox's face flashed like a knife in my memory, his cold gaze over the operating table, his heavy stare on my back as I walked through the wards. Maisie and Bertie were quiet and I wondered, for a moment, if they would abandon me. The train moved in jerks and hisses. Maisie put her hand on my knee.

"He's an evil bastard," she said. "But we'll get him."

"It's not possible." I couldn't bring myself to meet her smile.

"I was told that as a so-called 'half-caste' girl I couldn't even leave the mission. Yet I nursed in France in the war, married a diplomat, and now live in Paris." She raised her eyebrows. "That was impossible and I did it. You beating Fox? Definitely possible."

"Not at his own game."

"Oh no," said Bertie, "but who wants to win that? Make him play your game."

"And what game is that?"

"A game of love." Tom said this out the window into the rain-edged night. Maisie nodded and Bertie grinned. A game of love; perhaps Tom was right. That was a game that Fox could only lose. That was a game I had already won.

"L'AMOUR, TOUJOURS L'AMOUR"

It took a night and a day and a night to reach Paris. By the time we arrived we stank, the cabin stank, the "payment" from Fox was stashed at the bottom of my bag and not spoken of again. I cashed the check he sent with it and, once we had crossed the border to France, treated us all to meals in the dining car with every bottle of wine the waiters could find. I would have upgraded us to a sleeper car but there wasn't one, so we dozed against one another, living in the cabin like soldiers returning from the front. But I was formulating a plan, the rules of the game that Fox couldn't win. I wasn't sure yet how the game would play out, but I was not going to be subdued and made submissive by these revelations. If Fox thought he had won, then he didn't understand me at all . . . but I felt that he did understand me, more than was comfortable, and that's what kept me thinking. Did he expect me to fight back, to try and hurt him? Was this evidence just bait for a trap? He was too unpredictable; I couldn't second-guess him.

It really felt like we were soldiers on leave when we arrived at Gare l'Est in the fuzzy, drizzly dawn. We had bruises, literal and metaphorical. We had worked for the government but no one knew what we had suffered and how. We had bled, cried, drank, and fallen asleep together. My friends were now friends with each other and I loved, too much, to see Maisie hug Bertie so tightly, to see Tom lift Maisie off the ground and kiss both cheeks.

"Katie King," she took my face in her hands. "When you've had a good sleep and a couple of meals, you're coming to me for a check-up on that leg."

"Yes, Sister."

"And then regularly for some ordinary coffee and gossip." She kissed me, hugged me, and hailed a taxi.

Tom and I followed Bertie to the Ritz for a shower, after which we left Bertie to his seven messages from our editor Sir Huffandpuff, each increasingly irate, and a handful of work-related letters and telegrams.

Tom followed me back to Montparnasse. We barely said anything, just held hands in the street, on the Metro, up the road to my apartment block. We both needed sleep and I wanted some time just to chat about nothing, the weather, the drink in front of us, to read a detective novel in his company with a pot of tea between us. But that all evaporated before we had even left the apartment block foyer. In my letter box was a note in a scrawled hand I didn't recognize.

"Who's it from?" Tom leant against the doorframe and lit a smoke for each of us.

"To be honest, I'm more interested in that cigarette. Besides, it'd have to be pretty important to keep me from my pillow." I could feel Tom watch me as I read, as my energy ebbed, as I deciphered the scrawl.

"And? Will it keep you from your pillow?"

I handed him the letter. I was too tired; I could only watch our exhaled smoke entwine in the air between us.

"'Dear Mademoiselle Button,'" read Tom. "Actually, you know, my French is alright but perhaps not quite good enough for simultaneous translation . . ."

"Look at the signature."

"H-ma-ss . . . illegible."

"It's from Henri Matisse. He writes that he wants to talk to me about my mother. He says that I'm to see him as soon as possible."

"You aren't going to be able to rest with this ticking away beside you, are you?"

"Thank goodness we washed. Coffee?"

"Well, I can't change as I don't own another suit. So why not?"

꧁꧂

I could hear shouting as soon as the housekeeper opened the door to Matisse's studio apartment. The housekeeper, her face a mask of resignation, didn't even flinch at the insults flung about in the other room.

"Should we come back at a better time?" I asked.

"Oh no, he's in a good mood this morning. In here, mademoiselle, monsieur. I'll bring the coffee in directly." She opened the door but didn't announce us, leaving us to look around the crowded, colorful studio. A trail of brushes and paint, paper and discarded drafts led to a central podium. On the podium sat a curvy woman with masses of dark hair, her face on the brink of either anger or tears: Amelie, whom I had met at Gertrude Stein's. Standing at a canvas was Matisse. Dressed like a bourgeois accountant at a picnic, he glared at us through his glasses and his beard quivered when he spoke.

"Who the hell are you? Why on earth has Mathilde let you in? Get out, get out!"

"I'm the daughter of Cordelia King," I said. Amelie gasped and Matisse froze. "You asked to see me urgently."

"Yes, yes, of course." Amelie rose, drawing her red robe around her shoulders to embrace me. "How good it is to see you again! Henri, we met her at Miss Stein's, remember? Oh, doesn't she look like Cordelia? You must stay. Mademoiselle King . . ."

"It's Button, actually. Kiki Button."

"But of course, how silly of me. Yes, you absolutely have a look of Cordelia about you . . . sorry, are you a brother?"

Tom stopped staring at the canvases around the room and held out his hand. "No, a friend. I knew Mrs. Button, Cordelia, since I was a child."

"Ah, it is tragic. She was so young! Henri had commissioned her to sit for him on her next visit, he has a canvas of her that is only half complete . . ."

"May I see it?" I asked. Amelie looked to her husband. Matisse and his stare had not moved.

"Henri, *mon cher*," said Amelie, "the canvas?" She walked over to him and took the brush and palette from his hands, placing them on the table. It was only then that he seemed to come back to life.

"It's her," he said. "It's just like her, that look, that . . ."

"I know, *mon amour*, I know . . ." She stroked his face and fetched his pipe. "Do you remember now, Henri? Miss Stein's, the letter . . ."

"Yes, yes . . ."

"Mademoiselle Button—may I call you Kiki?—I'll fetch the canvas. Ah, Mathilde, coffee, just what we need. Please sit, help yourselves, I'll only be a moment."

We moved to a coffee table covered with scrap paper and cigarette butts. Mathilde poured coffee for all of us, leaving Matisse's cup on the table in front of him and the plate of biscuits in front of Tom. Tom shoved two in his mouth in quick succession but I could hardly even swallow my coffee. I felt Matisse's gaze on me like a searchlight. Eventually Amelie came back with a canvas.

"See?" she said. "So beautiful."

The painting was of a woman's face in a hat. The face was turned toward us, over the shoulder, the hat taking up most of the canvas with its enormous brim. The colors were not naturalistic, blue and green and lemon yellow, but the face was somehow more luminous because of this, the eyes imploring, or defying, or in some exultant emotion that demanded our attention. I nodded; I could see these were my mother's features but this was not a mother I had ever known.

"Throw it away." Matisse's voice cracked.

"Yes, I suppose we'll have to . . ."

"I'll keep it," I said. "I don't even have a recent photo of her. I'll pay for it."

"Pay for this?" Amelie frowned. "Absolutely not. It's yours, of course. Henri?"

He nodded, took a tiny brush from his wife's hand, and signed the painting.

"You are a Button?" Matisse said. "Not a Russell?"

"My father's name was Button . . ." I looked between him and Amelie. "Are you saying you know the name of my mother's lover?"

They shared a glance. Amelie nodded.

"I think you should know," she said. "Henri, sit down."

He plonked himself on a chair. "I'm not entirely sure, but . . ."

"Henri was so in love with her." Amelie smiled at her husband. "We all were, really. I would have been jealous, but by the time I met Henri, Cordelia was already married and living in Australia."

"I met her with Russell," he said.

"Who is Roussel?" I asked.

"Who is Russell? Who is Russell?" Matisse put up his hands in exasperation.

"The Australian, Russell—I think he says his name 'Rah-sel.'"

"Russell?" Tom asked. "Never heard of him."

"I've only heard of him in relation to my mother," I said, "but . . . he's a painter?"

"A brilliant painter," said Matisse, "in the Impressionist style. He made such a difference to my work. The way he used color, he made it sing, the waves shimmered, the sky danced, each blade of grass moved on its own over his canvas . . ."

"He met Russell on Belle Île."

"At the cottage that he shared with his wife. He was a true artist. He rarely exhibited—which is, I suppose, why he isn't widely known—he worked only for the work itself. I met Cordelia through him. I was jealous of Russell. Firstly, for his work. Secondly, it was clear that Cordelia adored him, and I wanted her to look at me the way she looked at him.

She . . . she was filled with joy. She made you feel that only you mattered in the whole world, she gave you everything. But then she'd disappear, leaving you bereft. I don't know how Russell withstood it."

"He didn't, really," said Amelie.

"No, well, who would? But he didn't leave Marianna."

"How could he? All those children."

"Hmmm . . . perhaps so. I would have though."

"I'm lucky you didn't get the chance." Amelie's smile was both understanding and wicked.

"So, this Russell . . ."

"Jean Russell . . . sorry, I should say it in the English way, 'John.'"

"He was her lover?"

"Oh yes." Amelie nodded.

"Were they though?" asked Matisse.

"Henri, she's dead, God rest her soul. You can't be jealous now."

"I'm not! No, I mean, they were close, absolutely, but were they lovers in the biblical sense? In the way the modern Mademoiselle Button means it?"

"Oh . . . I should think so. She was such a free spirit!"

"She became less free each time I saw her. It made her thoughtful and somehow more beautiful."

"Henri, you are such a sentimental fool sometimes . . ."

"Just a romantic . . . who likes to be exact. But you should really ask Russell himself."

"He's alive?"

"Oh yes! He lives in America now."

"No, Australia," said Amelie. "He went back to Sydney. Last year, I think? Yes, last year."

My mouth was dry. The coffee wasn't helping.

"Button's—ah, Miss Button's mother lived in Sydney," said Tom.

"Perhaps your mother met him there." Amelie shrugged. "Perhaps she died of a broken heart, after loving him for so long."

"That is a distinct possibility." It hurt to talk.

I could hear the traffic noises outside, cart wheels and car motors. The room smelt of paint and turpentine and linseed oil. The Matisses gazed at me intently; I felt they were looking for my mother.

"Is this what you wanted to tell me?" I asked.

"Yes," said Matisse. "I bumped into that crazy Romanian—"

"Tzara?"

"No, Brancusi. He said you were asking after Cordelia, that somebody should really tell you about Russell. He didn't want to say, he felt it was my secret to tell . . . I suppose because we were close, me and Russell and Cordelia." He fiddled with his glasses for a long time, until Amelie reached across and held his hand.

"We will miss her," said Amelie. "She was . . ."

"She was light," said Matisse, and in his long pause I understood: For him, light was life's most vital quality. To be light was to be the essence of everything. He shook his head and looked away. "You're very lucky to have had her as a mother."

"STUMBLING"

Tom and I sat at a terrasse table of the Rotonde, coats wrapped around us, Kir Royals in front of us, ankles locked together.

"How can she have been so different here to how she was at home?" I asked. "Matisse said I was lucky to have had her as a mother, but she was so . . . censorious."

"Maybe she wasn't censorious. Maybe you just assumed that she was."

"But Father would rant and yell at some minor infraction and she would say nothing! At most she would say, 'As you wish, Reginald,' when he asked for backup."

"So, she didn't argue against your father's censorship . . . but did she actually say, 'Do this, not that,' and so on?"

The dusk was falling briskly, the night clear, the lights of the city punctuating the sky. The fur of my peacock coat smelt of hot chocolate and my fingers smelt of a hundred cigarettes. Looking at Tom in his black overcoat, stained on the lapel, I couldn't call up a single memory of my mother admonishing me, just ones of her watching, impassive, as my father's face went red with yelling.

"She didn't do anything much, really. No help . . . but I suppose no hindrance either."

"Then that's the real question, isn't it? Why she wrote in her diaries how much she loved you, but toward you she was cold and remote."

"She was going to visit me here . . . oh yes, I told you already, I'm repeating myself. I wish . . ." I couldn't finish. Tom took the cigarette from my fingers to kiss my palm.

"It would have been a brave new world, Button. But at least now you know."

"Russell lives in Sydney . . . she didn't mention meeting him in her diaries."

"But you think she might have."

"She had an odd way of writing in those books, as though . . . almost as though she feared they might be read. I mean, if it's a private diary, why would you hide the name of your lover? And she's very lyrical, she writes a lot about street scenes and the sky and the sensations of her body in light . . . but after a while, I could see patterns. She used the same type of descriptions over and over . . ."

"Like a code."

"Like an idiosyncratic cipher for what was really going on. It was one of the reasons reading her diaries was so addictive. While I read them, I felt that I was part of her personal landscape."

"So, Russell is in those diaries as . . . a type of weather?"

"Yes . . . but I'd need to read them again to make sure. Her way of writing only really makes sense to me now." The last of my drink went down too easily.

"I could have met him," I said, "Russell."

"You still can."

"Not unless he comes here." I looked directly into Tom's dark blue eyes. "I'm never going back."

"Not even . . ."

"I went back for a funeral once and it took me a year to leave. If I go back for another funeral, I might never make it back to Paris. That place is Hades for me, Tom. It's no-man's-land."

He kept my gaze. He didn't even look up when the waiter brought us another round.

"It seems I'll just have to get a job on a London paper then."

"They're not sending you home, are they?"

"Not yet."

⌘

"More correspondence, Button? Don't you just go down to the café to get all your news?"

"This is a telegram, fooligan." I waved the yellow paper in his face. "That can only mean Fox and associates, or my father."

"Let's hope it's your father."

"Unlikely, as I haven't spoken to him since I left him after mother's funeral, when was that, November last year?"

"But he knows where you live, doesn't he? He'd have to, or you couldn't have heard about your mother . . ."

But I wasn't really listening to Tom, not with the telegram in my hand.

"What is it?" Tom looked over my shoulder. "What's the sad face for?"

I handed over the telegram.

JOHN RUSSELL 22 PACIFIC ST WATSONS BAY ADDRESS IN BACK
OF DIARY ENTRIES JUNE 12 TO 17 1921

"What the hell does that mean? Who's it from?"

"Look at the address."

"Westminster?"

"It's from Fox. He has my mother's final diary."

"How?"

"How indeed. That date is a few months before she died."

"But . . . she died in Sydney."

"She did. So how did he get the diary? How on earth did he get her final diary?"

"Alright, Button, it's alright . . ."

"No, it's not! It's far from alright!"

"Have a cigarette . . ."

"Fox sends me all this evidence of how he tried to get rid of you—then he sends me a note that says he knows all about me and my mother—where will it end, hmmm? When will he stop pulling my strings like a puppet?"

"When you stop letting him."

"How can I? How can I leave you in danger if I have any chance to stop it? How can I . . . my mother . . . how I can say I don't want to know? How . . ."

I sobbed then. It couldn't be helped. It had been such a fierce few weeks, after such a year. I hadn't slept properly for days, my leg throbbed, my head throbbed, I was hungry and thirsty and couldn't get a moment's peace. We stood in the stairwell and Tom took me in his arms, kissing the top of my head as I wailed into his chest, full wrenching sobs that seemed to come from somewhere outside of me, the noise of my cries alien to my ears. I couldn't work out how to inhale and almost choked. I hadn't cried like that for years, which meant I had to cry for everything, for my mother, for all the broken men I had nursed, for all the boys I had known and would never see again, for all the dead. Eventually Tom had to half-carry, half-drag me up the stairs to my apartment, still sobbing, wash my face and take off my shoes and push me into bed. He lay down beside me, holding me and stroking my hair with his sore hands, singing lullabies in his deep, rough voice, until exhaustion overwhelmed me and I sank into oblivion.

"JOURNEY'S END"

"Kiki, darling, how wonderful of you to see us off." Bertie kissed me on both cheeks. We stood just at the main entrance to Gare du Nord, the stone arches behind us, traffic swarming in front of us. Rain spat in fits and starts.

"In all that matching red, you're like my own personal firecracker."

"You seem to have missed her overnight bag there, Bertie." Tom pointed out my little suitcase.

"You're joining us?"

"Don't sound too disappointed," I said, "I might think you mean it."

"I'm not disappointed! This is a treat." Bertie linked one arm through mine and another through Tom's. "I always hate leaving Paris, but if the best part of Paris comes with me, what more can I ask for?"

"An explanation, maybe?"

We walked through the doors like we were in a movie, people parting for us, the marble floor rolling out in front of us. But it felt like a false note of cheer, my head still ached with dehydration and my toes were cold from where the rain had seeped in. The vaulting arches of the station, so welcoming when I arrived from London, seemed like a giant cage.

"You are the question and the answer, Kiki darling. Although I'm happy to hear an explanation, if there is one."

I didn't know where to begin. I felt a strong impulse to buy cigarettes, newspapers, postcards, bags of lollies, croissants in napkins, to grab as much Paris as I could before I boarded.

"What have I missed?" asked Bertie.

Tom scoffed. "Button can fill you in on all the colors of Fox's perfidy."

❦

The Blue Train clanked along, out of Paris and into the countryside I'd been looking at, in reality and in memory, since early 1915 when I was first sent to France. It seemed fitting that this would be the backdrop to my story, the trenches now full of birds' nests and poppies, rusting tanks coupled with farm equipment, temporary markets next to the temporary graves. Bertie listened closely to the tale of Russell and the diary, read the telegram and for once didn't interject with witty quips. The blue velvet seats of our private compartment made his skin look ghostly pale. I could only have looked the same.

"So, you're coming to London to collect the diary from Fox?" Bertie frowned.

"I told her she shouldn't," said Tom. "She could just write to Russell, now that she has his address. She can just call Fox."

"And have him read out my mother's diary over the telephone?"

"No, insist he sends it to you, in Paris," said Tom.

"It doesn't work like that."

"Why not?" asked Bertie.

"Yes seriously, Button, why can't it work like that?"

The windows showed farmland, gray and brown and black in the autumn, crows flying overhead. I could almost hear the guns again.

"The telegram . . . is a summons. He isn't just telling me that he has what I want, what I desperately need. He's telling me that I have to jump when he clicks, that if I want to hold onto this precious thing, I have to follow his instructions."

"How do you know this?" asked Bertie.

"From the war."

"It's not the war now," said Tom.

"This is what he would do when I worked under him as a nurse. Always giving with one hand and taking with the other. Then, his methods were cruder. If I wanted to eat, or sleep, once or twice even to live, then I had to carry out the mission. He . . ." Memories rose from the sodden fields outside the window, I had to voice them.

"He kept me working on the wards until I passed out, overpowering Matron by saying he needed me specifically in this or that operation, which were always when I was not on shift. At first I begged to be released, but then I learnt to stop begging and push through until I could no longer. I think once or twice I even held my breath to bring on a faint, just so I could be sent to my tent. Then he changed tactic, seeing me in the mess tent line and sending me off on some immediate, urgent mission. I began hiding biscuits in my pockets and my coat, I kept a store of bread and cheese and fresh water by two different gates, so when I headed out by bicycle after dark, I could still get a bite to eat. The boys started calling me Gretel as I trailed biscuit crumbs through the wards.

"But it was when he would leave me, after a completed mission, to make my own way back to the hospital, that were the most dangerous. One time . . . these fields remind me . . . after Passchendaele, after I had sent you home, Tom, he left me wounded in the snow.

"We weren't far from the front. An agent had messed up, he had been found out and beaten. He had crawled over no-man's-land back to our line with some scraps of information. He was badly wounded but, in a little alcove in a flooded trench, I patched him up. Then a shell exploded nearby, it killed him and left me with cuts all over my legs and arms. I sent the signal—'collect me'—but no one came. I had the intel and I couldn't walk properly. I sent the signal again, waited another hour, and still no one. What could I do? If I stayed in the flooded trench I would freeze to death; I could feel the burn of frostbite already beginning. I knew I didn't have long before I was in trouble.

"So I walked, limping for hours back to the casualty clearing station. Fox let me reveal my sorry state to everyone before he drove me to a hotel in town. Then he made me rest for three days, with cream and eggs and butter and other impossible treats brought to my room. He even sent Maisie in to take care of me as I lay back on the soft pillows.

"Fox claimed he never got the signal. But how could he have failed to get it, when he was expecting it? Stranger things have happened, of course, and I'll never really know . . . but I think it was punishment, for getting you help, Tom, followed by remorse when I turned up injured. I would have been permanently scarred without those days in the hotel, but I wouldn't have needed those days if he had been more professional, if he had searched for me when I failed to return.

"After that he became more subtle. He didn't need to threaten my life, he just had to intimate that my life was his for the taking. Which it was, until I left in 1918. That's how I know this is a summons. It's an old game and one I know well. Here is your life, he says, come and save it."

The sky darkened until it seemed indivisible from the fields, the endless gray disturbed only by a crow crying its loneliness, a rabbit running in fear, a tractor as it coughed its last. I stared out the window until the last light died and all I was left with was my reflection in the glass. I saw Bertie and Tom watching me, Bertie with pity, Tom with fury, both with love.

"I have to go to London. I have to play the game to the end."

"And you're near the end, yes?" asked Tom.

"I have a feeling this is just the beginning."

"LONDON, DEAR OLD LONDON"

This train ride was full of memories. I had only ever taken it with a full heart—going home to my mother's funeral, or leaving Sydney behind, or to and from the war. It wasn't transport, it was a journey of the soul, and each ride meant the difference between life and death.

We were all quiet, with tiredness, with tension, with the kind of emptiness that always found me after battle. Soon the farmland turned to coast, the clack of wheels replaced with the relentless pounding of waves as we boarded the ferry. All I could think of was my mother. How had she felt about this crossing? When she was young, was it a return to her gilded cage or was it another part of her bohemian adventure? How had she felt about it as a mother, when this crossing was the first step away from her true life and back to Australia and me? I must have looked appalling, as Bertie nodded to Tom, who took off my hat to massage my head, while Bertie took off my shoes to massage my feet. I fell asleep quickly and didn't wake until the clangs and yells and big-city buzz of Victoria Station.

London was much as it had been a few weeks ago, as it always was: ever-changing, secure only in its sense of being the center of the world.

A spiky place, a place where around every corner was someone waiting to overset my life, whether that was Fox, my aunt Petunia, my editor, Tom's editor, or more besides whom I had never met but could tell me that my mother was not who I thought she was, that Tom would suddenly be whisked off to the other side of the world, that I was never allowed back to Paris. I loved hearing the newspaper boys and flower girls, I wanted a sweet bun and a hot cup of tea, but other than that I didn't want to be here. It was the antithesis of home.

"I'm coming with you to Westminster," said Tom, looking firmly out the window at the steel of the station. The train squealed as we pulled into the platform.

"Yes, you need backup," said Bertie.

"It's best if I'm by myself."

"You can't be serious, Button."

"Kiki, are you going to turn up to Westminster at dawn, scruffy and smelly, on the off chance that Fox is walking around with your mother's diary?" Bertie raised an eyebrow.

"I have to go alone." The train screamed as it let off more steam, a fog outside the glass. "Tom, Bertie . . . trust me."

Both men looked at me, Bertie appraising in his pressed caramel check suit, Tom glowering in his worn navy one. The conductors rattled along the corridor, opening our cabin door with a brisk apology, forcing us out and onto the concrete platform with everyone else.

"We trust you, Kiki darling." Bertie straightened his shoulders and put on his hat. "Very well. I'm going home to my little boat for a moment of peace before I go in to see Sir Huffandpuff Himself and beg for a dark-room . . . and an assistant, as I've never in my life developed a photo." He kissed me on both cheeks. "But come and see me when you're done. We can look through some of the photos of the Casati party and write the copy together. Tom—share a cab?"

Tom looked at me for a long time, his posture as tired as his suit. "I'm just supposed to leave you here at the station? After all that's happened in the last few days?"

I pulled down his face to kiss each cheek.

"Go with Bertie. I'll call you at work in a few hours."

I watched them walk off down the platform, Tom looking back over his shoulder every few steps. I would have to follow them of course, there was only one way onto the concourse, but I needed to give them some distance. I needed the distance from them in my mind, to prepare myself for the thing I most dreaded: Fox. How else was I going to do it—get the diary, ask why he has it, berate him about Tom—except face-to-face? It was not a face I wanted to face, and my fear of him made me perversely want to run to him, to stand in front of his face, and my fear, and slap it. I couldn't have Tom or Bertie nearby when I did this. I had to do it alone.

Travelers clipped along in a very British manner, purposeful even when they were only walking to sit and wait. Trains grunted and huffed away. The station was all action, gearing up to the main part of the day when dozens of trains would leave Victoria for all over the country. I was wearing my favorite high red brogues, I couldn't seem to take them off. I strode toward the entrance, my thoughts flicking over details of the day's organization: I would check my suitcase into the luggage room, I needed the toilet and a cuppa, I had no idea where I was going to stay tonight, or if I would be finished by lunchtime and be on the train home this afternoon . . .

"Miss Button?" A man in a smart gray suit approached me, light gray eyes in a pale face, wreathed in gray smoke.

Who knew that I was here? Was this one of Charlie's fascist friends, come to take revenge? I kept walking.

"I have been asked to give you this." He gave no name, but before he opened his coat, he stubbed out his cigarette, his black, gold-tipped Sobranie. I stopped at the sight of it. No, it couldn't be, Fox couldn't already know I was here . . . The man held out a little package wrapped in brown paper and string. It looked very much like a book, it weighed about as much as a book, but before I could ask him about it, he nodded and left.

Surely that couldn't be it, that couldn't be everything. I looked in the direction he was walking. A broad-shouldered man stood by the station entrance, his overcoat perfectly fitted, his steel hair slicked perfectly in place, a scar on his cheek—Fox. No; the world paused for a moment, it held its breath. Then I grabbed my suitcase and ran toward him. The man smiled ever so slightly as I hopped, skipped, jumped through the crowds. He turned on his heel in a military manner and turned round a corner. I had no time to apologize to the people I knocked with my bag, I could only clutch the parcel and head after him. I found the spot where he had stood, I turned the same corner—was that him, that silver helmet, that upright bearing? I plunged after the man but it wasn't him—another gray head under a gray hat turned down the stairs to the Underground. I pushed forward, my suitcase flailing behind—but I caught his profile and it wasn't Fox either. I whirled around, I moved quickly to every corner and behind every cart, I ran up the street and then down again, but I couldn't see him. If it had been Fox, he was now gone.

Why was this the thing that made me want to give up? It was all I could do not to sit in the gutter and cry. It took all my presence of mind to head back into the station, to turn my frustration to action and work out what to do next. Fox had seen me, I was sure of it, and I had seen him as well. I closed my eyes and clutched the parcel. Where would he go now? I headed straight to the public telephone booth and rang reverse charges.

"I'm sorry, miss, but he won't be in the office today or for the rest of the week. May I take a message?"

"I'm sorry, Miss Button, he did not stay in the club accommodation last night. I will inform him that you rang."

"Yes, this is Greef . . . Miss Button, excellent to hear from you again. He is not here at present . . . No, I couldn't say where he was, but I will take . . . As you wish, Miss Button. I hope to see you again soon."

He wasn't at work, or at his club, or his home in Mayfair. He had disappeared, vanished somewhere, I felt, just so he could reappear and terrorize me once again. How did he know just how much to give and to withhold to keep me on tenterhooks, ready to do anything for him if only to relieve

my frustration? My clothes were sticky from the sweat of sudden running. My feet hurt from skipping on hard floors in high heels. My head
hurt from sleeping on a train, from too many cigarettes, from holding
back tears. My leg throbbed, my wound seared, my throat was raw.
There was nothing I could do now, except what that bastard had given
me permission to do.

I could only read the diary.

"ALONG THE ROAD TO GUNDAGAI"

I left my bag at the station and walked to the river. The pub I walked into was very surprised to see a brightly dressed, tear-stained young woman come through the dim doorway, order a pint, and light a cigarette at the bar, but I was far from caring what they thought. I wanted a drink, I wanted a view of the river, I didn't want any fuss. The publican insisted on giving me a plate of bread and cheese and pickles with my pint—"You're skin and bone, miss"—which I thanked him for but didn't eat. I took my necessaries to the window with the best view, opened it to let in the cold air and salty tidal smell of the river, and opened the package.

It was the diary and more besides. The more besides fell out of the leaves of the diary as soon as I opened it. First to fall out were the heaviest: photographs. They made me gasp: here was my mother, in an enormous hat on the ferry in Sydney. I knew it was Sydney, I recognized Circular Quay in the background, and the ferries as being the same ships I had seen from her terrace all summer. I had never seen my mother look so old and tired, so gaunt that her wrists were like twigs. This must have been taken just before she died. She sat at the prow, writing in a book; it must be this exact diary. My assumption was confirmed by the second photo, my mother a blur as she rushed out of shot, but in perfect focus was the diary, left on the ferry seat. So, that's how Fox got the diary; he had a spy in Sydney.

The next photograph was of me, on the balcony of my mother's terrace by the harbor. I was in a petticoat and dressing gown that were obviously stained. My hair was lank and down past my shoulders, I was as thin as water, barefoot and smoking. If that's how I looked, no wonder my aunt had had a fit when she came to collect me. No wonder everyone went on and on about my weight. It was obvious to even the most casual observer that I was sick, though I hadn't seen it then and I could barely see it now, not even with the bread and cheese in front of me.

There were two more photos of me. In the first, I couldn't tell if it was taken on the same day or months later, as I was still wearing that stained slip and dressing gown and nothing else. I was sprawled in an armchair, cigarette dangling from my fingers as I read. The photo was taken through the window, so I could see that the floor was covered in notebooks: my mother's diaries. The next must have been taken just before I returned to Europe, as I was dressed in a coat and hat, my new brogue heels shining in the winter sun, suitcase at my feet. I was waiting to board a ship, gazing into the middle distance.

I stared at the photos. I had never seen a candid photograph of myself. I had even been told that these were impossible to take, as I was always moving, laughing, talking, dancing. My mother's death had made me still, so that I found a position and stopped, frozen long enough for a surreptitious photo. I had no memory of anyone with even the smallest camera. I had no memory of seeing anyone interesting at all. Whoever the spy was, he knew his business.

There was no message on the back, no line of spidery Fox handwriting to entice, threaten, or bewilder. I suppose there didn't need to be, the fact of the photos said it all: he spied on me wherever I went in the world, I was never out of his thoughts, I couldn't hide. I suppose, with this diary, he was even trying to hint that he knew what I was thinking, but I wouldn't believe it. I couldn't believe it, as all this effort—the diary, the photos, the missions in code—was tinged with an unreality, a nightmarish quality. It reeked of denial; specifically, a refusal to see that the more he pushed me, the more I pushed back. The more he tried to entangle me, the more I resisted. Did he want it to be like it was in the war, when he dogged my every step, when he was in my every thought, when he dictated my every action even when he wasn't there, as he somehow lived inside my mind? I looked out the window at the water; ferries moved up and dinghies moved down, the boats modern but the actions of the sailors and watermen ancient. My beer was soft on my tongue. It wasn't like that now; it would never be like that again. He had scarred me and the scars had toughened me. I would never be a hostage again, as I saw him for what he was. However much he followed me, however much he tried to haunt me, he would always be foreign, alien, wrong. He could never be inside my mind again, so he could never fully triumph over me. My cigarette smoke was bitter as I listened to the traffic.

The next bit of more besides needed a bit of shaking to get out from between the pages. It was a letter, dated early 1921, from my mother's censorious older sister, my aunt Petunia.

Dear Cordelia,

I hope you're well in your antipodean hideaway. This is only a short letter to inform you that once again I have had to protect your reputation. At the National Gallery, of all places, I met Lady Emerald when I was caught in front of the Impressionists, such as they were. Lady Emerald asked after you, wondering, "Will Cordelia finally take up with that Impressionist, Russell, now that he's moved back to Australia? He's married, of course, but we all know that she has never had much respect for the marriage state." Naturally, I said what I could, that the rumors were all lies, that you didn't know a painter called Russell or any painters at all, anymore, that you were very firmly married . . . but, of course, we know that isn't true, don't we? We know that you knew a painter called Russell, that you had no respect for his married state then and little for your own now, with your endless trips away from your husband. That, despite the years, fundamentally you have not changed. Well, Lady Emerald didn't believe me but I did what I could and I hope you thank me for it. I don't know where she heard that Russell—whom no one has ever heard of—has moved back to Australia, but probably from one of her sycophantic American friends. Lady Emerald didn't mention where in Australia Russell would reside but I can't imagine that there are too many people who would make your mistake and think that a sheep farm in New South Wales would be anything like the Home Counties. I'm sure you can ask around and find out where he is, if you still believe you're in love with him.

My Robert has just started work in a bank and is an excellent prospect now for any sensible young woman. This rules out girls like Katherine, of course, who has chosen to spend her time going to parties in Paris. Cousins they may be, but a match, never. William has been elected to treasurer of his club and spends more time with his books now that he has retired. I would ask you to send my regards to Reginald, but I couldn't know that my regards would ever reach him. When did you see him last?

As ever,
Petunia

I had never liked Petunia, but after this letter I resolved never to see her again. My mother must have kept this letter as it alerted her to John Russell's return to Australia. They would once again live in the same country, twenty-seven or so years after their affair. I flicked to the back of the diary—yes, there it was in my mother's handwriting, Russell's address in Watsons Bay. I finished my beer, slightly acid at the bottom of the glass, the tidal smell of the river stealing over the traffic to join me at the table.

Did she meet him before she died? The only way I could know what happened was to read this, her final diary.

June 10, 1921
A summery winter, the chill in the air that creeps under the sun, that edges the warmth out of the rays. The harbor glitters, cold and inscrutable.

June 11, 1921

A wild storm last night. Tiles fell off the roof as the rain pummeled it. The wind keened and wailed and slipped past every bolt to enter the house and tear my hair, claw my eyes. The garden is a single large puddle.

This morning the city is panting, bruised and spent. The winter dawn limps forward, it must go on, it must rise against all inclination, against all desire. The water is flat steel and boatless. Not one seagull screams for its supper.

June 12, 1921

A letter to follow the telegram: X would like to see me.

Delie (he has always called me Delie),

I know you still love the smell of turpentine, so why don't you come and visit my studio? It's a shack at 22 Pacific St Watsons Bay, a Pacific Belle Île. Next week, maybe Tuesday? I'm all alone as Caroline goes off to Melbourne for some event or other, I can't stand that sort of thing, as you know. I love solitude but it is tiring. Please come.

Roo x

I've written it out as I can't believe it. He is here he is here he is here. Does the sun shine more brightly? Is Sydney somehow in summer, a northern French summer, perhaps, full of poppies and rosemary? I think those seagulls are the big British ones that coo like a ship's horn. I think those voices are cockney, are Breton, are nothing like the Australian drawl. I think they must be, yes, I can smell coffee and croissants in the air. I can smell wine and gentle French honey.

June 17, 1921

I have seen him. John Russell.

I will never see him again.

The light is . . . I can't do it. I can't write about the sun and the sea, the people as they slip along the streets.

I can only write what is.

I was not wrong; I was not a fool.

I worried that, when I saw him, the love I had carried for so long would disintegrate; would, when we could finally live in the same place, be shown as dust. It was not dust, it was not illusion, it was as strong and healthy as ever. It was as right as ever. And John, John, was as he ever was.

He didn't need to say it.

It was in the way he called me Delie, Delie to his Roo, took my hand, showed me his painting in detail. In the way he broke off listening to me to pick up his sketchbook and draw my face, once again. The way his pencil stilled, the sounds of the harbor outside the window, as he gazed at me.

It was in the way he talked about the rhythm of his days, of his life, of his children. Twenty-eight years and none of them included me. I am fifty-one, he is sixty-five. I could see, in his gaze, how he wanted me, how he still worshipped me, how he still saw me as unreachable, untouchable, unknowable. Our love wrapped around us like the salt air, it was in his breath and on my skin. It was the wood cracking in the humidity, it was the song of the tide outside.

And I knew—how, I don't know—but I knew, then, that we would never be together. It would always be like this: stolen moments, outside of daily life, outside of the social world. Our love was everywhere but I could see, in his face, that he could not conceive of it as other than it had been for the last three decades. It was a secret and always would be.

I promised to see him next week. I will not go.

I will not be his secret, his stolen moment, his hidden fire. Not anymore. I will not reduce myself and be his friend, his deniable muse. I will follow the example of my darling Katherine and live every moment out loud, proud and honest. I may even move back to Europe to be with her. Who says I can't live in Paris once more?

Only Reginald, perhaps, but our agreement is at an end. I have done as I promised. I never told Katherine about John. I never told Katherine about my life before Australia. I never gainsaid Reginald when he scolded her—much as I wanted to, he was so ridiculous and pompous and blind to the fact that his scolds were useless, they always drove her to do the very thing he forbade. I kept my promises and, to be fair, Reginald kept his too. But now Katherine is in Europe; thank heavens.

I was right, to stay for her, not to leave Australia completely. I know Reginald and his vulgar sister. If I hadn't been here, they would have locked her up, on the property and then in marriage, while she was still a girl. I insisted on her going to school, on her boarding in Sydney, on her being taught by those women who, while not nearly modern enough for me, were better than most of what was on offer in this small-minded city. Then, when she finished school, I got her out of Australia. Of course, she couldn't see what I was doing. I have Reginald to thank for that: he was always so bombastic. He oversalted every dish so Katherine could never taste the subtler flavors.

She survived the war and the pandemic. I was so worried for her. I wanted her home, then, when war was declared. My brave nurse. Did she know, I hope she knew, how proud I was of her, how scared and proud at once? Her letters were never frequent enough for me to be able to tell. I could tell, however, that something was off. Her surgeon, Dr. Fox, was mentioned far too frequently, not as a lover but as . . . well, he seemed like some kind of tormentor. She was clearly afraid of him, even as she wrote of him with lines of Keats. As soon as the war ended, I boarded a ship, intending to meet up with her, only to find her already on her way back to Sydney. Then Edvard got the Spanish flu, then I got the Spanish flu, then Petunia took charge of my convalescence until I ran away again. I only saw my lovely Katherine for a few months before she headed back to Europe. She was so vibrant, all her liveliness grown sure and strong, she was witty and able and in control. She was just as she should be. I know she thought I was sending her back for a husband, but that charade was only so Reginald would give her some money. My last charade.

That Dr. Fox was never mentioned. I only hope he was left behind with the war. Maybe she left him behind in London, just as I left behind Petunia and all the rest of them. That woman! Still trying to punish me more than two decades later. She was right in only one thing: I should never have come to Australia. Roo seduced me, I thought it would be bright and breezy and full of men like him. No, Roo went to France because there was no one like him in Sydney. Maybe one day this colorful country will adore itself, will let artists flourish, will provide good coffee and good conversation. Maybe one day, this country will not think of itself as an outpost of England (which it is not) or Empire (which it will be for *some time) and embrace its true history in the songs and stories of its first peoples. That time is not now, alas, and I won't be around to see it . . .*

But none of that matters. Now I can join Katherine in Paris, I can explain why I acted as I did. Money, always money, always the fear of the workhouse or prostitution. There were not many other options for women like me, if we didn't marry. I hope her generation, with their wartime experience and schooling and short skirts, can do better than we did, that they don't have to submit to some form of bondage, that they don't have such gorgons as Petunia breathing down their necks. I hope my darling Katherine can meet all the special people that one can find in Paris, all the artists, all the ambassadors, all the dodgy dukes, and beautiful beggars.

Why am I thinking like this? Why am I talking as though she is gone from me forever? I'm going to join her, I'm going to show her Maxim's and Angelina's. We're going to tour Montmartre and stroll the Champs-Élysées. She can live in her dingy garret and I'll stay in my gilded hotel, and we can meet up for gossip when she isn't too busy with all of her wonderful people. I can be myself, my true self, whom I have only been in patches for the last twenty or so years, and she can see it, and she can see how it was worth it, for her. It was worth it for her.

I have been riding this ferry, back and forth to Watsons Bay, for hours. I feel extremely weary, the sun is setting, the cold wind bites my ankles. My head aches, my heart aches, and a drowsy numbness pains my sense. I feel hollow and worn; I suppose a new heart sense will do that to one. I need to rest, to recover from the end of this affair, before I set off for my new life, my renewed life, in Paris.

I turned the pages, but that was it, just three little entries. June 17—that was only a few months before she died. Perhaps the extreme weariness never left her, perhaps the headaches and heartaches (oh, she quoted Keats, my mother) only increased and she never wrote another diary entry. She never joined me in Paris. I looked out at the water, the sky darker now, the clock hands had slipped toward afternoon. Would I have listened to her, even if she had explained in person? Would I have wanted any part of her "renewed life" in Paris, or would I have thought of her as an interloper, a spoilsport, a spy from my father? A boat rowed past with a grizzled waterman in the bow. I didn't know, but I suspected that I could only listen now because her death had left such a silence, and in that silence, I could finally hear her. I could hear how she loved me—how she interpreted Fox precisely, how she understood that my father understood nothing—I could hear how she valued her sacrifices as they were made because she loved me. She loved me. It started to drizzle, rain spotting the window, a drop slipping down the frame onto the sill.

In one year, I had lost my mother and found her again. The finding was incomplete but it was mine, more completely mine than anything else in my life. I stroked the black canvas cover of her diary. It was an artist's sketchbook—as were all her other diaries—I had only just noticed. She was an artist, I decided, an artist of the heart. And I knew because Fox had rescued, stolen, the diary. Was I grateful or annoyed about this? As always, with Fox, I teetered on a tightrope between the two.

'GOIN' HOME'

"Button! I've been waiting all day to hear from you!"

"I got caught up . . . her final diary . . ."

"You have it?"

"And read it. Can we meet?"

"Can we ever. Victoria? Half an hour? I have to be back there anyway."

"Why? Have you even been home?"

"No. I'll explain when I see you."

In just over half an hour we were in another pub, our pint glasses lined up in front of us. Tom wasn't lying when he said he hadn't been home. Not only had he not changed, his suit still smelling of the cleaning product they used on the Blue Train, he hadn't even opened his suitcase. I could see the string around it still knotted tight, doing the work of the busted locks. The pub was dark, stuffy, and warm, old wooden benches and frosted glass that looked like it had been around when Shakespeare was a boy. It was quiet, even at lunchtime, occupied only by a few old men muttering into their stout.

"As soon as I walked in to the office, Old Buffer told me to get my arse back to the former Ottoman Empire, there was still revolution to report on. And I got a telegram—I get them sent to the office—"

"I know."

"Of course, right, well, it's Sissy. Here." He pulled the telegram from his pocket. "'SERAPHINA GRAVELY ILL COME HOME AT ONCE PA.' It doesn't really leave any room for argument."

"What's wrong?"

"I don't know. There's no telephone on the property."

"Still?"

"Pa's too cheap to pay for the line all the way out there."

"Call my father's property. He'll know."

"Regardless, Pa wouldn't send a telegram unless my sister was already walking down the aisle to Death, waiting with a flower in his buttonhole. If I want to see Sissy alive again, I have to go home."

"You do." Then his heart-rent look crashed over me like a wave and I realized. "No. No, you can't go. I just got back. You can't . . ."

He grabbed both of my hands and kissed them hard, eyes closed. I must have kept murmuring "No, no," as he did so, because that's all I was thinking. He couldn't leave as I had done, for another family death, to be caught up in family business for months and months. When would he return? Would he return at all?

"You have to come back, Tom."

"Wild horses et cetera . . ."

"I mean it. You can't let your father persuade you to stay on the property and become a farmer. He'll try, you know."

"Oh, I know. But all my memories of that place have you in them and you won't be there. If I lived there, it'd be like you had died."

"Good, that means you'll return. Bring your sister with you."

"Sissy . . ." he frowned. "Why?"

"I told you, when I was there last year, that she was bored to tears. Now it seems she's bored to death. I have a feeling her illness can be cured by a trip on a ship, galleries in London, and cafés in Paris. Promise to look after her, promise your father I'll look after her, sneak her out in the middle of the night if you have to. Just come back. Leave nothing behind."

He had kept hold of my hands, playing with my fingers as he considered my words.

"You know, I was never as anti-home as you."

"Do you miss it?"

"A bit." He looked around at the dusty lithographs of Regency London on the pub walls. "When the sky's gray once again and London costs too much, when the memory of pineapple makes me cry, when so-called 'open spaces' don't even reach the horizon, when I've seen too much blood and heard too many dying children—then yeah, I miss home, I miss the warm sea and the big sky and the fresh fruit and the sun on my skin and hearing nothing but the warble of magpies. I can't get any of that here."

"That big sky, so deep blue it's almost purple."

"Sunshine that is actually hot."

Heat and space seemed very far away in this late autumn London pub.

"To be honest, Tom, apart from the heat, I couldn't have got much of the rest at home. Not as a woman, and particularly not as a married woman, which is what I would be if I'd stayed."

"And the pineapple?"

"I do miss the pineapple. And mangoes."

"And bananas."

"And days so balmy you don't need to get dressed . . . I can't live on sunshine though. Almost, but not quite." I untangled my fingers and slid across the diary. "Neither could my mother."

"What does it say?"

"Read it, and the letter, and the photos. I'll get us some food and another pint."

I stood at the bar and watched him read for a moment, emotions flitting across his face, but soon I couldn't bear to look. I took to studying the beer taps, the blackboard with its chalked-up specials, taking my time as I selected some local pale ale, pork pies, pickles, and a chunk from the enormous wheel of cheese that sat on the bar. The barman was gruff and spoke mainly through his moustache, but he took care to load everything onto a tray for me to carry it over to the table. Tom sat with the documents in his hands, staring at me, seemingly too stunned even to pick up his beer.

"I don't know whether to speak about Fox first or your mother first."

"Fox isn't important."

"He's very important. That man . . . he's unbelievable! How long has he been spying on you, trying to bully you into . . . what, being his wife? Being his slave?"

"Same thing, I think, with Fox." Thank God the pint was delicious, it saved me from tears. "How long? Ah, this will almost be the eighth year, give or take? I met him in 1915, when I first got to France."

"He even follows your mother on the other side of the world. He spies on your mother when you aren't there. Because you didn't know she was ill, did you? You didn't know you were going home. You had no idea you'd want this diary."

I could only sip my beer.

"I didn't realize the lengths he would go to control you."

"He doesn't control me." That thought gave me hope, which gave me strength. "Yes, that's right, he tries to control me and he fails. Unless you're suggesting that he killed my mother . . ."

"He could have."

"He could have, but I would say that was one step too far, even for him. He needs a reason to be brutal, and I've never known him to be vicious. No, he goes to these lengths because I left him behind. He can knock at the door, he can make noise outside the window, but he can never again take up residence in my head."

"Are you sure?"

"How can you doubt me?"

"I don't doubt you." He held my hand. "But I need to know you're sure."

"So sure. Because . . . because I have Paris, because I have Maisie and Bertie and Harry. Because I have you. Because . . ." I took a deep breath to steady my voice. "My mother loved me. I need never be prey to a surrogate parent again."

Tom looked at me softly. "Is that what it was?"

"In part. The war . . . it was a strange time, I was free and yet restricted, in ways that were so new I felt giddy. But when I first arrived in France, the sense of being alone in the world was very strong. I had Maisie, but we weren't always on the same shift, and we couldn't exactly chat when we were. I only saw you and Bertie sometimes and I worried about you all the time. I guess . . . I was scared—you know, soft and vulnerable and naïve under my bluster—and ripe for someone, a powerful commanding-officer type someone, to exploit."

I looked him in the eye; I saw him and he saw me. I raised my glass. "Never again."

"Never again, Button. I promise you that." He finally sipped his beer, licking the foam off his lips, leaning back against the wall of the booth. He lined up the photos in front of him, but I could tell he wasn't really looking at them.

"Cordelia sounds like she was a pretty special person."

"Doesn't she?" I couldn't help smiling, at this idea and all that went with it. "Doesn't she though."

"You're not sad? I thought you'd be full of regret."

"I was, I am . . . but how can I not also be glad? I'm not only Button, Kiki Button, Katie King. In Paris and London, I'm also Cordelia's daughter, imbued with her . . . what do people say, her expression, her essence? This special woman lives on in me. How can I not also be glad?"

❦

We finished our beer and snacks, we walked back across the road to his platform at Victoria Station. We were side by side, then arm in arm, then hand in hand. We didn't talk about anything in particular, just details of our upcoming days, musings on the weather and the other travelers, the various merits of English versus French beer. Then we were at his train, at his carriage, the horn sounded and it was time for him to board.

"I can't believe you're going."

"I can't believe I'm going. We were going to take in the town."

"And the suburbs and the country and everything in between. Hurry home."

"Is this my home?"

"Unless I'm in Paris."

The train whooshed steam and Tom jumped aboard.

"Give me something," he said, "some token, some memento, to help bring me back."

The guards were yelling. I had nothing in my purse but a pencil, a lipstick, and some loose coins. The guards were checking all the doors and waving their little flags. Tom leaned down, hand out, holding on to the rail, his face wide open. The guards yelled, I took his hand until the train wheels started to move and we were pulled apart. In the dim, drizzly dusk I watched him look at me stunned, then elated, then gutted, because as the train moved away, I kissed him.

ACKNOWLEDGMENTS

I would like to thank the team at Pegasus Books, in particular Claiborne Hancock and Tori Wenzel, for their work, help, and forbearance in getting this manuscript to publication.

I would like to thank my agent, Sarah McKenzie, for her unflagging support of Kiki in her adventures around the world.

Thanks, too, to my other champions: Hannah Ianniello, and Fyfe Strachan.

In terms of research, my thanks to Mick Chance for introducing me to Raven's Ait. My reading for *Autumn Leaves, 1922* had been a constant delight and the books too numerous to list here, but I will always be indebted to the vast research, fiction, poetry, and memoirs available on 1920s Paris.

This book is dedicated to my family, without whom barely a word could have been written. Thanks to Tania Disney, Dan Lunney, Tatyana Burmistrova, and Boris Frumkin, for all their awesome grandparental childcare skills. Thanks to Bridie Lunney, for the wealth of good words that supported me when I felt I might sink. Thanks to Rowan Lunney and Carly Williams, early readers. Thanks to my husband, Dima, for being my rock. Thanks to my eldest daughter, Penny, whose declarations of love keep me going. Thanks finally to Ellie, born in the midst of this manuscript, who spent her first weeks in a rocker as I wrote, who has never known a mother who isn't running off with her laptop.

Nothing could be done without you.